THE

CUTTHROAT

PRINCE

THE
CUTTHROAT PRINCE

BOOK TWO IN THE WILLIAM OF ALAMORE SERIES

BOOKS IN THE WORLD OF ALAMORE

- THE FALCON AND THE STAG

- SHADOW OF THE SWORD

- RANGER OF KINGS: BOOK ONE IN THE WILLIAM OF ALAMORE SERIES

- THE CUTTHROAT PRINCE: BOOK TWO IN THE WILLIAM OF ALAMORE SERIES

- THE FALLEN HEIR: BOOK THREE IN THE WILLIAM OF ALAMORE SERIES

If you have questions and would like to reach the author, please reach out through email at author@cjrisely.com or by reaching out through the website: www.cjrisely.com

Stay up to date on the news, new releases, characters, and more subscribe at www.cjrisely.com

For Gin,

My own personal Visra and Admere all rolled into one small and rather

murderous mare.

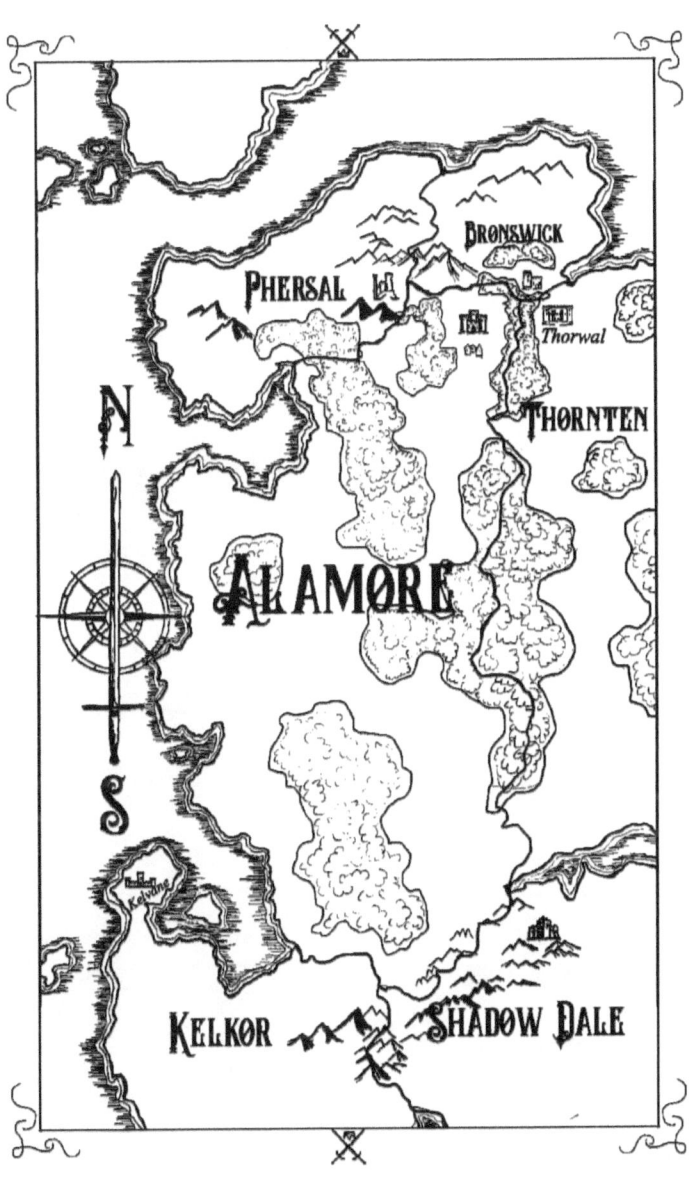

PROLOGUE

Heart slamming in his throat, threatening to strangle each rasping breath, the man ran harder, tripping over brambles and branches that caught at his clothing in the dark. His white-blond hair fell over his blue eyes; blood dripped over his arms through his clothing, down his face like scarlet tears. Somewhere in the tangle of trees around him, he could hear the hammer of hooves, a second pulse that beat a strange separate rhythm through his skin and chest. Hindered with exhaustion and the stale tavern spirits he could still taste on his tongue he stumbled, this time not catching himself before sprawling in the dirt on his chest. He felt blood leap to his skin where it had torn over his palms and knees. Swaying, he tried to push himself up. Run! He could hear the word screaming through his head. Run!

The hooves were nearing, getting closer and closer with each breath. The moon's silver light was filtering through the trees, showing nothing but branches and the sheen of the river only a few yards ahead, in the clearing of trees. Reaching it seemed impossible without being spotted and, even if he could, he couldn't swim well sober let alone in his current state. He closed his eyes, half hoping he might vanish. Perhaps they wouldn't see him here.

"Pathetic."

The voice above him sent a shiver through his body, deep and cold in his chest. He opened one eye and the world spun round him. He swallowed the panic and sick rising in him and lifted his face to the hooves that had stopped between him and the water, blocking his way forward. Black feathered hooves that led up the powerful legs of the fine animal, a horse the color of a clouded night, its eyes reflecting the distant moon in two faint stars so high above it may have been miles. The rider might have been the specter of death in his grey cloak, a sword swaying at his saddle, too far away to see if he even had a face.

"Mercy." The man's voice croaked, and he winced, his eyes stinging with tears. "Mercy, please, please have mercy."

Someone else in the shadows cackled, high and manic, but the rider before him merely cocked his head. "Mercy?" He sounded unimpressed, indifferent. "Surely the guards of Alamore are supposed to show more grit than that."

More laughter. The man on the ground squeezed his eyes shut, fighting the whimper that rose in his chest. "Please. Please don't kill me."

There was a faint musical note, the sound of spurs as the rider dismounted and approached him, each step shadow silent. "Look at me," said the rider, sounding bored.

The Alamore guard lifted his face, eyes still tightly squeezed shut, waiting for the death blow to slice through him.

"I said look at me," snapped the rider, impatience making his tone sharper.

The man opened his eyes and blinked up. Off his horse, the rider seemed small, yet not any less powerful. He stood straight like a King of Darkness that was ready to condemn the guard at his feet. The guard wished that he could close his eyes again. He had to clamp his teeth down to hold back his whimper of fear.

Unable to take the silence pressing down, waiting for the blade to fall onto his neck, the guard swallowed and spoke, his voice breaking with terror. "Who are you?"

"Never you mind." The rider laughed coolly, crouching down so that he could see the man on the ground better.

The guard blinked, bewildered. Was it the alcohol playing tricks or the moon? This rider looked like a teenager, a boy with a faint smirk on his lips, his dark hair falling loose around his black eyes under the shadow of his hood. Even if he couldn't be sure of the rider's age, he was certain of one thing; the pale face with its high cheekbones and the rider's regal stance spoke of power, something that the guard had never had, only seen and envied in the men that commanded soldiers and armies.

"Tell me, are you actually an Alamore guard or was that all an act back in the tavern to get the ladies to talk to you and the men to buy you drinks? It's hard to tell at times if people like you are telling the truth or if you're boasting the stories of others and are full of lies when you drink too much. So, which is it?" the rider inquired, tilting his head again, taking in the guard better.

The guard swallowed hard and nodded. "I–I am a guard of the castle, yes."

"Excellent." The rider leaned back, his smirk widening. "Would you say that you enjoy it?" He sounded calm. They might have been discussing the matter over a drink, as if this stranger was a friend merely curious about his life, but there was still something menacing about this boy and the shadows that shifted out of sight around them–more riders standing guard, silent and watchful.

"Ex-excuse me?" The guard blinked hard, trying to push himself off his stomach. A hiss of steel made him freeze, terror rising again. He was certain the slamming heart in his chest might break through his bones.

"I don't recommend getting up right now," the boy said, holding up a hand.

He wasn't certain if it was to stay him or the shadows that had drawn their weapons. He didn't move, too terrified by the prospect of death to dare more than breathing.

"My Cutthroats are a bit defensive of me."

"C-cutthroats?" the guard asked, his confusion evident across his face.

"Yes, but before you ask, no, we're not your common rogues and thieves. We don't deal in your stolen horses and money, that's not what we're interested in. Not what I'm interested in." The boy ran a hand over his smooth jaw, assessing the guard. "You see, I have those things. What I steal is information, debts, and loyalties. Stealing is a bit harsh of a word to describe it perhaps… it's more I accept them as payment."

"In exchange for what?" the guard asked slowly, but he had a horrible feeling he already knew.

"Are you this thick or are you enjoying playing stupid?" the boy asked, sounding genuinely interested. "If you want to live to see the dawn, you'd best think what your loyalties, information, and life are worth. Now, what's your name?"

"Oberoan," the guard whispered. He could hear the shake in his own words, the whimper. Another laugh, lower and more dangerous, hissed from the dark behind him, in the direction of the drawn steel.

"Oberoan…" the rider repeated the name and Oberoan had the sense he was mulling it over, making sure he would always remember it. "Well, Oberoan, let me ask you this: are the guards of Alamore as foolishly loyal as the knights?"

"Sorry? I don't understand what you-"

"I mean," the rider cut across him, a note of annoyance now edging his voice, and reached toward his belt, "do you happen to think that staying true to King Revlan is worth your life?"

A gleam of brilliant silver in the moon's light showed the ornate blade of a dagger in the shape of a diving falcon, its beak open wide to swallow the blade. "Think carefully before you answer, Oberoan. I don't give people the chance to change their minds."

Oberoan's eyes shifted from the black eyes under the hood to the dagger and he licked his dried and cracking lips, fighting to keep himself from screaming or getting sick. "I have th-three years on my time left for the King of Alamore…"

"And will you serve him or me?" The rider was annoyed now.

"You?" Oberoan heard it come out as a question from his own lips and flinched as the blade moved. A shrill scream broke from him before he could help himself, but the blade wasn't diving into his chest. It instead flicked closer, pressing up against his exposed neck. The horsemen in the dark laughed again, harder now.

"That didn't sound very certain. I'm feeling nice today, so I'll ask you again, who do you serve?"

"Y-you, my Lord."

"Very good, Oberoan." The boy pulled the blade away, thrusting it into his belt, and rocked backwards, rising to his feet and straightening. "You will serve me and, should you turn out to be lying, you will wish I had killed you here. Is that understood?"

"Y-yes, my Lord."

The boy laughed coldly, shaking his head. "I'm not a Lord, and don't waste your breath on that title. You will call me Your Majesty or Prince. You owe me your life now, Oberoan and, more important to me than your life, is the information and secrets you will risk your life to bring me."

"What information is that?" Oberoan turned his head up higher, panting, trying to see the Prince better.

"First of all." The Prince ran a hand over his jaw under the hood, a smirk playing over his mouth. "I want to know what you've heard of the uprisings in Kelkor. Is your King planning to send reinforcements?"

"Uprisings? We haven't heard anything about sending soldiers for any uprisings… months ago, they had discussed Shadow Dale pressing Kelkor, that the King's brother was concerned."

In the darkness, he heard the hiss of a voice, the shivering steel of a blade being drawn.

"What uprisings are you talking about, Your Majesty?" Oberoan hated the squeak of fear in his voice.

"Uprisings of those loyal to the Kelkorian crown and those seeking a new order. If you haven't heard of it, perhaps you will soon… I expect that the Ranger of Kings will be working to keep your King Revlan informed on the happenings in Kelkor. After all, Revlan will want to look after his brother's throne, won't he? But no matter. Should you hear anything you will be sure I find out. Is that understood?"

Sweat beaded over Oberoan's lip and he licked it away, a tremor running over his body. If his information was deemed worthless, then what? The world's edges spun and again he cursed the ale he could still feel burning his throat and tongue.

"I don't believe I've heard any guards say we are to be sent anywhere. The castle's hurting in terms of soldiers and guards after the winter battles with Thornten." He licked his lips again. "Might have heard some knights whisper of unrest in the south, but nothing strong, nothing worth the worry of sending us to Kelkor. But the Ranger's been away, and when he comes back, I could find out more."

"Excellent." The Prince chuckled. "You're learning your new role quickly, aren't you? It's good to see someone who wants to keep their end of the bargain…and their life. You say the Ranger's been away often? Have you heard any whispers of where he's been? Or why?"

"N-no. The Ranger doesn't speak to the guards, Your Majesty. He keeps to the council, to the King, and that's all. W-what do you need to know about the Ranger?" asked Oberoan slowly.

The Prince snorted, annoyed. "I need to know his movements, his plans, his plots, where he is going, what he is saying, who he is speaking with, when he's in the castle, and most importantly when he's away. You will watch his movements; you will let me know when he's gone and for how long he will be away. Is that understood?"

Oberoan shook his head, his temples throbbing, vision blurring. "I can't do that, it'd be impossible. He tells nothing, he arrives any day or time and there's no pattern, no reasoning, to how long he stays or leaves."

"You best find a way to, or you'll pay most dearly," the Prince replied coldly. "I'm sure a man as adept at hustling cards like you were attempting at the tavern can be clever enough to save his own life."

"How did you-" Oberoan started, but the Prince cut him off.

"Don't worry about how I saw you, only worry about how you'll be of use to me. I don't believe in keeping the worthless and if I could see you in that tavern without you seeing me, know that it would be just as easy to have you killed."

With that, the Prince moved to his horse and slid one foot into his stirrup. He was on the brink of lifting himself into the saddle and Oberoan felt a surge of relief. They were leaving, he was alive, and they were leaving. The relief vanished as the Prince hesitated, one foot resting in his stirrup. He turned to Oberoan, his face shrouded in the dark of his hood, impossible to see. "If you tell a word of this to the King or the Ranger, believe me, I will know. You will wish I had killed you here as you begged for your life. Is that understood?"

"Yes, Prince," Oberoan whimpered. He was starting to feel desperate. The others in the shadows seemed to be growing impatient. He could hear their breathing, the jangle of their tack, the hissing sigh of blades half drawn to strike.

"Additionally," the Prince started, then hesitated, as though considering his words carefully, debating what he could say. "You will bring me anything you know about the squire William. Anytime he leaves the castle, you will send a signal, anything you hear of him, you will bring that information to me. Is that understood?"

"A squire?" Oberoan furrowed his brow. None of this was making sense. The shadows at his back were moving past him, toward the Prince. "What use is there in a squire? Are you meaning the Greyhead squire? He isn't a Count until he's eighteen and-"

"I don't care about the Greyhead boy," the Prince snapped, pulling himself into the saddle. "Bring me information on the Ranger and William. That's what I need from you."

"Why? If it's money you want, neither of them-"

"I've already told you," the Prince said through gritted teeth. "I don't need money. Their titles mean nothing to me, nor does their wealth, is that clear to you, you dolt?"

"How?" the guard whimpered, trying to inch upright. "How will I tell you?"

"I have ears that can slip in and out of the castle," said the Prince and Oberoan could imagine the smirk under the hood. "You won't need to worry about how you will tell me or about finding me. They will find you and will get the information I need from you. If you're alive or dead when they are done is entirely dependent upon your cooperation."

Oberoan nodded, his mind sluggish with information, with bewilderment. "And why? Who are you? What does the Ranger have to do with a squire?"

The other riders hissed and snarled, hounds and snakes that mistrusted him, but the Prince threw back his head with a laugh, his hood falling from his face. He gathered the reins to his black horse, his handsome young face smiling dangerously as he stared down at the wreck of a man before him. "You're asking bold questions for a man on the verge of wetting his own pants, Oberoan. Consider it my interest for Thornten. There are times when heirs to a throne are useful, a future alliance perhaps or just another pawn to use from a place of power. That's all you need to know."

"Heirs? To Thornten?" The liquor and terror made everything harder to understand. "What matter is that to you?"

"Never you mind what matter it is to me," purred the Prince. He reined the horse in a tight circle as the other riders moved away from him, shifting toward the river, five other hooded figures on dark animals. The Prince eyed Oberoan assessingly again, his head tilting once more. "Don't disappoint me, Oberoan. You won't care to be on the wrong side of The Cutthroat Prince."

Oberoan listened to the hooves thunder into a gallop then fade to nothing. It was a long while before he dared to push himself to his hands and knees. He swayed, eyes shut against the terror of a moment before, and wretched over the forest floor, silently vowing never to drink again.

***

The teenage girl stared down from the high windows at the dark ocean that broke at the base of the cliff below. Storm clouds roiled overhead, blotting the stars from view, but their anger was familiar, tolerable. Nothing like the sight at the far side of the castle, the sight of the lands that stretched away from this kingdom. Their fury was different, something she'd never seen or imagined. Where lightning broke the sky here, there it was the distant fires on the horizon, growing nearer each night.

She closed her eyes as salty air blew through her window, fluttering the hem of her dress, lifting the hair around her face. For a moment, she felt she was escaping reality, racing back through time to when none of these fears had even existed, when she was play-fighting with the squires, racing horses with her friends, swimming in the ocean.

"Princess Kalia?"

Kalia started, whipping round, her dark blonde hair fanning in a curtain around her. Shoulders relaxing, she smiled at the sight of the two people standing in her doorway–a seventeen-year-old boy, dark shaggy hair falling over his tanned forehead, a few strands loose over his eyes, and his small shadow, a girl around twelve, her own slightly lighter hair braided over one shoulder, her hand resting on the hilt of the dagger on her hip.

"Storms of the sea, you scared me."

"Why are you sitting in the dark?" the boy asked, giving her a roguish grin as he stepped in, opening the door wider so the light of the corridor flooded over her surroundings. She blinked, taken aback by the shadows that had stretched over the room. Through the door behind the boy, light streamed into the room. It shone off the candelabra that hung overhead, the table set with a chessboard of silver and bronze figures. The light chased the shadows from her shelves of books, reflected on the bronze kelpie set on its sea green tapestry, and the ornate white and gold threads of the carpet shone. The empty hearth alone remained dark, swallowing the light in its depths.

"You'll laugh at me, Niet, but I hadn't even realized it was getting dark," she said, smiling sheepishly. Her smile slipped and she turned back to the window a moment, fighting the knot that had risen in her throat. She wasn't about to let either of them see her moment of weakness.

"Well then, let's work on getting this room a bit brighter, shall we? Eldin, give me a hand, get the lantern on the shelf lit, I'll work on the hearth."

When she turned again, the older was crouched beside the fireplace, the sword on his side clearly visible, striking flint and steel while the younger girl was crossing to the lantern. "Don't bother with that, Eldin. I haven't refilled it since last night," Kalia said quickly, reddening.

"Up late?" the younger girl, Eldin, asked quizzically.

"Aren't we all of late?" she asked, giving Eldin a wry smile. "Anyway, I figured if I was awake I might as well read up on my uncle's lands, just in case."

Light flickered to life and warmth spread through Kalia as the fire in the hearth ignited, growing quickly as it consumed the generous kindling around it. Niet stepped back, giving an appreciative nod at his own handiwork. "That should do." He straightened, brushing the ash from his hands, and turned to Kalia, a wolfish grin in place. "You read when you can't sleep, meanwhile squires all cause mayhem. I guess that's the difference between the royals and the protectors."

Kalia gave him a look of mock offense. "Are you implying the royals aren't protectors?"

"If he isn't, I will," Eldin retorted playfully. Kalia made a snatch for the younger girl but, with light-footed agility, she was already springing away into one of the plush chairs.

Laughing, Kalia crossed to another of the seats, sinking down beside the chessboard. "I was wondering when you two would get the chance to come visit. I don't think you've ever stayed away this long."

"Well," Niet said, flopping into the chair across from her, "we've been getting all the busy work now, helping mostly, and training's gone to the back burner." He moved a silver pawn forward, gesturing to signal her turn.

Kalia moved without much thought, pushing one of her pawns out two spaces. "I'm not surprised. The knights have a lot to do at the moment."

Instantly, she wished she could catch the words and swallow them whole. A shadow flickered behind Niet's dark eyes and his fingers, resting on the castle piece in front of him, visibly tightened. "Yeah, they have."

"She'll be back before long," muttered Kalia. "And you know you couldn't have gone. Father said it wasn't-"

"I know," Niet cut across her, moving the castle into the pawn's vacated position. "It's just frustrating. I don't even know if she's made it out of Kelkor or if…" He shook his head. "I should have been there. I'm her squire. She might need help."

"She thought you were needed here," Kalia said, her voice more commanding now. "And she was right. I'd lose my mind without you and Eldin, and Eldin would honestly probably just sneak out after you."

"She's not wrong," Eldin agreed, scooting her chair nearer to study the chessboard. "Anyway, now you get to see what it's like training a squire by helping Paxrin train me."

Niet snorted, but Kalia was glad to see the shadow of a smile return to his lips. "I'm pretty sure you've been training Paxrin. My poor brother probably thought you'd be simple to train after Serena's glowing review."

"If Serena gives a glowing review, I think it means the person will be an outstanding knight, not an easy squire," said Kalia, laughing. "Paxrin was a squire when you started. Shame on him if he doesn't remember the pranks."

"I told him always that it was your idea," Niet admitted, guiltily. "And don't go giving Eldin ideas on pranks or Pax is going to murder me."

"Pranks? Why haven't I been learning these?" Eldin demanded, sitting up straighter. "I've been a squire for four months and you haven't mentioned anything about these pranks! How come?"

After that, the conversation was interspersed with laughter as Kalia, then Niet, recounted to the younger girl their days of tricking knights, sneaking through the castle, and scaring the guards. She listened with rapt attention and Kalia could see the grey eyes were imagining herself pulling such trickery now that she was at last a squire.

The distant sound of yelling broke the warmth and laughter. They all turned toward the door and Kalia half rose, her heart sinking. "What's going on?"

"Not sure." Niet was the first to the door, the other two following. Kalia noticed Eldin was gripping the handle of her long dagger and could almost feel the girl's fear and excitement.

"Do we need to go to help?" she asked, turning to Niet.

"Might."

Another shout had all three racing into the corridor. They heard feet running down a stairwell to their right and charged toward them. Kalia wished she'd thought to change into something as practical as the other two's tunics after dinner, hiking her skirts up to her shins to keep from stumbling over them.

At the end of the hallway, she grabbed the railing that looked down over the open stairwell to the steps descending into the grand hall below. Knights and soldiers, men and women alike, were rushing downwards, pulling on cloaks and swords as they descended. Niet grabbed Kalia's arm and pulled her to the stairs. The three raced after the others, taking the steps two at a time. Kalia almost tripped twice but Eldin always was there to grab her other arm and steady her, never hesitating.

At the bottom of the stairs, the three stopped, panting, and took in the grand hall. It had changed over the last few weeks. Weapons lined the walls now instead of statues and art. The place where once the thrones had set now held a table ladened with maps and strategies. At the table, Kalia could see a woman, her golden hair falling loose of its knot at the back of her neck, barking orders while the man beside her had his dark head bowed, speaking to one of the soldiers.

Catching sight of the three of them, the man straightened, dark eyes flashing. "Kalia, Niet, Eldin."

Niet swore under his breath and Kalia bit back a mad urge to snort with laughter. Her father's stern tone scared most of the knights and squires but to her it was almost amusing, so seldomly used. They crossed toward the man, Niet and Eldin letting Kalia lead this time.

"Father, what's going on?" Kalia asked, hardly noticing her friends bow on either side, heads ducked forward, right hands held to their left shoulders.

"It seems Lord Casryn's decided he doesn't need the crown's favor," her father said, his jaw tightening as he spoke. He waved a hand to the two squires who straightened, still nervous.

"Lord Casryn," Kalia muttered, trying to place the name. "The one who looks like a beanpole."

"It doesn't matter what he looks like, Kalia, but rather what he controls and in this case it's the borderlands that hold the main route between us and Alamore," he said firmly.

Niet stepped forward, color washing from his face. "Your Majesty, King Azric, my knight-"

The King held his hand up to forestall his question. "We haven't heard anything, but I imagine Serena is already in Alamore at this point. She might have heard of Lord Casryn's change of heart, but she's not a fool, Niet. She'll be riding hard. What this mostly means for us is that the escape we had hoped for is meeting complications. Sending anyone from Kelkor now-" His eyes rested on his daughter. "is dangerous."

"So, I'll stay," Kalia said, stepping forward. "I'll stay, I can fight, I've been trained and-"

"No."

It wasn't her father who answered. The golden-haired woman was striding toward them, a commanding gleam in the clear brown eyes– Kalia's eyes. "You won't stay. When Serena arrives at Alamore, Revlan will know to send someone to help you, even if their forces aren't enough now to help us."

"Mother, I can't leave with this happening! My friends are here, you and father are here. I can't-"

The Queen of Kelkor silenced her with a sharp eagle eye. "You can't stay here either. Should something happen, the last thing I need is the knowledge that you're here and…" She stopped, shaking her head. "It's not for debate, Kalia. You'll leave as soon as we find a way for you to."

"Queen Paranella, why have the knights been mustered?" Eldin asked. Kalia was glad for the change of subject. Arguing with her mother was impossible at the best of times and now, with the flurry of wartime activity, it'd be impossible.

"With Casryn's change in his alliance to the crown, we face issues on a larger scale. We'll have to work to secure the roads we can from here to Alamore, as well as send for alliances to be strengthened with the

Lords on the north and eastern borders," the Queen explained. "We'll need to tighten the security around Kelvane and the castle, send word to Cale and see if King Prandus will send help. But, for now, I think you three need to stay upstairs. Go find a way to keep busy." The ghost of a smile lined her eyes. "Find a way to cause trouble somewhere, eh? Niet, Eldin, keep Kalia company. Once we've found a way for you to leave, we will send you away."

"All this changes is that we won't have the time we had hoped for, at least not enough for the Ranger to come for you," King Azric said, running a hand over the two-day beard on his jaw.

"The Ranger?" Niet asked sharply, straightening. "You were going to send Kalia with the Ranger of Kings? You trust him?"

"I would trust him with all three of your lives. The Ranger isn't a fool and Revlan has not been proven wrong to trust him yet. But I'm not as certain now that we have that choice. It may be best if we send you all with Paxrin instead-" Paranella's stony voice quelled argument and he bowed his head again respectfully.

"Yes, my Queen, I only meant…"

"King Revlan trusts him. I understand your knight's reserves, but in times of war, Niet, you must learn to do things that are difficult." Paranella's lips twitched into a faint smile. "Even when you know Serena would warn you otherwise. We can only hope she reaches Alamore soon and that we find some means of relief…but now, you three, get out of this hall. Niet, Eldin, stay with Kalia. We will discuss this more at the dawn. Casryn's fall means things are far darker than they seemed."

"Yes, Queen Paranella," Niet answered for them, bowing his head and grabbing Kalia's arm in one hand, Eldin's shoulder in the other, and steering them away. As they made their way up the steps again, Kalia couldn't help but look back one more time. She could see that all traces of humor were gone from her mother's face and replaced with strain and worry. Her father's dark eyes were shadowed. Her heart clenched and she gripped the banister tighter, turning away. It felt that Kelkor would never be as it had been again.

CHAPTER ONE

Sun poured across the courtyard, shining on the gleaming coats of horses, the shadow of the trees at the courtyard edge swaying gently in the late spring breeze. On the walls above, the Alamore banner–deep blue with a silver stag's head set across three slanted gold bars–waved in the lazy wind, the silver threads reflecting the western rays of the setting sun. The black double doors of the castle had been propped open, an attempt to free the castle of its last stale breaths of winter air. Leaning his back against the trunk of the tree nearest the doors, the brown-haired thirteen-year-old squire stifled a yawn behind his hand, turning his head up to the branches above him.

Will stared at the leaves overhead and listened to the sounds around him, already familiar as an old song, despite not even being at the castle a full year.

How had it been less than a year since the day that his two best friends–Colin Greyhead, the golden-haired Count's son, and Rowan Lonric, a Lord's heir–had come stumbling down the street where he'd been sitting? He'd thought that moment to be the best of his life, but it had only been where his luck began. By the end of that day, he'd been invited to train as a squire of Alamore, training to become one of the knights that defended the Kingdom. He could still remember the giddy feeling, the terror that he'd wake to find it all a dream.

Not that it all had been a perfect dream come true. Within months of becoming a squire, Will had faced dangers he had never imagined; murderous traitors living in tunnels beneath the castle, their enemy to the east–Thornten–turning their allied kingdoms against them and trying to set a trap for the King of Alamore, and worse still his own father–Marl–capturing him and trying to kill him. He might have succeeded in killing Will, and Rowan and Colin too, if not for the Ranger of Kings arriving to rescue them. The Ranger, with the help of several Alamore knights, had given Will, Rowan, and Colin the chance to escape.

It had been in that escape that Will had learned the truth. He squeezed his eyes shut a moment at the memory, unsure of whether it had been the pain of his broken rib that night, or the sharp edge of the spilled secret, that still could make him flinch. The squire of King Tollien of Thornten had followed them through the night to recapture Will. It had been he, Robin, squire of the King of Thornten, that had let slip the truth; that Marl was more than Tollien's spy. Marl, like the Ranger of Kings himself, was Tollien's brother.

Which made Will an heir to not only Thornten but, through the twists of his lineage, also one of the heirs to Alamore. He'd wanted to ignore this, to never consider these ties, but again and again Marl had proven that he would not so soon forget. He was fired by a determination to kill Will and, thus, eliminate a Thornten heir whose loyalty rested with Alamore.

Will hadn't been able to tell anyone, unwilling to accept the truth of the matter himself. If he lived in denial, maybe he wouldn't have to face what his blood made him.

It seemed a good plan and thus far he hadn't had problems in his decision not to tell anyone. The closest he had come to discussing it with anyone, other than those who knew–Rowan, Colin, their knights, Sir Laster, Sir Miller, and the Ranger–was with his knight, Haru. Marl had tried to kill Haru when he was still a squire and it had been Will who fought him then, determined to save his friend's life. After Haru had been knighted and asked Will to train as his personal squire, the reality had weighed on Will's chest. He knew he would have to tell Haru in time, to explain the dangers that surrounded who he was and how Thornten would never stop hunting him. But the words seemed to escape him. Each time he thought he might, it felt as though a hand gripped his chest, threatening to rebreak his ribs.

He had hoped that, childishly, he might be able to convince the Ranger to tell Haru, but that plan had proved in vain. The Ranger flitted in and out of the castle, a shadow that seemed to come and go without reason, never staying to talk before vanishing with the same silence and speed with which he had appeared. Rowan and Colin had tried to tell Will it was normal, that the Ranger had been that way for as long as they'd lived at the castle, and yet something felt wrong.

He couldn't explain it to them, he couldn't even explain it to himself properly. It was only that the way the Ranger came and went crackled with unspoken tension and a foreboding he couldn't understand.

None of it seemed to matter, however. Marl hadn't appeared in the long weeks since the battle of the crypt, where tunnel people and Thornten soldiers alike had rushed through The Crypt of Past Kings into Alamore. Though the tunnels had been fitted and sealed with iron gates so they couldn't be used as an entry into Alamore anymore, Will didn't think it had been enough to dissuade Marl from finding him. As much a relief as Marl's absence was, Will couldn't shake the gnawing sense that it wouldn't last. It felt bound to end and Marl would come hunting him again.

"Ouch! Dammit, that hurt!"

Will shook himself from his thoughts and, grinning, turned to the two figures hurrying across the courtyard toward him from the barn. Colin was shaking his head, struggling to look disapproving while doing his best to hide his smirk. Tall, his golden hair fell forward, and his green eyes were bright with suppressed laughter.

Beside him, Rowan either didn't notice or didn't care, his hand pressed to his mouth, muffling more oaths. Thin and lanky like his own knight, Rowan struck a contrast to Colin's composed manner with his disheveled brown hair and narrowed brown eyes. He pulled his hand from his mouth to inspect it for a moment, then pressed it back, swearing again.

"If Ross hears you, you'll be cleaning stalls another week," warned Colin, glancing back over his shoulder toward the barn. "He's been in a mood of late so you might not want to test him."

Rowan removed his hand from his mouth again, shaking it out. "When is he not in a mood? Anyway, he can bite me for all I care, the grouchy git."

"Watch it, the way he growls all the time, he might actually do that," Will said, patting the sparse grass beside him. "Pull up a dirt and stay awhile. How's fixing your bridle going?"

Rowan laughed darkly, flopping into the grass and holding his hand out for Will to see. "I nearly amputated my arm with that bloody needle! Look! Look at it! Pouring blood! I swear, had there been a lady there, she would have fainted. It's just that bad!"

16

Will fought the urge to laugh as he looked at the small puncture, the skin around it red. "I guess you'll have a scar to show off?"

"It's how he's going to impress ladies when he's older," Colin confided, lowering himself down with more grace than Rowan.

"Shove off, you bugger." Rowan aimed a swipe at Colin, which missed.

Grinning, Will shrugged. "I mean, if it's scars that are going to help you get a lady, you should break your bridle more often. You need all the help you can get."

Colin doubled with howls of laughter and Rowan whipped round to attack. This time he was faster, cuffing Will in the back of the head. "Twerp!"

Laughing, Will pushed Rowan away, flattening his hair again. "Knock it off. You'll hurt your hand, Princess."

"I don't know, Will," Colin chimed in, scooting out of Rowan's reach. "I don't think a lady would complain as much about a stab with a needle. Maybe Rockwood should ask for your father to send your sister to train as a knight instead?"

"You know," said Rowan conversationally, leaning back to sit on his heels and surveying them both through narrowed eyes, "I hate you. I hate you both. When I'm Lord of Lonric, I'm declaring war on you, Greyhead, and putting a price on Will's head. Or, worse, I'll make you two look out for my sister. That'd be a punishment alright. Crazy girl…"

"You know how bored you would be if we weren't here?" Will raised his eyebrows.

"If you weren't here, I'd be living peacefully," Rowan grumbled, grabbing a handful of grass and letting it float in the breeze.

"Peacefully? With you in the castle?" Colin snorted. "I'm pretty sure that Will doesn't cause half the mayhem you do."

"I feel attacked right now." Rowan sighed dramatically.

"And I feel restless," Will grumbled, pushing himself off the earth and brushing his hands free of dirt. His muscles were stiff from sitting, his body aching with the long practice he had had that morning with Haru and Robin, working on quarterstaff fighting. It had turned out that Robin was quite good at it, knocking both Will and Haru to the ground with ease.

After that, Haru had made Robin drill them both over and over until he was bruised and sweat-soaked, not giving him a chance to work on anything else before the two knights had been ordered onto an Eastern Forest patrol with Sir Don and his squire, Novin, the oldest squire and one of the few being permitted to the far east patrols.

Ever since the battles of the winter anyone not old enough to have their own sword–any squire under seventeen–had been banned from the Eastern Forest. They had to content themselves with the western patrols. Those were boring in comparison to the prospect of attack to the east, but Will had learned that boring wasn't always a bad thing.

"If you're about to suggest we go practice, I'll kick your teeth out and shave your head," Rowan moaned, laying back. Colin stifled a snort of laughter in a cough.

"You have such a lovely personality," Will commented dryly. "No, I'm not making you do anything. I just want to work Vis. You can stay here and rest."

"Fine, fine, I'll come, you can stop your begging." Rowan climbed to his feet, shaking the grass from his tunic like a dog in water. "Col, you up for some mayhem and horses? Watching Will try to tame the fire-breathing dragon?"

Colin glanced at the tree overhead and Will could see his hesitation. After a pause he stood with a resigned sigh. "If I don't go, I know I'll regret it later. It'd be like that time Rowan found the tunnels and talked you back into them. Actually, I somewhat do wish I'd missed that one. Not sure I fully forgive your stupidity for that, Will."

"Why just me?" Will demanded, laughing. "It was Rowan's idea in the first place!"

"Yeah, but he expects you to be the thinker out of the two of us," Rowan said, rolling his eyes.

"Exactly." Colin grinned, raising his eyebrows.

Will grimaced. "You've got a point. Perhaps not my best moment."

"We all make mistakes, Will." Rowan thumped him on the back. "You just made a bigger mistake than most by following me."

A clatter in the direction of the drawbridge made all three squires turn, Will's hand automatically reaching for the dagger on his belt, his muscles tensing after the months of always being on edge for the attacks from the tunnel people. There was no screaming horde in red robes, however. Instead, a single rider, slumped forward in the saddle, was barely managing to rein the horse to a halt in the courtyard. The sea-green cloak that hung from the rider's shoulders was mud splattered and torn, the tears revealing the dull gleam of chainmail hanging limply from the thin frame. The rider was doubled forward, one hand still clutching the horse's reins, the other clasped the handle of a sword that swayed at the saddle's side.

The warmth of the sun moments before vanished, replaced with a chill as every eye from the courtyard and the walls above turned to watch the rider. Taking a ragged breath, the rider straightened, the shadowed green eyes taking in the surroundings, the silent spectators. Out of the corner of his eye, Will saw the brown-haired and broad-shouldered form of Sir Ross, Colin's knight, striding from the barn. He paused several feet away, reaching for the rough-cut blue stone hilt of the sword on his side, blue eyes fastened on the rider.

"Revlan, I must speak with King Revlan," rasped the rider, sagging forward again.

Ross didn't hesitate but launched himself toward the horse, reaching the rider's side as her eyelids fluttered and the woman fell, unconscious, against the neck of her exhausted horse.

CHAPTER TWO

"Who do you think she is?"

Will sank onto the foot of his bed in the squires' chamber, frowning at his boots. Outside the window, the shadows of the castle stretched to darken the walls around it, the final moments of the day fading into the earliest breaths of night.

"How the blazes would I know? It's not like she and I caught up any more than you got to before she passed out," Rowan replied, lounging on his back on his bed, his head lolling off the foot of his mattress.

"I think that was rhetorical," Colin said, sniggering and leaning his shoulder against the wall between his and Will's beds. "I think the blood rushing to your head is making you a bit thicker than you already are."

"Watch it, Greyhead, or I'll knock your teeth loose."

"You're full of the best threats today, aren't you?"

Ignoring his friends, Will shook his head. "Where do you think she came from?"

"You want the long answer about the birds and the bees or-"

"Rowan!" Colin snapped.

"What? I'm trying to offer Will's restless mind some reprieve!"

"You're ridiculous." Colin rolled his eyes to the ceiling, pushing himself off the wall. He turned to Will, crossing his arms and frowning, though Will could tell it was more in concentration than annoyance. "All I can think is that she would be from Kelkor."

"Kelkor?" Will asked, bemused. "What makes you say that?"

"Don't you remember Laster telling us that Kelkor has lady knights?" Rowan lifted himself into a seated position, throwing out his arms to balance. "Bloody Thornten, I'm dizzy."

"Then stop hanging upside down, you're not a bat," Colin suggested, snorting with laughter as Rowan swayed on his bed, hands clamped on either side of his head. "If you fall off that bed, I'm never letting you live it down."

"You think she's a knight?" Will forced the conversation back on track.

"Probably." Colin shrugged. Will could tell he wasn't as interested in the subject as he himself was. "I can't think of another reason for the armor and weapon. Probably sent as a messenger or something."

"Why would she be sent in that state from Kelkor to here?"

"Come off it Will, don't be thick. She didn't leave in that condition," Rowan said, pulling his hands from his face. He gave his head an experimental shake. "She probably got either lost or met bandits or rogues or something."

"I've heard that path isn't the safest," Colin agreed sagely.

"But what kind of message could be that important to not take a moment's rest somewhere?" Will pressed on. It was frustrating him that neither of his friends seemed as interested as he was in this woman's appearance.

"I mean, the King of Kelkor is King Revlan's brother. It could be anything from catching up to something worse," Colin answered.

"Do you think it could be something worse?" Will asked, stiffening.

"Oh, drop it, Will, we will either find out if something's wrong or we will be kept in the dark," Rowan grumbled. "Blazes of Thornten, I could be sick."

Annoyed, Will opened his mouth to retort then closed it, running a hand through his hair and letting his shoulders sag at the realization that what Rowan said was true. They would either find out or they wouldn't. This burning curiosity wasn't going to get him anywhere. "Right... you're right."

"It always concerns me when someone says that Rowan is right," Colin said, grinning. "But more concerning still is when I agree that he is right."

"Been telling you two for a while now that I am a remarkable minded genius, you two just don't appreciate it with your minds of muck and moronic woes."

Will managed a snort of laughter, shaking his head. They were right. So far in his time as a squire, he had learned that the knights, the Ranger, and the King kept their secrets well-hidden until others needed to know them.

"Speaking of things only we need to know…"

Will turned to Colin who was grinning, green eyes alight with mischief. "Did you two hear that we're getting two new squires next week?"

"Oh yeah?" Will straightened. Apart from Airagon joining the castle after Will, Rowan, and Colin had pulled him from the tunnels, there hadn't been any squires who joined since he himself had come to Alamore. "Who?"

"Couple of the pages." Colin shrugged.

"Gabe and Jerram?" Rowan raised his eyebrows. Colin gave a curt nod and Rowan gave a maniacal cackle, rubbing his hands together. "Excellent! My guidance can begin again!"

"Guidance? Begin again?" Will looked between Rowan and Colin. "Colin, what the blazes is the crazy one on about?"

Chuckling, Colin ran a hand over his jaw, lost in some memory. "When we were pages, those two were a year behind us. Rowan always made it his duty to get them into as much trouble as possible. He called it teaching mischief or some stupid thing."

"It's called mentoring in mayhem and I don't appreciate you calling it stupid," Rowan grumbled, pushing himself to his feet. "But what I would appreciate is something to eat. I'm half starved."

Will nodded, his stomach growling appreciatively of Rowan's words. "I could go for something to eat now too, actually."

"How did you hear those two are becoming squires anyhow?" Rowan asked as they crossed the room.

"Sir Miller told me," said Colin, holding the door for Rowan and Will to pass through first. "He was working with Ross and me today on archery and mentioned that he'd be taking on Gabe as his squire."

Food wafted to Will's nose, causing his mouth to water and he turned away from Rowan and Colin's conversation and toward the massive dinner hall and, more importantly, the two tables. The nearer table–long and down the center of the room–was where the knights sat. This one was empty of food or people. He guessed that the knights were still attending to the stranger who had arrived, while the other table–

22

round and at the further edge from the squire chamber door–had been covered in platters and dishes, the smells of which made his stomach grumble louder.

Several squires were already seated at the table, serving themselves and talking animatedly when Will, Rowan, and Colin reached them. Will flopped into his usual seat, Rowan and Colin taking the chairs on his either side. All three reached for different dishes.

"I could eat an army," Rowan moaned, staring longingly at the plates around him.

"That's a good thing to keep in mind! Next time we've got Thornten knocking at the door to come in and kill us, we'll just send you to greet them then, aye?" cracked Loper, a red-haired and freckled boy, a couple years their elder, seated across the table from them.

"Send him on Will's fire breathing nag and we'll not only defeat their army but conquer their Kingdom," Saget, lanky and yellow-haired and seated on Loper's right, said wisely.

Heaping his plate, Will shook his head but grinned, listening to his friends discuss the fierce army they could create with a band of hungry Rowans and foul tempered Visra.

Before Will had finished his first helping of everything on the table, they were joined by two of the older squires, Delvin–shaggy brown hair falling nearly to his thick brows–and Novin–a burly black-haired boy with a round open face. They joined into the conversation eagerly. It grew louder and more ridiculous, the squires creating elaborate battle strategies based on Rowan's appetite.

"You lot hear anything yet about this woman rider?"

Will's attention broke from the conversation as Vancely, a tall squire with dark curls and clear brown eyes, sank into the seat next to Saget, brows raised.

"We were in the courtyard when she rode in," answered Colin, shaking his head. "She didn't seem in a good state."

"No, no, she didn't," Vancely agreed sagely.

"Have you heard anything about her then?" Will asked. Next to him, he heard Rowan's muffled groan and was certain his friend had rolled his eyes.

Vancely snorted, annoyed. "Not really. I was training with Airagon in the indoor practice court upstairs with Laster and the King, then Haru showed up to get them. The King told Airagon he should come along to the council. I tried to convince Laster, but you know him." He curled his lip in a mocking sneer and impersonated his knight's snide tones. "The knights' council isn't a matter for squires, as I would have hoped you understood by the name."

All of the squires at the table broke into laughter at this. Will had to thump Rowan on the back as he choked on a piece of bread he'd been eating.

"But Airagon got to go," pointed out Colin once the laughs had subsided. "He should have let you go."

"Well, what the King decides to do with Airagon is up to him, isn't it? He's the King's squire. I don't think Laster was going to tell him he disapproved of it," Vancely said, rolling his eyes. "But, either way, I'd have liked to go. I haven't been to a council in ages and this one was probably going to be interesting."

"I'd have liked to go myself," Novin agreed, nodding.

"Not much longer though and you'll be going as Sir Novin!" Loper punched Novin in the arm playfully and the older squire's face turned red with a pleased embarrassment.

"You can't leave us now!" Rowan slapped his palms on the table. "Who will be the voice of reason if you get knighted? Haru's gone, Robin's a knight too, and if you go I'll end up without any guidance or morals, wicked in my ways and-"

"Oh, shut up." Colin reached around Will to cuff Rowan in the back of the head, laughing.

The conversation shifted again, back to good natured dispute between the squires, but Will sank into silence, the uneasy feeling returning. He could tell Colin had noticed and, occasionally, his friend would shoot him a questioning look. Giving an almost imperceptible headshake, Will signaled that he didn't want to discuss it. Not now, when all the others were having so much fun. He wasn't about to be the one to spoil it for the rest of them.

Still, there was something going on; he could feel it. It was the sensation he'd noticed crackling through the castle over the winter when the advisor for Shadow Dale, Sir Dannix, had been brutally murdered. Then it had been the strife between Alamore and Shadow Dale that had coursed through the castle when Alamore refused to attack Thornten, guessing correctly that it was a trap. This feeling was the same as that had been. An uneasiness. Only this time he couldn't place it. The only thing that had happened was the appearance of the rider.

Will was so lost in his own thoughts that it was a moment before he realized the hair had risen on the back of his neck. A shiver ran down his spine and the sensation of being watched made him stiffen. He twisted in his seat and glimpsed the darkness in the doorway leading to the entry hall shift. A shadow that seemed to move apart from the others, darker than the rest, flitting out of sight.

"Oi, Will, where you off to?" Rowan grabbed his arm as he rose, raising an eyebrow. "We need your expert advice on the best way to battle Visra against King Kolt of Phersal."

"I'll discuss that in a minute…I, eh, I forgot something in the barn. I'll be right back."

Will pulled himself from his friend's grasp, grimacing at the suspicious glower both Rowan and Colin were now giving him. "Promise, I'll be right back."

"Aw, leave him be, he's been through enough here since becoming a squire that I think he can look out for himself some," Novin chided, grinning. "You two don't have to play at mother hen, you know. I think he can walk to the barn and back without a formal escort of soldiers, don't you?"

This broke their attention from Will and, moving quickly now, he heard Rowan make clucking noises behind him. Stifling a grin, he rounded the corner of the dinner hall, stepping into the entry hall. He stopped, the smile sliding from his face. Nothing stirred. The hall was empty, filled only with lengthening shadows. A few of the torches had burnt out. *Mind's playing tricks. It was just the torches, he's not here.*

Will made to turn away when a low laugh made him start, almost tripping over his own foot in his haste to face the shadows of a doorway. A figure, shrouded in a black cloak, leaned one shoulder casually against the wall of the corridor. In the darkness he'd been invisible at first and Will felt his face heat with embarrassment as the man before him crossed his arms over his chest.

"You should be a bit more observant." Even if he couldn't see it, he could hear and imagine the smirk beneath the shadow of the hood.

"Are you trying to scare me to death?" Will asked, trying to sound more affronted rather than shaken.

The man chuckled and straightened, stepping into the light of the remaining torches. Sure enough, a sneering smirk curved the lips, barely visible under the hood. "Perhaps. But, more concerning than that is that you're becoming predictable, Will," chided the Ranger in his imperturbable, almost bored, and familiar, voice.

"Oh yeah? How so?" asked Will, still trying to calm his thumping pulse. He tried to put the same cool inflection in his voice but judging by the twitch in the Ranger's smirk, he hadn't managed it well.

"Getting you to step out here without the others. I just had to stand there until you finally turned, until you noticed me, and they hadn't. Your curiosity is on the verge of a weakness. You should know by now that it's better not to wander off alone. It's unsafe at times. Rowan and Colin are right, you might need them as your, eh, mother hens."

Will scowled. "I don't need mother hens."

The Ranger gave a low laugh. "No, probably not but regardless, I'm surprised your cohorts aren't already out here to check on you."

"I don't need checked on," Will said brazenly.

"Continue to act in predictable ways, to follow patterns, to be easy to understand and guess, and yes, you will need checked on. You will need all the help you can get if you can't learn to keep yourself safe and watch your surroundings better than you did tonight," the Ranger growled.

Will gritted his teeth, biting back the retort he longed to throw at the Ranger. *He's going to lecture me on staying safe when he's been gallivanting off Alamore only knows where doing who even knows what?* In the months of the man's abcenses, he'd forgotten how much the Ranger could annoy him. Come to think of it, the Ranger seemed to have that effect on everyone, not just himself.

This brought questions to mind, and he frowned at the Ranger, crossing his own arms. "So, where exactly have you been then?"

The smirk turned into lips pressed thin in disapproval. "Have I not told you before not to ask about matters that aren't your business?"

"But you wanted to talk to me, so must be something going on that has to do with me," said Will.

The Ranger chuckled humorlessly. "You have a high opinion of yourself."

The squire waited, refusing to respond, still glowering at the hooded man until the Ranger sighed, uncrossing his arms and dropping one hand to rest on the hilt of his sword.

"You know, there are times when I find that you are refreshingly intelligent for someone who wants to become a knight. Then there other times when I feel you have just mind enough to make someone aggravated enough that they might murder you to simplify their lives," the Ranger said, his voice conversational. Will fought the urge to grin, half certain the mouth under the hood had given the ghost of a smile. "And right now, I can't decide which way I am feeling. But yes, I did want to speak with you. I'm not here for very long, but I hear we have a guest upstairs." He inclined his head in the direction of the stairs that Will knew from too much experience led to the healing chamber doors. "What happened when she arrived? Did she say anything?"

"She asked for the King, then passed out," Will said, shaking his head. He hesitated, furrowing his brow. "Why are you asking me instead of just going up there and speaking to her for yourself? I thought you were on the council, so shouldn't you be up there?"

The Ranger's smirk returned, though this time his voice was cold when he spoke. "My presence won't be necessary there, I am sure."

Bewildered, Will glanced at the stairs, then back at the Ranger. "You're the Ranger of Kings. I thought you normally bring the information. Isn't that what you've been doing? Don't you want to go report to the King and the council? Surely you just want to go talk to her yourself, don't you?"

"I would rather speak with a snake," the Ranger purred. Seeing Will's dumbfounded look, the man explained. "The woman that arrived is Lady Serena of Kelkor, a knight of Queen Paranella, and...an old acquaintance of mine."

"Oh." Will nodded. He'd seen how others reacted to the Ranger's presence. King Giltor of Shadow Dale had made his contempt obvious. Even some of the knights, Laster mostly, were openly hostile toward the Ranger. Still, that hadn't stopped him from stating his mind before. Will opened his mouth, and the Ranger held a hand up to stop him.

"Once more, William, we shall practice keeping your nose and curiosity to yourself, shall we? It's a lesson I feel I should teach you, so I don't finally tip over that edge where I murder you to simplify my life."

Feeling put out, Will scowled at his boots a moment. Why, exactly, had he even cared that the Ranger was gone? It should have been a relief to not have to deal with his snide remarks. If he'd missed the Ranger this much he might as well have gone to Laster and dealt with his arrogance. It would have been just like having the Ranger back then.

"Speaking of keeping things to yourself," the Ranger muttered, ignoring Will's annoyance. "I also wanted to know; who have you told about Marl's true identity?"

Will looked up, his face reddened at the thought of Haru. "No one…only people who know are those who found out when I did or already knew who Marl was."

"So not Haru?" the Ranger asked, frowning.

"Right," Will mumbled.

"Which means he knows that your father is Marl, just not that Marl is Tollien's brother?"

"Eh, yes, that's the general idea of it," Will grumbled, shoving his hands in his pockets. "I just haven't told him yet and-"

"I suggest then that you don't," the Ranger cut across Will's words before he could continue. Confused, Will stared at the hooded man, wishing he could see the face, read the expression.

"What?"

"Don't tell Haru. Do not tell anyone in fact." The Ranger's voice had lowered to a warning hiss. He reached forward, gripping Will's shoulder and lowering his face until it was nearly level with Will's own. "I don't want you to breathe that you even know anyone by the name of Marl, do you understand? Not in front of anyone but Rowan and Colin and especially-" he paused, inhaling deeply. "Especially not in front of our new guest."

"The lady knight?" Will asked.

The Ranger sighed. "No, the visiting jesters who have been juggling fire from the top of the barn for the past week… yes, of course I mean in front of the lady knight."

The sound of a door opening above them made Will turn his head up, listening to what sounded like the feet of all the knights leaving the healing chamber. He jumped as the Ranger gripped his other shoulder, his fingers biting into Will's skin through his tunic. "Listen to me, Will. You mustn't tell, do you understand? There isn't time to explain everything, and I don't know everything myself, not yet anyway." He spoke quickly, raising his voice slightly to cut across Will when he opened his mouth to respond. "You just have to promise me that you won't tell a soul. There are people that will want to use you for what you are, for who you are, and they aren't going to be stopped by walls. They will be searching for anything they can find on you, and I need you to promise you won't talk to anyone about what you are, who you are."

"But who-"

"Promise me!"

Will wasn't sure he had ever heard the Ranger sound more pleading. "Fine! I promise!"

The Ranger released him, stepping back in a swish of dark cloak. The footfalls were nearer, the knights on the stairs coming down to the entry hall. "I cannot stay here, I cannot protect you now, Will. There are things happening that I have to attend to, which means I can't stay here to keep you safe but-" He broke off, wheeling round as the first of the knights appeared, bounding down the steps.

Haru, red hair flopping over his pale forehead, paused with a bewildered expression at the sight of Will and the Ranger then bounded down the last two steps and strode toward them. He inclined his head to the Ranger in a silent greeting, which the Ranger returned stiffly. Grinning, he threw his arm over Will's head, leaning against him as if to rest.

"This is a convenient height for me, honestly, if you don't mind staying short, Will. Means I can take a break whenever and just lean on you."

"Get off." Will laughed, ducking out from under Haru's arm. He could feel the Ranger's icy glower on them and straightened again with a sheepish smile.

"Was he causing mayhem, Ranger?" Haru asked the hooded man, raising his brows and forcing a serious look onto his boyish face. "Perhaps opening tunnels again?"

Will shook himself free of Haru, grimacing irritably. "I don't cause mayhem."

The Ranger gave a derisive snort but didn't respond.

"I might be inclined to side more with the Ranger on this one," said Haru before turning back to the Ranger. "You missed the council; we were in the healing chamber. A knight from Kelkor arrived and…"

Haru cut himself short, glancing down at Will with the guilty look of someone who had nearly said too much.

"I only arrived a little while ago myself," the Ranger growled. "I didn't feel it prudent to interrupt. Anyways, I thought it best I speak with the King in private before addressing a council."

Other knights were appearing now through the entryway to the stairs, talking in low voices. Among them, Will easily spotted the dark hair and black eyes of King Revlan, his head inclined to his right to better hear the words of the handsome, if not somewhat arrogant looking, brown-haired and amber-eyed Sir Laster, speaking at his side. Laster's eyes flitted toward where Will and the Ranger stood, and Will was unsurprised to see his lip curl into a thin sneer.

Behind the King his squire, Airagon, was listening attentively, his brown hair swept back and away from his freckled face, a hand running over his uneven stubble. Nodding to Laster, the King straightened and surveyed the entry hall, his black eyes resting on the Ranger. He raised a hand, waving for the Ranger to join him as he turned, not toward the dinner hall, but back toward the courtyard.

"Keep your squire out of trouble, if you are competent enough, *knight*," the Ranger hissed under his breath. Before either of them could respond he had already wheeled round, black cloak swishing, and swept away after the King.

"Sarcastic prat," Haru huffed, shaking his head and scowling after the hooded man. "When he says stuff like that, it gets a whole lot harder to like him."

Will watched too, frowning. What had the Ranger been warning him about? What had happened? He wished he could sprint after him and demand answers. All he had done was prove that the uneasiness Will felt was right. There was something wrong and it seemed to have something to do with either who he was or, more likely, who Marl really was.

"What did he want anyhow?"

"What?" Will started and turned to look at Haru. His knight was waiting, a bemused expression on his face.

"I asked you what the Ranger wanted," Haru said, not quite managing to hide his laugh at Will's confusion. "Thornten, Will, I didn't think that Robin knocked you in the head today. What's got into you?"

"Oh, sorry. I'm just tired is all, long day. And the Ranger was, eh, was just seeing where everyone had got to and what was going on with the woman who arrived."

Lady Serena, the Ranger had called her. And she *was* a knight of Kelkor. Colin had been right on that one. But that only stirred more questions. Like why the blazes would she care about who he really was? Marl was from Thornten, not Kelkor.

"Wouldn't we all like to know what's going on!" Sir Rockwood, Rowan's mentor, was breaking away from his conversation with the sandy-haired Sir Don and moving to join them, his dark eyes shadowed with lack of sleep. Even so, they gleamed with good natured humor and there was a spring in his step that made his athletically lean build seem comical. Smiling broadly, he made a swipe to ruffle Will's hair, which the squire evaded with practiced skill. "But I think your squire here, Haru, is sneaking for answers."

"I wasn't!" Will protested, moving with the two knights back in the direction of the dinner hall. "The Ranger had a question, and I just was answering it."

"Sure you were." Rockwood rolled his eyes. "Because you, Rowan, and Colin are never out looking for trouble. Just a bunch of misunderstood squires that happen to find it." He winked at Will who did his best to look offended.

"Leave him be, Rockwood. You'll give him ideas," Haru warned.

"And my squire hasn't already given him ideas? You're off your rocker, Haru, if you think Rowan hasn't corrupted him!" Rockwood made another swipe and this time managed to mess up Will's hair, springing back with a bark of laughter when Will took a swipe at him.

"You're worse than your squire, Rockwood," Haru said, grinning.

"That's why I'm his mentor, still have to teach him the ropes of causing chaos, don't I?"

"I think he knows them well enough," Will grumbled, flattening his hair.

"Perhaps but, either way, if I'm to continue *trying* to teach him, I need dinner and sleep. Come on, you two."

They walked with the group of knights in the dinner hall. In the doorway Will glanced toward the squire table to see that several of the squires, including Rowan and Colin, had already left. His mind heavy with the Ranger's cryptic warning, he lifted a hand to wave to the knights then turned, striding across the hall. The Ranger had said he could talk to his friends and he needed someone to try to help him make sense of all of this. Now he needed to just find them and guessed that either they would be in the squire chamber, getting ready for bed, or upstairs in the Hall of Records working on an assignment from the knights. Knowing Colin, Will decided he'd check upstairs first and sprinted through the side door that led off the dinner hall.

***

"You've come to save me!" Rowan cried when Will rounded the corner of shelves that hid the spot where all three of them usually studied. He rose, arms outstretched, a heavy book falling from his lap and directly onto his own foot. "Blazes of Thornten and beards of goats," Rowan snarled, hopping up and down.

"Beards of goats?" Colin asked, half laughing and looking up from his own book. He nodded a greeting to Will. "I thought we'd try to get that assignment about the Wars of Maridia done for Richard and– Will, what's wrong?"

Will hesitated, trying to find the right words as he sank into another chair. "I…" He shook his head.

Colin took the matter from his hands, snapping his book shut and dropping it onto the end table at his side. "So," he said, raising his eyebrows inquisitively. "What did the Ranger want?"

Rowan spluttered. "What? The Ranger? He's here?" He sank back onto his seat, still rubbing his foot.

Will made a hushing movement, glancing round to see if he could see any movement between the shelves. Nothing stirred and, relaxing somewhat, he turned back to them and lowered his voice to a hushed whisper. Quickly, he relayed the Ranger's warning, his insistence that Will tell no one, not even Haru, who Marl really was and what that made Will.

As he spoke, Rowan became more and more confused while Colin's face shadowed. When he was done Will looked between them beseechingly.

"It doesn't make any sense, does it? I mean, why not tell Haru? Surely it's more dangerous for him–and for me for that matter–if he doesn't have a clue. So why is he telling me not to?"

"The Ranger doesn't make sense, mate, that's what I've learned," Rowan shrugged. "I would chalk this up to him being a half cracked admittedly good swordsman in a cloak."

"I wouldn't," said Colin, shaking his head and straightening. "If he's telling you that you need to keep that secret, then there's something wrong and it's got too much to do with Marl."

"Well, we already knew there was something wrong with Marl," Rowan grumbled, scowling. "Man's a bloodthirsty lunatic, isn't he? A moron in a beard?"

Colin ignored him and continued. "I think that what the Ranger's implying means he doesn't trust the people *in* Alamore."

"Like Haru?" Will demanded defensively. "Why wouldn't he trust Haru? He hasn't done anything wrong, he's my knight. I trust him and-"

It was Colin's turn to make hushing movements. "I know you trust him. I trust him, too, but there's something that the Ranger knows, and we don't, but, judging by what the Ranger said, he still isn't sure. If there's a spy in Alamore, someone working for Thornten, or trying to help Marl, the worst thing you could do is give yourself away by telling anyone."

"But a spy would know who Will is," Rowan pointed out.

"A spy might be able to figure it out but there are a fair few squires in this castle and there's no point in making it easier for them to find Will."

"Marl's done fine finding me on his own in the past," Will said coldly. He scowled at the book on the floor at Rowan's feet. "Why wouldn't he just show up himself and try to kill me?"

"I don't know," Colin said, sounding frustrated. He ran a hand over his face and sighed. "But whatever it is, the Ranger's worried and how often have we actually seen the Ranger worried? That's what makes me think this isn't something to take lightly."

"Who said we were taking it lightly?" Rowan asked, puffing out his chest. "I take the defense of this castle seriously."

"It's not the castle that the Ranger seems worried about, is it?" Colin snapped.

"And what about the Kelkor knight?" Will asked. "Why would I have to worry about her and why the blazes does he think I'd want to tell her anything? I don't even know her."

"Maybe he thinks you'll be so breath-taken by her stunning charm that you'll spill all your darkest secrets?" Rowan suggested, snorting with laughter as he avoided Will's swipe at the back of his head.

"Or he thinks that she's going to try to get answers out of you herself somehow," Colin said darkly.

Will snorted. "Like fight me? She's in the healing chamber, I don't think that'd be a fair fight."

"I don't know, Will," Colin moaned, burying his face in his hands. "I really don't know." He raised his head again, grimacing and fixing Will with a steely green gaze. "But, whatever's happening, whyever that Kelkor knight is here, the Ranger's worried it's going to come back after you."

"Which means," Will said slowly, cold dread running over his spine and making his skin shiver, "it's all got something to do with Marl."

"Oh, come on, what bad thing could be happening that's that important?" Rowan rolled his eyes. "We just got through a battle, for Thornten's sake, and you're going to tell me some random woman on a skin and bone nag is the bigger threat?"

"Not to the castle, but to Will maybe," Colin hissed. "Look at the knights even; whatever news she brought, whatever's happening, it's serious... and from what the Ranger's saying, I think that Marl might be involved in it."

CHAPTER THREE

"Pick yourself up, we try again," Haru ordered, stepping back.

Spitting out a mouthful of dirt, Will pushed himself to his feet, brushing the dust from his padded leather practice armor. Not that there was much point. He didn't doubt that he would, in a matter of minutes, be flat on his back again.

Haru, a few paces ahead, was already crouching into position again, spinning one of the short batons that they used as a practice dagger in one hand, waiting for Will to be ready to spar again.

It was the following day. Will's entire body ached with exhaustion. When he, Rowan, and Colin had finally gone to bed–when Rockwood found them and told them off for being up late–he had been plagued with his old nightmares of Marl. Nightmares where he approached the fallen rider only to have the face turn toward him and Marl's black eyes bore into his very being, that evil twisted smile rushing toward him until he woke in a sweat. Even now after a day of practicing footwork, swords, and now hand-to-hand fighting, he couldn't fully shake the haunting dream.

"I don't think this style of combat is my strong point," Will grumbled, spitting out a string of gritty dirt. "Disgusting…"

Haru snorted. "Even people who are naturally good at fighting start as beginners. You have to get better at the hand to hand and dagger combat, seeing as you don't get a sword until you're seventeen. If something happened, you'd be stuck with a dagger right now and, judging by this," he said and waved to take in Will's dirt covered appearance. "You'd be doing poorly."

Will had to bite down on the inside of his cheek to keep from snapping back. It was hard at times to remember that Haru wasn't just an older squire anymore. He was a knight now, commanding a certain level of respect. And he was not just any knight either but Will's knight, his mentor, the one in charge of seeing that he learned all he could before becoming a knight himself.

"I'll keep that in mind next time I fall, *Sir*."

Haru raised his eyebrows so they disappeared behind his sweat-dampened hair. "Was that a tone of sarcasm? Watch it, when I was a squire, Richard used to have me run laps around the jousting arena if I mouthed off. I might take a leaf from his book."

"If Rockwood did that, do you know how much running Rowan would do?" Will asked, grinning.

Haru chuckled. "He'd either be the fittest squire to have ever lived or he would run to death. Now, enough stalling, Will. Pick up the baton, we go again."

Will swiped up the short baton from the earth and braced himself, watching Haru carefully. The knight nodded and Will sprang forward, diving to strike with the baton like it was a knife. With a speed Will could not have imagined of Haru's muscular frame, the knight spun to the right and ducked, catching Will in the chest with his shoulder. Will staggered, twisting to catch him before he felt Haru grab his shoulder and push, shoving him, again, into the dirt.

The air knocked from his lungs, Will pushed himself gingerly into a seated position, wheezing slightly. "I'm getting worse."

"That one was, yeah," Haru agreed, nodding. "You didn't look for a strategy, you just attacked with your arm up like you thought you could stab me to death. Not how it works, sadly. You've got to keep your elbows close to your body, knife blade angled for quick strikes and swipes, none of this stabbing nonsense. Don't let your back turn to me for a moment, that's how you get a knife to the throat. If this was a real fight, I could have slit your neck right there or held you captive. It's better to fall because at least you can roll.

Once there's a blade at your neck, you're a goner. If your back is to someone and they've got a knife to your neck, about the only way to get out is if they're distracted and you can shove yourself backwards hard enough to knock them down or wrong foot them. Then you can try to get the upper hand, providing you did it right and aren't getting your throat cut instead." Haru held out a hand, helping Will clamber to his feet again.

Will snorted. "Does that actually work?"

"Not if you're fighting someone my size, but someone smaller than me, just a bit bigger than you, and then it would." Haru grinned and his eyebrows almost vanished in his disheveled fringe of red hair. "Maybe one day you'll get to practice it. Knocking someone backwards, maybe Colin? Rowan?"

"I don't see Colin falling for that." Will grimaced, running a hand over his back and wincing. "Still not sure I believe it works though because you pushed me right down."

"Only way to know is if you get to try some time." Haru shrugged. "Right, we give it another couple of goes and then call it a wrap because I've got to get to the barns shortly. I'm on the afternoon patrol."

"Am I going?" Will asked hopefully.

Haru shook his head with an apologetic grin. "Eastern patrol, sorry mate. No squires under seventeen still. I can't imagine that rule will last much longer though. We haven't had raiding parties on our lands in weeks and the ones we do have are pretty half-hearted, like they did it on a dare opposed to on orders…the morons."

Feeling somewhat disappointed, Will braced himself again, his feet apart, knees bent, body crouched forward like Haru had been doing. Once his knight nodded again, Will fought the instinct to lunge and strike. Instead, he circled, moving slowly to the left. Across from him, Haru moved the same way, matching his circle, the grey-green eyes calculating. Will's eyes flitted from Haru's face to his stance, trying to gauge what he should be looking for. If there was an opening, he had to find it but…

Haru moved, striking forward, and Will scrambled backwards, tripping over the uneven earth of the jousting arena. Catching himself with one hand, he brought the other hand holding the baton up in a block to catch Haru's next strike. The wooden cudgels made a dull cracking noise as they collided, sending vibrations down the bones in Will's arm.

"Nice one." Haru stepped back slightly, nodding at Will to straighten. "More thought out. But you won't win defending all the time. And watch your footing a bit better."

Sweat stung Will's eyes and he swiped his baton-free hand over his forehead irritably. The padded practice armor, heavy and uncomfortable in the beating sun, felt as though it were made of lead.

Haru was stepping back into position again and Will watched him calculatingly.

An opening. He needed an opening. Haru shifted his weight, turning the circle in the other direction and Will saw his chance. He sprang forward, twisting as Haru had done before, and trying to come under Haru's guard. The knight grunted as Will's shoulder collided with his chest. With a rush of giddy exhilaration at the idea of finally beating Haru, Will turned to strike with his club. Haru was turning away though, snaking aside and, next thing Will knew, he was flat on his back, coughing in the dirt once more.

"That was much, much better," panted Haru. He stepped forward and offered a hand to help Will to his feet. "Just don't let your head get you out of focus, got it?"

"Right."

Will shook dirt from his hair. He could feel clumps of earth congealing with his sweat and turning to mud along the collar of his tunic. "Are we done yet?"

Haru grinned, thumping him on the shoulder. "We're done. Just go wash off the practice armor and get it hung out at the hitching rail to dry, alright? Then you can take it easy. Richard mentioned something about reviewing your takes on the Maridia war later today with Rowan and Colin, but I'd like you to get Visra out for exercise before then. That horse doesn't need two days off in a row or he might decide to start eating people."

Will nodded, peeling away the leather padding and sighing in relief as cool air rushed against his sweat-soaked clothing. "I think this is the worst thing ever, you know that? It's like wearing a brick oven and expecting me to be able to focus on footwork."

"Wait till we practice without it," Haru said, laughing darkly and leading Will back along the side of the castle toward the barns. "You will miss the heat when you're waking up with bruises and busted knuckles. Sweat doesn't stick around as long as swelling."

At the edge of the courtyard Haru and Will parted ways, Haru heading for the barn and Will crossing to one of the horse tanks that stood at the courtyard edge. He slung the padded armor over one of the nearby hitching rails and reached for the cloth slung over the side of the tank, watching a group of soldiers unloading what seemed to be a new stock of arrows from a cart.

Turning away, Will scrubbed at the leather armor, gritting his teeth as he worked a particularly tough bit of dried dirt from one of the shoulder plates. For the second time in as many days, a shiver ran through him and he turned, glancing back around the courtyard. He felt again, like the night before, that someone was watching him. But there was no one there, just the soldiers, two of whom were now chatting animatedly some ways off, the taller one leaning on the cart, the shorter shaking his white-blond head.

His eyes darted to the shadows along the wall but then he silently chastised himself. *The Ranger isn't here, he will have already left on whatever it is that he keeps thinking is so bloody important that he can't answer a simple question,* Will thought bitterly. He redoubled his cleaning efforts, annoyed.

"You look like you bathed in a mudhole. You don't have to act like an animal. We've got perfectly normal human baths in the castle–you know, the ones that aren't full of dirt?"

Will started with a yelp and wheeled round. Rowan was sauntering toward him with a jaunty spring in his step, an evil grin stretching his mouth. He came to a halt on the other side of the hitching rail, propping his elbows on the post and watching Will clean.

"Aren't you supposed to be training on archery?" Will asked, trying to cover his embarrassment. Maybe the Ranger was right, and he should be a bit more observant.

"Rockwood is on the same patrol schedule as your knight this week, nitwit, so I get the same break you do. Colin does too, whenever he stops being a goody-two-shoes and gets over here."

"Where is he?" Will turned on the spot, not seeing the familiar tall squire amongst the jostling life of the yard.

"He's in the Hall of Records letting Sir Henry talk his ear off about the original treaty with Phersal," Rowan said, rolling his eyes. "I mean, like any of us truly give two damns and a rotten egg about Phersal. They're all a bunch of traitorous gits with a carrot as a King…I hate carrots."

Will snorted, wringing the rag out and slinging it over the hitching rail next to the padded armor to dry. "I'm taking Vis out, so he doesn't get two full days off. You coming along or you going to go hang out with Sir Henry and chitchat about carrots?"

"Like the blazes I'm staying here." Rowan pushed himself off the rail. "I've seen Phersal, met their King, didn't like him. History won't change that. Anyway, Naja needs a chance to stretch his legs. I've been riding in that stupid jousting arena for a week now it's getting real boring."

They walked together toward the barn, both laughing at the idea of Colin politely stranded with Sir Henry in the Hall of Records. At the barn, they skirted the edges of the alleyway to allow the knights leaving on patrol to pass them. Rockwood gave them a wink as he strode by with his lanky chestnut and Haru shot them a broad grin in passing. Ross and Don, the last two to be leaving, were talking in low voices. Noticing the two squires, they stopped, Ross giving them a stony glower but Don lifting his hand in friendly greeting.

"Getting out to ride, I hope?"

"Yes, Sir," Will answered politely.

"Excellent." Don nodded. "Just stay out of trouble," he said, chuckling.

"We always do," Rowan replied with his best attempt at an innocent expression.

Ross gave a low growl, shaking his head. "Don't lie, Rowan, it's unbecoming of a future knight." But as he turned away, Will could have sworn he saw the knight hide a smile.

"Grouchy git," Rowan mumbled when Ross and Don had followed the others out to the courtyard.

"He's not bad," Will said, shrugging. "And he's got a point. When was the last time you didn't go looking for trouble? You literally just said you're going to be the master of disaster, or whatever the stupid title was, for the two new squires."

"It's mentor in mayhem and it's not stupid," Rowan said with mock offense. "It's a vital position in this castle."

"Either way, we should probably get Strider saddled as well so when Colin gets free of history lessons he can come long," Will suggested, turning his attention to the lines of stalls. No matter how many times he came into the barn, he wasn't sure he'd ever stop being in awe of the place. The ceilings reached high above them, the tiles along the peak propped open to allow air and sunlight to filter through. Dust motes curled in the gentle breeze, glistening in the light like magic while horses leaned over their stall doors to take in the two squires. Horses in every color–dark bays, subtle greys, chestnuts with gleaming red coats, paints, roans, black, palominos, buckskins, and duns–all sizes, from pony to cart horse all attentive.

"Aw, your monster looks peaceful today," Rowan commented when they neared the stall of Will's large bay warhorse.

The bay flattened his ears to his neck, baring his teeth at Rowan who scrambled backwards. "Scratch that, he's still a monster."

"Visra, knock it off," Will snapped.

The horse snorted, raising his head to glower more menacingly down at Rowan who took another step away. "Always pleasant to see him. It's like being greeted with a knife to the neck, really wakes you up."

"He just likes to keep you on your toes," said Will, grinning. He reached for Visra's halter on its hook outside the stall. "Back up, beastie, so I can get this open."

"Right, so you deal with that menace and I'll get Naja, and Strider saddled," Rowan grumbled, taking several more steps backward. "I don't trust that he's not actually a dragon."

Will laughed, slipping the halter onto Visra's head. "Alright, I'll come help with Strider when I'm done getting Vis taken care of."

"If you can get him sorted. I think that horse is going to murder you. No getting things saddled when you're dead." With that he turned and hurried across the barn to where his horse, Naja, watched them curiously over the door of his own stall.

Visra pricked his ears forward again when Will shook his head, opening the stall wide enough for them both to leave. "Mind not being a git?"

The horse only huffed in response, shoving his nose roughly against Will's pocket to check for snacks. Laughing, Will pushed his head away and made to lead him toward a set of nearby crossties. He was reaching for the first rope of the crosstie when an almighty crash made him jump, almost letting go of Visra's lead. Whipping round, Will saw the commotion had come from two stalls away where a horse was raising his head, ears flat, seeming to challenge the bay that Will was leading.

Visra made to surge forward but Will pulled back, yanking on the line and quickly fastening the crosstie to the side of Visra's halter.

"Oh no you don't, we're not picking fights today, Vis," Will snarled. After a few more minutes of struggling, he managed to get Visra to stand still enough to connect the other side of the crosstie to his halter before turning to glower at the horse who'd caused the commotion. He had to bite down an urge to laugh.

The gleaming red chestnut that was watching Visra with ears pinned flat to his broad arched neck, his forelock falling to cover his eyes, was tiny in comparison to his warhorse. Visra flattened his own ears in annoyance but contented himself with biting the empty air in front of him, teeth clicking together.

"Don't bother yourself with him, Visra," Will told the horse firmly. "He's a large pony."

After that, the chestnut grew bored with Visra's lack of reaction and turned his attention back to his hay. Will forgot all about him while he groomed and saddled the bay, then hurried to help Rowan with Colin's red horse, Strider.

Colin sprinted into the barn, winded and red faced when Will was checking Strider's girth. "I'm sorry, I tried to get here faster, but I was trying to be polite, and Henry had a lot to say."

"Was it a good chat at least?" Rowan asked, smirking.

"Don't talk to me right now," Colin snapped. "Will, did he tell you he's the one who started Henry on his tirade? Asked him a question then pretended to need to use the bathroom. Next thing I see through the window is him running across the courtyard. Not funny, Rowan. He talked my ear off."

Will stifled a snort, trying his best to look serious. "Well, did you learn a lot?"

Behind him, he heard Rowan, who was in the process of bridling Naja, choke on his own laughter.

"You're both awful," Colin huffed. He glanced at Strider and grinned sheepishly. "But thanks for getting Strider saddled."

"You're welcome," Rowan called.

"Still not forgiving you though," Colin grumbled, stalking off to get his bridle.

It wasn't long before the three were leading their horses into the slanting afternoon sunlight. Will lifted himself into the saddle and his own body relaxed. All of the worries brought with the arrival of the Kelkor knight and the Ranger's warning vanished. This was what he'd needed: the freedom that only horses could bring him. He closed his eyes a moment, smiling.

"Come on now, Will, we haven't got time for a nap." Colin's laughing voice made him straighten, opening his eyes.

"Oh, but we had time for Henry's lecture on history no one cares about?" Rowan asked slyly.

"Why do I even hang around you?" Colin growled.

Rowan shrugged. "Because I'm brilliant probably, or because you're hoping to one day be nearly as good at sword fighting as I am."

Chuckling, Will urged Visra into a trot past his friends and toward the open drawbridge. As soon as the sound of hooves over the timbers echoed around him, he loosened his reins and Visra broke into a canter. Leaning into the horse's black mane, Will's heart soared. Air rushed over his face, making his eyes water. The long grasses at the edge of the road were swaying, brilliant emerald in the sun, waves of green that stretched all around him.

Only when he heard Rowan hollering behind him did he rein Visra to a walk again, turning to his friends.

"What?" Will demanded crossly.

"We can't go on the main road. Rockwood said it goes too far to the east, moron," Rowan called back. He and Colin were waiting at the edge of the bridge, watching him. "Get the monster back here and stop being stupid."

"If you bite him, I honestly might get you an apple or something," Will whispered to Visra. The horse's ears flicked back to catch the words. With a heavy sigh, Will trotted back toward Rowan and Colin. "Alright, if not the main road, where to then?"

"West, you know, the opposite of east?" Rowan offered. Will freed his foot from his stirrup and kicked Rowan in the calf, making him yelp.

"Knock it off you two," Colin chastised. "We can go to the river path."

"River path?" Will raised an eyebrow. "You mean the creek to the south of town? That'd be the main road and that's still too far east according to Lord Rowan here."

Colin blinked, bewildered. "I mean the river to the west. Haven't you been there?"

"No." Will shook his head. "I didn't even know it existed."

Rowan beamed; his prior annoyance already forgotten. "We'll have to show you then! It's the best place in the summer and spring. We can swim, have fights in the water, fish. We've got to show you!"

Without waiting for either Colin or Will to confirm, Rowan dug his heels into the sides of his horse and charged forward, galloping for the stand of trees that swayed in the lazy afternoon wind.

"Glad we made that decision as a group," Will said dryly.

"You didn't expect Rowan to wait on us, did you?" Colin laughed. "Come on, we better go after him or he'll do something stupid, no doubt."

"He'll do that regardless of us being with him," Will pointed out but he didn't argue. Instead, he turned Visra and felt the horse's muscles coil beneath him again. He and Colin surged forward together, the horses' powerful feet tearing soft earth as they launched after Rowan.

Their horses raced alongside one another, Colin leaning into Strider's red mane at Will's left side while Will urged Visra faster. It wasn't until they reached the edge of the line of trees that they leaned back, ducking the first branches and slowing to a trot. Visra arched his neck, stamping a hoof in irritation at the command to walk.

They had to proceed in single file, Colin ahead of him, as the trees thickened. Will felt twigs snatch at his hair and had to yank his cloak free of brambles several times. "I take it that this path isn't used much?" he asked through gritted teeth, struggling to again pull his cloak free without tearing it.

"Not of late," Colin admitted. "With all that happened with Thornten, I don't think keeping the paths clear was top of mind for anyone. But not much further now and we'll be in the clearing."

Sure enough, it was only a few minutes before the trees began to thin and Will could hear the distant rush of water. Standing in his stirrups, he glimpsed Rowan stopped ahead of them, swearing and yanking to pull his cloak off a snarling thorn bush.

"Having fun there?" Will asked innocently.

"The forest liked my fashion statement and tried to steal it," Rowan complained. He yanked the cloak free with a ripping sound and scowled. "But not today, forest, not today."

"Glad to see you can best a bush in battle with only minor casualties," Colin said, smirking.

"I am the master of all the forest." Rowan stuck out his chest theatrically.

"Alright, tree-master," Will said, rolling his eyes. "How far to this river?"

"Just ahead," Colin assured him. "Rowan, keep moving so we can get there today."

Rowan did so and a moment later they were passing between the last trees and into a clearing. Will caught his breath and stared at the rushing water ahead in the clearing. He had seen what the people in town called a river but compared to this they were creeks. Here the water was broader, far too wide to wade across and, with how the water surged past and broke over the rocks in its path, Will couldn't imagine anyone attempting to swim it. An old bridge spanned across it, seeming ancient and forgotten, the wood dark with decay and age. Will rode nearer, staring open mouth.

"Pretty great, right?" Rowan asked, swinging from his saddle. "Aw, how I've missed this place. The memories: trying to drown Colin, trying to drown Haru, trying to drown…"

"Yeah, I'm not trusting you near water," Will said decisively, dismounting. He moved to tie Visra to a tree several yards from where Rowan was affixing Naja's reins.

"Near water? You had to add the near water part?" Colin asked, also sliding from his horse.

"On land he can't drown me," Will pointed out. "In water, I'd drown myself. I can't swim."

Will was still tying Visra, struggling with his reins, by the time that Colin and Rowan were already at the riverbank, pulling off their boots. He had almost finished the knot when Visra jerked, the reins whipping from Will's hands painfully. He snatched at them, snarling in pain and annoyance.

"You nag." Will pulled on Visra's reins, trying to turn him again. "I won't make you get in the water. I'm just trying to tie you up."

The horse braced against Will's weight, lifting his head higher to stare into the forest behind them, his muscles rigid. Will followed the horse's gaze but could see nothing. Still, his hand reached instinctively for the dagger on his belt.

"Will, you going to chicken out or you going to get in?" Rowan called from the water, splashing along the river's edge. "Promise I won't try to drown you yet. We'll teach you to swim first, give you a fighting chance."

Not answering, Will studied the shadows under the trees, looking for anything that seemed unusual. Visra had alerted him to dangers before, warning him of attacks. This time, however, he couldn't see anything. Sighing in annoyance, Will shook his head and tugged the reins. "It's probably a squirrel, Vis. Get over yourself and just stand, won't you?"

Visra refused to budge. Will gave another heave on the reins, biting back the urge to use some of Rowan's choice swear words. He could hear his friends splashing through the shallows, laughing about something, and he was stuck fighting with a spooked horse.

With all of his strength, Will pulled again and Visra turned his head just enough that Will was able to loop the reins over a branch. "Aha!" He tied the reins before Visra could pull free again, feeling victorious. "Now, don't be an idiot," Will warned, turning to walk toward the river.

He had reached the edge of the bank when the horse snorted and Will turned, bewildered. "What is the matter with…"

The words died in his throat and Will froze, his hand reaching for his dagger.

A figure was stepping through the trees, his grey cloak swaying at his ankles, the lips beneath his hood curled in a smirk. One hand rested on the sword he wore at his side, the elegant bronze hilt twisted and set with a silver-grey stone that shone dully in the forest's muted light. Will noticed the stranger was shorter than Haru, but not by much, a few inches taller than Colin perhaps.

At his back, Will heard Rowan swear and the sound of both his friends drawing their daggers. Will drew his own, heart slamming in his throat and the figure let out a low laugh, shaking his head.

"If you're thinking about fighting me with that little knife, you might want to reconsider, William of Alamore."

CHAPTER FOUR

It was as though someone had punched him in the stomach. The breath had rushed from his lungs and Will stared at the stranger in disbelief, his hand lowering the dagger of its own accord.

"How do you know…" Will stopped himself and clamped his mouth shut, wishing he could snatch his words out of the air and swallow them.

"How do I know who you are?" the stranger asked. Will heard the laughter in his voice. "Or perhaps how did I know where you were? You see, I've been looking forward to meeting you for a while now."

"Well you met him, nice to meet you, goodbye, you can go now," Rowan snapped from over Will's shoulder. "Get going now."

The smile under the hood faltered, the lips pressing thin in annoyance. "You'll watch your mouth talking to me, or you'll regret it."

Anger flared in Will's chest, white-hot, and he stepped sideways between the stranger and Rowan, lifting his dagger again. "You take a step toward him and I promise you'll regret it."

The smirk returned. "Are you seriously going to fight me? With a knife against a sword?"

"He's not on his own," Colin snarled. "You'll have to fight all three of us."

Will saw the stranger's fingers slide to grip his sword's handle tightly. "I don't recommend you make me fight you. It's something you'll regret."

"We don't want to fight either," Will growled. "So how about you go your way, we'll go ours."

"I'm afraid I can't do that either," the stranger said, laughing coldly. "You see, I've wanted to meet you for weeks now, but it's been difficult. You're not an easy one to reach."

"Well, I've been busy, training to be a knight and all," Will said, taking a half step backwards. If he could get nearer to Rowan and Colin, they might stand a chance. Even if the stranger had a sword, there were three of them. The three of them armed with daggers might just be strong enough to overpower him. If they could just keep him long enough for the three of them to be ready to fight back.

"I'm aware of that. More problematic, however, has been the safeguard of your King's Ranger, so you can imagine my delight in finding out that you'd be here, and your Ranger would be gone." The stranger tilted his head to one side, the lips pulled from smirk to frown.

"Very nice." Another step and he glanced to his side. He was standing between Rowan and Colin now. They stood several feet on either side of him, both of them watching the stranger with tense expressions.

"But, you know what I find more interesting are the stories I've heard about you."

"Me?" Will asked, frowning. "What are you on about?"

"The stories of how much trouble you've caused King Tollien, the throne, Thornten. How well you've squirmed out of trouble. Honestly, it's that more than anything that makes me interested in you."

"I've been pretty lucky, yeah." Will shrugged and slid his left foot behind him, the better to launch forward. He glimpsed Colin mirroring his movement, readying himself for the attack. *Don't get hurt, please don't let them get hurt.*

"It'd seem so. That is, at least, what Marl calls it," the stranger was saying. "He thinks it's all luck, but he understands the intrigue I have now. He understands how I might find you helpful and that you might have your uses for us now. Tollien on the other hand seems to think you're like the Ranger–bound to be a thorn in the side until you're dead. And perhaps he's right, perhaps you will be a pain, but I think the potential benefit outweighs the risk for the time being. So, what do you say?"

"What do I say to what?" Will demanded.

"Come with me," the boy said coolly. "Come with me to Thornten and be of use. Stop running from what you are."

"I'm a squire." Will raised his voice, but even over his words he could hear the pounding of his heart. "That's all."

"Don't play stupid with me, William," the stranger scoffed. "You can't hide from what you are forever, so why not accept it? Why not embrace it? You could do so much, be so much, as an heir."

"I'll pass on that, thanks, but I appreciate your offer," Will snapped.

"Yeah, he's staying here because we're somewhat amazing, if you haven't noticed," Rowan added. "Your pitch was good, but not great. Work on it and try again later, maybe?"

Will expected the stranger to strike, to attack, but instead he laughed and somehow that cold sound was worse. It made the hair on the back of Will's neck rise and Rowan swore under his breath, Colin crouched low, eyes narrowing.

"I don't think you understand fully what I'm saying." There was a danger in the hooded stranger's voice that hadn't been there before. It was icy, shot through with purest loathing. "Either you come with me or you see your friends die."

"Not sure if Marl taught you how to count while you were being his precious lapdog," Rowan called and Will squeezed his eyes shut a moment, wishing he could kick his friend to shut him up, "but there's three of us, mate, and only the one of you. Sword or not, you're not winning that."

The stranger paused, watching them a moment before giving a nod. "You're right. I believe introductions are in order. I am The Cutthroat Prince and these," he said, raising a hand into the air and closing his fingers over his palm, the smirk rising to his lips once more, "are my Cutthroats."

For a moment Will thought, he hoped, nothing would happen. But then the shadows at the edge of the trees shifted and his heart sank. Rowan was swearing audibly now, and Colin was sidestepping to stand at Will's side, face drawn. Three more cloaked figures appeared, each astride a dark horse, swords swinging from their saddles. Visra screamed a challenge and twisted where he was tied, trying to break free, ears flattened at the horses and their riders.

"You have your friends, I have mine," The Cutthroat Prince purred, waving a hand behind him to the riders. "Now, we can do this simply or I can make sure you regret fighting. So, Will, which will it be? Risk your friends' lives or come easily?"

Will hesitated but Colin shook his head, stepping forward. "If you want Will, you'll have to go through us."

"Fine," The Cutthroat Prince hissed. "Have it your way. Draccart, take the smart mouthed one. We'll use him as a lesson to teach you what happens to those who cross The Cutthroat Prince."

Will launched himself between Rowan and the rider who was nodding, moving his horse forward. A moment later Colin was at his side, the two of them standing between the rider and Rowan. The Cutthroat–Draccart–gave a low laugh and reached for the sword on his saddle.

"Out of the way or you'll take his place."

"Draccart, no," The Cutthroat Prince snarled. "You're not to touch William, that's an order. I don't care about the other two but not Will."

"And the only way you'll get to either of them is through me," Will called, addressing The Cutthroat Prince even as he glowered at Draccart.

"You're playing a dangerous game there, William," The Cutthroat Prince sneered, watching Will closely. "If you don't stand down, someone's going to get hurt."

Will could feel his two friends at his back, ready to fight, ready to risk their lives. Risk their lives because of him... He glanced over his shoulder and could see the steely look in Colin's glower, the fire in Rowan's and knew: neither would back down. They would get themselves killed because of him. In that moment, a thousand thoughts rushed through his head–his friends falling, blood staining the ground, Visra pulling on his reins, the horse screaming into the fading evening light, and...

"Then let's negotiate," Will said, turning back to The Cutthroat Prince.

"Will, no!"

He ignored his friends.

"You're not in much of a position to do that," The Cutthroat Prince said, laughing. "You're outnumbered and out armed."

"But if you come at me, I'm going to fight, even if that means getting killed, before I'd let you near my friends," Will countered. "So, let's make a deal."

He could see The Cutthroat Prince considering, even if he couldn't see his face, and held his breath, waiting.

At last, The Cutthroat Prince nodded. "Let's hear what you have to say then."

"You let them go back to the castle, and I'll go with you." Will silently hoped his friends wouldn't do anything stupid. He wished they could read his mind, that he could relay his thoughts to them without the Cutthroats noticing. "Let them go back to the castle and I'll go with you, quiet as anything. I'll even ride my own horse, have you lead him, that way we can move faster."

The Cutthroat Prince paused and tilted his head once more, seeming to weigh Will's words. "I have heard you play the hero... how can I be sure you're not deciding to play at prankster now as well?"

"What the blazes am I going to do with a dagger against a sword?" Will asked, snorting. "You're right: we're outnumbered and underarmed. The best I can do for us now is get on my horse and cooperate with you so these two," he said, jerking his head to gesture at Rowan and Colin. "Can live."

The Cutthroat Prince paused a moment longer before nodding. "Very well. Draccart, stand down but draw your blade. You three, throw down your weapons and step away from them. Any tricks, anything at all, and the smart mouth will pay for it. Is that clear?"

Will's fingers uncurled from his dagger, the joints protesting, his mind screaming at him to hold on to the weapon. He had to battle his own instinct to let it slip from his hands and fall to the soft earth with a muffled thud. A moment later he heard two more thuds as Rowan and Colin's daggers hit the ground as well. He chanced another glance and could see Rowan's face was murderous, but Colin met his eye with a faint frown. Will broke his gaze away again, heart pounding faster now. Colin knew he wasn't giving up at the very least.

"There." Will held up his open hands, wriggling his fingers at The Cutthroat Prince. "Happy now?"

"Actually, I'm quite happy," The Cutthroat Prince chuckled. "That was much easier than I thought it would be. Now, step forward, away from the others."

"Not until I see that my friends get to take their horses again," Will snapped. "I can't trust you'll keep your word."

The Cutthroat Prince snarled, and Will imagined the eyes beneath the hood rolling. "Fine." He jerked his head again at the rider, Draccart. "Let them get their horses."

"What are you doing, Will?" Colin whispered harshly behind him.

"No plotting," The Cutthroat Prince snapped.

"We're not plotting," Will retorted sharply. He turned to Colin, fighting to keep his voice even and collected. "I'll go with them. I'll be fine, Strider and I both will be."

He saw the flicker of understanding in the green eyes followed by the doubt, but there wasn't time to say anything else. The Cutthroat Prince's impatience was palpable, and Will knew it would be a matter of seconds before he ordered Will away from them.

"I can't believe you right now," Rowan snarled, moving to follow Colin toward the horses. "I'm not forgiving you if you get killed."

"Mutual feelings here," Will grumbled, turning back to The Cutthroat Prince. He could see the Cutthroats watching Rowan and Colin closely as they crossed to the horses. Will shoved a hand in his pocket, his fingers crossed as he saw Colin reach for Visra's reins. "Right then." Will raised his voice and the attention of the Cutthroats all shifted to him again. "What do you want me to do then? Get my horse or…"

"Not so quickly," The Cutthroat Prince snapped. "Draccart, bind his hands behind his back."

"What?" Will's stomach tightened. This was something he hadn't bargained on.

The rider who had born down on them nodded and swung from his saddle. Under the hood, Will saw a round, leering face and beady eyes glittering with contempt as he approached, reaching into the folds of his cloak.

"Hands at your back and turn," Draccart grunted.

Will hesitated.

"Now!" Draccart barked, his face reddening under the hood.

"If you're tying my hands up, how the blazes am I going to ride?" Will demanded, turning to The Cutthroat Prince.

"You'll be fine and if you fall, I'm sure Draccart doesn't mind dragging you along." The Prince shrugged. "Honestly, I don't mind that option either. You're becoming somewhat annoying."

Will clenched his jaw and turned. He winced as his hands were yanked behind his back and pain shot up through his shoulders. Rough rope bit into his wrist, burning across his skin and he inhaled sharply, stumbling a step. Draccart swore, shoving him and Will managed to stagger a step to the side. He could see Rowan and Colin from his new stance. Rowan was in Naja's saddle, but Colin was still on the ground next to Visra, seemingly inspecting the girth with a confused expression. Will saw him give the smallest of nods before he was turned forcibly around again, his hands immobile behind him.

The Cutthroat Prince inhaled, turning his face upwards to the trees above them. "Are you quite done yet? I want to get ground covered before it's dark."

Will blinked, looking skywards. He hadn't realized that the blue overhead was now streaked with purples and reds. Light was fading fast, and the forest shadows were closing in around them for nightfall.

"He's set. Just need the horse," Draccart grumbled, shoving Will in the back so he tripped several steps forward. Losing his footing, Will crashed onto his knees and gasped at the throb of pain that ran through his legs.

"Well, then get it, won't you? And carry him for all I care, just hurry up." The Cutthroat Prince snapped. "Anyway you, squire, why are you taking so long to get in that saddle?"

Will tensed, eyes flitting back to Colin.

Colin turned with a convincing look of puzzled innocents. "Something's wrong with the saddle and I can't quite place it."

"For the walls of Thornten," The Cutthroat Prince snarled. "Resben, go get that one in his saddle and get them out of here before I change my mind on killing them."

A second rider dismounted. Will was struck again by how none of the Cutthroats seemed much older than himself. This one was thin and lanky, but still not much taller than Colin as he came to stand next to the golden-haired squire.

"What is the matter with it? It looks just fine!"

"It just seems off." Colin shook his head then clapped his hand to his forehead. "I know what it is!"

"What's that?"

"Well, this isn't my saddle."

There wasn't a chance for the other boy to respond as Colin loosed Visra's reins.

The horse struck with the speed of a snake and a scream of agony split the clearing, drowning the rush of water, the whisper of wind. Visra was drawing back, teeth bared, ready to sink them again into the Cutthroat.

The last horseman yelled, launching himself toward his companion, one hand diving for his sword but was nearly unseated as Rowan and Naja collided into him. Deprived of a dagger, Rowan was using the slack in his reins to attack, bringing the thick leather cracking down over the hooded rider's head. Colin scrambled away from the flailing hooves and toward Strider. Will tried to climb to his feet, to rush forward and help, but felt a hand shove him forward.

Before he could try to rise again, a weight dropped onto his spine and he gasped again, the air knocked painfully from his lungs. "Nice try," Draccart snarled. "You're not getting away that fast."

"Draccart, hold him, don't move!" The Cutthroat Prince's scream was almost indiscernible above the cries of his riders. Will saw him running toward them, reaching for the sword on his side. He hadn't gone more than a few feet when he was blocked from sight by the red body of a warhorse. Colin and Strider had joined the fray now.

Through watering eyes, Will could see that the Cutthroat that Visra had attacked was crawling away, his arm bleeding and clutched to his chest, while his bay horse battled against the unfamiliar horse of the last mounted Cutthroat. Rowan had turned his attention to chasing away the two other horses, waving his arms and bellowing, urging the animals back into the forest.

The pain in his back intensified and Will twisted, trying to free himself from Draccart's hold. Snarling through gritted teeth, he writhed, hoping to off balance the larger boy.

"Won't mean a damn thing to me if you die, scum," Draccart panted, leaning forward so Will could hear over the mayhem surrounding them. "I'm with Tollien on this, I don't see why The Cutthroat Prince or Marl is bothering with you."

Will didn't answer, panting in pain and trying to slip his hands free of the rope. It was too tight, and Rowan and Colin were preoccupied. Neither had seen that he was on the ground now. They didn't know what he was fighting against.

"Come to think of it," Draccart said, and Will could hear the muted laughter in his voice. "This might be the best way to ensure our protection."

Will saw the flash of steel from the corner of his eye and tried to pull back. A razor edge pressed against his neck and he froze, breathing hard.

"Call off your friends, or we'll see what color royals bleed."

"Like you'd hold to your word anyway," Will grunted. His ribs ached; his lungs felt about to burst.

"Have it your way!"

The dagger pressed tighter to his throat and Will braced himself, heart slamming in his ribs. He felt the skin break and a thin line of hot blood rise to meet it. This was it then. Whether he tried to stop Rowan and Colin or not, he knew that Draccart was going to kill him, with his hands tied behind his back, unable to help himself. He closed his eyes, silently begging Rowan and Colin to run.

A horrible, straggled cry rose from above him and Will felt the dagger drop away from his throat as the weight was lifted from his back. Eyes shooting open, he rolled onto his back, his shoulder protesting as his arms were caught beneath his weight. He struggled to sit up, to see where Draccart had gone. Another scream made him turn. Draccart was scrambling to his feet, reaching for his sword, and rushing backwards toward the river while Visra struck with hooves and teeth, ears flat to his neck. To Will's disappointment, he couldn't see any visible signs that Visra's attack had injured Draccart. He was still standing, hurrying away from the horse while not taking his eyes off the animal.

"Will!"

The cry snapped him back to his surroundings and his eyes darted to the fray. Colin was standing in his stirrups and turning wildly, looking for him. With all of his strength, Will struggled to sit up.

"Here! Over here!"

He wasn't sure Colin heard him, but he had seen him. A moment later the golden-haired squire was riding toward Will, reaching down.

"Can you ride?" Colin shouted over the sound of Visra's screams, Rowan's wild war whoops, and Draccart's bellows.

"My hands!" Will jerked his head to gesture behind his back. "I'm tied up."

"If your stupid plan gets us killed," Colin threatened. He swung from the saddle, snatched up Draccart's fallen knife and a moment later Will felt the rope fall away. Scrambling to his feet, rubbing his wrist,

Will turned to see Visra was pacing the water's edge, reluctant to dive into the river, but watching Draccart who had waded out of his reach.

"We've got to get Visra!"

"He's a horse, Will, he'll follow! He knows how to get back to the castle!" Colin barked. "We don't have time for this! Come on!"

There wasn't a chance to argue as Colin half pushed, half lifted Will over the front of the saddle. A moment later he'd swung up behind Will and was turning Strider round. Will grappled to cling to the front of the saddle, sure for a moment he was about to plunge off the horse.

"Rowan, leave him! We're getting out of here!" Colin ordered. Will twisted to see Rowan backing Naja away from where he'd pushed The Cutthroat Prince almost up a tree in his effort to escape Rowan's reins crashing down on him. Will wasn't sure where the last rider had vanished to and nor was he certain he cared much.

"You're dead," Draccart shouted. "You're dead, you beast!"

Whipping round the other way again, Will saw Draccart had drawn his sword and was trying to get to shore. Visra still blocked his path, head low, striking the ground aggressively each time Draccart took a step near him. With a roar of exasperation, Draccart lunged.

"Visra!" Will's scream made Colin turn as well. A moment later they were cantering toward the bay horse and Draccart. To Will's relief the sword blade was clean. It hadn't struck Visra. Still, the horse was watching Draccart closely. "Visra! Enough!"

Colin brought Strider nearer to the bay horse. "Grab him, Will! Grab him and let's get out of here!"

Will leaned across from Strider's saddle to snatch the reins. It was too late to do anything as he realized the mistake he'd made. He saw the idea flash across Draccart's face just as his fingers were closing onto Visra's reins.

Draccart sprang forward again, sword-free hand outstretched, reaching to pull Will from the saddle. Colin yelled and grabbed the back of Will's tunic to keep him from falling. Strider sprang sideways, and Visra struck again. His teeth sank into Draccart's left arm and the Cutthroat screamed, twisting to strike out. Will didn't see what happened next. Colin swore, pulling him upright in the saddle and urging Strider into a run. Rowan was on their heels a moment later and they were galloping toward the narrow trail.

"Visra! Visra!" Will craned to see behind them.

"He's coming!" Rowan shouted from behind them. "He'll catch up. Just focus ahead! Ride, Colin!"

Will jolted, nearly falling off the back of the saddle and grabbing the saddle tighter. They crashed back through the overgrown path, the twigs tearing at their faces. Will had to bow his head forward, squinting his eyes to keep anything from striking them. Behind him, he heard Rowan swearing, Colin urging Strider to keep moving.

Dusk was closing in fast now. The shadows of the trees blotted the last of the setting sun and Will's stomach swooped each time Strider moved to avoid an unseen obstacle or leapt felled trees. He heard Rowan yelp behind him and twisted to look back. He saw a horse and his rider. At least Rowan had managed to stay on. His heart leapt as he caught sight of movement behind Rowan, rushing to keep pace with them. Visra! The horse was a dark shadow in the gathering night, but Will recognized the broad white blaze.

Turning to face forward again, he felt another thrill of excitement. Ahead, across the valley, lights burned bright as stars in the windows of the castle. He could see a yellow shadow of torch light falling over the still open drawbridge like a beacon leading them back. They were going to get away, they were going to be fine.

The sun had gone, only the grey ghost of its light illuminating the faint outline of the track that rushed under Strider's hooves. It wasn't until they were nearly to the drawbridge that Colin began to rein in the sweating animal, slowing to a trot and giving Rowan and Visra time to catch up.

"I hate you, Will!" Rowan announced, reining Naja in beside them. "You nearly got yourself killed! Colin, I hate you too! How did you two think that was a good plan?"

"We didn't die though," Will pointed out, failing to swallow his grin.

"Well, night's not over and I might still murder you, you prat!" Rowan snapped.

Colin burst into laughter, shaking his head and running a hand over his face. "We just used your horse as our own army after all, Will. If Rowan had been hungry, we would have been unstoppable!"

Unable to help it, Will started laughing as well. The giddy relief of survival, of adrenaline, all washed over him. They had escaped, escaped something that had seemed impossible.

"You two need your heads checked," Rowan said, when he'd finally caught his breath. "And, coming from me, that's saying something."

"I mean, I took a pretty good knock to mine," Colin confessed, stifling a grin. "It's going to be nice and bruised."

Visra trotted to their side at last, his head on the ground, breathing hard. Will reached to pat his horse's neck from Strider's back, laughing shakily now. "Thank Alamore for the monster that got us through this."

He could feel sweat soaking the horse's coat in the darkness and felt a pang of affection and guilt. Visra had saved his life, attacking with the training of a full-fledged and seasoned warhorse and now he was exhausted, swaying slightly. Will stiffened. Swaying? He squinted through the dark, pulling his hand from Visra's coat and staring at the horse.

"Will? Everything alright?" Rowan asked, concernedly.

Will turned to answer, his hand still resting on Visra's neck, but the words caught in his throat as he turned his palm upwards. The distant silver of the moon showed dark over his palm, glistening darkness that clung to his fingers, staining his skin.

Visra staggered sideways, out of his reach and Will could only stare, frozen in horrified disbelief. "Vis?"

The horse's knees buckled, and he sank to the ground, slowly falling to his side. Before Will realized what he was doing, his boots hit the solid earth and he was grabbing at Visra's neck, trying to stop the horse as he made to lie flat across the ground. A new panic was surging through him as Visra's weight started to bring him to the ground as well.

"Visra!" Will knew he was shouting, could feel it in his hoarse throat, but it sounded distant to his own ears. A moment later he felt Rowan and Colin on his either side, both grabbing onto handfuls of Visra's mane as well, trying to keep him from sprawling flat.

The horse was breathing hard, foam dripping from the corner of his mouth. Will pushed harder against the broad neck. His boots slid over the ground, his body sinking lower.

"The blazes is wrong with him?" Rowan asked, bewildered.

"I don't know," Colin said, equally confused.

"Will? Rowan? Colin?" Will heard the growling voice but couldn't turn to see Ross running across the drawbridge toward the three of them, still holding Visra's head off the dirt. The dirt that Will was staring at, his head spinning, as it darkened with the horse's blood.

CHAPTER FIVE

"Sounds like some Thornten squires are getting a bit brazen in their training," said Rockwood. He readjusted his seat on the hay bale outside of Visra's stall, stretching his long legs out in front of him, and grimaced. "But how they got around the patrol is beyond me."

Haru, leaning on the stall door, his arms crossed, and his murderous glower fixed on the floor before him gave a low huff of annoyance but didn't answer.

"Soldiers have been getting lax and sloppy in patrolling is how," Ross growled. "I'll be bringing that up to the King."

"Well, honestly, they wouldn't think much of a bunch of kids, would they, Ross," Rockwood sighed, an exhausted shadow crossing his face. "They'd think either that they are our squires or that it's boys from the city playing at knights."

Next to Rockwood, Colin shook his head. "You couldn't have mistaken them for common folk. They had swords–good swords–and their horses weren't just common nags. They were warhorses and good ones at that."

"But luckily, not as good as ours," Ross growled. "How are you, Will?"

Seated on the floor next to Visra's stall door, Will didn't answer, still not entirely trusting his voice. He hadn't said a word since Ross had come to them outside the walls. He'd only watched in silence as Ross sprinted back to the castle, returning with Miller, Robin, Rockwood, and Haru. The five knights had worked in tense silence to sling ropes under Visra and, as they had managed to get the last one slid under his chest, Don had arrived leading a cart horse with a sleigh attached. It had taken all of them–knights and the three squires–to pull Visra onto the sleigh. They'd drug the horse into the barn and then pulled him into his stall before the healer had arrived, ordering Will, Rowan, and Colin out of the stall and out of his way.

And they'd been waiting ever since. The healer had set to work on treating the gash along Visra's side but had stopped Will and Haru at the door. He, Haru, Ross, Colin, Rowan, and Rockwood, had taken their stations outside, listening to the healer's low muttering voice, the words indistinguishable as he worked on Visra for two hours while Colin and Rowan filled the knights in on what had happened. Will was relieved they didn't ask for his input and more relieved still when Rowan and Colin glossed past The Cutthroat Prince's reasoning for approaching them. Instead, they made it sound like he had found them by accident and hadn't the slightest idea or interest in who any of them were. Ross's brow had furrowed at that and Will wondered if he had understood what wasn't said.

"He's got a good chance, Will," Ross said, his growling voice softening when Will didn't answer. "But he's exhausted and who knows what might have been on that blade."

Will nodded mutely, staring at the floor in front of him.

"And you say the only names you heard were Draccart and what else?" Rockwood asked and Will was thankful for the distraction.

"Resben," Colin answered, nodding.

"All of them shall hence forth be known as the Stupid Squire Squad," Rowan decided. "Because they're stupid."

Rockwood and Colin both stifled choking laughter and Ross growled and raised his eyes to the ceiling. "Alamore help the day you become a knight, Lonric."

"They didn't seem like squires." Will's voice cracked from the hours of silence. All of them turned to him, even Haru who hadn't taken his eyes off the ground since taking his stance against the stall door.

"What makes you say that?" Haru asked, frowning.

"Like Colin said," Will said, his voice hoarse, "their swords and horses were expensive. They knew…" he caught himself on the verge of saying *they knew who I was* but managed to stop the words from slipping. "They knew a lot about Alamore I think."

He knew by the flash that crossed Ross's eyes that he had understood what he, Rowan, and Colin weren't saying after all.

"Squires of higher-ranking nobles will have nicer things in Thornten," Rockwood offered, shrugging. "I mean, it's their tradition.

I'm sure Robin had the best horses as King Tollien's squire and, as for this lot, probably squires to Lords and Dukes."

And Princes, Will wondered darkly. Could The Cutthroat Prince be that? The squire of Marl? It made sense. It would be like Marl to send a squire to hunt Will down when he knew the Ranger and half the knights of Alamore were hunting him.

"The other weird thing if they were squires," Rowan said, breaking the silence, "is that they were in Alamore. I mean, really, do you think Tollien would order squires to Alamore?"

"They might not be here on Tollien's orders," pointed out Rockwood. "Don't give me that look, Rowan. Finding trouble and being where you shouldn't be is not a quality exclusive to Alamore squires."

"It wouldn't be the first time that Thornten squires have done something like this." Ross leaned his back against one of the stalls, his face darkening. "We've had attacks from young knights, older squires, those who have thought they could go rogue in Alamore and win some favor. More often than not they've gotten themselves killed or captured."

"I would like to kill them," Rowan snarled, scowling at the ground.

"Judging by what happened, that feeling sounds mutual," Rockwood rebuked, smiling sadly.

A sound behind Will made him turn and Haru hurried to straighten as the stall door opened. Will sprang to his feet, heart in his throat and stared at the healer, stepping calmly out of Visra's stall.

Wiping his hands on a rag, the round-faced man frowned at them, eyes shifting from the knights to the three bedraggled squires. "You didn't think that maybe you should take them to get treated while I treated the horse?"

"They weren't going to go even if we ordered it," Ross said flatly.

The healer rolled his eyes. "Alamore, all knights and squires are the same, I swear."

"How's Visra? Is he going to be okay?" Will demanded. He made to move around the healer, but the man stepped sideways, blocking his path.

"You're not going in there. No, not you either," he snapped as Haru stepped forward. "That horse needs rest. The wound will take some time to heal but yes–I think it will heal. We'll have to keep an eye for infection and check that the stitches hold. My bigger concern is that the blade that cut this horse seems to have been treated with Inanimus."

Will didn't understand and saw his confusion mirrored on Rowan, Colin, and Haru's faces. But Rockwood's face turned unusually grave and Ross's eyes hardened.

"Inanimus?" Will asked slowly. "I don't know what that is."

"Not surprising," the healer grumbled. "There's never enough focus on foreign medicines or poisons here... Inanimus is a toxin that, if inhaled, can render someone unconscious. It causes headaches when people wake but those tend to fade quicky which means it's often used to sedate people. But, if it is administered through the bloodstream, that pain sets in sooner and with more intensity. It spreads through the entire body. It can cause someone to lose control of their limbs and be unable to stand or walk. Depending on the amount given, it can be lethal." The healer blinked, seeming to notice their stricken faces and shook his head. "Your horse didn't get enough to kill it. That animal weighs a lot more than a man. No, it was only enough to knock him down by the time he got here. The mixture of exhaustion, blood-loss, and the toxin coursing through his body from running all caused him to fall."

"But he should heal?" Haru pressed.

"I said that didn't I?" grumbled the healer. "Let him rest. I don't fully trust how he'll act as he's waking up. I've not had much experience with Inanimus, especially not in horses. As I said, it's not from here."

"Where's it from then?" Will asked.

It was Ross who answered, his voice a low growl. "Kelkor."

Will saw Rowan and Colin exchange sharp looks and had to focus as not to let his own surprise show. "How would a Kelkor poison get into Alamore lands?"

"It's sold through black markets often enough to reach these parts," Rockwood added quickly, shooting Ross a questioning frown. "If I'm not mistaken, the Ranger said that's how you three got caught last year."

Will nodded. What the healer had described matched the means with which Marl had captured them the winter before. "Yeah, it must have been that." Still, he couldn't shake the dark thought forming in his mind.

"Now, if you'll excuse me," the healer sighed, closing the stall door behind him. "I'd like to go to bed. If you need treatment, go to the healing chamber. I'm not doctoring humans in a barn." With that he wheeled round, stalking out of the barn.

"Old wart," Rockwood said, laughing and clapping Will on the shoulder. "But you heard him, the horse'll be fine."

Will nodded, stepping toward the stall and peering through the bars. Visra was lying on his side still, eyes closed, but his sides rose and fell with a slow even breath. Will felt Haru come to stand beside him.

"I think it's time we all get some rest," Ross growled. "It's been a long enough day without this adventure on top of it."

"So, you're saying you don't want to go on anymore adventures?" Rowan asked mischievously.

"No!" Ross snapped.

Will turned away from Visra's stall, exhaustion washing over him.

"Yeah, I'm in agreement with Ross. If you three aren't needing the healer to look after you, it's time for bed," Rockwood grinned ruefully. "And try not to stay up all night telling the other squires of your madness and adventures. We don't need to be giving them any ideas."

"You're no fun," Rowan complained.

"He's right, Will," Haru muttered, gripping Will's shoulder tightly then stepping away. "You need some rest. It's been a long enough day and we're still going to have work to get done tomorrow."

Will hesitated, his hand gripping the bars that separated him and Visra. He wished he could stand there all night, guarding over the horse that had risked his life to save them.

Feeling the eyes of his companions heavy on his shoulders, Will pried his fingers loose of the bars and turned away. He fell into step with Rowan and Colin, leading the small party from the barn and into the courtyard. Night had truly fallen. Distant clouds blotting stars. The shivering shadow of silver moon was a hazy glow above, casting an eerie quality to the trees around them. The few lit torches along the wall distorted their shadows, stretching them far ahead of the three squires.

"Is it me or do the knights not seem real bothered by what happened? Like they're concerned cause it was us, but not worried about the Cutthroats," Rowan hissed in an undertone with a cautious glance over his shoulder. "Like do you think they we didn't tell them everything or..."

"I don't think so." Colin shook his head, scowling. "I think the reason they don't seem as worried as we are is they don't know the full truth. They don't know what that Cutthroat Prince was saying, or that he knew Will, or any of that."

Will nodded, guilt twisting inside him. "I feel like I need to tell Haru the truth now though."

"But the Ranger said not to," Colin whispered. "He's worried and this has to be part of why he was."

"He's worried because there's a spy. I don't think that's Haru," Will said flatly.

"I don't think we have any idea who it is," Rowan mumbled. "I mean, maybe an idea but…"

"You think it's her, too, then?" Will asked sharply. They had to wait to continue their conversation until they'd slipped through the black double doors and into the entry hall.

"It seems a bit fishy," Rowan admitted, shrugging. "She shows up and there just so happens to be a bunch of bone heads with cloaks? Not to mention the imadee, imaergus, imma-"

"Inanimus," Colin corrected, frowning. "Seriously, Rowan, do you not listen or is your memory that bad?"

"It's a weird name," Rowan said defensively.

"It is fishy," Will agreed. He heard the knights turning out of the corridor, through the side door that led up to the knights' tower. "You think the knights are thinking the same thing?"

"I don't think so," Colin muttered, shaking his head. "It seems too obvious. I mean, they might question her, but I don't feel like she'd be the spy."

"Ross just said that toxin, the weird name thingy, is from Kelkor!" Rowan said, smacking himself in the forehead. "And you aren't suspecting the rider who just showed up out of the blue from *Kelkor*? Come off it, Colin! You're supposed to be the smart one of us!"

"I'm trying to be the logical one," said Colin coolly. "And that's not a logical solution. It's too simple."

They stepped into the darkness of the dinner hall. Someone had extinguished most of the torches, leaving only the two that flanked the squire chamber door at the far end of the massive hall.

"What I want to know," Will said, pausing and turning to face his friends, "is who this Cutthroat Prince was. I agree with you two on that;

he wasn't old enough to be a knight. But I'm not sure I'm buying that he's a squire either."

"Unless he was Marl's squire," Colin offered.

"I've thought about that too, but why would Marl not have him kill me then? Why bother bringing me back to Thornten? They said it's because I'm an heir but that's just it. I thought that was the reason they wanted me dead, because he and Tollien see me as a threat and a future challenge for that stupid throne."

"You're probably the only person who would think the idea of taking a throne that you've got birthrights to is stupid," Rowan commented, smirking.

"Well, I don't want it," Will growled, scowling down at his boots for a moment. The memory of Visra crumpling flashed through his mind and he shook his head in a futile attempt to clear it. "It's not worth what they think it is." He could tell his friends had understood what he meant.

Colin sighed, running his hand over the back of his neck. "But you heard the healer. Visra will be fine. He probably wouldn't have even fallen if it wasn't for the Inanimus."

"But what if it'd been us," Will demanded, looking up sharply. "That took Visra down. If that was strong enough to knock down a horse, it could have killed you or Rowan and it would have been because of who I am." The truth of his words crashed over him and his shoulders slumped. "You two are putting yourselves at risk being around me, and so is everyone else, including Haru and he doesn't even know it."

"We're training to be knights," Colin said, and Will was surprised to see his friend was smiling slightly. "Not sure if you've realized it yet, Will, but knights tend to get attacked, injured, and killed."

"An occupational hazard," Rowan added, beaming. "So don't go getting all sappy and self-centered that it's your fault we got into danger. In case you've forgotten, I was the one to open the tunnels. Remember that? The tunnels? Full of murderous people and Airagon? Yeah, that wasn't anything to do with you so don't be so hard on yourself. Haru knows to watch his back and, honestly, we all know what being a squire means. Means a lot of thinking 'this could kill me or be a cool story.'"

Will couldn't help but laugh, albeit grudgingly.

"But Ross was right," Colin said, trying to hide a yawn in the crook of his elbow. "It's late. We've got to get rested up. I wouldn't put it past the knights to have us going through an exhausting training tomorrow."

They agreed and crept across the room and into the squire chamber in silence. Still, long after Will had climbed into bed and heard Rowan and Colin's breathing deepen, he couldn't sleep. His mind was alert, racing, spinning with thoughts and visions. Despite what Colin had said, he was sure that Haru couldn't have anything to do with what had happened. But, if that was the case, he wondered as he tossed onto his other side, why was it such a relief to hear Colin say he should listen to the Ranger and not tell anyone? Was he a coward for that? Was it fear of how Haru might react that made him so eager not to explain the truth?

And, what about the Ranger's other warning? He'd told Will to avoid this Lady Serena knight. Surely that meant something. How could Colin brush away those blinding facts so easily? The toxin that had nearly killed Visra was from Kelkor, where this woman was supposed to be from. Even if Marl had used it last year, it felt too coincidental.

The hours slipped by his mind, never slowing. Not even when his breathing deepened, and eyelids sank closed. The thoughts were there waiting in the darkness of sleep, already twisting into nightmares.

CHAPTER SIX

The following morning Will was surprised when Haru told him, Rowan, and Colin to wait at the breakfast table once they had finished eating.

"I thought we were practicing early this morning?" Will asked, bewildered.

"I thought so too," Haru grumbled. Will noticed that the young knight looked as exhausted as he felt. "Turns out, however, that your little adventure got the King's attention."

"Meaning we're getting an award or what?" Rowan asked, sitting up straighter, his fork halfway to his mouth and dripping yellow egg yolk over the table.

"Meaning you're going to a council," Haru said, raising his brows. "And you're also making a mess, so get that eaten and get to the council. Some of the knights don't care for waiting around."

"Yes, Sir," Colin and Will said in unison.

Rowan mumbled something but his mouth was now full of egg and it was unintelligible.

"You've the manner of a street rat," Colin said disgustedly, reaching to hand Rowan a napkin. "There's egg all over your face."

"Why do we need to attend a council?" groaned Will, dropping his forehead to the table. He was exhausted, his head was throbbing, and all he wanted to do at that moment was sneak away to the barn and curl up to sleep in the corner of Visra's stall.

"Probably because of the little thing of being attacked by prats yesterday," Rowan commented, swallowing his mouthful. "And I'm not a street rat. I'm a well-bred rodent of the finest lineage, as I'd have you know."

"Oh, because that makes it better," Colin grumbled, pushing himself to his feet and slapping Will on the shoulder. "Come on, it can't be that bad. Anyway, I haven't been to a council. Seems like it could be interesting."

"You haven't gone to one?" Will asked, straightening and looking up at Colin in surprise.

"Naw, we don't all get to be fancy like you." Rowan stood, shaking Will's chair side to side. "Now get up, let's go!"

Will rolled his eyes. He had attended the council. Only once, it was true, but it didn't mean it had been any more enjoyable. On that occasion, Ross had bellowed at the Ranger and Laster to control their tempers and he had ended up being asked to speak on behalf of all the squires. It had been intimidating.

Nevertheless, he rose with the others and crossed the dinner hall toward the door leading back to the squire chambers. Ross reached it a moment before them and held it open, gesturing them through.

"I take it you didn't go to sleep," Ross growled, taking in Will's appearance.

Will grimaced. "I tried, but there was a lot to think about."

The knight gave a gruff laugh, striding through the door after them and falling into step behind the three squires. "That gets worse as you get older."

Will didn't answer, instead fixing his eyes on the door at the far end of the squire chamber. Sir Rockwood was stepping through ahead of them, leaving it wide for the three squires and Ross to follow. Not for the first time, it struck Will as strange that the council chamber was tucked at the far end of the squire wing.

He nodded thanks to Rockwood who was holding the door and entered the unusually shaped chamber. This chamber was set at the bottom of a tower but, instead of having walls that curved all the way around, it had two straight edges. One of the edges held the door through which they had entered and the other held a large hearth. The high windows around the room filtered morning light over the chairs lining the walls and the two tables that had been pushed upright and out of the way beside the hearth.

Only two knights were already settling into seats. Haru and Robin, a young thin faced knight with brown hair swept back who sat on his right side. Haru was leaning over, muttering something to the other knight. The knight was nodding in agreement to whatever Haru was saying as he straightened and spotted the three squires entering the room, Rockwood and Ross behind them. He grinned and jerked his head to gesture to the chairs on Haru's other side.

"You three better take a seat, I don't imagine it'll be long until the others are in here."

"Thanks, Robin," said Will, dropping into the seat to Haru's left. "What's the point of us being here if we told you, Ross, and Rockwood last night."

"The King thinks it important to hear from the source," Haru answered, shrugging.

"It avoids details being lost," Robin explained, leaning forward to address Will across Haru. "We want to make sure we all get the story firsthand, from you three. And, you never know, we might hear something that Ross, Rockwood, or Haru here didn't catch."

Will nodded. A nervousness was stealing over him and he couldn't help himself from wringing his hands in his lap. There were details that knights hadn't been given but not because they weren't significant. He thought again of what The Cutthroat Prince had said about Marl and wondered if he was making a mistake listening to the Ranger's orders. He could tell Haru here and now. The only people in the room, apart from Haru, were those who already knew.

"And it's also procedure," Rockwood said, flopping into the chair across the room from the three of them. "Can't go having attacks that aren't heard and recognized by all the knights or you risk having one person who has no idea what happened and could get into trouble without realizing it."

"All the knights should be more observant than to fall into anything like that," Ross growled, lowering himself stiffly into a seat near the hearth.

"Should be, but people slip up," Rockwood shrugged.

Their conversation ended as the door was pushed open again and a group of knights filed into the room led by the sandy haired and bearded Don, who beamed at the squires before taking his seat. Behind him entered the rest of the knights; Sir Bane – black-hair and beard, white-ringed wild eyes; Sir Richard – his face lined with age, his brown hair streaked with grey, his eyes crinkled with years of smiling; Sir Henry – upright and rigid, his black hair swept back, peppered with white; Miller

– curly black hair, round faced, grinning at the squires and coming to sit next to Robin; Sir Laster – amber eyes narrowed, brown hair falling over his handsome face. Catching sight of Will, Rowan, and Colin, Will noticed his lip twitch into the shadow of its accustomed sneer.

Last to enter was King Revlan himself. Will rose with the knights around the chamber. He couldn't help but feel nervous as the King paused, raising a hand to signal all should be seated again. Will felt sure that even a blind man would sense the King's presence. Power emanated from him and his dark eyes flitted around the room, taking in each face. He gave Will a faint smile, inclining his head a fraction, then crossed the room to sink into the seat next to Ross.

"I take it that you know why you're here," the King said, turning to the squires.

Will felt some of the nervousness leach from him under the calm dark gaze. "Yes, King. The attack that happened yesterday."

All the eyes in the room shifted to Will and he swallowed hard, trying not to notice them. Instead, he watched the King, waiting for him to speak.

"Would you mind recounting what happened for the council?"

Will could tell that this question was more of a command than a request and inhaled deeply before starting. "We—me, Rowan, and Colin—rode out yesterday after training to get our horses some exercise. We've been focused on combat training for a few days now and needed to make sure they were worked."

Out of the corner of his eye, Will noticed Laster roll his eyes but pressed on, determinedly.

"We rode west, since the Eastern Forest is off limits still for any of the younger squires. Rowan and Colin decided to show me the river and, when we got there, we dismounted and went to tie our horses. That's when Visra, my horse, started acting up. I thought he was scared of the forest or something and didn't think anything of it. Once I'd stepped away from him though, a stranger appeared. He was wearing a grey hood, so I couldn't get a good look at his face, but I don't think he was very old, maybe a few years older than me."

"And how did you deduce that if you couldn't see him?" Laster asked, smirking.

"His height, voice, and mannerisms," Colin answered for Will, meeting Laster's arrogant glower with a defiant expression of his own. "I'd say he was around sixteen, like Will said, not much older than us."

"And what happened then?" the King pressed, shooting Laster a warning look. The knight crossed his arms, leaning back in his chair with a huff.

"He said he was from Thornten, or loyal to there," Will continued. He felt Rowan glance toward him but didn't turn to meet his friend's gaze. "Then he got annoyed that we didn't take him real seriously. He sort of signaled and three more hooded people showed up on horses. He said that they were his Cutthroats and that he was The Cutthroat Prince. They seemed to think it'd be funny I guess to catch one of us, so I bargained, told them to let Rowan and Colin go and I'd go with them. But Colin grabbed Visra instead of his horse and Vis attacked one of them which gave Rowan and Colin time to get on their horses and attack back."

"This is the horse the healer was treating last night?" the King asked sharply.

Will nodded, chest tightening. "Yes, King."

Understanding flickered in the dark eyes and the King shook his head with a faint smile. "You're lucky to have a horse like that, William. From what the healer told me; it sounds like he should heal."

"Yes, it does seem that way."

"Which brings us to the larger concern," Ross growled, glancing toward the squires then back to the King. "The blade used on the horse was coated in Inanimus."

A few of the knights stiffened. Will noticed Bane's brow furrow and Henry frowned. Laster snorted, lip curling again. "That's convenient timing."

"Laster," Rockwood said in a warning voice.

"I'm only stating what others are already thinking, Rockwood," Laster leaned forward. "We don't have a reason to trust her."

"We do," Bane spoke in his gravelly voice, shooting Laster a withering glower. "I've known Serena for years. This isn't anything to do with her. Anyhow, Inanimus is a banned toxin, even in Kelkor, and the plants used to create it aren't found anywhere near Kelvane."

"And she's a knight of Queen Paranella," Ross growled. "This isn't the first time we've dealt with this in Alamore, in case you've forgotten, Laster."

"I haven't," Laster snarled, eyes flashing.

"The part that concerns me is how easily they found you," Robin said, and the attention shifted to the young knight. "I'm in agreement with Ross. Inanimus isn't common in Thornten but people carry it. There was a roaring trade for weapons that had been treated with it for a while, because you didn't have to be a brilliant swordsman to win a fight. So long as you were able to get one cut into your opponent, it was your fight. But I am worried about how easy it was for them to find three squires." Robin leaned forward and turned his appraising gaze to Will. "Did they say anything else? Such as why they were here or what they were doing?"

Will heard the unasked question. Robin knew the truth. Robin had been the one to tell him. He'd been Tollien's squire until changing sides. Immediately, he noticed the attention of several other knights. Rockwood stopped bouncing his leg, Miller straightened, Ross's face grew stonier, and Laster's eyes narrowed. The knights who knew the truth also understood what Robin was asking.

Will forced himself to meet Robin's eyes with his best attempt at innocent ignorance. "No, not really." Out of the corner of his eye, he noticed the other knights relax. Only Miller still watched him, a faint frown between his brows.

"Squires have been riding to that river in good weather since I was a squire myself," Richard rasped, half laughing. "I wouldn't be surprised if they knew that and have been looking through these parts for a while and waiting for a chance to catch someone unawares. It sounds to me like some of the Thornten squires are getting a bit bold and labeling themselves with names to try to cause a stir and scare people."

"It could be bad luck on our part," Colin agreed, shrugging.

"Luck doesn't exist," Ross growled, crossing his arms over his chest. "What I worry about is how well they got into Alamore lands. It speaks of spies inside the walls."

It took all of Will's strength not to react to the words with more than wide-eyed puzzlement. At his side he could feel Rowan and Colin stiffen. "Spies?" Will asked, forcing his voice to stay even. "But you just said that Serena-"

"Not her," Ross growled. "It's possible for other people–those you'd never notice or expect–to turn against the castle."

"Which is a concern that's been growing," the King said, running a hand over his jaw. "The Ranger's reports have indicated that there's at least one person no longer loyal to Alamore in this castle."

"Like Vonnic and Danvac?" Rowan asked. "But how would we find them?"

Grimacing, Rockwood shook his head. "If they're any good, I'm afraid we wouldn't find them until they did what Vonnic and Danvac did and royally mess up. Perhaps the spy will try to pick a fight with you three again, eh?" He winked at the squires, his grimace changing to a grin.

"Don't give them ideas, Rockwood," Ross growled warningly.

"But spies who are tracking Alamore squires?" Henry asked, chuckling. "Ross, that seems a bit out of Tollien's usual scope of interest. Why not fight knights? Send someone to kill one of us or capture one of us? That would be the way to strike a chord in this country."

"I don't know," Rockwood countered, leaning his chair back on two legs, "What better way can you think of to dishearten and cripple a kingdom than taking their training squires? Without them, we'd all become old codgers working to keep the castle safe; no hope of retirement or rest. Plus, we've sworn to train and protect them as their knights, whereas all of us swore to protect the country or die trying."

"Some of us are already old codgers," Richard chuckled.

A few of the other knights laughed but it was Laster who turned to Ross, leaning forward to address him past Don and Rockwood. "It would be interesting if they have spies to select these three squires...wasn't it?"

Will stiffened. For one horrible moment, he wondered if Laster was about to tell his secret to the room at large. But the knight didn't say anything further, only raising his brows, lip curling into a smirk as he waited for Ross to answer.

"As Richard said, it sounds like this was convenience rather than a targeted strike for these three," Ross growled, glowering at Laster. Laster's eyes darkened and Ross continued, turning to the three squires with a nod. "And if it was targeted, they couldn't target much better than they did. Colin is the last heir from the Greyhead line, Rowan's father is the Lord of Lonric. Both of them would be high priced bounties for their return."

"Most of the squires come from noble lines and, yes, be it gold or loyalty that Tollien wants, we know he would use squires for it," the King said, cutting across Laster as he opened his mouth to retort. He turned to Robin. "Can you tell us of any plans Tollien may have mentioned in the past?"

Robin shook his head. "He often would discuss speaking with younger heirs in Alamore land–offering them their family holdings in exchange for loyalty–but I never knew who he was after with those plans. Rowan and Colin both come from prestigious families and…" Robin hesitated, eyes flitting to Will before continuing. "I know that they don't have younger siblings who are in line for their family seats. Perhaps this is a new way to gain their loyalties? Lonnac, Lonric, Finnwick–none have a long line of heirs left and all have a strong holding in Alamore. Rowan and Colin would be the end of the line in terms of obvious heirs. It'd be logical for him to go after them, and he can obviously get squires through our defenses easier than he could get knights into Alamore. So why not use squires to catch squires–better than getting his squires massacred trying to kill Ross or something."

"Very true, give the boy a biscuit," Rockwood said, clapping his hands.

Robin grinned, rolling his eyes.

"The Ranger has been hunting information down about this. He's told me that spies are a concern and how Tollien's reaching them, communicating. But, with the arrival of Serena, the changes to the south…" the King muttered, more to himself than the rest of the room. His voice faded to silence and he shook his head, sighing. "We can only wait for his return, however… and cannot rely on it for answers this time."

Cold tension seized the room. Every face had become serious, even Rockwood and Haru's usual grins were gone. Rockwood tilted his chair forward onto all four legs again. Will glanced at Rowan and Colin next to him and Colin gave the slightest shake of his head. They, like him, didn't understand. Whatever Serena had come to say, whatever the news from Kelkor was, it wasn't good. It seemed, too, to be the reason that the Ranger had left again.

"I want patrols out today without the squires," ordered the King, snapping out of his thoughts and straightening. "Check the forests, see to it that we are certain there aren't any of these Cutthroats, squires, whatever they are, out and about. Notify the soldiers—I want them riding out as well. Squires will be trained inside the wall until we are confident that this issue is resolved. I can't have heirs vanishing." He stood, clapping his hands together, and Will understood. They were dismissed.

Chairs scraped across the floor and the knights began to file through the door, some in silence, others exchanging quick and quiet conversation. A few threw the squires searching looks, including Laster, who paused before stepping out of the room after the King.

"You three going to sit there to try to get out of training or what?"

Will started. He hadn't noticed that Haru was standing, waiting for them with a tired smile.

"Right!" Will scrambled up, Rowan and Colin doing the same.

"Come on, Haru," Robin called, waiting by the door. "They're not going to run off and hide."

Haru gave a dark laugh. "Oh, just wait till you have a squire, Robin."

"Hey, I don't hide from training," Will protested indignantly.

Rowan held up a hand. "I do, I do that sometimes. Doesn't work, but I try."

"So I've heard," Haru growled but the threatening tone he'd been attempting was lessened by the smile he still wore. "Don't get any ideas, Will. Twenty minutes and you better be outside and ready for archery."

"I will be," Will promised.

Haru nodded and hurried to catch up with Robin, the last two knights to leave the room.

"Anyone else get a funny feeling that a couple knights didn't buy what Will was selling?" asked Rowan once the knights were out of sight.

"Laster," Will and Colin said together.

"Miller too," Will added.

"Yeah, but they already know the truth. They're bound to be a bit suspicious," Colin pointed out. "They're not stupid."

"Pity they aren't stupid, it'd make keeping things quiet like the Ranger told us to a bit easier," Rowan grumbled.

"Speaking of quiet, I noticed you didn't talk much," Will said, smirking. "What was up with that?"

"I decided that I should probably not say anything at all in the council." Rowan shrugged, starting for the door. "Some reason when I speak the truth, people see it as me being sarcastic or rude. Probably because they're all a bunch of spinach brained morons."

"That, that right there," Colin said, giving Rowan a disapproving look, "that's why people don't ask for your input. Now let's get to training before Ross gets moody about that too."

They entered the squire chamber, Will falling a step behind, lost in thoughts. So, the Ranger really was away, not working near the castle at all. How had The Cutthroat Prince known that? He hadn't and he and the Ranger had spoken only two days ago. And why had he gone? What had Serena said that made him leave like that? On what orders was he sent?

"Will? You okay?"

Will looked up. His friends were waiting at the far door, Rowan holding it open, and both watching him with concern in their eyes.

"Yeah, I'm fine, just was thinking," Will said, breaking into a jog to catch up.

"About the Cutthroats?" Rowan asked.

Will shook his head. "The Ranger."

Colin nodded. "I was wondering that as well."

"What about the Ranger? He's always gone," Rowan pointed out. "It's not a big deal."

"But it sounds like he left because of information Serena brought to Alamore," Will muttered, lowering his voice as they entered the dinner hall. Servants were clearing the tables of breakfast and he didn't care for the idea of being overheard, especially since all the discussion of spies.

"So, so what?" Rowan looked between Will and Colin. "Why does that matter?"

"It matters," Colin hissed, glancing around them covertly. "It matters because Kelkor's King is Revlan's brother, it matters because they're our strongest alliance and their messenger clearly struggled to get here. Which means, if the Ranger's been sent, there's something wrong."

Will saw the understanding wash over Rowan's face. "So that means…"

"It means Kelkor's in trouble and, if they're in trouble, we might very well be too."

CHAPTER SEVEN

Patrols rode out over the next two days. They searched the forests for any signs of The Cutthroat Prince and his riders, reporting that they hadn't seen grey cloaks or young riders. None of the squires were allowed to join, even Airagon, Novin, and Delvin, the three oldest, were ordered to train inside the walls.

"It's not forever," Haru assured Will when he returned from one of the patrols. "We're just trying to make sure Tollien's not up to something that could get one of you captured. I don't imagine that his squires are coming back. Bane is even starting to think it was done on a dare more than on any kind of orders. Ross and Miller are being a bit paranoid in my opinion, though. They think we need to go out again tonight, not staying on our normal routes to see if we can figure how they're getting in."

Will had to bite the inside of his cheek to keep from saying anything. He only nodded and hurried back to practicing staff fighting with Colin and Loper. Miller and Ross's paranoia made sense. They knew the truth and with each hour, Will wondered if he was doing the wrong thing by listening to the Ranger. Wasn't he putting Haru in more danger by not telling him the truth? As far as Haru was concerned, Will would be the least interesting target to Tollien. He thought Will's father was just one of Tollien's past spies. He didn't have the faintest inkling that he was an heir to their enemy's kingdom.

Still, he kept his secret and threw himself into training and practicing harder than before. If his silence was noticed by Haru, it was written off. All the squires were annoyed at being pent up in the castle while the sun shone tantalizingly above them.

The upside to being in the castle was that Will and the others could bask in the glory of what had happened. Rowan kept telling the tale of their ambush and escape, reenacting it with so much enthusiasm that he injured himself twice; once when leaping from the floor to his bed, over balancing, and toppling off the other side, and once when the chair he stood on at the squire table flipped. Laster had instituted a 'no idiots standing on the bloody chairs' rule after that one.

Another upside was that, with the knights busy on increased patrols, they were being set more studying assignments to fill their time. Will generally didn't care to read through old books about history, weapon care, horse training, and battle strategy, but he'd taken to leaving the castle with his stacked volumes and sitting in Visra's stall.

The horse was already showing vast improvement, standing without support though his shoulder was thick with white gauze and his head hung lower than usual. He ate at his hay while Will worked, occasionally coming to sniff his young charge's foot or check if Will had smuggled out anything more interesting to snack on. Will rarely disappointed on that front bringing anything he could sneak from the castle—toast, apples, carrots, and the occasional pastry.

Rowan and Colin had joined him once, but Rowan had been too distracted by the horses to pay attention to what he was reading, and Colin had found Rowan himself to be too distracting. After that, Colin had taken to studying in the Hall of Records again and made Rowan stay with him there so that Rowan would actually get his work done. Will didn't mind. He enjoyed the presence of his horse, the comfort of seeing Visra move—even stiffly—around the stall.

That's where he was the afternoon of the second day, lounging on a clean pile of straw, trying to find something to keep his interest in the dead boring book he was trying to learn from, when a soft tap made him look up. A smiling round face peered through the bars of Visra's stall back at him, curling black hair falling over dark eyes.

Will set aside the book, grinning, glad of the distraction.

"Mind if I come in?" Miller asked.

"Not at all," Will said, waving a hand to his surroundings. "Pull up some straw and stay a while. Anything to keep me from reading this."

Miller stepped through the door, patting Visra's neck gently as the horse turned to inspect him. After a moment, Visra seemed to decide Miller wasn't interesting or threatening and returned to his feed while the knight crossed to where Will was sitting. He turned his head to read the title of the book next to Will.

"'A History of Military Theory and Hierarchy.' Alamore, I remember that book. I'm surprised no one's burned it yet."

"I'm tempted to do it for the future of other squires who are ordered to read it," Will grumbled. "Dead boring."

"It is," Miller agreed, lowering himself to sit cross legged next to Will. "This is an interesting place to study. I thought you'd be in the Hall of Records with your friends."

Will shrugged. "I prefer it out here. Let's me see how Vis is doing and get my work done."

Miller nodded. "Yeah, I imagine it's less distracting. When I went in there, Rowan was in the process of seeing how many books he could stack on a table before they fell over."

"I'm sure Colin loved that."

"He seemed a bit preoccupied," Miller chuckled. "It was worse because the two oldest pages were supposed to be starting their studies to become squires and Rowan had recruited them."

Will snorted. "Doesn't surprise me. Aren't you supposed to be training one of those pages?"

"Yeah," Miller said, grimacing. "Wish me luck on that. Jerram's been corrupted by Rowan for years and it's clearly going to just get worse here on out."

"Good luck, you'll age a thousand years in the six years you train him."

"Thanks," Miller grumbled. Will watched him. The knight seemed to be considering something, running a hand over the two-day beard that had started on his chin. After a moment, he turned to Will, frowning. "From how you told that story the other day, I take it that there was more that you weren't quite willing to reveal in council, wasn't there?"

Even though it was framed as a question, Will knew Miller already felt certain. He nodded regardless, turning away from Miller and grabbing a piece of straw, twirling it in his fingers. "That obvious?"

"Only because I already know about Marl," Miller assured him. There was another pause then Miller continued. "And, from how it seems, I take it that you haven't told Haru any of that, have you?"

Will didn't answer, staring at the straw in his fingers, reflecting the sunlight pouring through the ceiling above. After a moment he shook his head. "No, I haven't told him. He's got no idea."

Miller sighed heavily, running a hand through his hair. "I thought as much. And I'm guessing that attack then, it wasn't some fluke. They weren't after Rowan and Colin at all, were they?"

"They knew who I was, but I don't know how. I know I didn't know them. I know I've never seen them, and yet they knew who I was and that I was leaving the castle. It was too well planned."

"And have you told the other knights about this? I'm not talking about the council," Miller added quickly. "I'm talking about the knights who already know who Marl is, like Laster, Rockwood, or Ross."

"No." Will let the straw flutter from his fingers back to the stall floor. "But I think they know even without me saying it."

"Well, Ross and Laster suspect it." Miller shook his head, leaning against the wall next to Will. "But that leaves us with larger concerns now, doesn't it?"

Will turned to him, raising his brows. "Like what?"

"Like how they knew who you were, that you'd be out there, that you'd just be with Rowan and Colin, those things for a start. They were too well placed, like you said."

"You think it was the spy who told them?" Will asked, turning to look at Miller again. The knight was frowning at the ceiling, eyes unreadable. "Or do you think that somehow it really was crazy luck?"

"Luck is good timing," Miller said flatly. "That they found you wasn't anything to do with luck. Will, I know you couldn't just outright say this in front of the council, that you aren't wanting everyone to know, but I'm not going to lie to you. I'm worried. That they knew you were out there…you know what that means?"

"Yeah, Ross said so. He said there's spies in Alamore, and that the Ranger was worried."

"That's part of it," Miller said, turning his head to fix Will with a searching look. "How many people knew you were going to ride out of the castle?"

"What?" asked Will, taken aback.

"When you left to work Visra, who all knew you'd be going out on that ride or leaving the castle?" Miller pressed.

Frowning, Will racked his memory, trying to recall all that had happened up to his departure from the castle. "Haru and I'd been practicing daggers and hand-to-hand fighting. He told me to take Visra out, since I hadn't worked him the day before when the Kelkor knight showed up. So, Haru knew, then I invited Rowan and Colin."

"You didn't talk to anyone else?"

Will shivered, sudden comprehension washing over him. "It wasn't Haru, he's not the spy."

"I didn't say that," Miller replied coolly.

"Yeah but you're thinking that he is," Will snapped, annoyed. "And I'm telling you he's not. Look, I was in the courtyard, I wasn't thinking about it. Literally anyone might have overheard me. It's not like it was a secret that we were riding out and anyone might have guessed that we'd head west. We're not allowed to go east."

"Calm down, Will." Miller reached over and gently cuffed him in the back of his head, grinning. "I'm not condemning your knight or anything. I'm trying to figure out who the spy, if we do have one, is."

"So, you don't think it's the Kelkor knight?" Will asked.

Shaking his head, Miller let out a long breath. "No, I'm with Ross and Bane on that. I've never met Serena, but her reputation precedes her. I can't imagine it would be her."

"But you'd suspect Haru?" Will demanded, unable to keep the accusation out of his voice. "How could you think Haru would do that before her? It was Kelkor toxin on that blade."

"And Serena is in the healing chambers on bedrest," Miller retorted, a flash of irritation crossing his boyish face. "I've already told you; I'm not blaming Haru for anything. I just want answers, the same as you." He pushed himself to his feet, brushing the dust and straw from his tunic. Looking down at Will, Miller's dark eyes softened slightly. "I'm sorry, Will, I didn't mean to lose my temper. I don't care to be in the dark, any more than I'm sure you do."

"It's fine," Will grumbled.

"It's not though," Miller said. He let out a hollow laugh, pressing a palm against his forehead. "There's something going on and I don't believe in this level of coincidence. That Cutthroat Prince didn't materialize out of nowhere and happen to show up the day that the Ranger leaves. He knew you weren't protected which means he might know other things, things happening in this castle. I would be willing to bet he's got ears in this castle–he or Tollien–and that makes me uneasy."

"Me too," Will admitted.

"Well, all we can do is try to watch our backs and keep our guard up," Miller said, shrugging. "Especially you."

"Why now, though?" The question slipped from Will before he'd even had time to consider it. "Why are they after me now do you think?"

A shadow crossed Miller's face and he turned away from Will, seeming suddenly interested in Visra's bandaged shoulder. Will waited, noting the red hue creeping up Miller's neck.

"What aren't you telling me?"

Miller snorted and kicked the straw, burying his hands in his pockets. "A lot, seeing as you're a squire."

"Is it something to do with Marl?" Will asked.

Miller shot a sharp look down toward him, eyes flashing. "And what would make you wonder that."

"Something the Ranger said," Will said slowly. "When you were all in the council with the Kelkor knight, he came and made me promise not to tell anyone that Marl was related to me. So, I want to know, everything that's going on, The Cutthroat Prince, is that anything to do with Marl?"

"I'm not sure about the Cutthroat," Miller admitted, visibly relaxing. "Look, I appreciate you telling me the truth, but I've got to go, Will. I drew the short straw of having a midnight patrol and I really need to get some rest first or I'm going to sleep in the saddle."

"Right," Will muttered, disappointed. There was something the knight wasn't telling him, and he was certain he was right. Marl was causing some of this chaos. Miller had to be lying about Marl not being involved in the Cutthroats.

"And Will."

He looked up. Miller had the stall open, and one foot raised to step out. He was watching Will, unusually serious.

"What?"

"Keep that promise to the Ranger, won't you?" Miller managed a half smile. "I don't think you need to be telling anyone the truth about Marl or you, not right now, anyway."

Before Will could respond, Miller gave him a curt nod, raised a hand in farewell, and stepped out of the stall, striding out of the barn without a backwards glance.

CHAPTER EIGHT

"Miller reckons Haru's a spy?" Rowan asked, wide-eyed. "I hadn't considered that. Think the Ranger did? Think that's why he told you not to tell him?"

"Haru's not a spy," Will snapped. "I trust Haru."

Colin, arms crossed over his chest, sighed. "That's just it, though, isn't it? A good spy could make you trust them as well."

"You two are being just as ridiculous as Miller," Will grumbled, turning away from his friends to scowl out the window of the Hall of Records, down into the courtyard where the afternoon patrol was returning. Even from here he could make out Haru's thatch of red hair bobbing through the group. A jolt of annoyance, guilt, and doubt ran through his stomach.

Half an hour had passed since speaking to Miller. Will had been too distracted to focus on studying again and rushed to find his friends in the Hall of Records. He'd needed to talk to someone, to have them agree and tell him that Miller was being an idiot. Instead, he was dealing with this. After a moment he shook his head, turning back to where his friends

"Look, he's not a spy," Will snapped, turning back to his friends again. "If anything, it's that rider from Kelkor we need to worry about. Even the Ranger warned me about her. Doesn't that seem a bit more like she's the one to worry about?"

"He also told you not to tell Haru anything," Rowan said. He chewed his lip nervously. "But I also don't know that I could believe it either. We've known Haru for years, he's never acted like a spy. He's always been a lot better person than Danvac or Vonnic. Or Marl, for that matter."

"They weren't brilliant spies," Colin countered. "I'm with Miller and the Ranger. We can't accuse Haru of anything, but we also can't let our guard slip around him, or the Kelkor knight," he added as Will opened his mouth to protest. "Because I agree with you. Her showing up and the Cutthroats appearance seems too perfect of timing."

Rowan groaned, dropping his head on the table that they were seated at. "And here I was thinking my biggest headache today would be how to build a tower out of all the chairs in this chamber. Now we've got this to contend with."

"Maybe I should just outright ask Haru if he's a spy," said Will.

"Right, because that wouldn't be an uncomfortable conversation." Rowan lifted his head, snorting with laughter. "I can imagine it now; 'Oh hey, Haru, Miller thinks you're actually trying to get me killed by my murder-happy father. Would you mind confirming or denying these details?'" When Will gave him a stony glower as his only response Rowan rolled his eyes. "The point is you can't just ask him."

"I can't just not trust him either," Will pointed out.

"But you've kept the truth from him this long, even without the Ranger telling you too," Rowan argued. "So, why's that?"

Will opened and closed his mouth, frustration mounting. They didn't understand, they couldn't understand, what it was like to be in his position, to have to face what he was facing. It had been stupid for him to even try.

"We're not trying to annoy you, Will," Colin said, his voice softer than it had been. "We're trying to help keep you alive."

"Yeah, well, the Ranger is too and all he's really done is make this worse," Will growled. He crossed to the table where his friends sat, dropping into the remaining seat between them. He sat back in the seat, digging his fingers into the faded blue upholstery of the chairs arms. "I want answers."

"We all do," Rowan said flatly.

"What I'd like to know," Colin said, frowning and closing the book that still lay open before him, "is what all this has to do with Marl."

"Marl's a prat, the Cutthroat is a prat, seems a good enough connection to me," Rowan mumbled.

"But Miller said that he didn't know if Marl had anything to do with the Cutthroat," Will repeated what he'd already said, more for his sake than his friends'. "And I don't think he was lying. He doesn't seem to keep a straight face well."

"Then what is it? Because now we've got Miller and the Ranger saying Marl's up to something," said Colin, watching Will carefully.

Will shook his head. "I haven't the faintest idea and I'm not sure how we'd find out."

"Didn't the King say that the Ranger left because of the Kelkor knight?" Rowan asked, straightening suddenly.

"Yeah, so?" Will watched his friend, noticing the excitement and dawning on Rowan's face.

"Well then, don't you think she'd know why he left? She'd know at least what's going on there, in Kelkor. If it was all somehow connected…"

"But we just said we shouldn't trust her." Colin shook his head. "So, I don't think asking her is any smarter than asking Haru. In fact, it's probably stupider. I'm with you, I'd like to think it's not Haru who's spying on Alamore. It's more believable to me that it's her, even if the knights don't agree."

"If she admitted to being a spy, though, that'd prove that Haru's innocent!" Will said, sitting upright.

"Hold up, not what I was going for," Rowan yelped. "We aren't doing that."

"Why not?" Will looked between his friends, a new energy coursing through him. "If I could talk to her, find out and prove she's the spy…"

"You'd get killed," Colin snapped. "And that defeats the point of us trying to keep you alive. The Ranger told you not to tell her who you are. How would you casually find out all of this without revealing you're Marl's son?"

"It'd be worth telling her the truth to catch a spy," Will pointed out. When neither of his friends looked impressed he slapped a hand on the table, causing them both to jump. "How can you take this not knowing?"

"We don't like it either, mate, but we also know we can't get killed trying to prove a point!" Rowan said, shaking his head. "And you've heard Laster talk about Kelkor knights–they are fierce. I don't even like to cross my sister and she's not a trained lady knight with a bloody sword."

"Rowan's right, Will." Colin's voice was decided. "You can't do that. All we can do right now is see what we find out through listening and focus on keeping our heads down. That's all."

Will sank back into his seat, crossing his arms and scowling at them. "I don't like this. I don't like not feeling like I can't trust Haru."

"We're not saying don't trust him," Rowan said, and to Will's astonishment his friend was grinning, hair flopping forward over his face. "We're saying don't trust anyone."

Will couldn't help but laugh, the knot of tension easing in his chest. "You're an idiot."

"You just don't appreciate genius."

After that, the three of them began talking about the Cutthroats again, Will's discussion with Miller sinking to the back of his mind in laughter as he watched, once more, spring to his feet and reenact the attack.

It wasn't until hours later, when the sun had cast a red shadow over the shelves the three descended the stairs for dinner, that Will's mind was pulled back to the idea of speaking to the Kelkor knight. They were sinking into their seats with the other squires, Rowan already trying to cause chaos by attempting to knock Novin's chair backwards as it balanced on two back legs, when a shiver like spiders ran over his skin. Turning in his seat, he stiffened as his eyes met the green set that were locked on him from the knights' table. There, sitting upright and proud, dark red hair pulled back in a braid and one arm cradled close to her chest in a sling, Lady Serena of Kelkor was giving him a searching look that gave Will the uncomfortable feeling that she already knew exactly who he was.

CHAPTER NINE

Grey clouds rolled across the skies over the night, sending shadows across the walls and courtyard. Their filtered light seemed to wash the color from the surroundings, and Will could smell the rain as he shifted foot to foot anxiously outside the barn.

Haru had told him at breakfast that the squires had been cleared by the King to practice outside the walls again, providing they had knights with them, and that they would be borrowing Ross's new hunting horse for him to practice with until Visra recovered. Rowan and Colin had been volunteered by their knights to help the two new squires, Gabe and Jerram, in their first day of training with Miller and Robin. Will had noticed both of his friends throw him anxious looks at the news they wouldn't be training together but had pretended not to notice. Haru wasn't a spy. He was sure of that and, not to mention, the idea of riding again was too tantalizing to resist.

The excitement of riding had been part of why he'd sprinted out to the barn before Haru. Part, but not the main motive. The more concerning and pressing reason had been Serena approaching Haru in the dinner hall. She'd shot Will a calculated look of loathing as she called Haru over and, not eager to be under her watchful gaze a moment longer, he'd slipped out of the castle. Whatever she was doing here, and whatever Will tried to tell himself, there wasn't any doubt in his mind that she knew more about him, and Marl, than the Ranger had admitted.

He glanced out the barn doors, hoping to see Haru rushing to meet him, and noticed the clouds slowly churning overhead. *Please don't rain yet, please, please, please. I need to get out of the castle for a bit, just get out and not deal with any of this for a few minutes.*

"Morning, Will!"

Will started.

Airagon was striding toward him, a spring in his step and hands buried in his pockets, a broad smile on his freckled face. He raised his brows. "You ready to go riding?"

"Are you training with us today then?" Will asked, confused.

"In a sort." Airagon shrugged, pausing next to Will. "Haru told us, the King and I that is, that you were going to try out Ross's hunting horse in the valley today. The King and I were already going to leave the walls this morning anyhow and he said we should go together. So, us, Sir Don, and Novin." Will noticed that even when not walking, Airagon was bouncing slightly on the balls of his feet.

"What were you leaving the walls for?" Will asked. He had to resist the sudden urge to laugh at how ridiculous the older squire looked, bobbing like a child awaiting sweets.

Airagon's chest swelled with pride and he straightened. "I turn seventeen today, which means, I get my sword."

"You do? Really? That's excellent!" Will beamed, some of the worry of seeing Serena melting away. "Are you getting yours from the same blacksmith that Novin got his then?"

"Yes." Airagon nodded. "I've been practicing with it a couple times a week and it's brilliant–the balance, the edge on the blade–I just hope I don't do something stupid when trying out the swords, like drop it."

"You'll be fine." Will rolled his eyes. "You've never dropped a sword in practice have you?"

"Not yet, but there's a first for everything."

Sir Don appeared through the double doors and waved a hand in greeting. A few strides behind him, Novin and Haru were the next to leave the castle, Novin laughing at something Haru had said. The King was last to appear, striding next to Sir Ross. Will noticed the King and Ross both looked unusually serious, more so even as the rest of the group ahead of them were in obvious good spirits. The King paused, saying something to Ross who nodded and turned away, toward the steps that led up the castle wall and onto the battlement. He didn't even glance in Will and Airagon's direction, frowning ahead.

Will's gaze moved back to Haru and he felt the knot of tension grip his chest again. If he was a spy...but how could he be? He was laughing now, thumping Novin on the back and shaking his head. Will relaxed. He was starting to act like Ross, Miller, and the Ranger—paranoid over nothing but empty suspicions.

"Ready to try out Ross's little horse with the big attitude?" Sir Don clapped Will on the shoulder as he passed him on his way through the doors of the barn.

Will grinned. "When you put it that way, I'm less certain about it."

"He's not terrible," Haru assured him, reaching him and ruffling his hair. "He's just a hunt horse. Different breed of animal from warhorses."

Will waved Haru's hand away, trying to flatten his hair again. "I'm not certain that's of much more comfort."

"Oh, you'll survive." Haru laughed, rolling his eyes. "Just don't come off the horse or I'm not letting you live it down."

A deep chuckle made Will turn. The King had clearly overheard his and Haru's discussion and smiled down at him, pausing to let Airagon and Novin enter the barn first.

"From what I've heard, your horse is a handful himself."

"Yes, he is, King." Will nodded, uncomfortably aware of his now disheveled hair. He tried again to flatten it. "But he's the only one I've really worked in a while."

"It's good to change horses every so often," the King said, stepping past Will and Haru and into the barn. "Though, I never much care for any horse that isn't my Talloe."

"See, even the King says it's good for you," Haru said, smirking when the King had walked out of hearing distance.

"And carrots are supposed to be good for Rowan, but he still thinks they're terrible," Will pointed out but he was laughing, walking into the barn with Haru. "You didn't tell me what horse I was looking for anyway, so I haven't saddled or anything. I've just been waiting."

"I'm sorry, Will." Haru clapped a hand to his forehead. "I forgot that! I got caught up talking to Serena, she had some questions about practice courts so she can start training again with her good arm. Hold on a minute, I'll get Ad."

"Ad?"

But Haru was hurrying across the barn already, not listening. Will shifted while he waited, watching Airagon saddle his grey horse while the King haltered his massive blue roan stallion. Visra was watching them through fiery brown eyes, his chest pressed against the stall door, clearly expecting to be worked. Will grimaced, turning away with a guilty twinge. It felt somehow like a betrayal to be working another horse.

He looked up to see Haru returning, and his stomach dropped at the sight of the animal walking casually at his other side. It wasn't the horse's height that took Will aback but rather that he recognized the deep red coat, the thick neck, the long wavy mane and tail and the thin white stripe that ran down the horse's curved face.

"Will, this is Admere," Haru said proudly, holding out the horse's line. "Don't mind the size–we've got a saddle that'll fit him in the tack room."

Will took the rope, not sure what to say. It was the same small stallion that had taunted and challenged Visra days before. Now he looked the picture of curious innocence, his breath hot on Will's hands as he smelled the squire's sleeve. "This is Ross's horse?"

"One and the same." Haru nodded. "Don't mind the size. As I said, he's built to be a fast mount for hunting or just light fighting, not carrying full armor or anything. Which is lucky because you don't do that right now."

Will didn't say anything, only looking over the horse's build. He was a fair few hands shorter than Visra, but his body was still muscular, the thick neck defined. His coat was a brilliant red and though he didn't have the thick feathers of most the war horses, he still had large hooves. Hooves that seemed almost too large for his legs.

"You know, strange as it is, looking at him isn't going to get him saddled," Haru joked, making Will look up, surprised to find his knight watching him carefully. Haru sighed, running a hand through his hair, making it stand up for a moment before flopping to the side again. "I know he's not ideal, he's just turned five and I'd prefer you be on something a bit more trained than him, but it was him or the ponies and I don't think either of us want to work with those beasts."

"I appreciate you picking him over a pony." Will grimaced. He forced a smile. "Then you'd really never let me live down falling off."

"No, no I wouldn't," Haru said, chortling. "Now, come on, let's get tacked up or the others will leave without us."

When saddling, Will felt like a complete fool, as though he hadn't gone through the motions of saddling a hundred times before. He fumbled with the straps of a borrowed and unfamiliar saddle that would better fit the smaller horse's back. Twice he tangled up the bridle so he had to step away to figure how it would fit on Admere's head again. The horse stood patiently the entire time, watching him with that same curious intelligence.

By the time Will had finally bridled Admere, the others were lounging against one of the stalls and watching him. Embarrassed, Will hurried to join them.

"Alright." Haru straightened, grabbing the reins of his roan from a nearby hook. "I think we can ride out now."

The others nodded and they traipsed out of the barn. Above, the sky was darkening, the air thick with the smell of an oncoming downpour. Will lifted himself into the saddle and had to grab at a handful of mane as he almost fell over the far side with his momentum.

"Smaller horse, smaller jump," Sir Don called. "And nice catch there. This courtyard isn't a soft landing."

Red with humiliation, Will only nodded, adjusting his reins in his hands. The red horse stood perfectly still, waiting for direction from his new rider.

The King chuckled. "Take it easy on the boy, Don. Airagon, come up here. I'm pretty sure this is your adventure, seems only fit you lead us."

Will felt his unfamiliar horse tense, his neck arching. Horses around him moved forward and, with a deep breath, Will loosened the reins. Admere broke into a trot, the movement strange, different from Visra's stride. It seemed to be less of thunder and more floating, long and even strides. Despite the freedom that rushed over him, the sense of flying as they left the castle, Will had to swallow the knot of resentment that the horse wasn't Visra.

***

The ride to the edge of the town was uneventful. Will rode at the back of the group with Haru, who made him practice different maneuvers with Admere. The horse was quite responsive, almost too much so, and Will had to catch himself twice from being thrown when the horse turned faster than he expected.

There was no comparing the animal to Visra. Where Visra pinned his ears and displayed his power, this horse seemed more interested in listening to Will, his ears flitting back to catch orders or words each time Will spoke. Not that the horse was entirely innocent. Will noticed he had a clever tactic of sidling up to the side of Haru's roan and biting him without any warning.

Haru's roan made short work of that on the second occasion that Admere tried. Will was listening to Haru describe their next practice maneuver when the roan twisted his head, pinning his ears at the smaller horse, teeth bared, and Admere danced sideways, making Will scramble for the reins.

Haru let out a bark of laughter. "Spirited little thing, isn't he?"

Their practice distracted Will through the ride. He hadn't even noticed their progress until Haru ordered him to rein in the sweating chestnut horse and walk him to cool down. Will slowed Admere from his trotting side-pass and looked up, taken aback.

They had reached the crest of the ridge that separated the valley that held Alamore and the city below. Ahead, the place where he'd grown up stretched out below. Will halted Admere, staring down at the streets, the buildings, the familiar place that had been his home most of his life.

Even from here, he recognized each building, could almost smell the bakery, hear the singing from the Dancing Stag Tavern. The place seemed unchanged and yet… yet strange.

It was like seeing a place he'd only heard about and, looking down over it, it seemed to fall short of the memories in his mind. Was this what happened then when a place became the reminder of the lies lived before? His fingers tightened on the reins and he had to fight a sudden urge to turn round and ride back to the castle.

"Miss it?" Haru had ridden up to stop beside him, watching his squire carefully.

Will shook his head. "Not at all."

"Don't blame you a bit," Airagon, on Haru's other side, said gravely. "If I had to go back to the tunnels." Airagon shivered. "Feels odd to think about…a past life."

Will nodded, watching the distant people hurrying down the streets, baskets ladened with shopping, people who hadn't known he lived there, hadn't cared he left.

"You two are just rays of sunshine aren't you?" Sir Don chuckled, his horse moving forward again. "Come on now. Don't look so worried, Will. You won't run into people because we'll be taking a side route, not the main streets."

"How come?" Will asked. He urged Admere alongside Sir Don, starting down the ridge and toward the sound of a market in full swing.

It was the King who answered, his roan falling into step next to Admere on Will's other side. "Because I am here."

"And, in case you didn't know, he's the King and people generally will flock to him." Sir Don grinned at Will and reached over to slap his shoulder. "Oh, don't be so sullen. We aren't about to leave you in the city again. We've grown fond of our common bred squire. If you're not in Alamore, I worry Rowan will burn it down."

Will gave a forced laugh. *He doesn't know.* Out of the corner of his eye, Will noticed the King's lips twitch into the shadow of a knowing smile. He was the only one in the group who knew the truth, other than Will himself of course.

When they neared the town, the King drew his hood to shadow his face and Sir Don led them east, away from the main road, and onto a familiar and empty dirt track. Will's throat tightened and he had to wipe his hands on his tunic to dry away the sweat.

The houses here were derelict, many staring at the riders through lifeless shattered windows, their yards overgrown and doors rotting. In spite of himself, Will found his eyes straining to see the houses ahead, hidden by a curve further down the road, desperate to see the house at the end of the street, the last one that lingered out of sight.

"This part of the city used to have a fair few people. The houses were built mostly for soldiers who didn't want to live at the castle, who had families or thought they needed extra space," Don said, noticing Will staring at the houses. "It was growing back in King Valren's day– Revlan's grandfather–but it lost popularity after Valren's death."

"Why's that?" Will asked, trying to sound interested. He was still transfixed by the twist of the road fading from sight. Each step toward it made his heart slam harder into his throat.

"Well," Don said, laughing coldly, "it turns out that they didn't just want the space for their family. They wanted to be away from the castle. The soldiers who lived here weren't loyal to Valren's heir, Paradon. They'd sworn loyalty to Prince Temrod instead, Paradon's younger brother. When that treason was found out, this place became rather unpopular, a slum even."

"What happened to the soldiers?" *Stop looking ahead, stop looking ahead, Will. You don't want to see it, you're being stupid.*

"They were cast to the tunnels with their families," the King growled darkly. Will at last turned, surprised. "What? That was your father who did that?"

"Yes, it was." The King sighed, the eyes under his hood narrowing. "I don't think he understood the problem he was creating at the time, though." He smiled slightly gesturing behind them with his head to where Airagon, Haru, and Novin were riding, still discussing swordsmanship. "I won't complain. I've had the honor of an excellent squire and a good page from the tunnels. As in life, not everyone turns out to be what people predict. Blood and past don't make a man, his decisions do."

Will nodded. He had the feeling that the King's words weren't only referring to Airagon and his page, a young boy named Mark. "Right, King."

"Yep," Don said, nodding. "That's the truth, but the superstitions continue to keep these houses empty for the most part. People still sometimes call it Traitor's End. Here, we turn here."

Bitter relief riddled with disappointment washed over Will as Don waved them through a side alley and off the road. Will couldn't help but glance back over his shoulder as they turned off the familiar dirt track. Traitor's End. A fitting name for the street where Marl had raised him before showing his true colors as a Thornten loyalist. As they rode further from Traitor's End, Will found the disappointment mounting. For some reason he felt drawn to the house at the end of that street. It was as though he needed to see the house at the end, the place he'd grown up before the world had been turned upside down.

Don led them through two more alleyways until they rounded a bend and were met with a solid wooden fence that blocked the street and the view beyond. They waited while Sir Don dismounted and knocked on the gate, the rap of his knuckles over the wood a loud cracking in the quiet still of the alleyway. Will barely noticed. The part of him that wanted to return to Traitor's End was consuming his mind.

He was still lost in thoughts when the gate swung wide, framing a teenager, his stocky frame muscled from years of hard labor, black hair falling across his soot-stained face. He greeted Don with a broad grin, reaching out a callused and scarred hand.

"Not 'xpecting you back again this soon," the teenager said, beaming and taking in the group of riders. "But I take it you're not here 'cause your own squire this time, less that sword needs an edge again."

"No, we're here regarding mine," the King said, swinging from his saddle and pulling his hood away from his face.

The boy paled and hurried to drop to one knee, bowing his head. "Majesty."

The King shook his head, chuckling. "Rise, boy. You must be Glimmern's apprentice."

"That's right, I am, eh, King Revlan," the apprentice said nervously, standing and brushing the street dust from his tunic.

Will frowned, taking in the teenager's appearance, temporarily forgetting about the street at their back. "Zudin?"

The boy started, looking over the rest of them. His face took on a bewildered expression for a moment on seeing Will, then the broad smile returned. "By the walls of Alamore, if it ain't Will!"

He seemed about to say more but Don cleared his throat then, hiding a smirk behind his fist. "If you don't mind, Zudin, I think it best we get the King off the streets. Can we come into the yard?"

"Oh, right." Zudin's face flushed with embarrassment and he scrambled backwards. "Come in, come in. I'll tend your horses and get them tied."

They dismounted in the street, Will sliding from Admere's back and patting his sweaty neck. Admere gave him a gentle shove, trying to itch his face against Will's shoulder while they waited for the others to file in first. Ahead of him, Will could see Airagon's hands were shaking on his horse's reins as he led the grey through the gate.

Stepping through after, Will glanced around, finally recognizing his surroundings. The gate made up one wall of a vast courtyard while the two walls on either side were the stone of shops and the wall at the back, directly across from the fence, was the back half of a stable. An old cart horse watched the newcomers with mild interest, a mouthful of hay dangling forgotten on his lips.

Will moved across to where the others were tying their horses. Zudin had already moved to tend King Revlan's large blue roan, tying him to the furthest end of the rail.

"If you want to go inside the shop, it's through that door there." Zudin gestured to the solid wood door at the side of the stable. "Glimmern's expecting you, I'd imagine, not that he told me who exactly was coming but he's got the swords set out."

"We'll meet you inside," Haru said when the King hesitated. "You and Don go on in, Will and I can help Zudin get horses taken care of. Anyway, I'm not sure there's enough room in the shop for all of us to hang around."

The King chuckled, gripping Airagon's shoulder. "Thank you, Haru, Will, Zudin. I think it best we get this boy a sword before he dies of excitement."

Airagon's face reddened as the knights and Novin laughed but he didn't argue when the King steered him toward the door. Novin passed Will his reins with a nod of thanks then darted to catch up with the others.

Will watched them go, smiling to himself at Airagon's obvious excitement. He was brought back to his surroundings by Zudin's low whistle.

"First name terms with the King, the King of Alamore! Blimey, Will, here I was, thinkin' you was dead and all along you're living large in the castle!" Zudin shook his head, in obvious awe.

"How do you know Will?" Haru asked, raising an eyebrow.

"Cause he lived here in the town, now, didn't he? Not far from this shop actually." Zudin seemed struck between awe and giddy excitement. "Didn't know he'd gone to the castle!"

"I've been there almost a year," Will explained, tying Novin's horse to the rail.

"Blimey! Really?" Zudin shook his head, whistling again. "I leave to train with Glimmern, then go to see you, and find your house empty, you gone and all that talk of Marl… never thought you'd be at the castle."

"I didn't think I'd get to go there either," Will said, half laughing. He saw Haru's brow furrowed with a bemused smile out of the corner of his eye.

"Can't blame you a bit on that." Zudin shook his head disbelievingly. "What a bit of luck. But, hey, I got to get inside. Glimmern told me I'd have to learn today how to better fit squires to blades." He grimaced. "And I don't care to make Glimmern mad. I'll see you in a bit then."

They watched Zudin dart across the courtyard and through the door before Will turned to Haru, laughing at his bewildered expression. "What's wrong with you?"

"I don't know," Haru said sheepishly, running a hand over the back of his neck. "I didn't think about it I guess."

"About what?"

"About you being from here." Haru waved an arm and Will knew he was trying to encompass the entire city with the gesture. "It's like an entire life you had before Alamore and I don't know anything about it."

"There's not much to know about it," Will said, shrugging. "It wasn't really interesting."

"Come off it, you have to know this place like the back of your hand! Short of Glimmern's shop and the Dancing Stag tavern, I've barely even seen the place." Haru laughed. "Alamore, I can't believe you never talk about it."

"I don't talk about it because I don't miss it," Will muttered.

Haru seemed to read his mind and his grin faded. "I'm sorry, Will. I forgot about Marl…"

"Don't apologize," Will said hurriedly. "I got the chance to become a knight. Even if I'd been happy here, I'd have left for that."

Haru's smile returned. "I get that. I just never think about it, you know? If I had, I would have said we can come down more often, let you see people."

"Other than Zudin, there isn't really anyone I know anymore. My mother left before I did and Marl…" Will let his voice drift then shook himself. "I didn't really hang out with anyone after Zudin got his apprenticeship. Glimmern's the best blacksmith in this place which means he's working most the time. Zudin is too."

Haru didn't answer, focusing on checking the knot he'd tied on Novin's horse. Will had the sense that he was weighing something. After a minute he straightened, eyeing Will with a mischievous look. "Since that shop's going to be crowded and hot as the blazes, maybe we should explore, eh? You can show me what I'm missing when I just come here for swords and to annoy Richard's wife at the tavern."

"There's not much to see," Will said, trying to keep his voice casual. The strange desire to see the place he had lived was rearing its ugly head again.

Haru raised an eyebrow. "You alright?"

"I'm good." Will shook himself. "Right, let's go see the city. Do we need to tell the others or…"

"They will survive, Will." Haru grinned. "I mean, I'm a knight, I don't need permission."

"Right." Will's mouth felt dry as he led Haru back across the courtyard, through the gate, and into the narrow alleyway they had ridden down. He and Haru didn't speak, Haru turning his head to look at the building on either side of them as Will retraced their steps. It wasn't long until they were stepping back onto the dirt track, onto the road they'd entered by. Will glanced in the direction of his old house, hidden around the curve of the road.

You don't need to go down there, Will told himself firmly. *Just go one alleyway down and you can turn onto the High Street, show Haru around the city where there's people. You don't need to go back there. You hated growing up there.*

Even as he thought it, Will found himself striding past the alleyway that he knew was the fastest route back to the crowded market and main road.

"Shouldn't we go this way?" Haru had paused at the alleyway's opening, bewildered. Will could hear the chaos of the market drifting down the narrow street toward them.

"If we go down further, we can walk up the road instead of passing all the same places twice, and it'll be faster without all the people." Will hated himself for how easily the lie fell from his lips. He waited for Haru to argue with him, to tell him that he was being an idiot. He hoped he would, that he'd grab Will's arm and drag him down the street and tell him off for trying to waste time.

But Haru only shrugged, grinning again. "Makes sense to me, mate."

They moved on. Will's heart slammed against his chest with each stride. Haru was taking in their surroundings with curious interest, gazing at the empty houses, the rotten and collapsing fences. They were nearing the curve and braced himself, pushing his hands into his pockets to hide their shaking. And there, ahead. His heart froze as his eyes locked on the familiar, grimy house.

The house looked as hollow of life as all those around it. The steps were coated in dirt, the fence collapsing, and the window that looked from the kitchen to the street had been shattered.

Haru brushed past him, unaware that anything was wrong until he'd gone several strides further and turned to Will, grey-green eyes concerned. "Will? You alright?"

Will didn't answer. He couldn't answer, as all the air seemed sucked from his lungs. All he could do was stare at the grey cloaked figure who had appeared in the broken window and turned to look directly at him. The Cutthroat Prince had found him again.

CHAPTER TEN

Life rushed back into Will's body and he sprang forward, seizing Haru's arm. "We have to go, now!"

"What? What's the matter, what's going on?"

Will pulled with all his strength but Haru was unmoving, shaking his head in annoyance and confusion. "Will, what's got into you?"

"Back to Glimmern's, we have to get back to Glimmern's shop. Please, Haru, we have to go, we have to go!" When Haru only stared at him, panic flooded Will. Miller was right then. Haru had to know, he had to be the spy.

Something of that horror must have shown on his face. Haru reached for his sword, tensing. "What's the matter, Will?"

"Did you...are you..."

"What?" Haru demanded. Will saw his own fear now leaching into the knight. "The blazes has got into you, Will?"

"Are you the spy of Thornten?" The question came out in a hoarse whisper.

Confusion, shock, anger–they crossed Haru's face in the span of a few seconds. He stepped forward and Will almost fell in surprise. "Of course I'm not! How could you think that, Will?"

The relief that flooded Will was short lived. Still gripping Haru's arm he pulled harder. "Then we have to go, we have to leave now. I'll explain later but Haru, please!"

"Wait just a minute!"

"We haven't got a minute!" Will shouted, pulling harder. "Haru!"

Swearing now, Haru started forward again, letting Will drag him back up the way they had come. He wasn't the spy. Will was sure of it but how could they have found them?

No matter. They couldn't stick around and ask questions. Will saw the street that he hadn't taken, and his heart leapt. There. If they just took that street and ran, they could make it to the main road and get lost in the crowds at the market. If they hurried, if they turned down there, they would be...

Hooves rattled the earth, the dust trembling at their feet and Haru grabbed Will by the shoulder, yanking him backwards and away from the mouth of the alleyway. A rider cantered onto the deserted street, shrouded in the hood of his grey cloak, sword drawn. Will didn't have to see the face. He recognized the jagged-edged sword the rider held– Draccart.

Haru swore loudly, drawing his own sword and shoving Will protectively behind him. But Draccart had stopped. He was blocking their path, stopping them from returning to Glimmern's shop or running down the alleyway he'd appeared from.

The beady eyes glinted with malice and the mouth beneath the hood stretched in an ugly leer. His gaze flitted from Haru to the sword in the knight's hand and he laughed, the sound bouncing off the walls of the houses that edged the street. "Oh, this should be fun."

"One more step and I'll make you wish you'd never been born," Haru snarled. Will tried to step out from behind Haru but his knight sidestepped, keeping his body between him and the Cutthroat.

"The theatrics of Alamore knights are rather boring."

Haru wheeled, almost knocking Will to the ground as he pushed him backwards again, trying to block him from the appearance of this new danger.

The Cutthroat Prince was stepping from the house as though it were the stairwell of a castle, his tone casual, bored even. He smirked, pausing to survey Will and Haru.

"You know, I always thought people were exaggerating when they said that Alamore knights will always play the hero. But, here we are, faced with a real Alamore knight and-" He tilted his head to one side, sighing sadly. "It proves disappointingly true. Just once, I would kill to see one of you sacrifice someone else to save your skins, or anything other than the predictable. It would make a much better story."

"If your mate there doesn't sheath his sword, the story will be short and end with you begging for your worthless lives," Haru snarled threateningly.

"Oh?" Will could hear the laughter in The Cutthroat Prince's voice. "That is intimidating. A novice knight, his barely armed squire, and no one to help them against myself, Draccart, and five riders who are waiting for me to simply cue them to join me. Really, I should have thought this through better, I am simply petrified."

Will stepped sideways, trying to move around Haru again. Again, his knight grabbed his arm. Haru turned his head to give Will a warning glower out of the corner of his eye. "You stay behind me, got it?"

"If we have to fight, I won't do a lot of good with you in the way," Will shot back in a whisper.

"Will, that was an order," Haru growled, eyes flashing.

Will gritted his teeth, biting back his retort. He saw Draccart waiting to strike and The Cutthroat Prince's hand resting on the hilt of his sword. His stomach tightened. If what The Cutthroat Prince said was true, then that was it. They were trapped. They couldn't escape let alone outrun seven horsemen. He didn't even see how they could get past these two.

"Perhaps introductions are in order?" The Cutthroat Prince asked.

"Yeah, that's not necessary as we don't intend to stick around for your hospitalities," Haru snapped.

"Oh, aren't we witty," The Cutthroat Prince drawled. "Alright, Sir Senseless, as I have manners more than a common hound, I'll introduce myself. I am The Cutthroat Prince, and I am going to make this simple for you, *knight*. Either you can give him up, let us take him with us, or we can fight you and still take him with us while you lie paralyzed on the ground, helpless due to the effects of Inanimus.

Now, before you answer." He held up his hand as if to stop Haru, descending the last stair. "I know you will be inclined to think you need to choose the latter because you are a knight of Alamore." Will imagined that The Cutthroat Prince was rolling his eyes. "But knight of Alamore or no, you will bleed red, and you will die. I've heard that the toxin causes excruciating pain."

Behind them, Draccart laughed again, and Will felt a prickle of hatred crawl up his spine as he reached for the dagger on his belt.

"Use your brain instead of your gallantry and you will realize that letting him go with us gives you a better chance of saving both of you. You attempt a heroic rescue after we go. Though, it will be worthless because we'll have ridden far away before you can, but I don't mind your trying. It could make the whole thing more…entertaining," The Cutthroat Prince said. His teeth flashed white in a smile under the shadow of his grey hood.

Haru snorted. "Yeah, like you'd let either of us walk out of here alive. You expect me to believe that you're here just to take squires on adventures or some other cracked logic? I'm not letting you touch him, got it? If you want to kill Will, you'll have to go through me first."

"Oh, but I don't want him dead." The Cutthroat Prince shook his head. "Surely you can understand how much of an advantage it would be if he was alive." He took another step toward them then paused, as if a thought had just dawned on him. "Or do you? Don't you know how much it could do for the Thornten crown to keep him alive?"

"What?" Haru asked sharply.

Will bit back an urge to swear. If it wasn't for Haru blocking his way, he was sure he'd make a wild run at The Cutthroat Prince to clamp a hand over his mouth. This wasn't good. This wasn't how he had ever wanted Haru to find out. The Cutthroat Prince's smile was broadening in amused understanding.

After several heartbeats that may have been years, The Cutthroat Prince threw back his head with a bark of manic laughter. "You don't know? You truly don't know? I know the Ranger's been seeing to it that things are kept silent, especially of late, but you? Of all the people in Alamore! The one who's teaching him, protecting him, and you don't have any idea who he is? What he could become?"

Will opened his mouth then closed it again, not sure of what to say. He was torn between telling the truth first and the more enticing idea of throwing every Rowan worthy insult at The Cutthroat Prince. Haru had gone rigid in front of Will but he wasn't speaking. He didn't try to block Will as he stepped sideways again. He saw the confusion and fury on Haru's face, but he was listening, waiting for The Cutthroat Prince to say more.

The chance to tell Haru first was lost in another laugh. The Cutthroat Prince was strolling toward them as if they were in a garden instead of a slum. Beneath the hood, Will knew he was watching Haru closely. "Tell me, *knight*; haven't you ever wondered why Marl wanted Will dead? We thought he was a threat to Thornten, we thought his change of loyalty made it certain he needed to be killed but matters in the south have changed this: the uprisings, the unrest."

"Get to the point or get out of the way," Haru snarled.

"Don't you see?" asked The Cutthroat Prince. He had come to a halt, a stride away from striking distance. What little Will could see of the teenaged face was elated, triumphant. "That boy's father is Tollien's brother. The squire you're hiding behind you? He's not just a squire. He's an heir."

The street fell silent. If not for his racing heart, Will might have thought time itself had frozen. Haru was staring at The Cutthroat Prince, the color washing from his face. The sword in his hand started to sag, the point lowering to the dirt.

"What?" whispered Haru.

When The Cutthroat Prince only smiled, he wheeled round to face Will, grey-green eyes blazing. "Is this true? Or is he lying? Are you an heir to Thornten?"

Hating himself, wishing he could vanish into thin air, Will nodded. Instantly, Haru's gaze became unrecognizable–cold with fury.

"Haru, I wanted-" Will started then stopped. He *hadn't* wanted to tell Haru, or he would have ages ago. If he had wanted to tell Haru, it would have been that day Marl tried to kill both of them before Haru was a knight. Before he'd become Will's knight.

The Cutthroat Prince broke into laughter again, echoed by Draccart at the other end of the street. "And here I was thinking that this day could not be better. You see, knight? Your squire has been lying to you, and you are willing to die for him. Now, that isn't worth your life, is it? So, why don't you let him come with us? I don't intend to hurt him, only to bring him back to where he belongs."

Will dropped his gaze to his boots. He felt he might be sick. He couldn't bear to see the betrayal in Haru's face. It was his fault. He should have told him. He had allowed himself to be a coward and hide the truth at first, then the Ranger and Miller's words had given him the perfect excuse. Never had he believed Haru could be the spy and yet...

Haru's voice made Will's head jerk up again, staring as the knight turned away from him, toward The Cutthroat Prince. "Alright, if you want him, take him."

Will could see the surprise on The Cutthroat Prince's shadowed face. After a moment of stunned disbelief, Draccart started to cackle, his head thrown back in wild mirth. The sound bounced off the surrounding walls, eerie, haunting.

Staring at Haru, all Will could hear was a ringing in his ears. He made to move forward and grab Haru's arm, but the knight sidestepped away, refusing to even look in Will's direction. There was cold steel in his eyes, a look that Will hadn't ever seen before.

"W-what? Haru, I-"

Haru shook his head to silence Will and glowered at The Cutthroat Prince instead.

"Go on then, get him. He's all yours."

He was sheathing his sword, stepping away from Will, his features a mask of cold fury.

The Cutthroat Prince looked between knight and squire a moment, frowning. It was evident that he had been as blindsided by Haru's change in attitude as Will had been. Then he straightened with a nod, his smirk returning.

"I'm glad to see that some of the knights of Alamore have common sense. You've made the right decision... I could use someone like you inside the walls."

"Don't push your luck," Haru snapped. "Just get your heir and leave."

Will was frozen to the earth. He couldn't believe what was happening. Again, he tried to catch Haru's eye, but the knight was staring at a point above The Cutthroat Prince's shoulder and Will understood. He'd betrayed his knight and Haru was returning the favor.

For one mad instant, Will considered running. If he sprinted now, he could try to get around The Cutthroat Prince. He had the advantage. These were the streets he'd grown up in, he knew like the back of his hand.

But what then? Even if he did, it would be Haru they killed and he couldn't do that, couldn't let Haru die. *He's handing you over though*, the whispering voice in his head spoke in Marl's snarling voice. *It would serve him right.*

"Throw your dagger in the dirt," The Cutthroat Prince ordered, striding toward them, chest stuck out with new confidence. "Or the knight dies."

Will hesitated a moment. He couldn't bring himself to look at Haru. If he fought... if he fought and ran, he might survive. It would cost Haru's life but...

Suddenly sickened that he would even entertain the idea of sacrificing Haru to save himself, Will drew the dagger and threw it into the dirt at his feet. He couldn't bring himself to look at Haru any longer, watching The Cutthroat Prince instead.

Haru stepped back, moving to stand behind Will, blocking the thought of turning and running away. It didn't matter though. Will knew he couldn't leave Haru here, no matter what he had done.

The Cutthroat Prince pulled a length of rope from his pocket. It might have been cut from the same length as the prior and Will's jaw clenched, remembering the bite of the fibers into his wrists, bracing himself for that pain again. That pain which couldn't match the tight feeling in his chest. Haru was really going to let them take him. He was handing Will over without a second thought.

"Nothing funny this time, Will, or I guarantee you'll regret it," The Cutthroat Prince hissed, coming to stand in front of Will. He grabbed Will's shoulder roughly and shoved him around. Will gasped in pain as his arms were yanked behind his back. A kick to the back of his knees sent him crashing to the earth. He closed his eyes. He wouldn't fight. He couldn't risk Haru's life. The rope bit into his wrists again, burning and tight. Already he could feel his fingers going numb.

"Anything you'd like to say to your *squire* before he comes with us?" The Cutthroat Prince sounded taunting, the words stabbing into Will's chest.

"Yeah, actually," Haru replied.

Will's eyes shot open, and he twisted as far as he could in a kneeling position. Haru standing behind him and The Cutthroat Prince and Will stiffened. Something in his knight's expression had changed. It was still cold, still furious, but he was watching Will and The Cutthroat Prince with a small frown creasing his forehead. He met Will's eye and gave an almost imperceptible nod.

Before Will could make sense of the action, his arms were yanked upwards, pain screaming through his shoulders. "Stand up, then, and face your knight," The Cutthroat Prince snapped, annoyed. Will stood, staring at Haru, heart echoing in his ears.

Will felt The Cutthroat Prince standing at his back, still gripping the rope that bound his hands. "Get your goodbyes over with then," The Cutthroat Prince ordered. "We haven't time to stand around all day."

"Right." Haru's eyes locked with Will's and Will could almost see the ideas tangled behind the grey-green set. "Only way to know is if you try."

Will frowned, bewildered. What was Haru on about?

"Inspirational." The Cutthroat Prince snorted. "Truly inspirational. Now, come on." He pushed Will's shoulder and Will felt the realization crash over him.

Taking a half step forward, Will stopped again, watching Haru. The Cutthroat Prince snarled and made to push Will again. Before he could, Will leapt backwards with all his strength. He felt his back collide with The Cutthroat Prince then they were crashing into the dirt. Somewhere behind him, Draccart yelled, Haru moved, and Will's bound wrists were crushed under his weight. The moment of heart slamming success died in an instant. The Cutthroat Prince was already climbing to his feet, snarling and swearing. Will rolled to the side to avoid a kick. Dirt blinded him, stinging his eyes, filling his mouth. Above him he heard a strangled cry of surprise, another string of swearing.

Blinking up through the settling dust, it took a moment for Will's eyes to focus on what he was seeing. He pushed himself onto his knees, staring at the sight before him.

Haru was gripping The Cutthroat Prince with one arm, pinning Prince's arms to his side. In his other hand, he was gripping the dagger Will had dropped, the blade pressed to the throat exposed beneath the hood. The Cutthroat Prince went rigid, his breathing shallow and panicked.

"Alright, I'll make this really simple, step by step," Haru called, and Will saw the arm pinning The Cutthroat Prince tighten. "Unless you want to see how fast a dagger can kill a Cutthroat, get off the horse."

Draccart didn't move, eyes flitting from Haru's snarling face to The Cutthroat Prince's shadowed one. It could not have been clearer that he was torn between obeying orders from his Prince and saving the Prince's life.

"Do what the moron asks!" The Cutthroat Prince snarled, his voice breaking slightly. "Get off the horse!"

Draccart sheathed his sword and slid off the saddle, his movements slow and deliberate. He held up both hands, wriggling empty fingers. "Let him go now."

Haru snorted. "Like Thornten. This rat is our ticket out of here. Will, get up."

Will struggled to his feet, nearly off-balancing with his arms bound but managing to steady himself, bracing his feet.

"Now, Princey, you're going to untie Will's hands, got it?" Haru said, voice crackling with fury.

"And how do you expect me to do that when I can't move?" snarled The Cutthroat Prince.

"You get one arm. Now, enough back talk." Haru half pushed, half carried, his prisoner toward Will. "Any funny stuff at all and you'll be painting the streets red with your blood. Got it?"

"You will pay for this." The Cutthroat Prince's voice was shaking with fury. "You are going to pay for this."

"Less chat, more untying. Will, turn so he can get you untied."

Feeling uneasy about having his back to The Cutthroat Prince, Will obeyed all the same, keeping his eyes fixed on Draccart. After a moment, the ropes fell free and he stepped away, rubbing his wrists and wincing.

"Right, Will, come over here and unarm our fine fellow. You need a sword, and I don't think he does," Haru ordered. "Careful of the blade, though. Can't guarantee that it's not like the one that hurt Vis."

"My other riders won't stand for this."

"Which is why I'll let you go very shortly," Haru promised. "In the meantime, if they appear, you're dead, is that clear?"

With The Cutthroat Prince's muffled oaths above him, Will hurried forward and reached for the sword at his side. He drew it carefully, the blade shining dully in the muted light of the grey clouds above. He stepped back, holding the blade as far from him as he could, feeling disgusted with the weapon and the poison it carried.

"Dagger, too, Will. He doesn't need it," Haru ordered, jerking his head to gesture to The Cutthroat Prince's other side.

Will stepped round to see the second weapon and froze. The hilt of the dagger was barely visible, tucked into a sheath under The Cutthroat Prince's right arm. But it wasn't how it had been hidden that made the air grow cold around him.

"What are you doing?" Haru demanded. "Hurry up!"

Will forced his hand out and grabbed the dagger, pulling it free from the sheath. The Cutthroat Prince was hissing like an angry cat. He barely noticed, stepping away, still transfixed by the weapon he was gripping.

He knew this dagger. How many times had he seen it? The ornate blade, the hilt in the shape of a diving falcon, wings outstretched into cross bars, beak opening wide to swallow the blade. He could remember staring at it in fascinated envy, wondering at the craftsmanship even when he was little.

The last time he had seen it had been in the house, that house, when Marl stared through the grime-streaked window at the sight of Rowan and Colin waiting for Will the day he became a squire. He could still picture it turning slowly in Marl's hands.

"Will!"

Will started, blinking hard to bring himself from his thoughts. For some reason, the presence of the dagger somehow felt that Marl was there with them. He shoved the blade roughly into his belt, trying to shake the cold sense that gripped him.

"What's the fastest route to the main road?" Haru demanded.

"This way." Will turned on his heel and broke into a jog, moving away from Draccart, toward the house at the end of Traitor's End. Behind him, Haru grunted with the effort of dragging The Cutthroat Prince along.

When they neared the house, Will refused to turn toward it. Part of him feared that if he did, it would be Marl who leered out of the window this time. Instead, he turned right, down the street he'd first seen Rowan and Colin race down a lifetime ago.

"Wait, let him go!" Draccart roared. Will spun. Haru was still pulling The Cutthroat Prince with him, Will's dagger still held ready.

"Like the blazes I will. You can come with and get him when I decide I can let his sorry ass go, how's that sound?" Turning to Will he raised his eyebrows. "Let me know if anyone else comes at us, got it?" He raised his voice. "Because if there are other riders, and they do show now, I'll kill The Cutthroat Prince myself! Understood?"

"They get it!" The Cutthroat Prince snapped, spluttering as Haru pulled him back another few paces. "They're not stupid."

"I wouldn't reckon on that kid," Haru retorted. "Will, get us to the main road. Now."

Each step seemed painfully slow, Haru dragging The Cutthroat Prince, Draccart following on foot, a silent shadow. They turned down the side street, Will turning back and forth, expecting to see someone attack at any moment. He gripped the sword in both hands so tight that his palms throbbed with his own pulse.

Each step brought them nearer the sound of the main road. Will glimpsed people hurry past the narrow alleyway opening ahead, never glancing toward them. This was the end of the main road, where people didn't linger, only rushing to get to the market and shops before the clouds, growling above, could pour rain over them.

"Stop here," Haru ordered.

Will obeyed. They were almost to the end of the alleyway. "We're almost there, Haru."

"I know," Haru said coldly. He was watching Draccart, eyes narrowed. "But we'll move faster without *him*."

In one swift movement, Haru pulled the dagger away from The Cutthroat Prince's neck and shoved him forward with all his strength. Taken aback by the sudden movement, The Cutthroat Prince fell, sprawling onto the street. Draccart screamed and sprang toward the Prince. Will watched him reach down to help his leader back to his feet but The Cutthroat Prince smacked him away, trying to sit up.

"Get your hands off me! Get them!"

"Come on!" Haru grabbed Will's arm, dragging him the remaining distance down the alley and into the street beyond. They almost collided with a woman carrying a basket of dirty clothing, Will pulling Haru to the side a moment before they knocked into her. She screamed, the basket flying into the air, clothing scattering over the street.

"Sorry!" Haru called over his shoulder as he and Will took off running again, sprinting for their lives down the street, toward the throng of market shoppers. "We need to get lost in the crowd! Keep your head down, don't let that sword hit anyone!"

Overhead thunder growled and the sky shattered. Rain started to fall, cold and biting. Still, they ran, through the driving rain, the wind whipping around them. Over the howl of the wind, Will heard the woman scream again and twisted round, panic rising. He caught sight of her running through the door of a nearby house, her basket forgotten on the ground. The reason for her flight was obvious, rushing toward them.

The riders had arrived. Five of them, riding hard, were streaming into the road from more alleyways. People were springing out of the way to avoid being trampled, shouts and cries echoing down the alleyway.

"They're getting closer," panted Will. He stumbled, almost dropping the sword he still clutched, but righted himself and ran on. Will found his boots slithering over the rain slick ground. "We can't outrun them!"

"We aren't going to try," Haru snapped. "Just a little further and we can…" Haru didn't finish his sentence, instead redoubling his efforts to continue running.

People were rushing from the streets, slowing their progress as vendors hastened to shelter their goods, mothers herding children out of the mud. At their backs, the horsemen were bellowing at people to move, their voices growing closer.

Will's lungs burned, his muscles jumping, and the sword in his hand felt like it was pulling him to the ground. He wasn't sure how long he could keep running and, with the streets emptying, they would soon be obvious.

"Here!"

Haru pulled Will to the side, almost falling over a goat being led by a portly man, who swore at them. The knight didn't seem to notice, too intent on shoving through the door of the building next to them. Staggering through the door, Will straightened as Haru snapped the door shut behind them, plunging them into darkness.

There was a muffled thud as Haru pressed his back against the door, panting. "Pass me that sword, Will."

"Oh, right."

He'd forgotten he still clutched the blade. Handing it to Haru, he took in his surroundings, water pooling at their feet. Now that they weren't running he recognized his surroundings. A stairwell led to a walkway that twisted above them while doors were set into the walls. Tables crowded the dark room, lanterns hanging above several and a line of candles burning on the bar that took up the center of the room. Behind the bar, reflecting the flickering flames, was a wooden sign depicting a silver stag on its hind legs, a golden mandolin tangled in its antlers.

The place was empty, eerie in its darkness. He'd never seen it without a crowd and rarely before night. The only times he'd entered were as a child, looking for Marl.

"The Dancing Stag?" Will asked, turning to his knight.

"Yeah." Haru nodded, still winded. The knight's face was drawn, his hair plastered over his pale skin. "And we need to keep moving.

They'll think to knock in doors before too long. See if you can't shove a table or two over here. We'll block them as best we can, give us some time."

Snapping back to his senses, Will darted toward one of the tables and threw his weight against the solid wood. It scraped against the floor, the timbers groaning in protest, and Will winced. The sound seemed enough to wake the dead.

"Hurry," Haru hissed.

Will pushed harder, straining to move the table when one of the doors burst open. He recoiled from the table, grabbing the stolen dagger from his belt.

"The blazes do you lot think you're doing, aye?"

A woman had appeared, eagle eyes flashing, framed in the light that poured from the door at her back. Despite being Will's height and thinly built, with grey streaking her blonde hair, there was something intimidating in her stance and the knife she gripped.

"We're closed another three hours, so get out of here," she snapped, taking a step forward. "I'll have none of this, making a racket and–what are you doing to that table, boy? Don't go moving my tavern round!"

"I…" Will stopped, turning to look desperately at Haru.

His knight however was straightening, his face flooding with relief. "Anryn, it's me."

The woman stopped. "Alamore, I thought you were a few more of the local loons trying to play at fun. What's going on? Knight or no, Haru, this isn't any hour for a drink and I'm not serving the boy."

"We're not here to drink," Haru said hurriedly. "We're running right now, we just got chased in here. I don't have time to explain but we need to get you out of here, we need to barricade the door, to-"

"That's not going to do," Anryn snapped. "If they can't get in they'll torch the tavern. Come on, quick, I'll hide you."

She turned back away from them, through the door. When neither Will nor Haru moved she spun back, planting her knife free hand on her hip. "Blazes you waiting on?"

"Coming!" Haru hurried forward, grabbing Will by the collar and dragging him after the woman.

"Hold on, Haru, who is this? What's going on?" Will hissed. He wasn't sure he liked trusting a stranger in this instance.

"She's Sir Richard's wife," Haru growled. "She and Henry's wife own this place."

They stepped through the door that Anryn had vanished through into what seemed to be a study. One wall held shelves, a heavy table was groaning under the weight of mountains of papers, and on the faded red rug an old dog picked up his white muzzle to survey the newcomers through drooping eyelids.

"Don't touch anything," Anryn warned. "Haru, make yourself useful and lift that rug–get off of there, Teldax."

The dog stood stiffly, moving off the rug as Haru crouched and pulled it up. A square door was set into the floor and Haru didn't wait for Anryn's order before picking that up as well, setting it aside.

"Where does it go?" Will asked, hesitant. Memories of the tunnels were freezing him to the floor.

"Under the tavern, you buffoon," Anryn said snippily. "Now, get under there and I'll send someone to the castle to get guards and-"

"No need to go that far." Haru shook his head. "The King and Don are at Glimmern's shop."

"And they're not being chased?" she asked, raising an eyebrow.

"No, just us." Haru nodded.

The woman tutted, rolling her eyes. "Alamore Haru, you ought to learn to stay out of trouble, you're making me grow old before my time."

Haru grinned sheepishly. "Sorry about that."

"And dragging the youngster into your wicked ways?" she demanded, eyeing Will. "I take it you're his squire then? Should've known Haru would get his squire into a mess like this before the year was out."

Will saw Haru's grin fade but to his relief Haru didn't say anything, kicking his feet down into the hole in the floor.

"Here, you'll want this." Anryn snatched up one of the lanterns from her desk, forcing it into Will's hand. "Don't come out till I'm back," she ordered. "Now, go. I need to straighten up the tavern, so it doesn't look suspicious. When the King and Don arrive, I'll come get you, until then, keep your heads down."

"Thank you." Haru gripped her arm a moment and Will saw the woman's eyes soften. Then she pulled away, waving her hands at them to hurry and tucking her knife in the belt.

Haru pushed himself forward, dropping into the darkness. Will's throat caught and he took a step nearer, lowering the lantern into the hole. He jumped as Haru's hand appeared, grabbing the lantern out of his grip, and stepping back out of sight.

Taking a deep breath, Will swung his legs over the hole and dropped in after Haru. His feet hit solid earth sooner than he'd expected and he stumbled with the impact, throwing out a hand to support himself on the freezing wall. Overhead the door dropped over the opening, casting them into the glow of the lantern. He straightened, nearly brushing the low ceiling. Ahead of him, Haru was seated on the floor, eyes narrowed, glowering at Will.

"So," the knight said, a frosty edge to his voice. "Shall we discuss your being an heir of Thornten or would you prefer to continue lying to me?"

CHAPTER ELEVEN

Stale air tightened and Will could have sworn the walls of the small chamber closed in around them. Under Haru's cold stare, Will lowered himself onto the floor out of Haru's reach, running a hand through his hair.

"I didn't want to lie."

"Then you shouldn't have," Haru snapped.

Will winced. He'd deserved that. Turning to look at his knight he felt burning hot shame wash over his face. "I'm sorry. It just...I couldn't..." How could it be that hard to tell someone?

"Alright, let's start simple." Haru sighed, shaking his head. "Why did you think I was a spy?"

Will looked away, face growing hot with shame. "I didn't, not really."

"But you accused me of that, Will, and that's not something I take lightly," Haru growled.

Will groaned, running his hands over face. "All I knew was that there was a spy and the Ranger seemed to know that before he left. He told me not to tell anyone, including you." He decided it best not to mention Miller's suspicions. That truth was one Haru didn't need to hear.

"So, the Ranger thought I was a spy?" He didn't have to see Haru to hear the angry expression he wore.

"I just said he didn't know. He just wanted me to keep my head down. I think he was worried something like this might happen."

"Alright." Haru sighed. "I can't get too mad about that. He's got a point and I guess your knight would make a perfect spy for someone like The Cutthroat Prince. We'll look past that for right now."

Will nodded, relieved. "Good."

"I didn't say we were done," Haru growled. "No, I want answers. Who all knows, Will? Does the King? Is that why he agreed to take you on as a squire in the first place?"

"I think so, but I didn't know that then. I didn't know anything about being related to the Thornten line until last fall, when Marl attacked Rowan, Colin, and me."

"He told you when he captured you?" Haru asked confusedly.

Will shook his head. "He didn't tell me. When we were making our escape, Robin found us and when he was telling me he needed me to come back with him, he said it."

"Robin knows? He knew? What, did everyone know and no one thought to tell me?" Haru demanded. Will glanced up and saw the hurt and betrayal in Haru's face.

"It wasn't his secret to tell, so why should he?" Will retorted defensively.

"Because I'm your knight! He should have." Haru shook his head and pushed himself off the ground, beginning to pace in front of Will, his head ducked to avoid scraping it along the low ceiling. "Alright, who else knows?"

"Rowan and Colin."

Haru snorted derisively. "Obviously."

"And the Ranger, Ross, Laster, Miller, and Rockwood, and the King."

"So, half the knights knew this, and it never crossed your mind that maybe, you should tell me?" Haru snarled.

Anger flared in Will's chest and he felt his hands ball into fists on either side of him. "It's not that simple."

"Oh? Isn't it? You couldn't have mentioned that your father is Tollien's brother? Because I don't see it as that complicated to tell the tru-"

"Do you think I wanted to tell anyone? Do you think that I have ever been proud of what I found out?" Will was on his feet, though he couldn't remember standing.

He and Haru glowered at one another, the anger coursing through Will's blood. "I don't want any of this! I didn't ask to be Marl's son; I don't want any tie to the Thornten throne. All I want is to be a knight!"

Haru stared at him, face unmoved, and as quickly as it had flared, Will's anger died. He slumped against the wall, exhausted, and let his forehead fall into his hands.

"I should have told you, I'm sorry... I couldn't do it, I didn't want to, and the Ranger told me not to tell anyone and-"

"When did he say that?"

Will looked up. Haru's face had changed. The anger was washing away, replaced with a pale look of dawning realization. Confused, Will frowned. "When he was last at the castle, when Lady Serena arrived."

Swearing under his breath, Haru came to lean on the wall next to Will. He gave a low humorous laugh, before groaning and turning his head to stare at the ceiling above them. "Alamore, I'm an idiot. With how the Ranger singles you out, talks to you, I should have realized there was something else."

"You didn't have a way of knowing this," Will muttered.

Haru shook his head, closing his eyes. "No, Will, I did."

"What's that supposed to-" Will's question was cut off by the distant sound of something crashing.

Haru straightened, reaching for the hilt of the stolen sword at his side. Somewhere above, footfalls clattered over the wood floor. Haru shot Will a sharp look and pressed his finger to his lips in a warning. The gesture was unnecessary. Every instinct in Will's body was telling him to be silent.

"We're closed," Anryn barked loudly overhead.

"Where'd they go?" Will recognized Draccart's gruff voice.

Haru whispered a string of oaths, moving toward the trap door, hand gripping the sword tighter. Will reached for the stolen dagger at his side.

"We get a lot of people through here," Anryn sounded unimpressed. "And I already told you, we're closed."

"Don't play games, you stupid woman. The knight and squire, where are they?" The Cutthroat Prince had obviously recovered himself enough to join the hunt. Will saw Haru's face go rigid with fury and grabbed the knight's arm to keep him from springing back out of their hiding place and attacking. "They came this way. Tell us or I'll torch the place to have done with it."

"Talk to me like that again and you'll be on your way out, either of my tavern or your life. I leave that choice to you."

"I've had enough of this. Draccart, grab this foolish female and…"

The Cutthroat Prince's words were drowned in a crash of breaking glass and a high-pitched squeal of surprise and fear.

Haru made to move but Will pulled with all his strength, stopping him. "Haru, no, we'll make it worse! If they see we're here!"

"But Anryn-"

"They'll kill her or use her as bait if we show ourselves."

Another crash and a yelp of fear and pain. They froze, listening.

"Quit throwing bottles at me, you lunatic woman!"

"Get out of my tavern and take your buffoon with you before I save myself the money on beef and serve you for the menu instead, boy." *Crash.* "And clean your mouth out, you disrespectful lout."

The door slammed and Will and Haru waited, holding their breath. A moment later they heard hurried footfalls and the trapdoor above them was yanked wide, blinding light pouring over them.

Anryn raised her brows at the two of them. "You both best get up in case they decide to burn the place. I've sent Senvren for the King's men but can't promise he'll get there fast enough."

"We won't let them burn it down," Haru snarled, pulling himself through the hole in the floor. He reached down, grabbing Will by the arm and pulled. They both fell onto the study floor and hurried to stand as Anryn dropped the hidden door back in place.

"Don't be stupid. We'll wait. They didn't stick around long, I guess they didn't much care for the cheaper liquor." Anryn smiled wickedly. "You and Miller didn't seem to mind it when you were younger, but I guess you had cheaper taste than those thugs."

"Anryn, if we can keep them away from the outside of the tavern," Haru insisted.

The small woman crossed her arms and Will was forcibly reminded of Sir Ross when he was in one of his immovable moods. "You think this is the first threat this tavern's got? Anyway, I've watched you grow up too long to see you die fighting for a pub. Anyhow, if they can burn this place down with that rain, I'll be more impressed than disappointed. No, Haru, not another word. The King will be here before too long and I told Senvren to get the city guard after that. They'll be here before long."

The sound of shouts from outside were followed by the crash of the door banging off the opposite wall. Before Anryn could stop him, Haru had drawn his sword and was rushing into the tavern, Will on his heels clutching the falcon dagger.

Glass shone across the floor, glittering in the light of the candles and lanterns. Will could see liquor spreading in dark stains like blood, reflecting the flickering glows. Someone had thrown the door wide and was shaking his head in a dog-like manner, water spraying from his hair and beard.

Hearing them enter, he straightened and grinned, his brown eyes laughing as he took in Will and Haru, Anryn hurrying into the room behind them. "A little early for a drink, isn't it Haru?" Don asked, beaming. Then his eyes fell on the bottles and he frowned, shaking his head. "Anryn, if this is a new way of mixing drinks, I'll have to take my business to the Piper's Pub."

"Oh, shush you." Anryn snapped, pushing past Will and Haru to embrace Don. Stepping back, she sighed. "I best get it cleared away, though, before you start rumors and drive my drinkers to Piper's." She hurried away through another of the doors and out of sight.

Don turned to Haru and Will, brows raised. "How is it you two always find the adventure?"

Haru snorted. "I'd rather it not be that way."

"Well, what do you expect when you take your squire to a tavern for the first time?" Don winked at him. He took in their appearances and Will noticed of the mud that had smeared over his clothing in the hidden cellar. He tried to wipe his hands clean on his tunic, stashing the dagger back in his belt. "The blazes were you doing? Wrestling pigs while running from ruffians?"

"Not exactly," Will grumbled.

"Aw, so the pigs were the ruffians," said Don understandingly. "We best get back to the castle. The city guard got here just before me and, instead of being sly, announced their presence and all of your dear friends in the grey cloaks took tail and ran. Any idea who they were?"

"The Cutthroat Prince." Haru sneered. "The same band of Thornten loyalists that went for Will, Rowan, and Colin."

Don whistled and pulled his hood over his head again, waving them toward the door. "Oh, that will make all of this more interesting. I decided you'd probably not want to walk so I've got your horses with mine. Novin and Airagon are escorting the King back to Alamore and I'd like to avoid being too far behind them. Novin is good but can be a bit overeager and Airagon is so obsessed with his new sword I'm afraid he might not want to risk getting blood on it if someone attacks them."

"We'll be right out, Don." Haru nodded. "I just need a quick word with Will."

Sir Don shrugged. "Make it quick or I'll drown."

He pulled the door shut behind him and Will turned, bracing himself for the explosion. Haru's eyes were unreadable, a faint frown between his brows.

"An heir of Thornten then…" Haru said slowly, shaking his head.

Will dropped his gaze to the floor, the water gathering at his boots. "Yeah."

Silence fell again and Will waited. He couldn't stand the quiet, the feeling of Haru's eyes boring into him. Swallowing, Will wondered how his mouth had gone so dry. He dared a quick glance at Haru, then dropped his gaze again. "So…so I take it you won't be training me from now on."

"What?" Haru asked sharply.

Will flinched. He hated this. "I mean, I lied to you, I didn't tell you what I was…and I guess you won't want to be my knight."

"Will, look at me."

Will squeezed his eyes shut a moment, refusing to lift them, fighting the burning that had risen in his throat. Was he seriously about to cry? Right now?

"Will, that's an order."

Will obeyed, straightening to his full height, fighting to keep his face cool and composed. Haru was glowering down at him, grey-green eyes stormy.

"Don't ever say anything that daft again or I'll box your ears. Is that understood?" Haru uncrossed his arms, his demeanor relaxing.

The knot in Will's chest moved upward to his throat and he forced a shaky laugh. "Alright."

"Alright, *Sir*," Haru corrected, a grin splitting across his face.

Will nodded then hesitated. "You're sure you want to be my knight? I'm an heir to Thornten and-"

"And I don't care," Haru said flatly. "Is that why you were scared to tell me before? Why you didn't tell me before the Ranger ordered you to stay silent? You thought I wouldn't want to train you or would hate you for it?"

Will nodded, and Haru's brows nearly vanished under his damp fringe of red hair as he looked at Will in astonishment.

"That doesn't matter to me, Will. Seriously, don't look at me that way. As far as I'm concerned, the blood in your veins is red, just like mine, just like anyone else's. I don't give a damn that Marl is a Thornten by blood. I wanted to be your knight because you try your heart out, because even knowing Marl was loyal to Thornten and your father, you were willing to fight him to save my life. You're loyal where it matters, to the people who do good, who help others, and that's worth a whole lot more to me than blood."

Will opened his mouth but closed it again, not sure what to say. The knot was loosening in his throat and he managed a half grin of his own.

Haru chuckled, ruffling Will's hair. "Let's just make sure there aren't any more surprises like that, alright? Just tell me the truth here on out."

Swiping away Haru's hand, Will stiffened, glancing at his knight. "Which does bring up something else too, I guess."

"What?" Haru narrowed his eyes. "Are you also King of some random powerful country or..."

"No, nothing like that." Will shook his head. "But the Thornten line, well that means I'm somehow related to Alamore's royals and am an Alamore heir." Haru's mouth fell open and Will hurried on. "I don't quite get how, but I just wanted that out there."

After several seconds of gawking at Will, Haru closed his mouth, rolling his eyes to the ceiling. "Here I was thinking I was taking on a squire, not a Princeling."

"Don't call me that," Will grumbled, flattening his hair once more.

"So, is that it for secrets?" Haru asked quizzically.

"Yes." Will grinned. "*Sir.*"

"Great, because another stunt of lying like that and you'll live in the kitchen for a year, that's a promise," Haru said, frowning at Will with his best attempt at a scowl. The frown deepened and he tilted his head, his expression becoming unreadable once more. "Also–I want you to do what the Ranger told you to. I don't want you telling anyone about this.

Not right now, anyway. Things are too complicated with Kelkor and, well I'd like them to settle down before you decide to tell anyone else. Got it?"

Will snorted. "I'm not really in a hurry. Anyway, what's going on in Kelkor? What's too complicated?"

Haru raised his eyebrows, smirking. "Not your concern, mate. If I tell you anything, you'll find trouble."

"Hang on, that's not fair! What happened to no secrets?" Will demanded.

"Are you wanting to work in the kitchens?"

Holding up his hands, Will rolled his eyes upwards. "Alright so that only applies to the squire, not the one who's been knighted."

Haru laughed. "Clever of you to catch on that fast! But we better run, or Don will drag us out by our collars like dogs."

Outside Don was already mounted on his horse, his fingers tapping the front of the saddle. Next to him, hunched against the rain, Admere shoved Will lightly in greeting as the squire made to untie him and mounted up, being careful not to swing off the other side.

None of them spoke as they left, cantering along the streets, puddles splashing mud over their horses and cloaks. Leaning his head forward to keep the rain from stinging his eyes, Will slid his rein-free hand to his side to feel the dagger's presence.

Marl. This all came back to him again and again. But if it was Marl, why hadn't he been there today? Why had he sent a boy in his place to try to capture Will? And why capture? How many times had Marl wanted him dead instead?

Heir. The Cutthroat Prince had called him Marl's heir, he had mentioned that Marl needed an heir. But why? And the spy. That spy had to be how they'd been found today. *It has to be her, it's the only thing that makes sense,* Will thought. She'd arrived before The Cutthroat Prince. Her arrival had driven away the Ranger. By the time they'd caught up with the other three riders, Will had already made his decision. Ranger's warning or not, he needed answers. He needed them from Lady Serena of Kelkor.

CHAPTER TWELVE

Will couldn't rest his mind in the days that followed. He had tried to carry the falcon dagger tucked inside his tunic, hidden from prying eyes, but felt as if it weighed him down. It was like carrying Marl's watchful dark eyes on him all the time. After several days of hiding it, he stowed it safely in the trunk at the foot of his bed, under his winter cloaks.

Still, it seemed to press against his mind, distracting and ever present. This made studying harder. Practice too was more difficult with his mind fixed on finding out more about Lady Serena and why she'd come to Alamore. This meant that by the end of the week he had more bruises than usual from not paying attention, two assignments about battle history that were late, and a map that Haru had ordered him to redo as his first attempt had been so abysmal. The worst of it was that he still didn't have answers.

Thankfully his strange behavior went relatively unnoticed. Gabe and Jerram, the two pages, had officially become squires and spent a majority of their time bouncing with excited energy and wanting people to tell stories of the fights they'd been in. This gave Will the chance to tell of the latest attack from The Cutthroat Prince and pretend his frustration was only about the fact they hadn't caught The Cutthroat Prince or Draccart.

He was relieved whenever Haru would save him from these interrogations and take him to train in the courtyard or jousting arena. His knight hadn't said anything else about Will being an heir and was his normal casual self. Even so, Will noticed he was constantly selecting to ride the eastern patrol, giving him an excuse to leave Will inside the walls.

On the rare occasions that he rode western patrol, he always had an excuse or a task to keep Will inside the castle. The walls were beginning to feel like a prison where Will was the only captive.

Haru wasn't the only one acting oddly. Rowan and Colin now refused to let Will out of their sight. He knew that they both blamed themselves for what had happened, despite his explaining they couldn't have done anything about it. They ignored this and took to flanking him everywhere and making sure at least one of them was always in the same training that he was.

This made the idea that had been forming in his mind more difficult. He couldn't imagine that they'd let him search out his answers from Serena.

Because that, more than anything, had been haunting him. The Kelkor knight had been moved from the healing chamber to a wing of the second floor normally reserved for visiting dignitaries and their guards. Will had seen her several times, often speaking in low voices to the other knights, or watching them train.

Colin and Rowan had noticed this too and this only redoubled their standing protectively at his side like a couple of mean dogs. The one time he'd brought up his thoughts that they should try to find out why she was there, both Rowan and Colin had shot him down. They seemed to think it more important to keep the truth about Will hidden rather than find out what she could be doing there.

"If she knew, that would be different," Colin had said flatly. "But if she doesn't know, we need to keep it that way."

Even Rowan agreed, which was evident when archery practice with Will. He'd noticed Serena watching them from the edge of the jousting field and ordered Will switch sides with him so he could stand between them.

"I want to shoot the green target, it's easier."

"How is the color of the target going to make a difference?" Will demanded, frustrated with his friend's antics.

"Just switch."

"Rowan, she's about fifty feet away. Unless she can fly, she's not getting over here," Will snapped, reaching for another arrow from the quiver at his hip. He looked toward the Kelkor knight then rolled his eyes, notching the arrow to his string. "Plus, she's still wearing a sling, so I think I'd stand a chance if she decided to attack me in front of you, Rockwood, Laster, Vancely, and Saget. So, knock it off."

"Rowan, Will, less chitchat and more firing arrows," Laster barked from several targets over.

"And now…" Will growled. "You're getting us in trouble."

"I always do that." Rowan rolled his eyes. "Don't think it's about to bother me now."

Will snorted, trying to focus on his stance as he drew the string to the corner of his mouth, eyes fixed on the green banner draped over the straw bales ahead–his target. He could almost feel Serena's eyes burning him as he let his fingers slip from the string. The arrow sprang into the air, striking the bale about six inches to the left and down of his target.

"Focus, Will," Rockwood called. "Just aim smaller, you'll miss smaller."

"I hate when he says that" Rowan grumbled, pulling back his bowstring and firing his arrow. Will watched it strike only inches above the target.

"And you claim you need the easier one."

"Oh, bite me, Will."

Will grinned, reaching for another arrow. He glanced toward the fence, but Serena wasn't there. Relaxing slightly, he drew back and tried to focus all of his attention at the white ring in the center of the target. The arrow hissed free of the string, closer but still left of the target.

"You're not pointing your toe straight, fix that."

Will jumped, Rowan springing into the air beside him and swearing, arrows falling from his quiver to scatter in the dirt at his feet. Neither of them had noticed Serena approaching but she stood behind Will, green eyes unreadable, fixed on the arrow Will had just fired.

"Is it custom in Kelkor to creep up on people?" Rowan asked hotly, scowling at Serena.

Serena raised her eyebrows, shifting her green eyes to stare unblinkingly at Rowan. "Is it custom in Alamore not to pay attention to your surroundings?"

"Honestly, no, but I don't follow customs so in my world, yeah, I shouldn't have to," Rowan grumbled, stooping to collect his fallen arrows.

Serena ignored him, turning to Will instead. "Your feet, you're pointing your leading foot to the left and it's throwing off your aim. Focus on your stance then try again."

"Right," Will said distractedly. Turning back to the target, he couldn't shake the uncomfortable feeling of her eyes piercing the back of his neck. He set his stance, trying to seem unphased, and turned his foot to point straight toward the target. Fixing another arrow to his bow, he pulled back the string and fired.

It struck an inch below the green fabric.

"Nicely done."

He turned to find that Serena was nodding approvingly and, despite the smile she gave him, he couldn't shake the uneasy feeling that she was assessing him.

"Thanks."

"You're welcome." Her green eyes narrowed slightly, and she frowned. "I apologize, I haven't introduced myself."

"Oh, right." Will's face flushed, and he hurriedly extended his hand. "I'm Will."

"Will." The curious frown deepened as she shook his hand then recognition dawned over her face. "The squire from the city that I've heard so much about."

"Probably nothing good," Rowan growled. Will shot him a look and Rowan shrugged unapologetically. "What, if it was good, it wasn't true. It's one of the two, can't have it both ways."

Serena smiled coolly. "Perhaps that is so. Unusual for a squire not to come from a powerful family."

"Yeah, well, we were short on squires," Will mumbled. That had been the excuse Rockwood had given him when first offering Will the chance to train.

"So I've heard," Serena said slowly. She nodded to the bow in Will's hand. "Focus on your stance. It can break a good archer not to have his feet right. My squire in Kelkor, Niet, has been known to do that very same thing. Practice your footwork and then you can try to aim. It was good to meet you, Will, Rowan."

She turned, striding away before either could respond, and leaving Will with a cold knot in his chest.

"You didn't introduce yourself to her, did you?" Will asked Rowan, watching the Kelkor knight slide between the rails of the fence and out of the arena.

"Nope."

Will swallowed the sickening taste rising in his mouth. "So that means she knew who you were."

Rowan nodded and said the very thing on Will's mind. "Which means we've messed up. My money says she already knows who you are, mate."

Will couldn't help but feel that Rowan was right, and that the Ranger's warning had been in vain. Turning toward the target again, he focused on his stance, fighting the sickening churn in his stomach. His silence hadn't mattered. Serena knew exactly who he was.

As soon as they had finished archery training, Rockwood ordered them to saddle their horses for training with Ross and Colin on swords. Will and Rowan hurried to the barn and found Colin already there. They wasted no time in conveying what had happened with Serena and their suspicions.

"How could she know?" Colin demanded worriedly.

"Well, it's not exactly uncommon knowledge that Marl attacked us, or that he's Will's father," Rowan pointed out crossly as he struggled to lift Naja's leg. "Look, you beast, either you let me clean your foot or you don't complain when you get thrush."

"That's true," Will muttered, leaning on Admere. "But others haven't figured it out, which is weird to me. Does no one know that Tollien's got a brother?"

"I'm guessing Marl was a false name," Colin said. He eyed Will, furrowing his brow. "Did he ever mention another name? Because if Marl was a fake name or a middle name or something, then that might explain part of this."

Will shook his head. "Nothing. He didn't really talk to me about the fact he was a spy, or a Prince. Pretty sure I'd remember if he brought it up."

"Fair point, mate," Rowan grunted. He was still struggling to get Naja to lift his leg. The horse was watching his small handler's battle with interest.

"I'm not sure we can be certain she knows then," Colin said, waving Rowan aside and running his hand over Naja's leg. "I mean, she might have heard Rockwood use Rowan's name or something. Alamore knows he gets yelled at enough that it's not a hard one to learn." He lifted the horse's hoof effortlessly and reached to snatch the hoof pick out of Rowan's hand.

"Naja, you're dead to me right now," Rowan huffed, stepping away.

"You weren't there." Will shook his head, annoyed. "She knew. And that makes me think that she really is connected to all this. Why else would she bother knowing who Marl was if it wasn't to do with The Cutthroat Prince? I want to find out more; I want to know what she's doing here."

"Why do I feel like you've got a terrible idea planned?" Rowan asked, grinning. "Please say you do."

Will hesitated, watching Colin clean Naja's hoof but not really seeing it. "I want to find what she's hiding, who she is, but I don't think we can ask her."

"So, we'd need to know what she's hiding, if she's got written messages from Kelkor or things like that?" Rowan asked eagerly.

"I don't like this," Colin mumbled, lowering Naja's leg from his knee and straightening. "Rowan, I thought you were on my side. I thought we'd agreed we need to keep Will away from her and safe."

"I said I agreed we needed to make sure Will didn't do anything stupid that would let her know who he was," Rowan explained. "Big difference. Now we're talking about the fact she already knows, and I think Will's right. We should make sure we know what we're up against with her, and what better way to do that then to make sure we know as much as possible about her and about why she's here?"

Will grinned hopefully at his scowling friend. "I mean, it'd get answers."

"And it'd be fun," Rowan added. "Come on, Colin, let's do it. I've behaved for almost a solid week and I'm bored with it. Honestly, I don't know how you do it."

"And it would totally go against the fact that the Ranger told Will to avoid Serena and, if she is a spy, we'd be risking your neck because you can't handle not knowing everything," Colin snapped. "Absolutely not. That's insanity."

"I won't risk my neck because I won't get caught." Will's smile widened and, for the first time in days, he felt a rush of excitement awaken in his blood.

"Oh yeah? And how's that?" Colin growled.

"Because Rowan is going to keep her distracted."

***

Between sandy-haired Gabe and the chestnut-haired Jerram, the dinner table could not have been noisier. The distraction was welcome for Will, who found himself glancing at the knights' table every few mouthfuls. Serena seemed deep in conversation with Bane and hadn't looked their way. Maybe this was a mistake; maybe she didn't know and him doing anything now would be a dead giveaway.

"We'd best get set to move," Colin hissed, following Will's gaze. "I'm not sure that we'll get a chance when it starts."

"And there isn't a better way to keep the knights busy?" Will asked in a whisper.

"Don't be a spoil sport, this is my time to influence new squires to do bad things, this is my time to shine," Rowan snapped. "Anyway, get out of here."

Will nodded and he and Colin rose. Will immediately felt Serena's eyes shift toward him and stifled a huge fake yawn.

"Hey, Gabe, Jerram, you want to know the best way to prove you're fearless?" Rowan was saying.

Colin grabbed Will's arm and marched him toward the squire chamber. They had just shut the door behind them when they heard the unmistakable crash of a diversion starting. A second crash was followed by a yell.

Opening the door a crack, Will and Colin saw Rowan leaping away from the squire table, which had been flipped over, holding a serving spoon like a sword and pretending to battle away Gabe and Jerram—both armed with similar utensils.

"Away you fiends, you dogs, you hounds!" Rowan roared.

The knights were springing to their feet, Rockwood fighting to yell over his own laughter, Laster swearing, and other squires were launching themselves out of the way of Rowan, who started to throw great handfuls of mashed potatoes at anyone who tried to approach. Serena and Bane were the last two knights to their feet, sprinting to help the other as Jerram wriggled free from Robin and leapt back into the fray.

"This is it!" Colin grabbed Will's arm, pulling his attention from the spectacle.

They ran, skirting the far wall, unnoticed in the chaos of a food fight in full rage. If it hadn't been for his burning curiosity, Will might have wanted to stop and watch, maybe even join in with Rowan who had just thrown a boiled carrot with expert aim at Laster's face.

Instead, he and Colin sprinted into the entry hall together. Colin led the way toward one of the doors that led out of the corridor, yanking it open. "Through here!"

They dove through, slamming the door behind them and running down a second hallway, this one lined with banners of different countries and courts. At the far end, a grand staircase led upwards, toward the second floor.

Taking the steps two at a time, they skidded into the guest wing of the castle and paused, Will gripping a stitch in his side, turning to look at the doors that lined this new passage. Between the doors were more banners. "Which one? How do we know which one?" Will hissed. How hadn't he thought about this?

"Don't be thick," Colin pointed toward one of the doors ahead. "The Kelkor banner, that's where we're going. It'll be one of those doors. Then we just have to find which one of those it is."

"Right!"

They dashed toward the section of doors designated with the Kelkor banner—sea green with its rearing bronze Kelpie—and began trying to force doors. Will almost fell when the first one he touched sprang open. He stumbled into a dark square chamber. The only light was the grey of the darkening sky through the window, casting shadows over the bare bed, the dust covered desk, the sparse bookshelves. The room didn't look like it had been touched in ages.

Springing back out of the room, Will rushed to the next. It opened just as easily. Again, empty. Across the hall he could hear Colin bursting into more rooms.

Really starting to panic now, Will launched himself at the third door and was knocked to the floor as it didn't budge. Aching all over, he scrambled to his feet again, excitement racing through him. "Colin! This is it! It's got to be!" He shook himself and tried the door again. It didn't move.

Colin ran to his side, panting, hair falling over his face.

"It's locked," Will grunted, shoving his shoulder into the door again.

"Hold on." Colin drew his dagger, sliding the blade between the door and the wall. "Stand back. I think I can get the latch to...lift...if I can just..."

The click made them both jump. Will slapped Colin on the back, laughing. "Brilliant! How the blazes did you learn that?"

"Thanks!" Colin grinned sheepishly. "Ross told me even nobles should know how to pick a lock."

They ducked into the room, shutting the door at their back and turning to take in their surroundings. Will had no doubt at all now that this was Serena's room. A fire crackled in the hearth, throwing warmth and light over the blue carpet and the sea-green cloak that hung on a hook from the door. Like the other rooms, there was a bed, desk, and shelf but this bed was made, the desk scattered with parchment, and the shelf held an assortment of books that Will recognized as having come from the Hall of Records.

"Where do we start?" Colin asked, face draining. "We don't have a lot of time and-"

"Check if there's anything in those books," Will interjected, crossing to the desk and rummaging through the parchment. As he did so, he strained to hear any sound of approaching feet over the slamming of his heart in his ears. If Serena came back up here, if she walked in, they would be cornered, trapped.

Most of the papers appeared to be maps, covered in red and green circles, but he didn't recognize them. The land they showed was mountains and oceanside, nothing like what he'd seen in Alamore. After a few panicked seconds, he found one that made him hesitate, turning his head. A large map of Kelkor, marked with more red and green. He squinted down at the map. One of the dark lines that he had thought was part of the illustrated terrain was different. The ink wasn't black but dark blue, snaking a path through the land. He glanced back at the others, understanding dawning on him. These were all maps of different parts of Kelkor then. But what were the red and green supposed to signify? And what about the blue line? He traced his finger over it, perplexed. It seemed to be weaving away from main roads, a trail that led directly to Alamore.

"Hey, Will, look at this."

Will looked up from the map to see that Colin had stooped to pick up something that had fallen out of one of the books. A thin parchment, folded over like a letter. Will hurried to his side, peering over Colin's shoulder as he unfolded it.

Lady Serena Delfane, Knight of Queen Paranella's Guard– Permissions to cross line of war in order to reach Alamore as granted by King Azric of Kelkor, Lord of Vanrel.

"Line of war?" Will asked, frowning slightly. "What line of war? I know that Bane mentioned that Shadow Dale had been pressuring their border with Kelkor, but she wouldn't have to cross that border to get to Alamore."

"No, she wouldn't." Colin stuffed the note back into the book, worry making him look older. "There isn't anything between Alamore and Kelkor but miles. That means, if she was crossing war lines, they would have to be in Kelkor."

"But against who?" Will shook his head. "Unless they're fighting themselves, which would be stupid. Alright, never mind that for now, let's keep looking. If we see anything that mentions Marl or looks like it might be connected to The Cutthroat Prince, we'll be on the right track."

Colin nodded and started shaking more of the books as Will returned to the desk. It was as he was reaching for the maps that something else caught his eye.

Words were bleeding through the top map. Flipping it over Will found himself looking over a list scrawled with the names of all the knights and squires. Lines had been drawn through most of the names, some blotted as if Serena had been annoyed when scraping a quill through them.

Of the knights, three names remained uncrossed–Ross, Robin, and Laster. Will's eyes flitted to the next row of names, the squires. Almost all of these names were scratched through. Only one was left and Serena had circled it in the same red ink she had used to mark the maps.

William.

He stared at it, so focused on his own name, outlined in red, that it was a moment before he noticed the distant sound of feet. He looked up at the same moment that Colin was opening another book.

For a moment Will was uncertain if he'd imagined the noise, before crossing the room and peering through the crack in the door. His blood ran cold at the sight of a shadowy figure mounting the stairs at the far end of the corridor, a hood drawn low over the face.

"Colin, we have to go," Will said, turning, heart slamming in his chest.

"Hold up, I think I found something," Colin muttered, running his finger over the page he was reading.

"Not time for it now, Colin, we have to go! Someone's coming! Just take the book!"

Colin snapped the book shut and hurried to Will's slide. Glancing out the door, he swore under his breath. "What do we do?"

Will hesitated, watching the figure's approach. If it wasn't Serena, they might be fine hidden here but…

One of the torches reflected on a gleam of silver in the person's hand and Will's body went rigid. Whoever it was, they were moving too stealthily and holding a knife. He didn't need another moment to consider their options.

Grabbing Colin's arm, he wrenched him out of the room and started to run. To his relief, Colin didn't hesitate, launching himself into a sprint. Behind them, Will heard the feet gathering speed.

Not bothering to glance over their shoulders, Will and Colin ran like their lives depended on it. Colin pulled Will through an off branch of the corridor, down another hallway. They both almost fell as it led onto a steep flight of stairs.

"Down!" Colin ordered, springing down the first steps. Will followed. Behind them, Will heard a clash and looked up just in time to see a knife strike the wall above them and fall to rest on the top step.

After that, Will didn't bother with turning around. Instead, he ran faster, hardly keeping up with Colin, until they were bursting through another door that Colin slammed behind them, plunging them both into darkness. Neither one moved, holding their breath and listening.

The sound of running feet neared the door and Will reached for the dagger at his side, bracing himself, ready to fight. But the steps moved past their hiding spot, running past them.

The air rushed from his lungs in relief, and he took a tentative step backwards, feeling the wall press comfortably against at his back. "She's gone."

"Shhh," Colin hissed. "Might come back."

They waited for what seemed an eternity. When the footsteps did return they were running again, back up the way they had come from, past the door. Neither Colin nor Will moved from their hiding spot for a long while, anxiously waiting to see if Serena would find them.

CHAPTER THIRTEEN

Will and Colin lost no time in recounting the chase to Rowan when they finally made it back to the dinner hall sometime later. They'd been surprised to find that Rowan was waiting for them there rather than asleep like the rest of the squires. The reason had become clear rather quickly though when they noticed the bucket of murky water that Rowan was using to clean gravy from the walls.

"But there wasn't anything that might help us know why she's here?" Rowan asked, not able to quite hide his disappointment.

"Nothing much." Will shook his head. "Something about war lines in Kelkor, a list of the knights and squires names–mine was circled so I would bet anything we're right and she knows who Marl is–and then Colin found a book."

"A book?" Rowan asked, bewildered and turning to Colin. "That's your evidence? A book?"

"It's not just *a* book," Colin said, indignant. He pulled the small leather-bound book from his pocket, holding it up for them to see. "It's a book she's been writing in. Most of it's about the royal lines, old history about Alamore, but she's got a lot of notes in here. Only issue is–she's written it all in Kelkorian. I know a bit from my mum, but I haven't tried to read anything in years."

"For the love of Alamore," Rowan complained, crossing his arms and scowling at them. "I pull off the distraction of a lifetime and all you two get is the chance that there's issues in Kelkor and a knight's diary that you can't even read? Seriously?" He pointed an accusing finger at Will and Colin. "Next time, you two distract and I-" He stabbed himself in the chest with a finger. "Will be the useful one."

"Don't get ahead of yourself," Colin said, stashing the book back in his pocket. "I shouldn't have to remind you that this book isn't just about Alamore royals."

"It's Thornten too," Will muttered and Colin nodded.

"Well, Kelkor, Thornten, Alamore, or a group of one-legged mules, I seriously don't care. You two can help me get this place cleaned up since it was your idea."

"What?" Colin stared at Will. "You told him to do this?"

"I said cause a distraction, not wreck the dinner hall," Will said, laughing at the horrified expression on Colin's face. "Rowan, pass me a rag then. Colin, you see if you can't make any headway on what she's written there while we clean up."

***

Will held out hope that what Colin had found would be of use. However, by the end of the first week, some of that hope had started to wane. By the end of the second week, he couldn't help but agree with Rowan–their heist had been a complete waste of time. Most of what Colin had translated seemed mundane, just notes about King Revlan's father and his brother, the same story that Don had already told Will when they went to the city.

"It's got to be relevant!" Colin insisted whenever Rowan and Will showed a lack of interest. "They keep talking about Right of Blood. That's how Temrod tried to take Paradon's throne."

"Yeah, well unless Marl is challenging Tollien for the Thornten throne, I don't think that's it," Will used this protest for what seemed the thousandth time.

"And," Rowan pointed out, smirking. "If he is challenging Tollien, I don't think that's a bad thing. Let them rip each other apart."

The feeling that their raid had been a complete waste of time, however, wasn't Will's largest concern now. He had noticed that Serena had taken to watching him, Rowan, and Colin during their training almost every day. At first he had thought it might be coincidence but, after the fourth day, he knew that wasn't the case. There was no way she didn't know.

"If she tries to kill us, my vote is we run straight to Ross and hide behind him," Rowan had announced when Will pointed this out. "He's the only one who stands a chance against her."

"You think she could take down all the knights in Alamore? In a sling?" Will asked, grinning in spite of himself.

"Have you seen girls when they're royally ticked off? Because I have a sister and I can tell you–I'd rather fight Tollien with a dead fish than defend myself from her."

"She doesn't have proof it was us anyway," Colin had assured him. "She can suspect but Rowan was in the dinner hall–clearly–and the others saw us go to bed."

There wasn't much they could do anyway; Colin and Rowan were right. Without proof, Serena could only watch them with a glower and Will knew that their best chance of answers was either in the book Colin was still translating or else in Serena's own mind.

No. Overall Will's suspicions that Serena knew were only a discomfort until the second week after their break in and his and Colin's escape. It was the sight of Haru striding into the barn with Serena the morning of the eleventh day while Will carried Admere's saddle toward the horse, sent a thrill of panic through him.

"Change of plans today," Haru called, reaching for the halter of his roan. "Serena's offered to work with you, and I've been asked to fill on the eastern patrol."

"What?" Will stared at his knight, openmouthed. Trying quickly to cover his panic, he shook his head. "I can go work with Rowan and Colin if you're busy."

"No." Haru shook his head. "Serena volunteered to work with you when the King asked me to take Henry's place on the patrol this morning. Turns out his horse broke his foot yesterday so he's not going to be riding for a bit. It'll be good for both of you, as she needs to work her horse now her arm is healed, and you can learn some new tactics of battle." Haru's voice was too jaunty, too eager. It seemed he was trying to remain casual in front of Serena, hiding the truth of who Will really was.

Seeing Will's horrified expression, she raised her eyebrows, a smirk playing at her lips. "Don't tell me Alamore squires are scared to learn a bit of Kelkor fighting."

"I'm not scared," Will grumbled, turning back to adjust Admere's girth.

"Good." Haru was striding toward him now, having tied his roan at the far end of the barn alleyway, well out of Admere's reach. When he was next to Will, he paused, gripping Will's shoulder and lowering his voice to a whisper. "Watch your back, got it? Just listen to what she says and stay alert. The King and knights trust her, so there shouldn't be anything to worry about."

Will bit his lip, longing to tell Haru his suspicions but knew it was impossible. Serena was already stepping from her horse's stall and, anyway, what ground did he have for his fears? That the poison used on Visra had been Kelkorian? That he'd broken into her chamber and found his name on a list? Come to think of it, Haru might be more terrifying than Serena if Will told him that.

Haru let go of Will's shoulder, ruffling his hair and grinning ruefully. "Mind yourself, mate, and try not to be an idiot."

With that he turned toward the tack room, leaving Will to ready Admere with a sick pit of tension in his chest.

To his relief, Serena didn't say much as they prepared to leave the barn. Haru was the first out, hurrying to catch up with the other knights who'd already left the castle walls. Even without him, though, Serena only paused long enough to ask Will simple questions about his training, what he had worked on in the past, what he wanted to do.

When they had both finished saddling their horses, Serena ordered Will to the courtyard and followed a few moments later. "Have you ever knocked someone from a saddle without a weapon?"

He shook his head. "Not intentionally, no."

"Then we'll do that." She nodded curtly and urged her horse forward, not toward the jousting arena but in the direction of the gates.

"Hold up, aren't we going to the arena?"

"Are you afraid of riding without a fence?" Serena demanded, leveling him with a piercing green look.

"No, but-" He stopped himself. He'd been on the verge of mentioning The Cutthroat Prince but remembered. If he did that, he would be as good as admitting to her that he was worried about them. None of the other squires had been ordered to stay in the walls.

"Good, then stop holding us up," Serena snapped. "The fences of the arena are a good way to get your leg broken should you hit one when vaulting. Anyway, the ground is too deep to get your footing."

Will didn't have a chance to think of a response. She had already urged her horse into a canter, clattering over the drawbridge. Will waited a moment, glancing around the courtyard in the hope that another knight might come out and tell him off for leaving, or that Rowan and Colin might appear. When neither happened he grimaced, feeling slightly sick, and leaned forward. "Well, Admere, I guess we're going on another ride outside the gates." The horse needed no further encouragement, launching into his floating trot after Serena.

Outside the gates, the air was warm against his skin, heavy with the smell of green grass and spring. Birds perched in the notches of the walls, singing and fluttering upwards when he appeared, only to resettle again as he passed. Will had to grudgingly admit that he felt a sense of relief leaving the courtyard again. Serena was waiting along the path, some ways ahead.

She didn't turn to look at Will when he stopped beside her but rather spoke with her eyes on the distant trees swaying to the east. "Perhaps I've underestimated you and the Ranger."

"Excuse me?" Will asked, frowning. "What are you talking about?"

Her green eyes flashed and the hand gripping her reins visibly tightened. Before Will could think to react she spun, her rein-free hand grabbing his shoulder while she kicked out, striking Admere's side with her boot. For a horrible moment, Will's insides lurched, the horse springing sideways, out from underneath him, then Serena let go of his shoulder and he crashed to the earth, sprawling in the long grass on his back.

"Don't play games, squire," Serena spat, glowering down at him. "I know you were the one who helped yourself to searching my chambers."

"You're mad," Will panted, pushing himself back up to his feet. Admere, wide-eyed and startled, was standing several yards away. "Thanks for that, beast," Will snarled. The chestnut horse only nodded his head and reached to grab a mouthful of grass.

Serena gave a dangerous laugh, backing her horse away from Will and nodding to Admere. "Watch your accusations. Get on the horse and this time, pay attention."

"My accusations?" Will demanded in his best attempt at an indignant tone. "You think I'm the accusing one? You just practically accused me of breaking into your room, which I didn't do!" *Colin did that, I just followed him through the door,* he added to himself.

Serena gave a disbelieving snort, shaking her head. "Lying tends to run in your blood."

"And what's that supposed to mean?" Will demanded hotly.

"It means," Serena sneered, leaning back in her saddle and watching him carefully. "That you're no different from your Ranger. Did you think I didn't know who you are? What you are?"

Will turned his back to her, pretending to focus on trying to get his foot into his stirrup and lift himself onto Admere again. A tremor was running through his body, making it almost impossible to balance on his other leg. "I've no idea what you're talking about."

"Don't insult my intelligence," Serena snapped.

Will pulled himself into Admere's saddle, tightening the reins as the horse tossed his head, attempting to turn and leave. He glowered at Serena with as much defiance as he could manage, hoping that she couldn't see the slamming pulse in his throat, the panic rising. "You've lost your mind."

Anger flashed over her features, but she inhaled deeply and forced a smile. Somehow that smile made Will feel in far more danger than her snarl had. Would it be considered cowardice to gallop Admere back to the castle?

"Your Ranger must have thought it smart to try to get you to hide what you are from me. He is probably the one who told you to spy on me as well."

"Spy on you? Me?" Will retorted. "That's pretty bloody bold of you to think that."

"And what's that supposed to mean?"

"The Inanimus, The Cutthroat Prince, it all came about when you did." Will gritted his teeth, kicking himself as soon as the words escaped him. *Why do you talk? Why can't you keep your mouth shut? Why are you, William of Alamore, a moron?*

Serena raised her eyebrows, leveling him with a cool gaze. "You think I'm the spy? You think for a moment that I would care to have anything to do with what your father is doing?"

"What?" Will asked, taken aback. He sagged in the saddle, feeling completely wrong footed. "What? What does any of this have to do with my father?"

Her fingers tightened on her reins and a frown creased her brow. She seemed to be sizing him up, debating if he was telling the truth or not.

"Focus on your weight being in your heels," she said after a moment.

"What?" Will blinked, bewildered.

"Your heels." She nodded toward his feet in the stirrups. "If your weight had been in your heels you would have stayed in the saddle better. Come now, if you are knocked to the ground, you're an easy target. You can't learn how to get people out of the saddle until you know how to stay in it yourself."

"What–what?" Will shook his head. "No, don't change the subject. I want to know what's going on."

"Ask your precious Ranger," Serena snapped. "That is, if he actually decides to return. As far as I'm concerned, he's probably there now, with your father, betraying your King in exchange for his own brother."

Utterly disbelieving, it was a moment before Will realized he was again shaking his head, staring at her with a cold anger rising. "He'd never betray the King. You don't know what you're talking about."

"Enough of this," Serena retorted. "We came out here to train, so let's focus on that. Perhaps you're right, perhaps your Ranger has changed enough that he will choose his King over his own agenda, but I doubt it. The moment rumors reached Kelkor about his brother's son being taken in as a squire, I knew the truth."

"The Ranger serves the King of Alamore," Will growled. "And that's it."

There wasn't time to react as Serena swung round, kicking her horse so it sprang sideways into Admere. Will felt fingers close over his upper arm, pulling it up and another hand shoved into his side. For the second time, that morning he crashed from the saddle, the air knocking from his lungs.

"Pay attention to your surroundings," Serena said, smirking down at him. "And maybe you'll learn to see who's good and who's evil, who is working for the King of Alamore and who is working in their own self-interest, and that sometimes they are one and the same. The people you think are trying to save you have reasons for keeping you in the dark as well."

"You are insane," Will grunted, pushing himself to his feet again and wincing. "For the love of Alamore, quit knocking me off my horse."

"Learn to keep your eyes open then and be alert."

Will opened his mouth to retort but a shout made both of them whip round. Snatching Admere's reins, Will felt his stomach drop. Four riders were galloping from the western trees, their horses stretching out, charging across the valley and toward the castle. Their appearance shattered the peace of the valley and sapped the warmth from the sun.

In the span of a heartbeat, Will recognized the rider at the back of the group, the dark horse surging across the grass.

"Will, wait," Serena barked but he was already in his saddle, digging both heels into Admere's side and galloping toward the riders. He wasn't thinking about the Cutthroats, not thinking about the danger of being outside the wall. All he could do was push Admere to run harder as the cloaked rider on his dark horse began to slump sideways, hardly managing to clutch his saddle. One of the other riders was slowing, grabbing the reins of the black mare and trying to keep the cloaked rider from falling.

Admere stretched further beneath Will, flying over the ground, the air deafening Will's own shout. He saw the hooded rider try to straighten, turning, looking for him, then the Ranger of Kings slid sideways, collapsing against his mare's neck, the other rider still gripping his arm to keep him from hitting the earth.

CHAPTER FOURTEEN

Will was out of his saddle and running to the Ranger before Admere had even come to a full stop. But as he reached the Ranger's side, the rider that held the Ranger twisted to face him. Will saw the flash of silver blade just in time to leap backwards, away from the dark-haired teenager on his palomino horse.

"Don't come any nearer!" the older boy ordered, struggling to keep his sweat-soaked horse from prancing forward.

Will took a hurried step back, reaching for the dagger at his belt. "What the blazes happened to him? What's wrong with the Ranger? Who are you?"

"Who are you?" snarled the older boy and Will caught the sounds of the inflection in his words. He knew that accent. It was the same slightly musical accent of Serena.

"I'm Will, and I'm not trying to hurt you, I swear! Look, all I've got is a dagger and I'm not about to fight you. But I need to know, what happened to the Ranger? What's wrong with him?" Will demanded, trying to step closer again. He was forced to step back once more, swearing in frustration, as the older boy leveled his sword at Will's chest. "Stop being stupid. What's going on with the Ranger?"

"We were attacked," the teenager snapped. "I need to get to Alamore, I have to get us to Alamore."

"Calm down, this is Alamore," Will said hotly. "Look, I'm not trying to hurt you, I want to help the Ranger. I don't give a damn who you—any of you—are! Just let me help the Ranger!"

Will saw the hesitation in the teenager's face before he lowered the sword. "This is Alamore?"

"I just said that didn't I?" Will shot back, stepping closer. His heart slammed in his ears, a deafening beat. The Ranger hadn't moved.

He was slumped over his mare's sweat-darkened neck like a corpse. *Don't think that way. He's not dead, he can't be dead.* Will reached for the arm dangling over the mare's shoulder, gripping the wrist. His heart leapt. There! He could feel a pulse, but it was faint, slow. "What happened to him?"

"We were attacked."

Will turned at the sound of the unfamiliar voice. The other two riders were approaching, their faces flushed with exhaustion, hair falling over their eyes. He stared in momentary disbelief. The two girls were both dressed like squires–tunics, breaches, boots, with short swords at their sides–but the older one sat like a noble, her heart shaped face, framed with dark blonde hair, was regal, her thin frame erect in the saddle and the other girl was small, too small for her grey horse. Even so, she gripped the hilt of her short sword in white knuckles, shadowed eyes narrowed.

He looked between them all again. Their cloaks, though filthy and torn, had traces of sea-green fabric showing through. Sea green…the same color as Serena's cloak when she had arrived from Kelkor. So, the three had to be from there but none of them were old enough to be knights, surely.

"In the woods, as we came this way," the older girl spoke again, and Will could now hear the slightly musical accent in her words. "Grey riders. They ambushed us; the Ranger was struck with an arrow before we got away. As we were riding, he started to grow weaker and…" She shook her head, looking helplessly from Will to the Ranger.

Will's chest tightened. "Inanimus."

There wasn't a chance for the strangers to respond. Serena had reached them and was reining in her horse, eyes flashing as she took in the riders. "What has happened? Why are you here? And without a guard? You three should know better than to ride without-"

"The Ranger was my guard," the older girl cut across Serena, a daring gleam in her clear brown eyes. "As were Niet and Eldin and Paxrin."

The teenager with the sword looked away but not before Will saw the pain cross his face.

"Where is Paxrin now then?" Serena demanded.

"Dead."

It was the last girl who answered, shrinking lower into her saddle as she said it, glancing sideways at the boy. Will saw an icy tension run through all of them, and Serena's fury was replaced with horrified disbelief.

"Paxrin is…"

"We will explain everything when the Ranger has been treated," the older girl said, straightening again. She had all the appearance of someone trying to keep a brave face, but Will couldn't help but feel a grudging respect for her.

"Very well. Will, Niet," Serena said, nodding toward the teenager who was keeping the Ranger from falling. "You two get him to the castle. My priority is Kalia's safety."

Will opened his mouth, not sure what he was going to say–that Serena needed to explain what was happening, that the Ranger should be her focus? But she was already wheeling away, ordering the two girls to her side and cantering back across the valley toward the castle.

"It's Will, then?"

Will turned. The teenager was glowering down at him assessingly. "Yeah, that's right," Will grumbled, moving to the Ranger's other side, bracing so he wouldn't fall from the saddle. Admere, standing several paces away, ambled back toward him curiously. He snatched at the reins, looping them over his dagger hilt. "And you're Niet?"

"Yes. I train under Serena's mentorship in Kelkor." Niet nodded. Will stiffened a moment, not certain if he should trust this newcomer but Niet was sheathing his sword, relaxing, and Will did likewise. Niet didn't seem to have any idea who he truly was and why should he? He hadn't had more than a few words with Serena in weeks. Not of course since she'd figured it out for herself. "We better start moving. I don't think we can go fast, or we risk him falling."

Not fast was an understatement. Each step felt a painful crawl. The Ranger's mare was spooked by her flight through the woods, her rider's collapse, and occasionally shied either away from Will or away from Niet so that the other would have to scramble for a better hold. Will was glad he hadn't climbed back in the saddle as he wasn't sure he would be able to keep the Ranger upright if he wasn't on the ground.

By the time they were approaching the drawbridge, Will could hear the muffled shouts of mayhem from within. The arrival of the others had brought a change to the quiet courtyard. Already he could see soldiers racing along the top of the walls and two people were running over the bridge toward them: the lanky black-haired Rockwood and Ross's broad shouldered figure.

"What are you doing outside the gates?" Ross demanded when he reached Will's side. His eyes flashed in a dangerous way that made Will take a half step back.

"I was practicing with Serena and-"

"Not the focus right now, Ross," Rockwood said in an unusually snappy way. He reached slowly toward the Ranger's mare, Hemcole, one arm grabbing the Ranger. "Give me a hand with him. We got to get him to a healer and fast or it'll be in his veins and causing damage."

"What?" Will asked, bewildered.

"Inanimus. That's how it attacks the body." Rockwood grunted, staggering as the Ranger slid into his side. "Blimey, looks a lot leaner than that when he's standing on his own feet."

"We'll discuss you being outside the walls later," Ross growled at Will, reaching to grip one of the Ranger's arms and heaving it over his shoulder. "As for now, you help the Kelkor squires get their horses dealt with. Rowan and Colin are already in the barn with the Princess's horse."

"Princess?" Will asked. But the two knights ignored him, heaving the Ranger over the drawbridge. He inhaled sharply, fighting the frustration that was rising with panic in his chest. Was anyone going to explain what was happening?

"Kalia," Niet muttered, swinging from the saddle of his golden horse and reaching to take the reins of the Ranger's horse from Will. "She is Princess of Kelkor."

"What?" Will stared at the other squire in utter disbelief. "She's a Princess? Like the King's daughter."

"I mean, yes?" Niet said cautiously, giving Will a sidelong look. "I would expect that is what most people mean by Princess. What is going on here? Were you not expecting our arrival?"

"No." Will shook his head. "I haven't heard any of this."

Niet nodded slowly. "Interesting. I would have expected that the Ranger's mission to come to Kelkor for the Princess was common knowledge."

"That's where he's been?"

"I need to tend my horse," Niet cut across Will's question. "We perhaps can talk then?"

"Right." Will pulled on Admere's reins and led Niet across the bridge. In the courtyard there was more movement than even on the walls. Will saw Miller barking orders to soldiers saddling horses; Henry, his foot in a heavy bandage, was limping up the steps to the wall; and Richard was herding a group of gawking squires back toward the path that led behind the castle, toward the jousting arena.

With a low whistle, Niet turned on the spot, craning to look up at the walls and towers around them, seeming not to notice the chaos their arrival had sparked. "This is Alamore then."

"Yeah, pretty impressive when you first see it," Will admitted, turning left, toward the towering barn.

Inside the barn the world was strangely calm after the melee of the courtyard beyond. The only people in the barn were Rowan, Colin, and the younger girl, all three of them working to unsaddle the three Kelkorian horses that had arrived first.

"Will!" Colin dropped the girth he'd been unfastening, straightening as Niet and Will entered the barn. "Where have you been?"

"Training with Serena," Will said dryly. He noticed Rowan start and exchange a panicked look with Colin. "Nothing to worry about, just working outside the walls a bit when they all arrived." Will jerked his head to gesture to Niet at his side. "Rowan, Colin, this is Serena's squire, Niet."

Niet inclined his head politely then nodded to where the small girl was unsaddling the large grey horse. "I take it you have met Eldin."

"Yes, we have. She's making me remember that your country probably has to be one of the scariest places to fight." Rowan scowled. "Girls look all small and innocent, but I saw her handle that horse when it spooked. Even a half ton animal finds a girl intimidating."

"That's because the horse has a brain," Niet said, chuckling.

Will relaxed slightly. Niet didn't seem as aggressive as Serena but as he turned to unsaddle Admere, he felt eyes following him. Glancing over his shoulder he noticed that the small girl, Eldin, was frowning, watching him. Catching his eye, she turned away quickly but not before Will had time to wonder if she perhaps knew more than she was letting on. *If someone could tell me what's happening, that would be brilliant. I hate being in the dark like this.*

He didn't speak as he groomed Admere down. Instead, he listened as Colin asked Niet a thousand questions about Kelkor–the difference in the castle layout, the difference in the breeds of horses they rode, what it was like to defend a castle by the ocean rather than one surrounded by land. Niet answered all of them and fired back his own questions about Alamore. He seemed particularly interested in their lack of knowledge that the Princess of Kelkor had been riding for Alamore.

"I would have imagined your King would announce the visit of a high ranking royal," he mused as he set his saddle on the ground beside the door to the tack room.

"Well, as you saw when you were attacked," Will said, breaking his silence at last, "it's not exactly safe in Alamore."

"Safer here than in Kelkor right now," Eldin muttered darkly.

"What's going on in Kelkor?" Rowan asked interestedly. "Pirates? You guys get pirates there?"

Niet's face darkened and he gave a humorless laugh. "Pirates we've dealt with. What we're dealing with there now is nothing like the invasions from the sea."

"Is Shadow Dale pushing the border lands? We heard rumors about that over the winter when we sent word that we might need aid from Kelkor," said Colin.

"That's how it started," Niet explained, unbuckling the lead of his palomino and urging the horse forward, toward one of the empty stalls awaiting the visiting animals. "But we've dealt with that for years. No, something's changed in the last few months, a stirring in Kelkor itself. Fathers against sons, brothers and sisters at one another's throats."

"What?" Will nearly dropped the brush he was holding, gawking over Admere's low back at Niet. "People are just attacking one another? Like your own country is attacking itself."

"Yes," Niet muttered, shutting the stall door. He ran a hand through his shaggy dark hair and sighed. "Kelkor is in a state of civil war."

"But why haven't we heard anything about this?" Rowan demanded. "Surely we need to send help, we need to do something. I'm sure that Revlan has a plan, that we can send soldiers or knights or-"

"This is exactly why none of you have heard this."

They turned. Ross had returned, his face a mask of emotionless stone. He jerked his head at Niet and Eldin. "Lady Serena and Kalia request you two get to the castle and get fed. From what Kalia has said, the journey has pushed all of you hard. I'll give a hand getting the rest of your horses dealt with."

"Thank you, Sir," Niet muttered. He and Eldin gave low bows, their right hands pressed to their left shoulders. Will noticed Rowan suppressing an evil grin at the unusual custom. Thankfully no one else seemed to notice and there was silence as the two squires left the barns.

"The Ranger?" Will asked as soon as Niet and Eldin had gone. "What's happening with the Ranger? Is it Inanimus again? That girl, that Princess, she mentioned the riders were in grey. I bet it was The Cutthroat Prince and-"

Ross held up a hand, silencing him. "Listen," Ross growled. "And don't interrupt me. Yes, the attack was The Cutthroat Prince—we are almost sure of it. We've sent out a patrol to see if we can't find them because this is far graver than just an attack. They had to have been on that path for a reason. The Ranger mapped out a trail to and from Kelkor that hasn't been used in my lifetime, if ever before. They should have been invisible. From what Kalia says, however, the attack wasn't prepared for four riders. They must have expected that the Ranger would be returning with Kalia and Kalia alone.

The Ranger must have realized what was happening a moment before they were struck. He managed to get himself between Serena's squire and an arrow. Thankfully he managed to turn to avoid the brunt force of the arrow through his chest and it instead got him in the leg. But it was poisoned, just like the blade that was used on Visra. The healer is tending to him now but has asked everyone to stay out of the healing chamber a while."

"Is he going to live?"

Ross gave him a silencing look. "Right now, he needs the healer, Will. The larger concern is how the attack happened, how they had that information."

"How do you think they knew? I mean, we didn't even know," Will said, shaking his head.

"Yeah, which I'm a little bit sour about," Rowan grumbled, crossing his arms.

"That was kept silent by intention, but it seems we truly do have at least one spy in Alamore. How they found out the direct route that Kalia was taking is still unknown– the only people who knew were the senior knights, the King, the Ranger, and Serena herself, of course," Ross growled. "Serena arrived to tell us that Kelkor was falling into civil war, that they were losing alliances within their own land and would need to bring Kalia to safety in order to avoid a hostage situation. That's where the Ranger was sent."

"Why didn't they send Kalia with Serena then?" Will asked, bewildered.

"Because when Serena left Kelvane–that's the city where the Kelkor castle resides–when she left there, things did not seem as dire as they were. Serena was attacked in the mountain border trail. The injury to her arm was also inflicted by a weapon with Inanimus. Thankfully, that dosage was low and she has enough sense that she was able to treat herself. But enough of Kelkor, that's not what I'm concerned with." His blue eyes swiveled to glower down at Will. "What I wanted to talk to you about is your reckless behavior in leaving the walls."

"What?" Will raised his eyebrows, taken aback. "Are you telling me I'm not to leave Alamore again or-"

"I'm not saying that," Ross cut across him, drawing himself to his full and considerable height. "But I am saying that we are in times of uncertainty and after the two attacks you have managed to somehow escape from, I'd have thought you smart enough to stay in the walls. You should know that they are after you, Will. These Cutthroats, Tollien, Marl, they are after *you* just as much as they were after Kalia."

"I was training with Serena," Will protested. "How was I supposed to avoid leaving without making a big deal of my blood?"

"You think she hasn't already deduced that?" Ross snapped. "She was testing you."

"And I was supposed to just argue with her? If she knows who I am then she shouldn't be dragging me out of the walls!"

The injustice of it all was making him bold and he glowered back into Ross's hard features. "If you want to bring it up with anyone, it should be her."

"I'll bring it up with her and Haru both," Ross snarled. Will took a half step back, surprised at the rage that crossed the knight's features. "She doesn't trust you, Will. She doesn't trust you because of what you are and there are others that, if they knew, would be on her side. Especially right now, with what Marl is-" He stopped himself and Will could see the knight was regretting what he'd nearly said.

"Marl is what?" Will asked slowly. "What's Marl doing?"

"It's not your concern right now," Ross growled. "No, your concern, the only concern for the three of you, is training to become knights and not getting killed in the process. Colin, Rowan, don't let him out of your sight and don't do anything stupid. I haven't the time to keep the three of you alive."

With that the knight wheeled round and stalked from the barn, leaving the three squires in an uncomfortable silence.

"Well," Rowan said after an awkward moment. "I don't think he's a really happy camper right now. We should probably have offered him a hug or some sweets. Colin, he's your knight..."

"I don't really care to be brutally murdered today, Rowan," Colin said waspishly. Then he sighed, shaking his head. "He's right though, we've been reckless. We broke into Serena's rooms when we thought she was a spy and nearly got Will and I killed."

"I nearly got killed making a diversion," Rowan added. "You didn't see Laster with mashed carrot all over his stupid face!"

Colin ignored him, leveling Will with a stern green gaze. "We can't keep trying to figure out this for ourselves. For all we know Serena is a spy and she might have tried to kill you today."

Will shook his head. "She's not a spy."

"What makes you say that?" Rowan asked.

"She knows it was us, or at least suspects it was, who were in her rooms." Colin inhaled sharply but Will continued as if he hadn't noticed. "She told me that I needed to be more alert of my surroundings and that I wasn't right to trust the Ranger." Will frowned, struggling to remember all the knight had said. It was a blur; the conversation had been so unimportant when he'd seen the Ranger. "She told me that I needed to see when people were working for the King versus their own self-interest, that she didn't believe that the Ranger had changed...but changed from what?"

He looked up to see his friends seemed as confused as he did. After a moment Colin shook his head, running a hand through his hair. "Not sure. But this means we risked our necks going after the wrong person. Ross is right, Will. We've been reckless, trying to take this into our hands instead of leaving it for the knights."

"Yeah, but it's hard to leave it for the knights," Rowan said darkly. His unfocused gaze shifted to the door and his brow furrowed in

152

thought. "Really hard to leave it to the knights when it seems one of our own knights might really be this spy after all."

CHAPTER FIFTEEN

All Will could think about was the chance to see the Ranger. He'd hoped that night he'd be permitted but, after scarfing down his dinner, barely joining in the conversation of the other squires with Niet and Eldin, he'd raced to the steps only to be met by Ross, waiting for him.

"I said he needs time, Will," Ross growled warningly, stepping to bar his way.

"Is he not conscious yet then?" Will asked, not quite managing to keep the dread from his voice

The knight shook his head, dark eyes unreadable. "He's awake but he's not quite aware of his surroundings. The healer fears that questioning him now will cause him to panic. The toxin is still working through his body." Ross must have seen Will's face fall because the corners of his lips twitched into the ghost of a grave smile. "The Ranger isn't weak, Will. Even the healer thinks he'll be ready to meet with the council by tomorrow night."

"Then I can come back then?" Will asked hopefully.

The knight shook his head again. "I said the council and last I checked, you're still a squire. You'll have your chance to see him, Will. You can speak with him after he's well enough to fill us in on what's happening in Kelkor."

"Why not ask the others who just arrived?" Will demanded hotly. "They can answer that? Come on! I want to see the Ranger…Sir," he added quickly when Ross's glower hardened.

"The Princess and her squire guard aren't in a position to know fully what happened either. The Ranger will have more information than they will. Now, get out of here before I lose my temper and set you to something useful."

Will slunk back to the squire chambers in a poor mood. There he explained his conversation with Ross to Rowan and Colin in a low whisper.

Rowan groaned, throwing Colin a scathing look. "Your knight is a real piece of work."

"He doesn't want us involving ourselves in any of this," Colin replied snippily. "Besides, I thought we just agreed we'd be best off not trying to find trouble."

"You said that," Rowan stated, rolling his eyes and sinking onto the foot of his own bed. "I never promised anything."

"Rowan," Colin said firmly. "We can't go encouraging Will to find trouble."

"I'm not looking to find trouble!" Will grumbled, turning away to hide his annoyance as he set his dagger on his side table. "I want answers."

"I know you do, but it sounds like Ross doesn't think anyone but the Ranger has those answers," Colin's voice softened sympathetically. "And I bet we're not the only ones tired of being left in the dark. Think about the two squires from Kelkor, and about the Princess. If no one's given them answers, I'm sure they want to know what's happening in Kelkor too."

Will stiffened. He glanced toward Rowan and saw his own idea reflected on his friend's face. He gave the smallest shake of his head, signaling Rowan to keep his mouth shut. Then, forcing his voice to remain even and casual, asked. "Speaking of those squires, are they staying in here or not?"

"Of course not." It was Airagon, passing Will's bed, who answered. He paused, grinning roguishly. "They're up on the second floor, aren't they? In Alamore or not, they were still sent as the Princess's guard. Plus, they're guests, not Alamore squires. They get their own rooms."

"Lucky dogs," Novin moaned from his bed several yards away, planting a pillow over his face. "If I had my own room, I might get some sleep because I wouldn't have to wait for everyone else to shut up."

"Oh? You want me to shut up?" Rowan asked, an evil gleam lighting his eyes. He bounded off of his bed, springing to Novin's side. "I can do you one better. I can sing you off to sleep with the song of my people."

"I swear, Rowan, you sing one note," Novin warned, yanking the pillow from his own head and launching it at Rowan's face.

That was a mistake. Rowan caught the pillow and sprang out of reach, gasping in a breath and belting out at the top of his lungs. "Egghead sleep, and egghead dream, egghead do egghead things!"

Will couldn't help but fall onto his bed laughing until his stomach hurt as Novin launched himself from his bed with a roar of fury and chased Rowan around the room. Soon Gabe and Jerram had joined in the fun, adding their own refrains to Rowan's song. There were tears of mirth rolling down Will's face and his chest ached with laughter before Rockwood and Miller appeared, Rockwood grabbing Rowan out of the air as he leapt off a bed, and Miller seized Gabe.

"Alright, that's enough!" Miller said, fighting to keep his own face stern. "Bed, all of you."

Rockwood, who hadn't bothered with disapproval, put Rowan in a headlock and cuffed him in the back of the head. "You are the best of the pest," he announced, before pushing Rowan toward his bed. "Okay, lights out and get some sleep, for the love of Alamore, or we'll send in Ross and Laster. They won't be as fun as us."

Once they left, Rowan rolled his eyes, climbing into his bed. "They just think they're fun because they aren't mature."

"Bold words from you," Will commented dryly, stifling a yawn and sinking into his own bed. Despite the tangle of thoughts, the questions running through his head, he was asleep even before the last candle had been extinguished, plunging all of them into darkness.

***

It was an unwelcome surprise when Will, waking before all the others, rushed to the stairs that led to the healing chamber and found them again blocked. He was running so quickly he almost tripped over the man seated on the bottom most step, an exhausted bored expression on his face.

The man yelped in surprise when Will appeared, scrambling upright to block the corridor. Red-faced with embarrassment, the soldier blinked down at Will through a sheet of unkept white-blond hair.

"No one's permitted up here without permission of the King," the soldier said after a moment.

"Oh." Will took a step back, shoulders sagging. "Right, sorry about that."

The soldier nodded and Will could feel his gaze burning into his back as he crossed toward the dinner hall again, head hung in disappointment. Not wanting to try to get more sleep, Will chose to wait at the empty squire table for his friends. When they had arrived, bright and early thanks to Novin extracting his revenge before morning patrol and beating Rowan with a pillow to wake him, Will explained the guard at the steps.

"Blimey!" Rowan whistled. "They must really be determined to keep you out. Wonder what the Ranger knows that we're not allowed to know."

"Probably a lot," Colin pointed out. "But it won't be long till you can go see him, Will."

"Tomorrow," Will grimaced. "Seems forever."

"Unless…" Rowan said slyly, rubbing his palms together.

Colin groaned. "Is this going to be a stupid plan?"

"Not stupid!" Rowan snapped. "My plans are brilliant. This was a trial, a gauntlet thrown at our feet. The battle cry of Ross's challenge still echoes in our ears!"

"Oh, don't start this, Rowan." Colin rolled his eyes.

Ignoring Colin, Rowan thrust a fist into the air. "And we shall heed its call, accept our destinies, and get past Ross's guard!"

Heartened by Rowan's attitude, Will started plotting ways up the stairs with Rowan in an undertone through breakfast, ignoring Colin's doubtful snorts and grumbling at their ever more drastic ideas. It was only slightly disappointing that Colin wasn't interested in joining in. Will imagined that if any of them were to have a plan that would actually work, it'd be Colin. Still, he maintained his stony disapproval and didn't offer more than condoning scowls when Will asked his opinion.

"Depending on who guards next, maybe I can tempt them away with some excuse? Say something like the barn is on fire?" Rowan offered. "Then you can get up the steps, talk to the Ranger, and we will all be happy again."

"I don't know the guard who was there this morning." Will shook his head. "And if it's someone we know, that won't work. They'll not trust you, no offence."

"Don't you think it'd make more sense not to end up in a load of trouble?" Colin asked at last.

"Don't go shooting down adept style and skills," Rowan replied waspishly.

After their first practice of the morning Will and Rowan slipped away from the others under the pretext of needing to grab practice swords from the weapons shed. Once out of sight of the jousting arena, they broke into a sprint, racing through the double doors. Inside they immediately skidded to a halt, Rowan swearing under his breath.

Standing at the base of the stairs, brows raised and sneering, Laster's amber eyes locked on the two squires.

"Don't you have lessons to attend?" Laster demanded.

Will turned away. "Let's leave it, Row."

"Hold on, I've got a plan," Rowan hissed back, narrowing his eyes at Laster.

Laster cleared his throat and Rowan turned toward the knight, not bothering to explain himself to Will. "Well, we would but..." Rowan shoved his hands into his pockets, sidling forward. Will thought he looked the picture of fake innocence. "We wanted to come check on you, see if you're doing okay with guarding and all and-"

With a sudden lunge, Rowan launched himself at Laster, reaching to grab the knight around the middle in a tackle. Unfortunately for Rowan, he seemed to have forgotten two small matters; that Laster was much bigger than him and that Laster was a fully trained knight.

The knight stepped back, reaching out a hand to grab Rowan by the back of the tunic before he could collide with him. Snarling, Laster dropped Rowan to the ground with a crash, Rowan letting out another string of oaths.

Will wasn't sure whether to check on his friend or laugh and reached out a hand to support himself on the wall as Rowan climbed up, brushing the dust from his tunic. "Excellent, had to check, and your instincts are on point, I might add. Now, Will and I'll just be off, leave you to it then, shall we?"

"Not so fast," Laster snarled. The sneer had been replaced with a look of absolute fury. He stepped from the stair, towering over Rowan.

"Actually, forgive us, Sir, but we've got to do something really quick," Rowan said, turning to Will.

"And what would that be?" Laster hissed dangerously.

"RUN!" Rowan sprang back down the corridor toward Will. Will threw open the doors and both boys bolted into the courtyard, around the corner, and launched themselves into the shed of practice weapons. Rowan barred the door and Will sank against the wall, panting. Outside in the courtyard they could hear Laster swearing at the top of his lungs.

"So." Rowan flipped his hair from his face, grimacing. "Not quite as successful as we might have hoped."

Unable to help himself, Will started laughing. "Alamore, Rowan, that was your brilliant plan? What was it? Get killed?" He doubled over, his stomach hurting with laughter. "First the carrots to his face, now you tackle him? Laster's going to murder you!"

"You know what, I didn't think it quite through, but that's the risk you take in brilliance!" Rowan announced, striking a post like he was holding a sword above his head. Will sank to the floor, choking on his laughter at the ridiculous antics of his friend. "Oh, knock it off, it was a good idea!" Rowan scoffed, reaching to cuff Will in the back of his head. "Though," Rowan said, sinking to the floor as well, stifling his own mirth. "I'm not sure if I'm brave enough to show my face again."

"We'll have to go into hiding forever now."

"Maybe he'll forget?" Rowan asked, hopefully.

Will wiped his streaming eyes on his sleeve and pushed himself to his feet, shaking his head. "I'm pretty sure he's never going to forgive or forget."

"Well, someone ought to tell him it's not good to hold onto anger that way."

Still grinning, Will reached for three of the practice swords; their excuse to even leave training in the first place. "I'll let you tell him that but, come on. If we don't get back soon we'll be in worse trouble still."

"Fair point," Rowan chuckled. "Alamore, I know I should be worried, but it was so worth it to see his face."

Will and Rowan lost no time in recounting Rowan's wild attack to Colin when they got back to where he waited in the jousting arena, lounging in Strider's saddle. Despite his best attempts to be disapproving, Colin shook with suppressed mirth.

"Wish I'd seen that!"

"Told you that you would regret missing out on this adventure, this quest," Rowan ranted, swinging back onto Naja. "But, no, you had to be the responsible one. Responsible ones are boring!"

"Yeah, well the responsible one will live to be a knight," Colin said, shaking his head and grinning. "But yeah, it might have been worth the risk to see that."

"I'll have bruises for a month, I swear," Rowan lamented, wincing as he readjusted in the saddle. "Now I just want to go lie down."

"Hold on, didn't you get any punishment?" Colin inquired, frowning.

"Not a one," Rowan said, sticking his chest out proudly. "Escaped without so much as a warning."

"And how did you do that?" Colin sounded dubious.

"My charm."

Will snorted, settling onto Admere's saddle. "Not hardly. We bolted. Ran like the blazes to get out of there and we hid out in the practice weapon shed."

"You realize you two are going to be in bigger trouble for that?"

An image of Laster's furious face flashed before Will's eyes and he had to bite the inside of his cheek to keep from laughing again. "Worth it for the look on Laster's face."

The sound of someone else laughing made the three squires turn. Kalia, Eldin, and Niet were approaching the fence. The two squires were leading their horses but Kalia, laughing at something Niet had said, was not leading a horse or even dressed for practice in a long blue-grey dress.

At the gate, she raised a hand in farewell to them before trotting along the fence to stand by where Rockwood, Ross, and Haru were waiting for their squires to start practice. Will smirked, noticing even from this distance the red hue creep over Haru's face when the Princess joined them.

"They're not practicing with us, are they?" asked Rowan, groaning. "Oh, come on, I was hoping we were about done."

"Don't be a prat, Rowan," Colin hissed under his breath

"What? Come off it, that's Serena's squire! Even if she's not a spy, she's a git and honestly can't say that her squire will be any better."

Though Will silently agreed with Rowan, he shrugged. "Honestly, practicing with Kelkor squires, even if Serena was a spy, would be safer than trying to tackle Laster."

Colin snorted. "He's got a point, Row."

They stopped talking as Niet swung onto his palomino and trotted toward them, still beaming. Eldin, who seemed to shrink once in the saddle of her grey, was a half-step behind. Will was forcibly reminded of a small shadow in how the girl watched the older squire, concentration written over her face as she mirrored his movements.

"You haven't started on sword practice yet, have you?" Niet asked, drawing his horse to a halt beside Admere.

"Not yet." Rowan shook his head.

"These two have been procrastinating," Colin grumbled, rolling his eyes.

On Niet's far side, Eldin laughed. "Judging by that knight in the courtyard a bit ago, they've been doing more than just procrastinating." Her grey eyes met Will's and she beamed. "Did you really try to tackle a knight?"

Feeling sheepish, and all too aware of Rowan smirking beside him, Will grinned. "Don't bunch me in that. That was entirely Rowan."

Across the jousting field, Rockwood gave a piercing whistle and all three Alamore squires straightened to attention. "Are we going to practice or die of old age waiting on you lot?"

"Both!" Rowan called back. Will noticed Eldin and Niet seemed taken aback by Rowan's gall and even more surprised when Rockwood gave a bark of laughter.

"Right then, Rowan, you've volunteered to be first. Eldin, how about you and Rowan get up here and face off."

"You heard him," Niet said, jerking his chin in Rockwood's direction and grinning at Eldin. "Go show the boys how to fight like a girl, eh?"

"Just don't kill me," Rowan said, winking. "Come on, let's get up there and show these lazy louts how to fight."

Eldin smiled mischievously. "I make no promises." She moved her horse to trot forward with Rowan, out of the way of the other three squires.

As they were riding away, Will noticed Rowan lean over, showing Eldin his hand. "Want to know how I got that killer scar? Bet you would've fainted because there was blood everywhere, and I know how ladies are with that sort of thing."

"So, you're saying you fainted?" Eldin asked interestedly.

Snorting with suppressed laughter, Will turned away from them, shaking his head. Beside him, Colin was frowning slightly, watching Eldin's horse rather than Rowan's antics. After a moment he turned to Niet, brow furrowed. "Isn't that horse a bit big for Eldin?"

Niet nodded, all traces of his smile vanishing. An icy tension filled the air and the older squire's knuckles whitened on his reins. "He wasn't meant to be her horse."

"He wasn't?" Will asked, frowning. "Then what…" He stopped, wishing he could swallow his words again. Hadn't they mentioned something about one of their knights falling in the journey?

"Sir Paxrin was Eldin's knight and…and my brother." Niet turned to them, his face grim and dark eyes unreadable.

"When we were told to leave Kelkor, he was our guard. The plan had been to wait for Revlan's Ranger, but something happened, a message arrived at the castle, and Paxrin snuck us from the castle a week before we had planned.

We met with the Ranger two days into our journey, along a mountain pass. It was that night. We were in the mountains, on a trail that we didn't think anyone else would find but he found us and got worried. He tried to talk us off the trail, but we didn't go… I argued with him even.

That night, Eldin's pony stumbled into a trap, and they attacked, rebels against the throne. Paxrin and the Ranger started fighting them while Kalia and I pulled Eldin out of the trap. By the time we'd freed her, there were too many of them. Paxrin ordered us to ride and…he was killed trying to defend us." A spasm of pain flashed over the older squire's face and he turned away, his eyes fixed unseeingly on Eldin and Rowan, now sparring from horseback, Rowan yelping each time Eldin struck toward him. "If the Ranger hadn't been there we would have died. He managed to hold them off long enough for us to get Eldin on a horse then he came riding after us. After that, we followed the Ranger off any trails."

"I'm sorry," Will muttered. Colin nodded beside him, green eyes filled with grief. Like Niet, he'd lost his own brother years before.

Niet shook himself and straightened in his saddle, forcing a faint smile. "He died a warrior, defending Kalia and us, like a knight of Kelkor. But now it's up to me, it's up to me to see those two stay safe. I just wish I'd found out why we left the castle when we did, why he thought it was time we leave, you know?"

"So, he didn't ever tell you?" Will asked, frowning.

"No." Niet's eyes flitted to Will again. "But I'm sure your Ranger knows."

Will grunted noncommittally. Niet seemed nice enough but he wasn't certain he wanted to discuss these things with Serena's squire. "Might."

"He saved my life, Will. Mine, and Kalia's, and Eldin's too. Serena might have her reasons not to trust him, but I've got my reasons now to trust him. I wish I'd trusted him sooner," Niet muttered. Colin shifted uncomfortably but Will met the older squire's piercing glower. "I know you want answers too, I heard you talking to Ross. They're planning a council tonight and I think we can get our answers there."

"Councils are only for knights," Will said flatly, shaking his head. "And that stairwell is being guarded."

"You've already considered that though, haven't you?" Colin said, startling Will as he broke his disapproving silence and frowned at Niet. "You already know that."

"I do. Kalia already tried to get an invite as Princess but was told no," Niet said hesitantly. "But I've got to know I can trust you two if we're going to try, because the plan will help us get answers, but it isn't the…um…safest."

Will turned to Colin, brows raised in silent question. After a moment, Colin groaned, running his hand through his hair. "Fine, I'm in. Rowan will probably be too. But I swear, Will, Niet, if you two get us killed…"

CHAPTER SIXTEEN

Training with the Kelkor squires was actually more fun than Will would have wanted to admit. Eldin was quite good with a sword, though it was a bit too large for her, much like the horse, and she ended up doing best with one of the baton daggers. She also had Serena's skill of getting a rider off their horses, knocking Colin into the dirt twice, much to the amusement of Will and Rowan. As far as they were concerned, it was good for Colin to fall. He won too often.

Niet, far too large and skilled to make a fair fight, ended up training against Haru. The two were a relatively even match–Niet was quick but tended to get bold in his attacks, Haru was stronger and more deliberate–and by the time that Ross announced it was time for all of them to quit, Will and the others had cheered and yelled themselves hoarse. Even Kalia, who had sat on the fence to watch, was breathless and red when they were all dismounting.

Will and Colin were eager to fill in Rowan on what Niet had discussed–the plan to somehow overhear the council–but that opportunity was lost as soon as they left the jousting field and found Laster leaning on the castle wall, glowering at them.

"Oh no," Rowan mumbled, hunching in an attempt to hide behind Will, seeming to forget he was leading a massive horse. "I'm so dead."

"Told you so," Colin said dryly.

"Shut up, Greyhead."

"Rockwood, Rowan, a word?" Laster called, straightening.

Rockwood turned to look at Rowan, rolling his eyes. "Alamore, what did you do now?"

"It was nice to get to meet him before he dies," Eldin commented, coming to stand next to Will while they watched Rowan slink toward Rockwood and Laster.

The others moved toward the barn where Will was hopeful to find out more about Niet's plan but was disappointed when Haru joined them and began talking to the Kelkor squire about the battle tactics more often used in the coastal country. Not until they had entered the hall, where the tantalizing smells of dinner made Will's mouth water, did Haru depart from their side to join the knights. The four squires moved toward their own table, where any chance of a covert discussion was impossible. Gabe and Jerram were eagerly telling everyone about their training, Gabe bouncing in his seat, Jerram trying to act more refined but making sure he showed everyone the bruise he'd given himself when he'd accidentally punched himself in the face.

They were almost finished eating before Rowan joined them, throwing himself into the seat next to Will and snarling as he reached for any plate near him.

"Nice talk?" Will asked, grinning wickedly.

Rowan gave a dark bark of manic laughter. "You know what that son of a-"

"Rowan," Colin said warningly.

"Is making me do?" Rowan continued, as though he hadn't heard. "He's making me write him an apology letter and told me I have to help in the kitchens."

"That's not all bad," Will said consolingly, grabbing up a slice of bread and dropping it onto his plate.

"For a week!" Rowan slapped his hands on the table, causing the cutlery and the two youngest Alamore squires to jump. Novin, across the table, threw Rowan a bewildered frown. "Seriously! What gives him that right to do that?"

"The fact that he's a knight?" Colin suggested. To Colin's other side, Niet snorted into his sleeve and tried to play it off as a cough.

"He doesn't respect the lesson I was trying to teach him in survival."

Will smirked. "I think he's teaching you survival too. Do it again and he might kill you."

"I'm going to die working in the kitchens anyway," Rowan lamented sadly.

Movement at the double doors made Will turn away from his friends. The guard he had seen that morning was hurrying into the room, shooting nervous looks into the shadows of the dinner hall, before darting to where Sir Ross sat. He leaned in to address the knight in a low voice and Will noticed Ross's frown deepen. To Ross's far side, Lady Serena had gone rigid, her head tilted the better to hear what the guard had to say.

After a moment, Ross waved a dismissive hand to the soldier. "Thank you, Oberoan," he growled and pushed himself to his feet. At the far end of the table, the King rose as well, a grim expression on his face. "King, it seems the healer thinks he is ready for us now."

"Very well." The King sighed, shaking his head and gripping Kalia's shoulder briefly as he moved past her seat. "Niece, I would ask that you have your squires escort you back to your chamber. I must borrow your knight for a while."

"Yes, Uncle," Kalia said, nodding.

"I'll escort her back to her rooms," Serena said stiffly, nodding to Revlan.

The King gave a respectful bow of his head and moved toward the double doors. Chairs scraped over the stone flags as other knights moved to stand and follow, Ross the first to the King's side. In the confusion of movement, the soldier had somehow vanished as if into thin air.

Rowan, his mouth full to bursting, lifted his face from his crouched position over his plate. "Where er dey gong?"

"You know, it's concerning how much better you're getting at talking with your mouthful," Colin said, looking revolted. "It's actually quite disgusting."

"Must be time for their council," Niet muttered. His eyes flitted to Will who nodded, understanding. This was it then. This was when they would have to act.

Kalia, at the knights table, was fixing Niet and Eldin with a piercing gaze. She raised her brows and mouthed. "Time to go."

"Right." Niet stood and Will, Colin, and Eldin did the same.

"What? Where are you going?" Rowan asked, choking as he forced himself to swallow his too-large mouthful.

Will opened his mouth to explain but Laster's voice carried across the hall, interjecting.

"Rowan, kitchens, now!"

Tossing his fork down with a murderous scowl, Rowan rose as well, grumbling something unintelligible.

"I'll explain everything when I get back," Will promised quickly.

"You better," threatened Rowan.

Not wanting to risk anything being overheard by the other squires and all too aware of Colin bouncing nervously on the balls of his feet behind him, Will only nodded before Rowan was stalking through one of the side doors leading out of the chamber. Spinning round, Will caught sight of Princess Kalia. Across the dinner hall, Princess Kalia was striding toward the doors after the knights, but more slowly. She seemed to be struggling with a tie on her belt and shook her head at Serena, who stood guard at her side.

"Go on, Serena. Niet and Eldin can watch me well enough. Or have you forgotten that they got me here alive? I don't doubt they are more than capable of helping me get to my rooms," Kalia insisted.

The knight's green eyes flashed in Will's direction and Colin grabbed Will's arm, steering him toward the squire chamber. "Keep your head down," Colin warned.

"She's such a pleasant creature," Will grumbled. He made a point of not looking toward the Princess until he heard Serena's footfalls leaving.

"And now we catch up with them," Colin whispered, glancing back over his shoulder. "Serena's gone and they're waiting just in the entry hall."

Will and Colin turned and walked quickly back across the dinner hall with expressions of forced calm. The tension rising in Will's chest was making it difficult to keep from sprinting after the knights. Whatever Niet's plan was, it had to work. He needed answers, to know how Marl might be involved, and most of all, he needed to see the Ranger, hear him, know that he wasn't close to death.

"Ready for an adventure?" Kalia asked when they'd reached her, Niet, and Eldin in the entry hall.

Colin laughed hoarsely, a flush of color flaring in his cheeks. "Not entirely sure, eh, Your Majesty."

Will turned his face away a moment, pretending to cough in order to hide his laughter. Judging by the flash of a grin Eldin shot him, she had noticed Colin's red face too.

Kalia grimaced. "Don't use titles right now. I don't want to be reminded of my status when scheming against my uncle the King of

Alamore." Turning to Niet, she raised her brows, smirking. "You have everything you need for this?"

"I got it all up there this afternoon." Niet shrugged. "I wanted to be prepared."

"Then can we go?" Eldin hissed, glancing around the corridor. "We're going to miss information."

"Got all of what up where?" Colin asked suspiciously.

"Never mind that right now," Niet muttered. "Eldin's right. Let's go."

And with that he wheeled round, striding down the corridor. Will thought at first that they were about to turn toward the stairs that led up to the healing chamber and wondered how on earth Niet had thought that a good idea. They were sure to be guarded still. Sure enough, drawing level with the steps, Will saw the same guard as that morning standing a few steps up, just out of sight of the end of the hall, his face almost entirely in shadows. But Niet ignored him, either not seeing him or not caring that he was there. Will couldn't quite manage the same and shivered, the feeling of eyes making him glance over his shoulder. The soldier was watching them from the dark. There was something eerie about the gleam of his eyes in the flickering torch.

Discomfort mounted when Niet instead turned and pushed through the door Will and Colin had gone through the night they had broken into Serena's room. A quick look at Colin out of the corner of his eye told him that Colin was thinking of that night as well. His face had gone gaunt, his jaw tense, and the fingers of his right hand were gripping his dagger hilt.

They climbed the stairs and Will's unease was cut with confusion. Surely this wasn't the plan. What on earth were these Kelkorian's thinking? Were they going to just go hang out in the Princess's rooms maybe and hope Serena gave them news when she got back? Or, and Will's stomach clenched at the unpleasant thought, maybe these squires thought they should try to break into Serena's room. They didn't know Will and Colin had already done that.

But then they were passing Serena's chamber and cutting toward the stairwell that Will and Colin had escaped down. Now feeling utterly bewildered, Will hesitated, looking down the twisting steps, thrown into shadow by the sparse torches.

"We're going the wrong way if we go down there," Will said, turning to Kalia. "They're in the healing chamber."

"We know that," Kalia whispered. "And we're not going down. We're going up."

Will nodded uncertainly and turned, colliding with Colin who had frozen beside him. Taking a staggering step backwards, Will scowled at his friend. "Blazes, Colin."

But Colin wasn't looking at him. He was glowering at Niet suspiciously. "Up? Why are we going up? All that's up these stairs are the battlements."

"Which is where we're going," Eldin said in the same soothing voice that Will imagined she might use for a fussy toddler. "But you're blocking the way."

Will and Colin exchanged suspicious looks, but the others were already slipping past them, mounting the spiral stairwell. Starting to think that he had made a mistake in convincing Colin to go through with this, Will shrugged to Colin and followed them.

Shadows slanted through the windows that lined this tower stairwell, casting their own grey light in-between the dancing orange of the sparse torches. Will forced himself to focus on the next step to keep from getting dizzy. Whoever had invented these twisting steps really deserved a punch to the face, he thought bitterly as they climbed higher. Behind him, he could hear Colin muttering to himself, a consistent hum in the soft padding of their feet.

"What's the matter?" Will asked, glancing back at his friend.

"I don't care for heights," Colin hissed, swallowing. His eyes darted from Will to the drop beside them and he squeezed his eyes shut a moment. "Actually, I hate them"

"Well then," Will said, grinning in spite of himself, "don't look down."

"Alamore, why do I hang around you and Rowan?"

Their conversation was cut short as Niet pushed through the door at the top of the steps and cold night air rushed over them, lifting the hair on Will's forehead and sending a shiver through his body. Taking the last few steps two at a time now, he rushed through the door after the three Kelkorians.

Immediately he wished he had taken his time on the last steps as he straightened and took in his surroundings. They were under the canopy of dark stars and wispy clouds. Wind rushed over them, making him wish he'd thought to bring a thicker cloak. But even as the hair rose on the back of his neck and over his arms, Will knew it wasn't due to the cold. Instead, it was the sickening drop, only feet away over the low battlement wall, that drew his eyes. They had to be six stories or more above the courtyard, where the first torches were being lit, orange candle flames from their vantage. He could see the small figures of guards roaming the ground, horses being led from the barn for the night patrol. It looked as if they were playthings.

"You good there?"

Will turned to see Niet watching him, a frown creasing his forehead. Forcing himself to swallow, Will nodded. "Why are we up here?"

He had to raise his voice to keep his words from being whipped away in the wind.

Niet gave his wolfish grin and jerked his head toward where Eldin was rummaging through two bags Will hadn't noticed before. "We're going to listen in."

"Listen in?" Will asked, bewildered. Understanding struck with the force of a dulled practice sword to the stomach when Eldin straightened, a long length of rope in one hand. "Are you mad?"

"You've got to be joking," moaned Colin, still standing in the doorway. "We can't go down the side of the castle."

"We're not all going." Niet shook his head. "But there isn't really another option. We just have to lower a couple of us down to the window of the healing chamber. It's dark enough that the soldiers shouldn't notice. I figured Eldin is small enough and good enough at grappling that one of you and Kalia can handle her weight and then I can help the other of you..." His voice drifted, taking in the green tinge in Colin's face and Will's apprehension. "Have you two never scaled a building before?"

Colin let out an unnaturally high laugh. "No! Why the Thornten would we be that raving mad?"

"In Kelkor we're trained on buildings as squires," Niet said, seeming confused. "Then we learn on the cliffs outside the castle...oh" His grin faltered. "Right, you don't have cliffs."

"I'm fine going alone," Eldin said, already knotting one of the ropes firmly.

Worry flashed over the dark eyes and Will could see that Niet was beginning to reconsider his plan. But one look at Kalia, her face falling, made Will step forward, shaking his head. "No, I can go. Eldin can teach me, and I can make sure we get to the right window."

"You sure?" asked Kalia.

"Of course I am," said Will, beaming. His eyes drifted toward the drop and he wondered for a moment what would happen if he puked while scaling a building.

There wasn't time to reconsider though. Niet was already grabbing up the second rope, twisting it into complex knots, and talking about the proper way to adjust the makeshift harness. Will nodded, barely hearing him, his full attention tangled in that drop. That drop that he was about to willingly go down. *You've lost your mind you idiot,* he thought, taking the rope that Niet was offering him and stepping through one of the two loops. Niet ordered Will to put one leg through the first loop before creating a second. Will found himself at an utter loss as Niet twisted the rope around his back

"The one at your back is for your support, but you'll still want to hold that front rope," Niet was explaining. "Just act like it's a chair."

"A chair over a tremendous drop," Kalia offered, laughing.

"Not helpful right now, Princess," Niet called over his shoulder. "Anyway, how are you and Eldin coming along with her harness?"

"We're set," Eldin said, grinning as she took in Will's appearance. "It's not that bad, I swear. You start to like it."

"I'll just take your word on that," Will muttered.

Colin had finally left the doorway, looking on the verge of being sick, but grabbed up the end of the rope holding Will and glowered at him. "Are you sure this is a good idea?"

"I have to know what's going on," Will said firmly. "It's to do with Marl.." he glanced beyond Colin, to where Eldin was lifting herself onto the battlements, letting her legs kick out over the drop.

Colin didn't need to hear the rest of his thought. Instead, he ran a hand through his golden hair with a Ross-like growl. "Fine, I get it. But remember what I said, if you get killed, I'm not forgiving you."

"I'm not going to die, but I appreciate the optimism," Will said dryly. He stepped past Colin, slapping him on the shoulder. "You're on my rope with Kalia then. So, just don't drop me and we should be good. My life is literally in your hands, but no pressure."

He grinned as he heard Colin's low whisper of insults, turning to Eldin. "Right then, you're in charge."

"Then get over here, we're wasting time," Eldin ordered. Will hurried to obey, wishing he'd thought to skip dinner as he swung himself onto the wall next to her. Kalia and Colin were pulling his rope taut, bracing in the same stance Niet had taken up with Eldin's rope. "Now, when we push off, you'll want to have your back to the ground. Use your feet to push off the castle, but don't do it too hard or you'll smash into the wall again and that hurts," Eldin warned him. "Hold onto your main rope–that one going up–yeah that's it. Grip that. When we get to the window, just let me know. Until then, kick off the wall to signal to our rope holders that we need slack to go lower. When we stop kicking off is when they stop loosening."

"And how do we get up?" Will asked, the realization dawning on him.

"That's their problem. Come on." She didn't give him another chance at questions but twisted and pushed herself off the wall, over the edge. Will's heart caught in his throat as he watched her drop a few feet before stopping and waving him to follow.

Closing his eyes, Will wondered one more time why on earth he had considered this a good idea before pushing off. The world rushed around him, the cold air stinging his throat as he opened his mouth to cry out. This was it, this was how he was going to die, falling to the courtyard like an idiot!

The rope went tight under his fingers and he was pulled to a halt, the stop far more gradual than he had expected. Twisting round, Will saw he was a few feet to Eldin's right now and she was watching him, brows raised.

"Did…did I scream?" Will asked, feeling sheepish.

"Do you really want the answer to that?" Eldin asked sweetly.

"Shove off," Will grumbled, scowling at the wall. He braced himself for another drop and pushed off with both feet. Again, the world rushed around him for several feet of controlled fall, but this time Will allowed himself to look around, taking in the torches growing brighter in the courtyard, casting faint shadows up the stone he was scaling down.

Several of the windows cast their own strange glows to the mix, their light breaking through stone, fracturing the darkness. Will glanced down at the windows below him, and his heart skipped a beat. There. They were nearly to the healing chamber window.

Turning to Eldin, he pointed frantically toward the narrow window until she nodded, shooting him a toothy smile that seemed ghostly in the darkness. "Got it."

The last few drops seemed agonizingly slow now that they were so near. Will glanced up again to see the wall above them, the top out of sight. He had to suppress a laugh at the thought of Colin looking down. Maybe it wasn't his own urge to puke he should have worried about.

"Stop. They'll see you!"

Eldin reached out a hand and grabbed the rope above Will, pulling him to the side as his feet dropped to the height of the sick room window. Will pulled them up, heart slamming in his ears. In his worry about the drop and being vomited on, he hadn't considered what would happen if the knights saw them dangling outside the window.

"Careful now. Small push," Eldin muttered. "We just need to be able to see and hear…and that, stop, there."

The window's light glowed beside them, the soft murmur of voices adding a new cold to the night. Will was careful to move slowly, bracing his hands and knees against the wall in a bizarre crawl toward the window. Peering through, Will's mouth went dry and his muscles rigid. There they all were–the knights, the King–each seated and standing around a bed.

From this angle it was impossible to see the person in the bed but that didn't matter. Even hoarse with exhaustion, rasping, he knew the voice that was saying; "…don't you understand? There is no going back, Serena. Kelkor has fallen."

CHAPTER SEVENTEEN

Will twisted, clamping a hand over Eldin's mouth as she gasped, her face draining of all color.

Pressing the finger of his other hand to his lips, he shook his head desperately. "They'll hear us," he mouthed. But he couldn't blame her. His own mind was reeling with those three words. *Kelkor has fallen.* But how? A civil war had, in a matter of months, brought down the crown?

The King's voice carried from the chamber, breaking the silence and making Will drop his hand from Eldin's mouth to peer around the edge of the window, back into the chamber. "He's right, Serena."

"How can you say that?" Serena turned, her face visible from the window, twisted with grief and anger. "Azric is your brother and-"

"And not a swordsman capable of fighting him," Ross finished, shaking his head. "Azric is a powerful King, a great King, but he is not a warrior, Serena. Even before the raiding party attack crippled his leg, he wasn't a swordsman."

"And if he were alive, he would have already had a messenger here, someone to bring back Kalia," the King murmured. He lowered his head and Will stared in horrified silence at the pain that aged the King's regal features. In the span of a few hours the King of Alamore had aged a thousand years.

"Maybe the messenger was delayed or..." Serena pressed on, voice rising in desperation.

"Did you listen when I told you what Paxrin told me? The letter than arrived before he left?" the Ranger rasped. "He said that Azric knew he wouldn't win. He'd already given up. Nothing else would have made him send his daughter away with only a knight, and a new one at that. He knew that there were spies at his court, that people he thought were loyal were betraying him left and right. If he had thought he could win, he would have waited for the dawn, for me to arrive."

"Not unless he thought he couldn't trust you," Serena spat.

Will expected to hear the Ranger retort but was surprised to hear a low humorless laugh instead. "I have no doubt you tried to make sure that was the case."

"Serena, Ranger," the King barked, straightening. "There isn't time for your squabbling. Serena, if you cannot handle being here, I invite you to leave and have another of the knights fill you in later. For now, we can't be focused on if Azric somehow won. What we need to do is figure out our next move while we are a day ahead of the news reaching the rest of the Kingdom."

"Our next move?" Haru asked, turning to the King. His face had gone white, the red hair a stark contrast as he turned between the Ranger and the King. "What can we do?"

"What Azric was no doubt planning to do or had done." The King began to pace, and Will pulled himself away from the window, heart slamming as the dark eyes flitted in his direction. But, to his relief, the King didn't seem to see anything, too preoccupied in his thoughts. "We will have to send a message to the west, to King Prandus, to reaffirm that we can rely on them. Perhaps one to Shadow Dale too."

Will inched toward the window again and saw Laster's lip curled in a sneer as he shook his head. "Giltor?"

The King grimaced. "I know, Laster, but it must be done. Giltor is not my favorite of people either, or I his for that matter, but we need to know which side they will stand on."

"It's their fault we are here in the first place," Bane snarled. "How can you want to ally with them when it was their rogue men who gave that chance for an uprising?"

Will started as the King gave a roar of fury. Beside him, Eldin let out a string of words in Kelkorian that he didn't understand, gripping her rope tighter.

"Do you think I have a choice? There are times, Bane, for me to mourn my brother and there are times for me to defend a Kingdom! If I lapse now, it will be more than Kelkor that is lost."

The room fell silent. At his side, Eldin was trembling–whether with the cold of the air or the same cold Will could feel coursing through his own blood he wasn't sure. Inside the chamber, Will could see Miller

175

running his hands over his face, Ross's thumb running over the blue stone in his sword's hilt, Rockwood rocking back and forth on his feet. After a painful silence that stretched an eternity, Serena broke it, narrowing her eyes.

"And what of the boy?"

All eyes broke from the King and shifted to her. Ross straightened, gripping his sword hilt. Haru's face tensed and Will saw his hands ball into fists at his side.

"What about him?" the Ranger growled dangerously.

Serena snorted, eyes flashing. "He's a threat, that's what, Ranger. You've already seen they were prepared to attack Kalia to get to him. They probably hoped to use her as a bargaining chip to get him."

"So, because that failed, you think we should hand him over freely?" asked Laster, raising an eyebrow. "That logic is the same logic that would make someone suspicious of you."

Serena's hand flew to her sword handle. "And what's that supposed to mean?"

"It means that someone in this room clearly had loose lips regarding the Ranger and Kalia's arrival," Laster pressed, seemingly unphased by the lady knight's obvious rage. "Someone knew he would be taking that route even though it's not the direct path to the castle, it's not even a path really but a deer trail. They didn't just happen to stumble upon the Ranger and the Princess of Kelkor."

"How dare-"

"Laster," Ross growled warningly. "Serena, don't draw a blade in here or I'll be forced to confiscate it. Laster, Serena is no more a spy than you or I."

"Probably even less so," Serena snapped. "Considering your own past, Laster, I think you've been much closer to the King of Thornten and his brother than I ever have."

Anger masked Laster's face and he made to move toward Serena, his hand gripping his sword hilt, but Haru had launched himself forward, grabbing Laster's arm. "Not worth it, Laster. She's not worth it."

Laster spun and raised his other arm to strike Haru away, but Miller was faster, gripping it as well. "Don't be an idiot."

"Serena, if you continue to cause mayhem, you will lose your invitation to this council," the King barked. "Laster, stand down. That is an order."

With a narrowed eyed look of purest loathing at Serena, Laster obeyed, shaking off Haru and Miller and stepping back, out of Will's line of sight.

"She's right though," Henry spoke, seeming older and more exhausted than ever before, stretching his bandaged leg ahead of his chair with a wince. "We can't keep living in denial... The Cutthroat Prince, he's made his intention clear."

"And we can try to get prisoners from Kelkor, to save people in Alamore, all if we just hand him over," Serena pressed on.

"Prisoners in Kelkor?" Miller demanded, half laughing. "Haven't you listened to the reports of the war since you arrived? No one is being spared. He won't save a single prisoner. And, as for Alamore, don't think that Thornten is a new threat to us. They've been a danger to us for more years than I've been alive."

"Then we save him for when they make demands, or bargaining for peace," Serena said flatly.

"And since when do we cave to blackmail?" Rockwood asked, frowning. "Or has that changed in the last twenty minutes and I just missed the news?"

"We don't cave, nor will we," the Ranger spoke, and all eyes shifted again to the bed out of Will's sight. "All we can do is keep him in training and find our ways to deal with Kelkor. Bargaining with him will do nothing. He means nothing to Tollien. He wouldn't give us any alliance for the boy's life."

"And what of his brother?" asked Richard, running his hand over his jaw. "How long will it be until he comes to claim his heir and tries to negotiate with peace?"

Frozen to the wall beyond the room, Will waited. The air in his mouth was stale from being held, his heart was slamming.

It was Ross who answered, face contorting with unreadable emotion. "He will be here before long. But King of Kelkor or not, if Marl wants to take Will, he'll have to get through me first."

CHAPTER EIGHTEEN

Surely the world had stopped turning, the days no longer inching through their light and dark. This night would press on him forever, the rope numb against his skin until the end of time. Because those words had to spell the end of all.

But the world hadn't stopped. Beyond the window, the knights were still standing, speaking. The words meant little now. He wasn't sure he wanted to hear them. He wanted to unhear all he'd already learned. He saw each familiar knight, those he looked up to, those he learned from. And they were discussing him, discussing what to do with *him*. They didn't have any idea that he was there, listening, dangling from a rope above the courtyard. That he knew the truth now.

The truth…so this was it then. This explained everything. It had been Marl who sent The Cutthroat Prince after all, but not to kill him, never to kill him. He'd sent him to capture Will as his heir now that he knew he would be claiming his own throne. He'd been the one inciting the uprisings, causing the mayhem in Kelkor and Right of Blood… he'd been so stupid. Stupid not to make the connection with that simple phrase, not to understand what that meant in Serena's ledger. She had been tracing the family line, keeping track of which power strongholds he had in Kelkor. She had been tracking the moment that he held enough power, enough of a right, to challenge King Azric for his throne.

"They mean you?"

Will turned. Eldin was staring at him in horrified fascination, her eyes wide as she shook her head. "You're the son of the traitor heir, the man who's been murdering my people."

Will opened his mouth, not sure what to say. "I didn't know."

It sounded lame, stupid even. Of all the things to say, those three words seemed the worst.

Eldin snorted. "As if!"

"I swear." Will shook his head. "I didn't know. I don't want-"

"Shut up," Eldin snapped. "They're speaking." She jerked her head at the window and turned away, scowling in the glow of the torches.

"We can't keep this from the Princess," Haru was saying, shaking his head. "Not any longer, not if we know there's no chance Azric won."

"Would you rather I inform her that her parents are dead, and her Kingdom has fallen?" Serena demanded. "And what if it hasn't?"

"If it hadn't then her parents would already be here looking for her! The Ranger and them were delayed getting here and you know it!" Haru was raising his voice, stepping nearer. "She deserves the truth from us rather than a messenger riding in to announce that Tollien's brother has murdered her family. She thinks she has a Kingdom! She thinks she has a family! You can't let that be broken by the brutal words of someone who's loyal to Marl, belting it out to the courtyard. She has a right to know, she's got to know!"

Will's head spun. Eldin was hissing what he knew had to be oaths in Kelkorian again, a steady string of musical words spiked with panic. Will paid little attention. He was already using all of his energy to focus on the conversation in front of them instead of the ringing that filled his ears. *King Marl of Kelkor, King Marl of Kelkor, King,*

"He's right," the King spoke, silencing Serena with her mouth open to retort to the younger knight. "Serena, she deserves the truth, and you should be the one to tell her. She trusts you. I will come with, of course. And you and her, and your squires–you are all welcome here. Should you choose, I would be honored to have you serve the Alamore court."

Serena took a step back and, for the first time, true grief softened her features for the span of a heartbeat. She looked away, at her feet a moment, then straightened and the fire had returned to the green eyes. She gave a stiff nod. "You're right. She should know. My King...I mean King Azric...isn't, wasn't..." She swallowed hard. "Fighting was not his strength in recent years. I, and my squire, and Eldin too, would be honored to serve Alamore. Thank you, my King."

"And what of The Cutthroat Prince then?" Bane asked, running a hand over his black beard.

"What of him?" demanded Laster.

Bane shrugged. "He's getting more dangerous. We know there are spies in this castle and a good number of them must be his, Laster and Serena were right about that. We can't be fully sure our spy isn't in this room. Only knights knew of that route and they knew who the boy was before many of us knew his tie to the Thornten line."

"Thank you so ever kindly for telling the world that fact," Miller growled at Serena. She snorted, refusing to look at him.

Bane didn't seem to notice, his dark gaze shifting instead to the place the Ranger rested. "If Marl is crowned King then…"

"Then The Cutthroat Prince will continue to hunt Will," the Ranger rasped. "He will continue to act as a hound, searching for Will, under Marl's order. Why The Cutthroat Prince listens as well as he does, what he has to lose, is a form of power, not gold. If my suspicions are correct, if what I have presented to you, King, is true, then he stands to gain a new generation of power by taking Will."

The King nodded. "Power that's making him bold, unfortunately."

"It always comes down to power," Bane scoffed, shaking his head "He's getting dangerous for the power. He nearly killed you. So far he hasn't killed anyone but now…"

"Oh, now he would certainly love to kill–though whether he was intending to kill me and the Princess or more hopeful to take us hostage. The second arrow I took was intended for her. They didn't know the squires would be with me, that was the only reason we managed to escape. But I wouldn't put it beyond Marl to want Kalia dead. A martyr isn't as concerning to him as a returning heir in the future."

"She won't return," Robin said, breaking his silence.

"And why do you say that?" Serena demanded harshly.

"In Kelkor, your women can become knights, but your power still rests with a King." Robin shook his head. "Marl is Tollien's brother. He has an alliance with Thornten that Kalia couldn't match, and Marl will continue to push Thornten beliefs on Kelkor–that women can't lead an army. Which," he added, inclining his head toward Serena, "is one of Marl's weaknesses in his failure to understand."

"And I can only hope it comes back and murders him," Henry said, wincing as he stretched out his cast leg. "But, regardless, this isn't a matter for us today. No. All we can do is prepare a messenger in the morning to travel to King Prandus and, for now, rest."

"You're right." The King nodded and pivoted to Serena. "We best go speak to Kalia. Haru, if you would join us?"

"M-me?" Haru stuttered, taken aback.

"We need to go!" Eldin pinched Will's arm, making him start.

He glowered at her. "Don't pinch. I hate being pinched."

"I don't care, you weren't listening to me," she snapped. "Now we signal to go up."

"What? How?"

Muttering under her breath, she leaned across the gap between them and gave his rope two solid tugs before doing the same to her own. He felt a jolt of movement and the dark stone began to slide in front of him. Next to him, Eldin was walking her feet along the wall and he mirrored it as best he could, his mind humming with all they had heard.

"Look for finger holds, toe holds, any way to make it easier for them to pull us up," Eldin hissed.

Will nodded, barely listening. He wanted to be sick. The height didn't bother him anymore. He wasn't sure that it could ever again. Instead, he could only imagine Marl laughing over the body of a King who looked like Revlan, a bloodied blade in one hand, a crown tilting over his brow.

A sharp intake of breath made him look to the side. Eldin was shifting on the wall, her knuckles white on her rope. "You okay?"

"Fine," she hissed back. "My knot must have just tightened, went down a few inches. But I'm fine. Now shut up, I don't want to talk to you…traitor heir."

Anger made Will's face burn. He opened his mouth to retort then closed it, disgusted. She would think that. And let her. What she thought didn't matter and she wasn't wrong either, which made it worse. No. All he could do was get to the top of this way and get away, somewhere he could think.

Will's fingers were tracing over the wall of their own accord, seeking purchase, when movement out of the corner of his eye drove all thoughts of Marl from his head. With a gasp of fear, Eldin was dropping, her hands sliding down her rope, falling.

Instinct born of training to fight made Will lunge sideways, one hand on his rope, the other grabbing her wrist. Her fingers were sliding down the rope, her weight pulling him painfully backwards.

"Grab my arm!" he snarled. "Let go of the rope with this hand, let go of the rope and grab my arm!"

To his immense relief, she obeyed, holding the rope with one hand while the nails of her other bit into his arm. The main supporting knot at her back had given way and she now clung to his hand with one of hers, the rope with the other, fear making her ghostly white.

"Don't let go," Will grunted, pulling her upward with all his strength, still gripping his own rope in his other hand.

She yelped, grabbing his arm tighter as the second knot on the rope she held began to slide free. Will could hear the distant panic above them; Niet was swearing, Colin calling something down to them. Will glanced up and instantly wished he hadn't. They were still stories below the three faces peering down, too far to see their stricken looks which meant their chances of reaching the top were minimal while the ground below was too far to survive a fall. They were trapped, dangling from his rope as hers gave way more, his arm starting to shake from holding her.

"Hold on, hold on," Will hissed through gritted teeth, looking around. He knew he was speaking more to himself than to her. "Don't let go."

"Thank you, I had no idea," Eldin snapped.

Will gritted his teeth. Leave it to her to still have breath for sarcasm at a time like this. His eyes roved along the wall, his mind racing. They needed a way out, something to grab onto or rest on before his arm fell off his body.

There! Several feet below them and further to his left was a darkness different than that of the wall, deeper in its blackness. An open window. He glanced back up, feeling the rope tugging him. They wouldn't make it. His arm wouldn't, he knew. No. They needed down.

He pushed off the wall with both feet, letting his full weight and Eldin's tug on the rope. He heard Eldin scream, someone above them howled in pain, and he made a note to apologize to Niet for the rope burns he could imagine on the older squire's hands.

They were jerked to a halt, the rope cutting into Will's fingers with the force of their stop and the muscles in his shoulder screaming from Eldin's weight. Below him, she was whispering a string of Kelkorian that sounded like panicked song but that didn't matter. The window was now at their level and to his left. But, holding Eldin and his rope, he didn't have a way to reach for it, to stretch that tantalizing few feet between them and a solid castle floor.

"We need to get to the window." Will turned to Eldin. "We have to swing over there, but you have to let go of that rope. Grab me with both hands. Your rope won't let us swing out that far. Do you think you can do that? Can you trust me?"

"No!" Eldin hissed, petrified. "I don't trust you, I don't want to fall, I…"

Will clenched his jaw, fighting the retort he wanted to throw back at her. He should have known better than to ask. Part of him felt a mad urge to let her drop a few more inches, truly scare her, but the idea made him instantly feel ill. That would be enough to give her a reason to despise him. And, if he dropped her, then he would be proving himself no better than Marl.

"Please, Eldin, I swear I won't drop you." Will's muscles were jumping in his arm, up his shoulder to his throat. "But if we stay here, I will."

She hesitated and he squeezed his eyes shut a moment. They were going to dangle here until either their strength gave out or the strength of those holding them from above failed.

The feeling of her other hand grabbing his arm made his eyes fly open. Next to him, the empty rope made a dull thud against the castle wall. Looking down, he could see her pale fingers tightened around his arm, clinging to him as her feet dangled above the nothingness, the endless space that separated them from death.

He turned away again, fighting the pain in his arm, and began to inch sideways, walking along the wall. Each step was an eternity, threatening to slip him sideways, to give away. His hand gripping Eldin was starting to sweat, their grasp becoming weaker. Her fingers were shaking, a muscle in his arm was jumping. If they didn't reach the window soon…he couldn't let his mind think that way. No. one more step and…there!

The solid feel of the window ledge sent relief flooding through his body. His second foot met the ledge and he twisted, letting go of his rope to reach down with his second hand and grab Eldin's arm. Muscles screaming, his breath snarling through clamped teeth, he pulled upward with all of his strength. She was trying to climb with her feet, lift her body, and he braced himself, lifting harder, certain his shoulder would dislocate. Then her feet were on the window ledge and she was falling backwards, knocking both him and her through the window.

With a sickening thud, they crashed onto the unforgiving floor of the dark corridor they'd entered. The pain in his arms was immediately matched by the pain in his head, back, and leg. For a moment, he wondered if he had broken bones, but he was struck with a new worry as the rope tightened around him, pulling him back toward the window. The others thought he needed help, that he still needed pulled up!

Will scrambled to sit upright but Eldin was already on her feet. In a flash of silver, her knife sliced the rope. With a lazy movement, the rope drifted from the window and out of sight.

"Hold on? Really? That was your amazing advice?" she demanded, spinning round to stare down at him, brows raised. "Do you think I'm daft or did you think I'd decided to take up flying lessons?"

Will snorted, pushing himself upright. "A thanks would have been fine."

She gave him a strange look, somewhere between a grin and a grimace. "Well, thanks for not letting me fly. I might have deserved that."

"Honestly, I can't blame you," Will muttered, detangling himself from the remaining rope. He glanced out the window and a thrill of dread that had little to do with the drop rushed through him. "This explains a lot at least then."

"So, you really didn't know?" Eldin asked tentatively.

Will wheeled round. "Of course I didn't! Do you think I'd want Kelkor to fall?" He glowered at her with enough intensity that she took a hurried step back.

"No, I," she was babbling.

Guilt flooding his insides, Will shook his head. "I'm sorry. I just…" Running a hand through his hair, he glanced around the unfamiliar passage. "Look, we better find the others. Kalia needs to be in her chambers."

"You're right," Eldin agreed"Let's go."

They ran, rushing along the dark hallways, pausing at doorways to listen for approaching voices or feet. Will found that the harder he ran, the more he focused on his burning lungs, his aching muscles, the less he had to dwell on the reality. The reality that even now his father might be King of Kelkor. That he might be Prince of a Kingdom he had never wanted or seen.

A door to their side flew open and he and Eldin both leapt sideways in alarm as a pale haired someone crashed through it in the pool of torch light beyond it. He staggered into the hall and spun toward them, relief vivid on his face.

"Will!"

Colin grabbed him in an embrace, his own muscles shaking as bad as Will's had been on the side of the castle.

"Let go, Colin!" Will grunted, pushing him off. "I'm alive, aren't I?"

Colin stepped back, white faced and trembling but grinning embarrassedly. "Alamore, you scared us! Eldin, Niet and Kalia might murder you. Will, I might kill you as well, come to think of it."

"Where are they?" Eldin asked, doubling and clutching a stitch in her side.

"Niet's coming right now. We sent Kalia back in case Serena comes looking for her. Once we realized Will's rope was cut, we knew you had to be in the castle." Colin explained. He turned to Will, brows raised. "Well? What did you find out, what happened?"

"Yeah, we did," Will muttered. He was relieved by the distraction of Niet stumbling into sight, panting and swearing.

Shoving past Will and Colin, Niet launched himself toward Eldin, lifting her in a bone cracking hug and ignoring her string of protest. "You idiot! I thought you were dead!"

"Let me go, Niet, I'm fine!"

He released her and stepped back, his hands visibly shaking as he crossed his arms and glowered at Will and Eldin. "What happened?"

"Rope slipped, my knot was wrong," Eldin mumbled. "I really thought I had it, I really thought it was right." She glanced at Will, giving him the shadow of a smile. "But I guess it's a good thing that Alamore squires have at least some brains in their heads."

Colin laughed darkly. "Some of them..."

Niet turned to Will and, to Will's surprise, stepped forward and embraced him as well, his arms feeling like iron vices. "Thank you, thank you for not letting her fall. You've saved her life. I thought..."

Will struggled to budge free of Niet's grip, throwing a desperate look at Colin. To his immense relief, Colin cleared his throat pointedly. "Perhaps we should stay on task? Remember what we were doing and get out of here before we're all found out?"

"Right." Niet stepped back, grinning sheepishly. "What happened? Did you hear anything about Kelkor? About the King? Are we sending Alamore troops?"

Will swallowed hard, not sure what to say. Niet's face was transported still with the relief that Eldin was alive. Now he would have to end that. He would have to fill that face with the loathing Serena had for him, to explain that his father, Will's own father, had killed King Azric. *And then he will want to hand me over, just like Serena.*

"Niet." Eldin stepped into the pool of golden light still pouring from the open door at Niet's back. Her jaw jutted with forced defiance, but her eyes were overly bright. "Niet, Kelkor has fallen. The King is dead."

"What?" Colin wheeled on Will. Niet turned to him too, the relief morphing to horror when Will didn't deny it. Colin stared a Will a long moment before asking. "Is that true?"

Will nodded, the pain in his aching body rushing back at the small movement. "And, what's more," Will muttered. He ignored Eldin's panicked look, her shake of the head. They had the right to know. Niet had a right to know. Meeting the older squire's dark eyes, Will pressed on doggedly. "King Azric was killed in a battle of Right of Blood, by his own cousin."

Understanding washed over Colin's face, his mouth falling open, but Will refused to look away from Niet's gaze. He wouldn't hide from it. He couldn't.

"That cousin is Tollien's brother, and my father. I swear, I didn't know…but now Marl is King of Kelkor."

CHAPTER NINETEEN

None of them wanted to return to their chambers. Instead, Colin led the way to the Hall of Records where they sat in near silence, staying at the orange glow of embers dying in the hearth. Eldin curled, cat-like, in a chair while Niet stared unseeingly at the sinking flames.

That was how Rowan discovered them sometime after midnight, splattered in food from dishes. He looked between the four of them in bewilderment. "You lot look like someone died. What's happened?"

Colin explained their adventure to Rowan in an undertone. Will was glad of this. He didn't want to go through it again. It was hard enough the first time.

It was a mark of how terrible and serious the matter was that Rowan didn't even joke. He couldn't even bring himself to swear, only sinking into the chair next to Will, cupping his face in his hands, and groaning.

To Will's tremendous disbelief and relief, Niet didn't shoot him the cold looks he had expected. Instead, he started breaking the silence with simple questions about Will–how he had come to Alamore, his life there, his past, and Marl. How Marl had hidden the truth, how he had acted as spy, as Tollien's warrior.

It was astoundingly easy to tell Niet and Eldin everything. The story of the last year poured from him without much effort; from his first suspicions of Marl betraying the Ranger, to Marl attacking him, Rowan, and Colin, and then finding out the truth for himself. Niet's face turned to stone but Will understood. The anger brewing behind black eyes wasn't for him. It was for Marl. Each story he told, with assistance at times from Rowan and Colin, was another reason to hate the man that had raised Will. The hate he could see was the same loathing he felt for Marl, only lacking the fear Will had.

"So," Rowan said after Will had finished telling of the last time he'd seen Marl, when he had saved Haru in the battle of the crypt. "What we can all agree is that Marl is the worst."

"That we can," Colin muttered hoarsely. He groaned, running a hand over his face. "I should have realized, with the Right of Blood in that book, what was going on."

"What book?" Niet asked, sitting upright curiously.

"Eh…" Colin's face burned red, and Will grimaced at him.

"We thought…I thought," Will said, and shifted as Niet and Eldin both fixed him with stern gazes, "that Serena might be the spy," he finished, somewhat sheepishly. When neither of them interrupted, he hurried to add. "But that was just because of the Inanimus that The Cutthroat Prince used on my horse, since it's from Kelkor."

"What book?" Eldin asked, cutting across him with a faint smile. "You don't need to explain that part, just tell us about the book that I'm assuming you stole from Niet's knight."

"What?" Niet looked between Will and Eldin, clearly torn between confusion and disapproval. "Serena's?"

Colin pulled the book from his pocket, face bright red with embarrassment. "This. We've been trying to translate it, but I don't know much Kelkorian and those two don't know any. All I made out was Right of Blood…"

Niet took the book, flipping through the pages with a frown creasing his brow. "It's a book of family blood." He flicked through another page. "All she has in here are the ties of the royals and a list of the powers that turned traitor to the crown before she left."

"Alright, but what the blazes is Right of Blood?" Rowan demanded. "And how does Marl have any right to anything? He's a git!"

"Right of Blood is when an heir can challenge a rightful King," Colin explained in a low voice, face grim. "If an heir has a following and the ability to turn the country to civil war, then he can issue what is known as a Right of Blood challenge to the rightful King. This is done to avoid the bloodshed of a country, the theory being only the King and the challenger might die. Well, one of them at least."

"But how can Marl challenge Azric?" Rowan pressed.

"Revlan and Azric are both sons of King Paradon," Colin continued patiently. "Paradon's brother, Temrod, challenged him to Right of Blood when he was crowned. Paradon won but didn't kill

Temrod. Temrod fled to Thornten, where he married the Princess of Thornten and had-"

"Marl," Will finished flatly. "So, they're cousins."

"Which gave him that Right of Blood," Eldin muttered. She shivered. "After all you've told us, he sounds like he's awful. I can't imagine him as King of Kelkor."

"He's an arse, alright," Rowan huffed, scowling. "Not sure why any of your people would follow him."

"Because he's bloodthirsty," Niet said bluntly, straightening in his seat and, at long last, shifting his eyes from the book to their faces. "Our country has been uneasy for years. Shadow Dale has always pressured the bordering lands. Neither Giltor nor his father have been able to control them well, nor saw issue with that control. It didn't matter to them." His musical accent was shot through with venom now. "And Marl approached that border first. He promised what Azric didn't promise–he used a sword to lead rather than diplomacy."

"And they don't know the truth of Marl either," Colin added, grimacing. "I mean as far as they are concerned, he's Tollien's lost brother. He's related to one of the most powerful Kings in the lands. That promises well for them and probably causes fear in Shadow Dale."

Niet snorted disgustedly. "Disloyal cowards unwilling to have a backbone for their throne. Should I get the chance ever, I'll go back to Kelkor and kill every last Lord, Duke, and Count who has ever turned their back on the crown...and I'll kill that King."

"Go for it," Will said, grinning. "Save me a lot of headache if you do."

"No one is killing anyone tonight though," yawned Eldin, stretching from her curled position in one of the cushy chairs. "We should go to bed before someone comes looking for us."

They had agreed and left the Hall of Records, Niet giving Will a one-armed hug as they parted at the stairs that would take him, Rowan, and Colin to the squire chamber.

"Get some sleep," Niet muttered. "And thank you, again. Eldin's like my little sister. Paxrin would have been so thankful for you. I know you're nothing like him, just by what you risked to save her."

Will had no words and left in silence. But, even after the three Alamore squires returned to their rooms, he laid awake. He stared at the ceiling until Rowan and Colin's breathing had deepened to peaceful slumber.

Tonight was supposed to bring him answers but, lying in the dark, more questions were chasing themselves through his mind. This must have been the Ranger's reasoning for trying to hide who Will was from Serena. But what about what she had said? About how he shouldn't be so fast to trust the Ranger? That the Ranger had his own agenda? Was this what she'd meant? That she thought he would use this shift in power…for what? For bargaining Will to Marl? But the Ranger wouldn't do that. He had been one to advocate in Will's protection tonight, he and Ross especially. *But how well do you know him?* said an unbidden voice in Will's mind. *He hid all of this from you. Perhaps he does have motives he's using you for. He might just not share them with you.*

He didn't tell me this because he was trying to protect me, Will thought fiercely. *He wanted to keep me alive.*

What he wanted more than anything now was to speak with the Ranger. He glanced out the window beside his bed. Night was still gripping the castle, the grey of dawn not yet starting to fade the eastern sky. Would there be a guard there now? Probably. No, he'd risked enough for one night. Squeezing his eyes shut, he forced himself to breathe evenly, to try to fall into sleep.

All he found, however, were the twisting nightmares of old. Marl leered from the darkness, blood oozing down his face from the crooked crown he wore.

***

A hand gripping his shoulder made Will start from his uneasy sleep, sitting upright and diving for the dagger at his bedside.

"Easy, mate!" Haru said, stepping back in surprise. "Don't go killing me quite yet."

Will blinked, breathing to slow his racing heart. "Sorry, bad dream."

Haru frowned and took in Will's exhausted appearance. "You feeling alright?"

"Yeah, I'm fine." Will forced a grin. "Just didn't sleep well is all."

Judging by Haru's shadowed eyes, his disheveled hair, and drawn face, Will realized his knight must not have either. With a stab, he remembered that Haru had been ordered to accompany the King and

Serena to deliver the news to Kalia. That must have been what kept him awake.

"Worrying about the Ranger?" Haru asked seriously, stepping back to sink onto the foot of Rowan's bed. Rowan made a muffled grunting noise of annoyance and attempted to kick the knight, who deflected the strike with long practiced ease. "Don't be a prat, rat."

"Yeah, guess so," Will lied, sitting upright. "Are we training already?" Judging by the grey outside, it couldn't be much after dawn.

"Not exactly," Haru ran a hand over his jaw, grimacing. "I'm actually on the patrol again this morning and Niet volunteered to train you on some Kelkorian hand to hand. He's in the courtyard right now practicing with Robin." His face broke into a broad smile. "Who is losing spectacularly. I must say, it's doing wonders for Robin's ego to be beat by a squire."

Feeling annoyed at Niet for suggesting training, as well as at Haru for waking him, Will reached for a clean tunic. "I'll be out in a minute."

"Brilliant." The knight stood, crossing the room and closing the door before Will had finished climbing out of his bed.

From Rowan's bed came a low evil chuckle. "Guess who gets to sleep in this morning?"

Snatching up his pillow, Will brought it crashing down on Rowan's head with as much force as he could muster. It was almost worth getting up early to hear Rowan's yelp of surprise and the string of snarled gibberish that followed them.

But by the time Will got to the courtyard, scarfing down a piece of toast while he jogged out the doors, he would have taken a pillow to the head to trade places with Rowan. Overhead, storm clouds were growling while, ahead, Niet and Robin were trying to wrestle one another to the ground under the unimpressed eyes of Sir Laster.

"This is the kind of thing that makes me think that eighteen is too young to knight anyone," Laster sneered when Will reached his side. Robin was trying to kick out Niet's foot, which wasn't working well considering Niet had taken up a wide and low stance and was using his back to shove Robin across the courtyard.

"It looks like practice to me, Sir," Will commented.

"If you are ever resorting to this fighting, just know you've already lost," Laster snapped. "You should be using a blade, not your brawn."

Niet shoved upwards in a sudden move, rolling Robin over his shoulder and flat onto the hard ground beneath the same tree where Will had sat weeks before. Several of the soldiers on the wall hooted with laughter or clapped, only stopping when Laster threw them a scathing look.

"Nicely done," Robin grunted, climbing to his feet and brushing the dirt from his tunic. "Alamore, I thought they taught us well in Thornten."

"We learn in the ocean," Niet explained, giving his wolfish grin and holding out a hand to Robin. "It's harder to keep your stance when the waves are hitting your head, back, and knees."

"I bet so," Robin chuckled, gripping Niet's hand briefly.

"Robin, if you're done acting a fool, I'd like to get this patrol out of here," Laster called, striding away from Will and toward the barn. "Niet, your next victim is over there. Please refrain from killing him."

Will had to stifle a grin at Niet's affronted look at being addressed in such a manner. Robin on the other hand, rolled his eyes and hurried to catch up with the older knight.

"Is that knight always so…unpleasant?" Niet asked, striding to join Will at the double doors.

"Yeah, he is," Will admitted. He hastened to wipe the crumbs of toast from his hands, watching as Laster and Robin reemerged from the barn with Haru in tow, each leading their horses. "So, you got up early and wanted to share the suffering, eh?"

"I actually didn't sleep at all. Eldin's room's next to mine and she's been having nightmares since Pax…well, Kalia couldn't sleep either so we sat in Kalia's room and played chess. But that's not the point. I didn't wake you now to make you suffer," Niet said slowly, glancing down at Will and grinning. "I wanted to train with you this morning for a different reason."

"And what's that?" Will asked suspiciously.

Niet glanced toward where the knights were mounting their horses, calling to the guards on the wall, then turned back to Will and lowered his voice. "They're no longer guarding the healing chamber, which means you could talk to the Ranger."

Will stiffened, heart catching in his throat. "Really?"

"Yeah, really." Niet nodded. "The guard who was there part of yesterday, he was saying this morning he refused to watch it another second, that he was too bored there."

Excitement and anxiety congealed in Will's chest and he ran a hand over the back of his neck, thinking. This was his chance to speak with the Ranger. Especially with Haru away from the castle, he could get his answers and find out more about Marl and... he frowned, a new thought dawning. "Why does it matter to you?"

Niet's smile slipped several notches, replaced almost instantly with a grim determination. It was his turn to look away, glowering up at the towers that rose above them. "I want to know more of what's happening. I owe it to Kalia, to Eldin, to Kelkor... I have to know what's happening, more than what...what Eldin heard last night." He lowered his gaze to Will again, frowning. "Does that make sense?"

"What more could you want to know?" Will asked, grimacing.

"What's happening in Kelkor, which Lords, Dukes, and Counts betrayed Azric, anything I can learn about the *traitor King*," Niet spat the last words. "I want to know what he's planning, where he is. It's up to me to defend Kalia now. Paxrin told me it was my duty. I have to keep her safe and I can't do that if I don't know what's happening."

"But you're in Alamore now and if she's not the heir anymore," Will started but stopped, shaking his head. "Do you think he'd go after her?"

"Wouldn't he?"

Will thought of Marl, his cruelty, all the times he had tried to bring suffering to Will either through physical pain or hurting those close to him and nodded. "But you're still in Alamore."

"With a spy," Niet pointed out. "Please, Will. I need to know what he's doing, where he is. If anyone knows, it'll be the Ranger."

"Niet, he's in Kelkor. If he's there then I can't see that-"

"How can you be so sure?" Niet demanded, cutting across him. "Look, I'm giving you a chance to go speak with your Ranger. I'll be your cover story later, I'll say we were practicing. When you get back, we can train."

Will hesitated. Something about Niet's determination was intimidating and made him nervous. Niet seemed to think that he could stand between Marl and Kalia, that he could defend her on his own. He had no idea of Marl's brutality and didn't seem to understand that Marl now had armies at his command. If he wanted Kalia, then what did it matter if he came in person or sent someone?

But Niet seemed unwavering, glowering down at Will. *This is your chance after all,* said a voice in Will's head. *You can ask the Ranger about anything, talk to him about anything, get your answers. You can ask him about The Cutthroat Prince, Serena, Marl, the fall of Kelkor...*

"Alright, let's go," Will said, making up his mind and wheeling round, back toward the double doors. Niet let out a relieved laugh, breaking into a jog to catch up.

"I'll wait for you down here then and hide if I hear anyone coming. But please, just try to find out what Marl is doing, if he's staying in Kelkor, if I need to go there-"

"Yeah, I get it," Will cut across him. He was already regretting agreeing to doing this, but he was at the steps. Sure enough, they were deserted. Inhaling deeply, he nodded a stiff farewell to Niet and mounted the steps. The buzzing that had filled his head the night before was returning with the thoughts of Marl and the Ranger's secrets. As he approached the door, he realized his hands were shaking at his sides, his breathing uneven. He was going to get answers at last. He was going to see the Ranger and get his answers to everything.

The door to the healing chamber was unlocked and swung with almost too much ease under his touch. Stepping over the threshold, Will let it click shut at his back before blinking in the darkness of the room. Someone had drawn the curtains, blotting away the stormy grey of the sky. The only light was the crackling glow of the hearth and, squinting, Will took a step further into the room. His heart sank.

Each of the beds was neatly made, empty. The Ranger had gone. Bitter disappointment welled in his chest and he began to turn when a low laugh made him start. Leaping backwards, his knee collided with the footboard of one of the beds.

"It's good to see you haven't changed too much while I've been away. You still haven't learned the wisdom of not going places you ought to avoid." The Ranger stepped from the darkness beside the door, his cloak drawn about him, his hood low over his face. Despite the shadow thrown by the cowl, Will thought he saw the faint gleam of a white-toothed smile. "I was wondering when you would find your way here. It's good to see you're in one piece."

"Yeah, despite The Cutthroat Prince's best attempts." Will snorted, trying to compose himself. His knee was throbbing in time to his frantic heart. Did the Ranger really have to lurk in the darkness like that? Annoyed, he ran a hand over his leg and sank backwards to sit on the foot of the bed that he'd smashed into. Now that he was here, he wasn't sure what to say. How much could he ask without giving away that he'd been at the window listening?

"I'm guessing you didn't only come to see if your darling uncle was alive and breathing," the Ranger rasped, stepping nearer. Will noticed he drug his left leg, limping slightly. "So, how much have you found out then?"

"What?" Will asked blankly.

"Come now." The Ranger sat gingerly on the bed across the chamber from Will, his injured leg held out straight. "You're not adept enough at lying for these games."

Those words struck flint and steel, sparking an anger Will hadn't even realized he was suppressing. His fingers tightened on the footboard of the bed. "Yeah, well, you seem to be good enough at lying for the both of us."

"Watch your mouth, Will. Squire for a year doesn't mean you can disrespect me without consequences, regardless of your lineage."

"That's all anyone cares about, isn't it!" Will burst, throwing his hands in the air. He noticed the Ranger lean back, seemingly surprised. "All anyone bloody cares about is who my father is and now what he's done! How could you have hidden this from me? Why is it that everyone else knew what Marl was doing but not me?"

"We have spies in this castle who would have made it their job to attack me and the Princess," the Ranger snapped. "Don't you think telling any old squire what was happening and where I was going might have been a giveaway?"

"I'm not any old squire! I'm the son of the man who's killed the King of Kelkor!"

The Ranger stiffened. "How did you..." He paused and groaned, running a hand over his face. "It wasn't just the girl outside the window, was it?"

"What?" Will faltered, surprise breaking the flare of rage. "You knew we were there?"

"Well, I knew at least she was, but I didn't know you were. I heard her swearing." The Ranger let out a humorless laugh. "I don't think anyone else noticed. And I saw the corner of a face through the window when the King rose, but I couldn't make out features."

"Then why didn't you," Will started but the Ranger cut across him.

"Because I don't believe in keeping everyone in the dark. Those two squires and the Princess went through misery on our journey here. They had a right to know."

"And I didn't?" Will demanded. The rage was returning.

"Did I say that?" the Ranger snapped.

"You don't have to. If you'd wanted me to know, you'd have told me before you left," Will growled.

"Before I left, I was working on finding who the spies in this castle are. Serena brought us the first true concerns of the uprising as the last four messengers that Kelkor tried to send were slaughtered. All I knew before her arrival was that Marl had left for the south," the Ranger explained in a tone of forced calm.

Will hesitated, the memory of Haru encouraging to keep his silence flashing through his mind. "How did the others not know then? Is Marl a false name or…" He shook his head. "If he was after Kelkor, how come no one knew that it was the same Marl who tried to kill me last year? My father? What was the point of my being silent?"

"Marl is a second name," the Ranger said, shaking his head. "So clever of you to figure that–though I've no doubt that it was Greyhead that came up with that suspicion. No. When he started this campaign to the south, started the uprisings, he decided to label himself with his regnant name–Prince Temrod of Thornten. He's named after our father, and growing up, Marl was the named used among our family–the name of my mother's father."

"Then Serena didn't know," Will muttered. Then he shook his head, fighting the frustration mounting again. "But she did. And she doesn't trust you or me. But she's not the spy, so why did you care if she knew."

"Because she's the one I knew would make that connection and tell the rest of the knights. How many times do I have to tell you? We have a spy who is getting information from the council, information that should be impossible to reach. What I did was to protect you. I knew I was leaving you in danger. You see, when she arrived-"

"You didn't want me talking to her because you thought she'd tell me the truth?" Will cut across. "Is that it?"

"Didn't I just tell you? My concern was that she'd sell you out to the knights and, therefore, the darling spy who's been doing his best to see you killed or captured," the Ranger snarled through gritted teeth. "Additionally, if you haven't realized, Serena doesn't trust us because of who we are. But, speaking of Serena, it seems you and her charges have been getting along well. I suppose it was her squire who let you know that Oberoan had shirked his guard duties this morning."

"What does that matter?" Will said evasively.

"And what was Niet wanting to know?" the Ranger smirked beneath his hood. "Marl's secret weakness? The way to win a war? Or was he perhaps hoping you'd get information from me for Serena as she seems to think I'm the very spy who passed on the information that nearly got me killed."

A prickle of annoyance ran down Will's neck, but he shrugged, keeping his expression passive. "I wanted to see that you were actually okay…and we were curious if you knew Marl's next plans."

The Ranger laughed coldly. "Brazen of you to come outright with that. I appreciate your honesty but I'm afraid to disappoint you and Niet both. Despite Serena thinking Marl and I are the best of friends, we haven't really caught up on his plans of late. We're more interested in killing one another than renewing our brotherly bonds. If you heard all of what we said last night, you should already know my suspicions that Marl will be on his way back to Thornten to secure his brother's alliance and celebrate his new throne. But I think it best we stay well away from that. Sometimes it's safest to guess and stay in the dark."

Will frowned slightly. The Ranger's words had stirred something in the back of his mind: *the people you think are trying to save you have reasons for keeping you in the dark as well*. Serena had said those words when telling him to pay more attention to his surroundings, to not trust the Ranger. "How does she think you're going to use my tie to Marl?"

"What?" the Ranger stiffened.

"She said that you'd use me for your own gains, that that's what you wanted," Will said, now fighting to keep his own voice even. "What does that mean? How does she think you'll use me?"

Cold tension filled the room, crackling between the Ranger and Will. After a moment, the Ranger gave a huff of laughter, shaking his head. "She will cause mayhem and strife however she can where I am involved. I've given her reason enough not to trust me in my past but that doesn't mean that there is anything you need to worry about."

Will glowered at the Ranger. "I want the truth."

"And I've told you that some truths are not mine to tell," the Ranger hissed.

"You left and with everything that happened, you expect that you can just keep hiding everything? I want answers, Ranger. I'm over the secrets, I never asked for any of this and-"

"And do you think I did?" the Ranger hissed dangerously. "Do you think that I would have wanted this for you or myself? With Marl's shift in power, you're in new dangers and I'm not just referring to The Cutthroat Prince. Tollien and Marl both have a reason to need you, to use you."

"And what's that?" Will demanded.

The Ranger sighed, running a hand over his jaw. "Now that Marl has his own throne, he'll need an heir to keep his people from worrying. He can't claim Tollien's son as his heir-"

"Tollien has a son?" Will interjected.

"Didn't I just say that?" snapped the Ranger. "If he named Tollien's son his heir, the country would uprise against the crown again. They have a history of not caring for Thornten as more than an uneasy alliance and, to make matters worse, Thornten Castle is over a two-week ride from Kelkor's gates. A King could not easily rule both kingdoms. So, Marl will want to bring you to Kelkor as his heir and Tollien will want to ensure you become a puppet for his own heir."

"And why would I ever listen to them? I'd rather die," Will snarled.

"Then they'll see to it that you do die, but not before they try to break you." The Ranger pushed himself to his feet and began to pace, one leg dragging on every other step. "Don't you see, Will? If you are captured, they will torture you. There are things worse than death, worse even than Inanimus. A crippled King who is loyal to Thornten, cowed by them, is better than any King who might rise against them."

Will sat in stunned silence, the Ranger's words sinking in. "But I don't want to be any King," he said slowly, shaking his head. "Surely they could find another heir or…"

"They won't ever believe that you don't want to be King," the Ranger said, waving a dismissive hand. "They only see you as they themselves were when your age–power hungry from the start, willing to murder for a crown, and with your tie to the thrones."

"I don't want any of this!" Will shook his head. "I don't want a tie to the crown, and I don't want to be King. I don't-"

"They don't care what you want!" the Ranger raised his voice, wheeling round on Will. "They won't care! You are either with them or you are against them. Until either you lie dead or sit on a throne, they won't be satisfied. The only way of winning would be to see that you take the throne of Thornten. Only if they're dead can," the Ranger stopped, and Will knew he had said too much.

Staring at the face shrouded in shadow, Will saw the lips press into a thin line and icy understanding settled onto his shoulders, pressing him down. "That's why Serena said you're trying to use me…because you are. You want me to take the Thornten throne."

"I didn't say that," the Ranger countered. But his voice shook slightly, the lie transparent in the dimly lit and deserted room.

Will ran a hand through his hair, feeling his fingers shaking. "That's why the King let me stay here to train then, isn't it? You told him I would be your pawn instead of Tollien's, that you'd be able to put me on the Thornten throne because I'm Marl's son and I have a tie to it."

"That's not true," the Ranger started but Will pressed on, the rage growing in his chest, dark and suffocating.

"You haven't cared about me, have you? It's been about you this entire time! How you can use me to get power! You thought you'd be my right hand or something if Tollien fell and Marl? You could put me on that throne and control me and still live how you want to because you'd shirk the royal line."

"You're being a child," the Ranger snapped. "That's not why it has to be you."

"Has to be me? Has to be me?" Will gave a slightly hysterical laugh. "It won't be me!" He felt his legs shaking beneath him but couldn't recall standing. "You want Thornten to be in an alliance with Alamore? You want Tollien off the throne? That's fine. But you better be ready to wear that crown yourself because I'm not going to. I won't be your puppet any more than Marl's or Tollien's."

"Will, it's got to be you. I can't, it's not my-"

But Will was already turning away. He cleared the distance between the Ranger and the door in a few bounds, throwing it open with such force that it crashed off of the wall. He heard the Ranger say something, but it didn't matter. He wasn't listening. Instead, he was leaping down the steps two at a time, rushing into the entry hall where he nearly bowled through Niet at the foot of the steps.

"Will, what's happened, what's?"

He didn't answer. He pushed through Niet and out the double doors wishing for the first time that he could leave the castle and never see the blue and silver pennants atop the walls again.

CHAPTER TWENTY

Will took refuge in Visra's stall, his back pressed against the wall, watching the bay horse move stiffly over his bedding. The stitches had been removed but the scar was still vivid, the hair barely starting to grow. The bay turned his large head to survey Will between mouthfuls of hay, a curious concern in the dark eyes.

The calm presence of his fiery horse made Will's heart rate steady, his breathing even. Even so, his mind still was tormented with what the Ranger had said, this newest truth. The Ranger was using him. He wanted Will to take Thornten's throne. Despite his fury with the Ranger, his anger that anyone would want to use him like this, Will knew that the Ranger had a point. It would be best for Alamore, but he didn't want it. He didn't want a crown and, clearly, the Ranger didn't either or he wouldn't be trying to push it off onto Will.

"Are you wanting to talk about it?"

Will looked up, startled. He hadn't heard Niet enter the barn and Visra had, uncharacteristically, not pinned his ears at the older squire's approach. He was leaning against Visra's stall door, watching Will with a faint frown.

Will grimaced, pushing himself to his feet and brushing the straw from his tunic. "Not sure if I want to talk or if I feel more like punching something."

"Well," said Niet, laughing and opening the stall door for Will, "That's a benefit of being a squire, isn't it? We can talk while you throw punches. Come on, I'm supposed to be training you anyhow. It's a good distraction."

This seemed an inviting compromise and Will nodded, following Niet from the barn and back toward the jousting field. He was relieved to find it was still deserted. No doubt the other squires were just sitting down to breakfast.

"Footwork is the first thing with any training tactic," Niet explained, vaulting the low fence into the arena. "Make sure you always keep a bend in your knee. A locked leg is a good way to hit the ground hard and get hurt in the process."

"I know that one," Will grumbled, climbing over the fence with less grace.

He was glad when Niet didn't press with talk but rather pointed to his stance, correcting it only slightly, before raising his hands to chest height and lifting his brows. "Ready?"

"Yeah."

Quick as lightning, Niet sprang forward, lifting a hand to block Will's first strike and grip his wrist. With a spin, he twisted Will's arm up and behind his back, knocking his knee into the back of Will's so he crashed to the earth.

"You sure you're ready?"

Panting in annoyance and surprise, Will wriggled free of Niet's grip and straightened, flexing his fingers. "Blazes, I thought I was till you turned into a bloody assassin."

Niet chuckled and stepped back, nodding to Will's stance again. "You have to keep your eyes on my movements. You tried to think of my move before seeing it. So, step back, and we can try again."

Will managed to get one strike in the next round before he was flat on his back, more annoyed than ever. Niet held out a hand to help him out but he ignored it, waving his own hand dismissively and climbing to his feet. "I'm fine."

"Whatever happened with the Ranger has you too distracted to practice with your head," Niet commented coolly, frowning. "If you don't manage to shake it off, you're going to get hurt, even if it is only practice."

"Well, not exactly something I can just shake off," Will snapped. Niet took a step back, surprised, and Will immediately felt a pang of guilt. "Niet, I'm sorry."

"It's alright." Niet shook his head. "It can't be easy to be in your position, with Marl and this Cutthroat Prince after you."

"Wish it was that simple," Will said, sneering at the dirt and placing his feet again.

"Did he mention where Marl was?"

Will looked up to see Niet had paused, his dark eyes narrowed, his face rigid.

"Well, he doesn't really know," Will said, shrugging. "He said he figures he's on his way to Thornten from Kelkor but that's not much help now, is it?"

"No," Niet said slowly, seeming to mull it over. He shook himself and gave Will his wolfish grin. "I suppose not. Now, come on. If you're not going to talk about what's bothering you, why don't you start actually getting in a punch or two? I promise it will make you feel better."

***

It did help. By the time that Haru returned from his patrol two hours later, Will was sweat-soaked, bruised, and too exhausted to feed his own fury at the Ranger. A small amount of shame was even gnawing at the edges of his mind, reprimanding him for his attitude to the Ranger. He shouldn't have been surprised and shouldn't have attacked. The Ranger was, after all, probably acting on Revlan's own orders. But he couldn't shake the pit of anger that still rested in his chest. No. He'd talk to the Ranger but not now. He needed a chance to collect his thoughts.

"Blazes, Niet, did you drown him in dirt?" Haru laughed when Will and Niet met him in the courtyard as he dismounted from his roan. He took in Will's appearance, grinning and reached to brush the dirt out of Will's hair. "You look a mess, Will."

"Knock it off," Will grumbled, batting away his knight's hand.

"He learned how to fall with grace," Niet offered, shrugging and shooting Will a smirk. "Maybe someday you will learn to strike with it, too, eh?"

"Shut up."

Haru laughed again, shaking his head. "Well, get yourself ready for more training. Ross said we can train with him and Colin this afternoon and Rockwood should be about done torturing Rowan with court manners by now. They might join."

"Court manners?" Will asked, frowning.

"Yeah, Rockwood decided he should teach Rowan the proper ways of conducting conversation," Haru explained, his grey-green eyes dancing with mischief.

Laster, passing on his way to the barn, snorted derisively. "By which he means that Rowan is learning not to launch unprovoked attacks on the knights."

"Unprovoked is questionable when it's Laster," Haru muttered but not loud enough for the older knight to hear. "Right then, thank you for training with him this morning, Niet. I appreciate it. Will, come give me a hand getting Thunder tended then we can hunt down the rest of them."

"Right." Will nodded and made to leave with his knight. He caught himself and turned to Niet. "Thank you, Niet…" he hesitated, trying to find the words to express his gratitude to the other squire without giving away what had happened.

Niet seemed to understand however and only inclined his head. "Thank you too, Will. I needed the…practice."

For the span of a second, a shadow crossed Niet's face, darkening his features, stiffening his jaw. Will faltered, bewildered. There wasn't time to ask, however. Haru was calling for Will to catch up and Niet had already turned away, striding toward the double doors of the castle.

Wheeling round to chase after his knight, though, Will couldn't shake the feeling that Niet, like himself, was hiding something more about that morning's meeting with the Ranger.

CHAPTER TWENTY-ONE

Throughout training, Will's mind kept flitting back to the conversation with the Ranger. The idea of challenging Tollien for his throne sent a sick feeling through him, weighing on his mind and distracting him several times so that he was knocked off Admere twice by Rowan when practicing with swords.

"Pay attention, Will," Rowan hissed, reaching from his own saddle to help Will up. "You're making me look good and it's suspicious."

"Sorry," Will mumbled, clambering to his feet again. At the fence, he saw Ross, Haru, Laster, and Rockwood watching him. Embarrassed, he brushed the dust from his tunic and picked up his practice sword. "Sorry," he repeated when he realized that Rowan was still watching him.

Several strides away, Colin gave a hoot of victory as he disarmed Vancely. It was enough to distract the knights attention and Rowan leaned in again, frowning.

"What's going on, Will?"

Will hesitated. He was still torn if he wanted to tell anyone but, at the same time, it felt like the truth might strangle him if he didn't. He was on the verge of speaking when Ross clapped his hands together, making them both start and turn toward the knights.

"That's enough for this evening. If Will takes another fall like that he might get hurt," Ross barked, scowling. "Get the horses tended, all of you, and get into the castle. It's about time for dinner anyhow."

Will glanced upward. He hadn't noticed time passing, too preoccupied in his own thoughts.

"Oh, sweet dinner, how I love thee so," Rowan lamented, clapping his hand over his heart and pretending to swoon from his saddle.

"Do you ever think of anything other than food?" Will asked, grabbing up Admere's reins and pulling himself onto the small horse again. Admere reached round to grab gently at Will's boot, pinning his ears a moment when Will shoved his face away. "Knock it off, horse."

"I think of food and swords, like a true man," Rowan announced proudly, sticking out his chest.

Will gave a grudging snort of laughter, turning Admere toward the gate. "Yeah, that sounds about like you."

"What were you going to tell me anyhow?" Rowan said, trotting Naja to Admere's side. Will tightened his reins as the small red horse reached to nip at the larger animal. Naja bared his teeth threateningly and Admere arched his neck. "Quit it, tiny horse. Naja could eat you for breakfast," Rowan snapped at Admere. "But what was it?"

"I'll tell you and Colin later," Will muttered. They were approaching the fence and he could see Rockwood watching them closely. Catching Will's eye, the dark-haired knight gave his usual grin and turned away. Still, it made Will's chest tighten. Was this going to be his life? People knowing secrets about him first?

In the barn, Vancely began telling them about the patrols along the Western Forest, which he had just been permitted to join that morning with Laster, Robin, and Haru. "It's crazy how silent the woods are over there now," he was saying, brushing down his large chestnut. "I mean, nothing is stirring, not even the bird, but there aren't tracks of the Cutthroats either. Laster thinks that they've moved on to another part of the forest, that we've realized they're there, you know? But, I don't know, it feels eerie. Like I just know that they've been hiding in that wood so well. We rode to the town and tried talking to people there about him, but they seem scared. They seem to think that The Cutthroat Prince is some dark ghost or something."

"He's a fart, that's what he is," Rowan grumbled.

Colin tried and failed to look disapproving, owing to his own snort of laughter. "That's disgusting, Rowan."

"The truth is gross at times."

"What are the town people afraid of?" Will asked, turning from Admere, the saddle cradled in his arms.

Vancely shrugged. "I guess he's been harassing them, riding through the streets at night. The city guard has implemented a curfew to see if that can keep people safe but at least once a night, they get reports of hooded figures riding or walking past windows. People are terrified and they don't even seem to know why."

"Makes you wonder what they're up to," Colin muttered, voicing Will's thoughts. "Like why are they in the village?"

"Beats me, but rogues will be rogues," Vancely said, shrugging.

By the time they had put away their horses and stepped out of the barn, the sky was turning indigo shot through with brilliant reds and fiery orange in the west. Their shadows stretched before them on their way to the double doors. Will lapsed into silence, barely listening to Colin and Vancely, now on the topic of border security and defense.

Defending the border of Thornten and Alamore wouldn't be an issue if Tollien wasn't King, an unbidden voice hissed in Will's mind. He quashed it, gritting his teeth. He didn't want the stupid crown and responsibility for Thornten, he didn't want to be destined to kill Tollien or Marl. He wanted to be an Alamore knight. That was all.

In the dinner hall, the smell of food made Will push all other thoughts to the back of his mind. Rowan beside him gave a groan of longing and started to walk faster. "Come on, Will. I need to eat before I get called back down to the kitchen for my completely ridiculous punishment. Seriously, it's absurd."

"You did tackle Laster," Will pointed out, sinking into his customary seat. He accepted the plate of roast venison from Gabe with a nod of thanks and started to pile food in front of him. In his focus of training and thoughts, he'd somehow forgotten about eating almost all together that day, with the exception of the single piece of toast that might as well have been in another lifetime.

"You lot hear that the King turned down the request of a bounty hunter to search the forest for The Cutthroat Prince?" Jerram asked, wide-eyed. "A real bounty hunter! Came here! Asked if he could hunt The Cutthroat Prince in exchange for payment. Said he had all sorts of traps he could set but the King said no."

"Why would he do that?" asked Vancely, frowning.

"Probably because he's worried someone else like one of these fine young idiots would stumble into it and get killed," Airagon said, sinking into a seat and ruffling Jerram's hair. "Or Rowan," he added, almost as an afterthought.

Everyone except Rowan laughed. "Rude, Airagon," Rowan huffed, scowling. "Are you saying I'm not young? Is that it?"

207

"You're a nitwit," Colin commented dryly.

"Where are your Kelkor friends?" Airagon asked, frowning at Will, Rowan, and Colin. "You were training with them today, weren't you?"

Will noticed his two friends shift uncomfortably but managed to keep his own features bland as he shrugged. "Not sure. I trained with Niet this morning, but I haven't seen the Princess or Eldin today."

"Well, speak of the crown," Gabe said, climbing up to kneel on his seat, the better to see the double doors. "Isn't that them now?"

Will twisted round. Eldin and Kalia were stepping into the hall, both dressed in simple tunics, though he noticed that Kalia wore a black sash around one arm and Eldin's eyes were shadowed with exhaustion. Will expected Kalia to join the knights' table but was surprised when she nudged Eldin toward the squires, smiling faintly.

"Coming to sit with us? Hasn't anyone told you yet that we're trouble?" Airagon said, rising and pulling a chair out for the Princess.

Kalia smiled, the expression not quite reaching her sad brown eyes. "I've survived this long amongst squires such as Niet and Eldin, I think I can handle you all."

Eldin sank into the seat on her other side and Will felt a stab of pity. Up close, both Kalia and Eldin seemed much the worse for what they had heard the night before. Kalia's eyes were slightly puffy, her pale cheeks tinged with red, and her blonde braid was uneven with wisps escaping to fall about her face. Eldin's eyes were shadowed with exhaustion and she wore the look of someone who had seen too much in too short of a life. It reminded Will forcibly of the expression he'd first noticed on Colin's face when he'd met him the year before–a squire starting his journey to become a knight after losing his entire family. Eldin was much the same now. A squire chasing her title as knight without a country, without her mentor, with only those who she had arrived with.

"Where's Niet at anyway?" Colin asked, breaking Will from his thoughts.

Kalia shrugged, reaching for a slice of bread from the tray at the center of the table. "He seemed exhausted. He said he wasn't feeling too well. Perhaps Will was too challenging an opponent for training?" she suggested, giving Will the shadow of a wink.

He grinned sheepishly. "Doubt that. I think I ate more dirt today than I've eaten the rest of my time in training combined."

"If you'd been training in true Kelkor fashion, it would have been seawater instead of dirt," Eldin added, smirking, a ghost of her former self showing through the grief.

"That's disgusting," Rowan grumbled, grimacing. "I mean, that water is the worst."

"What's so bad about seawater?" Will asked, feeling somewhat left out.

"You've never seen the sea?" Kalia asked, wide-eyed. "You're missing out."

"Imagine a lot of water, imagine it tastes salty. It's like licking dirty sweaty padded armor," Rowan explained.

Beside him, Colin gagged on the piece of potato he was eating, and Will thumped him on the back, grinning. "That sounds delightful."

"Don't listen to Rowan, he's clearly bitter about the ocean," Eldin said, rolling her eyes. "It's marvelous. Water as far as you can see and…"

Will forced himself to focus his entire attention on the stories of Kelkor. It not only helped to distract him from thoughts of Marl, but he noticed it seemed to bring both girls out of their dark thoughts. More squires joined the table and soon Kalia and Eldin were being asked question after question–everything from how to properly defend a country so near the ocean, to how to sail a boat, and how the castle was situated. Will could see the homesickness in both of their faces when discussing Kelkor. Still, they plunged into stories of training, tales of the land, while most their audience sat in silent awe. Only he, Colin, and Rowan knew the truth–knew that they were telling of a place that they would most likely never see again.

"Alright, you lot."

Will looked up, taken aback to find Rockwood standing behind him, grinning, arms crossed over his chest.

"If you're about to send me to the dungeons again," Rowan growled warningly.

"They are kitchens, Rowan, and you deserve that punishment. You're just lucky it isn't something worse." Rockwood laughed, reaching to mess Rowan's hair. "But yeah, that's part of it. It's getting late and I think it's time for all of you to get set to turn in. No, Rowan, that doesn't mean I'm letting you off tonight. Get on downstairs and give a hand in the kitchens."

Rowan rolled his eyes and made a rude hand gesture under the table where only Will noticed it. He had to suppress his own laughter. Rowan clambered to his feet, saluted the squires, made a ridiculously low bow toward Kalia, then skipped from the room. Rockwood turned away, shaking his head, eyes raised to the ceiling. "Alamore help us all the day that boy gets a sword. Right, rest of you." He lowered his gaze to the other squires and Kalia. "You best get off to bed. Most the knights have already turned in, but I don't trust you won't bother the Princess and Eldin all night with questions."

Will turned. He hadn't noticed how long they had sat there. Sure enough, the light was gone from the windows, the only glow that of the torches, candles, and hearth. Only Ross, Haru, Serena, and the King still sat at the knights table, speaking in low voices.

"Come on, Will."

He started. Colin was already on his feet, pulling Will's chair from the table. "Up we get."

Rockwood waved to them and departed for the double doors. Will stood with the rest of the squires, said his goodnights to Kalia and Eldin, they followed the others toward their chambers. His silence was unnoticed in the conversations around him. The others were still talking about Kelkor in apparent fascination. None of them knew, none understood.

Colin mirrored his morose quiet and, when they climbed into their beds and the candles were extinguished, Will laid awake, listening to the others sink into the steady breathing of sleep. Exhausted as his body was, his mind wouldn't slow. It replayed his conversation with the Ranger and the rage, hurt and betrayal tightened around his chest. He squeezed his eyes shut, begging his brain to stop thinking, to let him sleep. Sleep didn't come. The minutes dragged on, one after the next, the light under the door that led to the dinner hall fading to shadow.

He forced himself to breathe deeply, to sink into the darkness. On the outskirts of sleep, Will could feel the nightmares pressing at the edges of his vision, waiting to torment him throughout the night.

The feeling of a small hand clamping over his mouth brought Will back to abrupt consciousness, jerking free of the outskirts of sleep, eyes shooting open. His hand had flown for the dagger on his bedside table before he recognized the dimly lit figure crouched next to his bed. Relaxing slightly, Will pulled away from the hand.

"Eldin! What the Thornten was that about? Is it normal in Kelkor to try to scare people who are sleeping or…" He stopped, sitting upright and blinking at her.

Standing in a pale shaft of grey light from the window, he could just make out her drawn features, her haunted eyes. "Eldin?" he asked, softening his voice. "Eldin, what's wrong?"

"Do you know where Niet is?" Eldin whispered.

Will stiffened. He could hear the whimper of fear she was trying to hide in her voice. He shook his head, glancing around the chamber to check if anyone else was awake. "Why?"

"I'll explain, but not in here." She straightened, a pleading look on her face. "I need to find him."

"I'll be right there. Just get out of here so I can change," Will muttered, waving a tired and dismissive hand.

He dressed silently, pulling his cloak over his shoulder and grabbing up his dagger last. For a moment he toyed with waking Colin, as Rowan's bed still appeared empty, but then shook his head. He didn't need to ruin his friend's sleep. Afterall, they'd figure out what was going on and it'd be fine.

Will crossed the squire chamber and stepped into the dinner hall, softly closed the door, and turned to see Eldin pacing before the orange glow cast by one of the large hearths.

"What's going on?"

She started, turning to him, wide-eyed. It was a moment until she seemed to register his question and shook herself. "He's not in his room."

"Are you sure?" Will frowned. "Is he maybe with Serena or…"

"No." Eldin shook her head. "I know he's not. Serena's sleeping in Kalia's room now–I think she knows Kalia was out last night with us and doesn't care for that. I couldn't get to sleep and wanted to talk to Niet, so I went to his room and all I found were maps of Thornten and…" She shook her head again and a little of the fear on her face leached into Will's chest.

"Thornten? What the blazes would he be doing in Thornten?" Will hissed.

"I don't know," Eldin groaned. "But I'm scared."

"Did you tell Serena?"

Eldin snorted. "And have her murder me for waking her then murder him? I don't know if that's where he went and if it isn't…"

"Let's go start looking, shall we?" offered Will, fighting to keep his voice casual. "I'm sure he's around here somewhere. Afterall, there's a wall and a gate, so he's probably inside like us."

Eldin nodded and together they strode across the dim dinner hall, into the entry corridor. Their footsteps rose eerily in the deserted space and Will couldn't quite suppress the shiver that ran over his spine. *Surely there are supposed to be guards here or something,* Will thought, glancing at the doors on either side. But nothing stirred. They might have been the only living souls in Alamore.

At the black double doors, Will reached for the ornate handles but Eldin grabbed his wrist, her nails biting into his skin.

"Ouch!" Will hissed. "What was-"

"Someone's in here," Eldin whispered.

Will turned, eyes straining to see through the shadows that lined the wall, dancing pools of darkness cast by the sparse torches. He wasn't sure if it was Eldin's words or instinct catching up, but he could feel the hair rising on the back of his neck. Someone was there, someone was watching them.

"You're not having adventures without me, are you?"

Will jumped, his feet leaving the ground and Eldin let out a string of Kelkorian that Will was certain she wouldn't have used in front of Serena. Whipping round, he glowered at the figure stepping from the shadows, a wide grin already evident on his face.

"Rowan, I'm going to murder you."

Rowan laughed, shaking his head. "Seriously, are you scaling towers again or what? Because I am not letting the Alamore kitchens keep me from the sweet call of a quest!" He stuck out his chest and struck a pose, as though holding a sword aloft.

"We're not on a quest," Will grumbled, still embarrassed by his own reaction to Rowan's appearance. "We're looking for Niet."

"Have you seen him?" Eldin asked hopefully.

"Funny enough, he didn't come visit me in the kitchens," Rowan said, rolling his eyes. "But I'll come with you two. You know–I'm a master tracker."

"I'm sure you are," Will grumbled, turning back to the doors. He pulled them wide, stepping aside for Eldin and Rowan to leave first before following them into the courtyard.

The first thing Will noticed was the same eerie still that had echoed about the corridors. He blinked, his eyes straining to see through the light of a barely-there moon.

"Shouldn't the guards have lit torches by now?" Rowan asked slowly. Will felt a small amount of smug satisfaction that Rowan now sounded apprehensive. The satisfaction died immediately, however, as his words sank in.

Will turned on the spot. He wasn't sure he had ever seen the courtyard this late, but anytime he had seen it at night there had been orange glows of torches along all the walls, illuminating the stairs up the wall and around the barn. Their absence was unnerving. "I don't know but maybe..." Will started but Eldin was darting forward, sprinting across the darkness.

"Eldin!" Will hissed.

"Girls don't listen that way, Will," Rowan snapped. "Come on."

They raced after her, toward the dark shape of stairs rising along the castle outer wall to the battlements. Eldin was scrambling up the stairs, whispering a string of Kelkorian under her breath that Will couldn't make out. Trying to ignore the open plummeting drop to his left, Will scrambled after her, Rowan, ahead of him, taking the stairs two at a time.

Wind bit through Will's tunic as he straightened on the top step, panting, and turned to see Rowan and Eldin were standing together a few feet ahead, at the edge of the wall. Both were staring down, at the drop that led beyond the wall. A thrill of panic ran through Will and he moved forward, terrified of what he might see lying on the ground in front of Alamore.

He peered over the battlements and blinked, bewildered a moment by what he was seeing. There was no corpse, no broken Niet on the rocks at the base of the castle. Instead there was a rope, trailing downward, a pale line that had been neatly coiled and abandoned at the base of the wall.

"He left?" Rowan asked, bewildered. He turned to Will, raising an eyebrow. "Why would he just leave?"

"How am I supposed to…" Will started then stopped. He took a step back, away from the wall's edge, feeling sick with the realization that was crashing over him. He clamped both hands over his face. *Stupid, stupid, stupid!* He should have seen this coming, he should have understood! Why else would Niet be so fixated on finding out where Marl was? Kalia was here, where she had Serena. Niet didn't need to guard her any longer.

"Will?" Eldin asked tentatively. Her hand rested gently on his arm, pulling his hand down from his face. She fixed him with a steely gaze that reminded him forcefully of Serena. "Will, where's he going?"

Swallowing the panic rising like bile in his throat, too aware of Rowan and Eldin's eyes on him, Will inhaled shakily. "He's going to find Marl. He's going to try to kill the King of Kelkor."

CHAPTER TWENTY-TWO

"What?" Rowan demanded. "You think he's that daft? He's going to walk to Kelkor? On foot?"

"No." Will shook his head, hating himself for the look of dawning terror that was taking over Eldin's face. It was his fault. He'd got the information that Niet needed, he'd questioned the Ranger–not for himself, but for Niet. "Marl is coming back from Kelkor."

The color drained from Eldin's face, her mouth falling slightly open. Beside her, Rowan swore loudly, running both hands through his hair and making it stand on end. "Seriously? And he thinks he's going to cut him off or…how did he even find out?"

Will couldn't bring himself to look at Eldin. Instead, he dropped his gaze to his boots, hating himself. "I spoke to the Ranger and I told Niet and…"

Eldin didn't wait for him to say anything else but took a step back. Will lifted his gaze in time to see her stepping away, shaking her head. With the speed of a fox, she whirled round and sprang back toward the steps.

"Wait, Eldin! Where are you going?" Will called after her, forgetting for a moment they weren't supposed to be outside the castle, that they were in an empty courtyard after midnight.

"To get the horses!" she barked, not bothering to pause.

Will turned on Rowan, astounded. "Is she serious?"

"Well if she is, I guess she intended to jump them over the damn wall," Rowan said, grinning. Noticing Will's complete lack of amusement, he rolled his eyes. "Right then, I'll get the gate."

"The what?"

"The gate? The big iron thing that blocks the drawbridge? Better get the drawbridge too, come to think of it, so we aren't all leaping the wall. You get Naja," said Rowan, nodding decisively.

Will's mouth fell open. "Rowan, we need knights, we need to-"

"We need to get Niet before he runs into The Cutthroat Prince," Rowan snapped. "Eldin's right on that one. Come on, go help Eldin get horses saddled, I'll get the gates."

The reality of Niet's predicament sank through Will's skin like an icy knife. Before he could fully stop to think about Niet and The Cutthroat Prince, he was leaping down the stairs after Eldin. He no longer cared about staying silent. The courtyard might as well have been a grave. Nothing stirred, no one moved. All that mattered now was catching up with Niet and who knew how far a head start he had. An hour? Three hours? He hadn't been at dinner. Had he left then? surely not. Surely someone would have noticed him then...

In the barn, Will almost collided with the side of Eldin's horse as she led him from his stall, the saddle already slung over his back. The grey shied sideways in surprise at Will's appearance and he took a step back, giving a hasty apology, and crossed to Admere's stall. The small red horse was staring at him, head high, ears erect. He nickered a greeting, tossing his curved face, his long forelock falling over his arched nose. Across the barn alley, Will heard Visra's hoof strike his own stall door in annoyance.

"Vis, not the time to be a prat," Will snapped, grabbing up Admere's halter and thrusting it over the horse's face. He wasn't sure he had ever moved so fast to saddle an animal. By the time that Rowan appeared, panting, a streak of grease smeared over one side of his face– Will had already fully tacked Admere and was tightening Naja's girth.

"You would not believe how hard it is to figure your way around the gatehouse. Seriously, I don't know if our port keep is blind, daft, or drunk, but the organizational skills are lacking and oil on everything and..."

"Not time for this right now," Will cut across him, thrusting Naja's bridle into Rowan's hands. "Get this on him and let's get out of here."

Eldin was climbing into her horse's saddle and, across the barn, Will could see Visra leaning against his stall door, ears flat to his neck and teeth bared in frustration.

Launching himself toward Admere, Will was glad when the small horse didn't hesitate to take the bit from his shaking hands. They needed to find Niet. They needed to get to him before The Cutthroat Prince.

Swinging into Admere's saddle, Will twisted round to see Rowan already straightening on Naja, grim face set and determined.

"You ready?" Will asked, fighting to keep his voice even. *Don't let The Cutthroat Prince find Niet, don't let…*

"Born ready, good Sir." Rowan sketched a mock salute.

"Let's get out of here," Eldin ordered. She lacked any of Rowan's levity, her eyes blazing in a way reminiscent of Serena. Will and Rowan didn't need telling twice.

All three squires urged their horses from the barn, out into the courtyard. Admere arched his neck, prancing sideways as they approached the drawbridge at a walk. Behind them, Will heard the crash of hooves against a solid stall door. Visra's fury at not being included.

"Should we be worried about leaving the drawbridge open when we leave?" Will asked, hesitating a moment.

Rowan shook his head. "We've made enough racket someone will be out before long. So, we will not only have backup and the gate closed, but we will also get our necks wrung by Ross and that is the part I am really excited about. What an honor, to die by strangulation of the finest knight in all the realm."

Will didn't answer, only nodding and, together, the three of them loosened their reins and charged forward. His stomach clenched uncomfortably as hoofs clattered deafeningly over the wood of the drawbridge. Surely that sound would be enough to muster whatever guards should have been in the courtyard.

Though none of them spoke, Will urged Admere to take the lead down the path that twisted to the left–away from the dark Western Forest and instead racing in the direction of the other stand of trees. The trees that stood between Alamore and Thornten. That, he was sure, was the route that Niet would take. Marl would be aiming to return to his brother's fortress and Niet meant to kill him on that road.

Admere didn't hesitate, his arched neck stretching to catch the air, speeding beneath him. Had it been any other time, Will might have marveled at the freedom of galloping, the cool night air on his face.

As it were, all he could envision were grey shadows flitting through the night on either side. Twice, he turned his head, releasing one hand from his reins to grab at his dagger but both times it had been either Rowan or Eldin alongside him for a few strides.

None of them slowed until they reached the outskirts of the woods, where the moon's feeble light reflected off the leaves and the path ahead vanished into the blackness.

"The adventure continues?" Rowan asked when Will hesitated, pulling Admere to a halt at the edge of the trees.

Will glanced at Rowan and Eldin. Rowan was grinning nervously, his rein-free hand gripping his dagger so hard that his knuckles stood out white even in the barely-there light of the moon. Beside him, Eldin's face was scared but determined, her jaw jutted in a defiant manner. She gave him the smallest of nods, which he returned, twisting back to the forest path ahead.

"Okay, Ad, onward we go then."

The horse didn't need more encouragement and, seeming to sense Will's discomfort, moved with slow and deliberate strides, ears swiveling to catch any sounds. The further they rode into the forest, the more Will wished they could turn round and go back for help, but Rowan was right. Every moment Niet was out was another moment where he could be killed by The Cutthroat Prince.

Still, he couldn't keep himself from starting at small noises: the wind rustling the branches above them, the flutter of wings as a bird flew between trees, the crack of a twig under Admere's feet, the breathing of their horses. In the dark, the sounds seemed to reverberate, telling the world that they were there. *What if The Cutthroat Prince finds us before we find Niet?* an unbidden voice seemed to ask, over and over, inside his head. *What if...*

The world jerked him from his thoughts as Admere came to an abrupt halt, throwing his head high in the air, his muscles coiling beneath Will. Behind him, he heard Eldin gasp in surprise and Rowan give a string of whispered oaths. It seemed their horses had stopped as well, catching them unaware.

Will reached for his dagger, heart slamming in his ears, eyes straining to make out anything in the night. The trees around them were looming shadows, the thicket impossible to see through. Nothing seemed to be moving but Admere was still standing rigid, his ears pricked forward.

After a moment that might have contained a lifetime, Rowan's voice whispered forward, "Will? You see anything?"

Will shook his head, still staring in the direction Admere was searching. "Nothing. You two?"

"I can barely see my nose in this forest right now and that's on my face," Rowan grumbled. "Eldin? Anything on your side?"

"Not that I can see," she replied slowly. "Might have just been a squirrel? Something that just ran past, and the horses got scared?"

"That's it," Rowan said decisively, making Will start and twist in his saddle, expecting to see an attacker. Instead, his friend was shaking his head, scowling around them. "I don't think I like this much."

"Then turn back," Eldin snapped. Will could tell by her own colorless features that she, like him, had thought Rowan had seen something approaching. She scowled at him, clearly annoyed. "But I'm finding Niet."

Rowan returned her glower. "Did I say I was going to wimp out? I said I didn't like it. You need me here anyway, to protect your fair maiden self."

"Rowan, Eldin, shut up," Will retorted in a sharp whisper as Eldin opened her mouth to argue, eyes flashing.

"Don't you tell me," Eldin started but Will spun, lunging sideways to clamp a hand over her mouth.

"There's something ahead of us!"

They all froze, listening. Even the wind seemed to hold its breath, waiting. Waiting. Then, through the darkness, Will saw the slightest shift of shadow, something moving toward them ahead and he raised his dagger, ready to strike, heart deafening in his ears. Behind him, he could feel Rowan and Eldin do the same. There was a moment of painful realization that he'd led them into this, that they were about to be attacked and...

The figure stepped nearer and gave a snort of disgust, lowering the sword he gripped in one hand. "Storms and seas, you three!" Niet snarled, his features melting from cold fury to annoyance. "What are you doing here?"

"What are *you* doing here?" Eldin demanded hotly. "You shouldn't be here! Did you seriously think you could take on Marl? Alone? And now that he's a King?"

Niet's eyes flitted from Eldin, to Rowan, and finally to Will and his shoulders slackened. He sighed, sheathing the sword at his side once more. All of the fight of a moment before melted away and he ran a hand over his face, groaning. "I want to kill him."

"In case you haven't noticed yet, mate, there's a line and you best get in the back of it," Rowan said, laughing. "We all want to kill him."

Niet looked between them, stormy eyes darkening. "If I find him now, though, before he gets to Thornten…"

"He'll be with soldiers, Niet," Eldin snapped. "He's a King now. Don't you think they'll be expecting something like this?"

"She's right." Will nodded. "He'll be ready for someone to come after him. If they don't know the Ranger is injured, they might even think it's him. Even if he didn't have soldiers around him, even in a one-on-one fight, Marl isn't someone you'd want to duel. He'd still kill you."

Niet straightened, narrowing his eyes at Will. "Are you saying I'm not a good enough swordsman to fight him?"

"He's saying you're being an idiot," Rowan interjected in a sweet voice. "Now, come on. This forest gives me the creeps and, I'm not so sure about you all, but if we could get back before Ross realizes we're gone, I'd appreciate it. Marl is scary and all, but Ross is a short tempered, well-armed, git, who is in the walls that are there to protect us. I think he's the bigger threat right now."

Niet hesitated, glancing back over his shoulder, toward the darkness, and Will saw the internal battle playing out over his features. Sighing, Will shook his head. "Please, Niet. Come back with us. You can't walk all the way to Thornten anyway. Kalia needs you guarding her at the castle."

"But Marl is why I don't have a brother," Niet snapped, turning back to Will, grief washing over his face. "He's why Paxrin is dead."

"And Paxrin wouldn't want you dead." Eldin's voice was so small that Will thought he had imagined it a moment. All three boys turned to her, slunk down in her saddle. Even in the darkness, Will saw the tears reflecting in her overly bright eyes. "Please, Niet. We all miss Paxrin…please come back to Alamore. We'll go after Marl, we'll kill him, I promise, but not right now. Paxrin died to save us. We can't just throw that away.

"Please…please get on Kelpie with me and we'll ride back."

Niet nodded and turned his face away and made a fuss of adjusting the straps of his sword sheath. He was hiding his face, Will knew. Hiding the pain, the grief, the loss. A knot rose in Will's own throat as he imagined Niet's suffering, what he and Eldin had gone through. He had seen what grief could drive a man to do the year before when King Giltor of Shadow Dale had led his army to slaughter over the death of his best knight. His friend Treck had nearly died in that battle, starving for revenge. But this was different. At that time, Will had thought Treck insane, Giltor a fool. Now, however, glancing at Rowan's unusually serious face in the darkness, Will felt a stab of hate and pain toward Marl stronger than ever before. Part of him wanted to break free of logic and charge into the forest, find Marl, and make him pay for what he had done. He hadn't even known this Paxrin, he didn't have brothers, but imagining Rowan or Colin... he swallowed hard and shivered. He couldn't think that way. He had to stay focused.

"Right." He turned Admere to see Niet swinging into the saddle behind Eldin, adjusting himself on the grey's back. "We need to get back to Alamore." He forced a grin, raising his brows. "Or Rowan's premonition of Ross killing us might just come true."

"And then we will need someone to avenge us instead, and that is just going to get exhausting to keep score of," Rowan pointed out. "So, let's chop chop and trot trot back to the walls, shall we?"

A low laugh whispered in the trees surrounding them, making all four squires start. Admere sprang forward several steps, almost unseating Will in his surprise.

Will reached for his dagger again, blood running cold. He didn't need to see the shadows drawing toward them or hear the hiss of steel drawn from sheaths to know. He already knew what to expect even before the cool voice spoke from the pathway behind them, blocking their retreat. "And here I was, imagining I would have to ride all the way to the walls myself. How thoughtful of you to save me the journey."

CHAPTER TWENTY-THREE

"Oh, not this prat again! Come off it, can't you just buzz off and find something better to do with your time? Seriously?" Rowan demanded. Will wished he could throw his elbow into Rowan's ribs to get him to shut up.

The Cutthroat Prince laughed coldly as a low hiss of fury rattled from the forest around them. "Oh, not only do we get the heir to Kelkor, but also two squires and a jester? Lucky us."

"Don't you dare touch any of them," Will growled, tightening his grip on Admere's reins. The small horse shifted, arching his neck and pinning his ears at The Cutthroat Prince's larger black horse. "Let them go and-"

"You'll come quietly?" asked The Cutthroat Prince, the sneer evident in his voice. "Do you think I'm that thick as to fall for that a second time? No. You've used your good graces with me, Will. I won't have you continuing to make a fool of me."

"Don't need Will to help you with that, you do it just fine on your own," piped in Rowan. Will heard a quiet thud and Rowan's grunt of pain. "Eldin, don't punch, it's not ladylike."

The Cutthroat Prince's head turned away from Will to the others and seemed to only now take in Niet and Eldin on the grey horse. Every muscle in Will's body was on edge, his frantic heart echoing strangely in his ears. He didn't like the way that The Cutthroat Prince was eyeing Eldin and Niet, watching them closely.

"A lady in your midst?" he asked slowly. Will braced himself to strike, noticing Niet reaching for his own sword. "Draw that blade and I promise you'll be holding a dead damsel," The Cutthroat Prince snapped. "I've archers in this forest and her life means nothing to me, but I can't imagine that any such noble Alamore squires would be able to stand."

His head turned slowly back to Will and Will could feel the eyes boring into his from under the hood, "the murder of a girl."

"You want to get to her, you'd have to kill me," Will snarled. "Any of them, touch any of them, and so help me I'll-"

"Stab me with that needle you call a knife?" asked The Cutthroat Prince sweetly. "Oh, I am scared now. Let's make this simple then, shall we? I don't want to be bothered with the task of taking all of you back to Thornten but you're coming with us. As the new heir to Kelkor, I think it best you keep your loyalty where your blood is, don't you?"

Will didn't answer, only waiting, teeth gritted, and dagger raised. It took all of his self-control not to recoil at The Cutthroat Prince's words. Behind him, he heard Eldin's gasp and Niet give a low growl. They had known this, they had all known this, but The Cutthroat Prince's words were confirmation. It seemed that he knew already that King Azric was dead.

"I'm sorry, I guess word hasn't reached Alamore yet," The Cutthroat Prince laughed. "I forgot that Marl has been ensuring it wouldn't. You see, if you had just waited in Alamore, you might have heard word from him. I don't imagine it'll be long before he's seeking a meeting with King Revlan to discuss alliances in Kelkor. Pity so many of the messengers sent by the rebels in his country failed to keep their heads long enough to reach you. Entertaining, isn't it? How quickly power can change?" When none of them responded, he snorted in annoyance. "Alright, keep your silence. What's going to happen is this– the girl is getting onto Draccart's horse and riding with him. Will, you will ride with us of your own volition but, so help me, the slightest sign you're going to fight us and she's dead. The other two can ride back to Alamore. If they attempt anything, again, Draccart will kill the girl. Are we clear?"

"You underhanded son of a two bit," Rowan started but Eldin reached across her saddle to cuff him in the back of the head.

"Don't," she hissed. "You're going to make it worse."

"Wise move, girl," The Cutthroat Prince chuckled. "Now, Draccart, why don't you assist the fair lady in changing horses? If we ride out now we can reach Thornten by early morning."

"You're not taking Eldin," Niet snarled.

The Cutthroat Prince sighed dramatically. "I don't think I was asking your permission. You see, that's the benefit of being the one with the upper hand. I've got nine armed riders, there are four of you sharing one sword. I'll let you figure the odds of who would win a fight."

"If your even try to take her, I'll…"

"Niet," Eldin hissed, throwing the older squire a sharp look. Facing forward, Will could see the determination fighting to hide her fear as she turned to The Cutthroat Prince. "You'll let them go."

"Naturally, my lady." The Cutthroat Prince sketched a mocking bow from his saddle, head tilting upwards to keep his eyes on her. "We'll even let them keep their horses."

"Eldin," Will said warningly. "Don't,"

"We don't have a choice," Eldin cut across him, her narrowed gaze still fixed on The Cutthroat Prince. "Niet and Rowan can ride back to Alamore for help."

He could hear the false hope in her words and icy fingers gripped his chest. She knew what they were getting into. She knew, like him, that Niet and Rowan would race to the castle and lead a charge for them but that it'd be too late. The Cutthroat Prince and his riders could have them miles away by then.

"I'll go," Niet turned to The Cutthroat Prince, dark eyes blazing. "You can take me instead."

"And let you and Will find a way to overpower us? I highly doubt that would be as entertaining as you hero type always portray it." The Cutthroat Prince sneered. "I've had enough of this. Hand over the girl now or we resort to blades."

There was a soft crunch of leaves, the sound of Eldin sliding from the horse to the ground before Niet could stop her. "Eldin, don't-"

"Get to Alamore," she ordered firmly.

Will turned away, hating himself for being the reason for all of this. Hating himself for the blood in his veins.

"Good girl," The Cutthroat Prince purred, shifting in his saddle, one hand falling to rest on his dagger. "Draccart, come collect the girl. Make sure she's not armed–you know Kelkor arms their women…the morons."

A shadow detached itself from the dark with the faint song of tack jingling and Will recognized the hulking form, the strange, jagged edge sword swinging from the saddle.

"Alright, girl, get over here," Draccart barked.

"So help me, you lay a hand on her, and I'll rip you apart with my teeth if I have to," Rowan snarled.

The Cutthroat Prince snorted. "If I had the time, I'd ensure you couldn't by knocking your teeth down your throat. You two, step away from Will and the girl. Now. It's time you leave."

"I'm not leaving Eldin," Niet said steadfastly.

"I don't think you understand that you don't have a choice," The Cutthroat Prince said, and Will could hear the irritation tainting his words. "I said go."

"Get out of here." Will turned on Niet and Rowan. "Please get out of here." He could sense the riders around them shifting, uneasy, preparing to strike.

"Will," Rowan started.

"Go!" Will barked, loud enough to make Admere start in surprise.

Rowan threw Will a scathing look before loosening Naja's reins. "Get killed and I promise, Will, I'll never forgive you."

"Fine," Will snapped, barely listening. All he could truly hear was the slam of his heart, the rush of blood in his ears. They needed to get out of here before The Cutthroat Prince changed his mind. He had to find a way to save Eldin and the best chance he had was Rowan and Niet getting help.

Niet said nothing, passing Will with his head bowed, his expression one of the utmost loathing. Will thought it was directed at him until Niet paused, moving past The Cutthroat Prince, and lifting his gaze to the hooded figure.

"Should anything happen to Eldin…"

"You'll no doubt kill me in a painful way, yes, I understand the way that threats work. I get it," The Cutthroat Prince said coolly. "But let me make a promise of my own–do anything to stop us, and she'll be dead."

Niet growled, turning his horse to follow Rowan back toward the path. Will watched them riding away, his heart sinking. They hadn't succeeded. There wasn't any way of escaping, no brilliant ideas rushing forward. He wished that he had woken Haru, brought him along. At least Haru had the brain to get them out of this.

The Cutthroat Prince seemed to read his mind and laughed, shaking his head. "Pity the redhead wasn't with you. I had ideas of how to make him pay for our last encounter. Shame. But there will still be chances to get to him, like we did the guards."

"What?" Will asked, jerked from his thoughts. "The guards?" he thought of the empty courtyard, the silence in the castle. "What did you do to the guards?"

"*I* didn't do anything. I just saw to it that they wouldn't do anything either." The Cutthroat Prince shrugged. "Such as wasting their breath guarding."

Draccart let out a cruel chuckle, reaching down to grab Eldin by the back of her tunic. "Drop your dagger and come on."

"Yes." The Cutthroat Prince nodded. "You're right. We've wasted enough time. Will—you ride by me. That's an order."

Will waited until Eldin had half lifted herself, half been drug up, onto the horse in front of Draccart before he moved Admere to The Cutthroat Prince's side. The faintest gleam of silver in Draccart's hand had him on edge. It seemed that the bigger teenager was more than willing to carry out the execution of an unarmed squire.

"We lead," The Cutthroat Prince purred to Will. "You'll get used to it. It's how royals ride—at the front of the group."

Will didn't answer, only tightening his legs on Admere's side so the small horse pranced forward several steps, arching his neck. For the thousandth time, he wished he had Visra. The warhorse was as good as having one of the knights fighting with them. But he didn't. All he had was this small hunt horse who kept glancing around them in the dark and, on a few occasions, snaking his head to the side to snap at The Cutthroat Prince's dark warhorse.

"Keep that beast on its leash," The Cutthroat Prince ordered the second time Admere's teeth clicked together, a breath away from his own mount. "Or we'll go ahead and dispose of the worthless pony here."

Time was acting most strangely. Each step seemed to take them a mile away from Alamore, away from help, but the night was clinging to them, the day refusing to inch nearer. Will guessed they had been riding for around thirty minutes, and he had glanced over his shoulder to see Eldin and Draccart about fifty times by now. It was almost a nervous twitch.

But she seemed fine, her face pale in the darkness, washed of color by the fear, yet unharmed. Draccart's knife was gripped in front of him, ready to swipe forward into her chest. Will turned away again, disgusted.

"You know, if you let her go, I'll come quietly," he said, breaking his silence at last and turning to The Cutthroat Prince.

The Cutthroat Prince snorted. "And I imagine that if I wish really hard, I might sprout wings and turn into a bird? Is that the game we're playing?"

"She doesn't need to come."

"She's my guarantee that you will come," snapped the hooded boy. "I've had enough of your games. If it wasn't for Marl returning as soon as he will, I wouldn't bother. But I made a wager."

"A wager?" Will demanded, gaping at The Cutthroat Prince. "You're doing this all because of some stupid bet?"

"It's benefitting you and me both, so I'm not certain why you won't just agree to go to Kelkor and be heir. Seriously, you're acting as though being a Prince and serving under Marl will be torture."

"You mean serving as a pawn for Marl and Tollien," Will snarled. He could feel his temper mounting. If not for Eldin behind him, he was certain he would have punched The Cutthroat Prince straight in his stupid face by now.

"I mean doing what your blood dictates." The Cutthroat Prince paused, turning his face toward Will. It was impossible to make out the features in the shadow of his hood, but Will could feel the gaze raking his face. "I can't imagine someone of your status settling for just a knight. It's remarkable that Revlan has eaten that lie as well as he has."

"It's not a lie," Will had to grit his teeth to keep from shouting. "I want to be a knight."

The distant shriek of an owl made Admere dart forward several steps, head jerking upwards. Several of the other horses spooked around them, and a flurry of low oaths rose up in the darkness.

"Keep those beasts under control. If one of you gets thrown, I'm leaving you here," The Cutthroat Prince barked. "We don't have time for this kind of-"

Draccart's horse jerked forward, and he swore loudly, scrambling to grab his reins better. Eldin let out a terrified squeak and moved to tighten her grip on the front of the saddle.

"Draccart!"

"It's this stupid animal," Draccart snarled, shifting his grip on the dagger to tighten his reins. "If he would just-"

"Don't you dare try anything, girl," The Cutthroat Prince whirled round, drawing his sword and Will spun to see Eldin had one hand reaching back, toward Draccart's sword. "If you touch that blade, I'll kill you. Draccart, hold your prisoner. I shouldn't think a horse and a girl too much for you. It's an embarrassment."

Snarling under his breath, Draccart jerked his horse's reins and grabbed Eldin by the back of her tunic. He dug his spurs into the side of his horse and the animal lunged forward with a grunt of pain, gasping and snorting, the white ring around his eyes shining in the night.

A second owl scream made Will turn his head again, stiffening. Something felt off. He could sense rather than see movement in the trees. If this was Niet and Rowan trying some mad scheme to rescue him and Eldin then he would murder them both.

The movement settled, the forest falling silent around them. The Cutthroat Prince snorted derisively. "You are all jumpy. Come on, we've got miles to cover and-"

He didn't get to finish his sentence. Something flew through the dark, missing him by inches, and collided instead with the side of Draccart's horse. The animal screamed in pain and surprise, rearing up on its hind legs. Will and The Cutthroat Prince shouted in unison, both lunging forward to grab at the reins which had whipped out of Draccart's hands. In the chaos of others shouting, the horse striking out, movement in the shadows, Will saw the gleam of the dagger in Draccart's hand fly through the air. Eldin had seen it too. His next shout was drowned by the sickening crash of Draccart falling to the earth. For one wild moment, Will's heart leapt, certain they could break free and gallop.

Then the horse was rearing again, higher now, and Eldin was clutching a handful of mane, swearing in Kelkorian. One of the other riders sprang from his saddle, running to grab the flying reins of Draccart's mount.

"Get that animal under control!" The Cutthroat Prince howled. "Get it under control!"

Another rider moved in their midst. Will's heart froze in his chest at the sight of the small black horse, the white star on the animal's brow. No one else had noticed, they were too busy with Draccart's horse and trying to pull Eldin from the saddle, despite her kicks.

Will forgot about the rider as Draccart sprang to his feet, grabbing Eldin by one arm. She brought the other hand across, smacking him in the face. With a roar of fury, he pulled her from the horse, throwing her to the forest floor. A sickening crack rang through the night, the unmistakable sound of breaking bone.

"Eldin!" Will dug both heels into Admere's sides but another of the Cutthroats was grabbing Admere's reins. The small horse jerked sideways, trying to bite the stranger, but they couldn't get past him to where Draccart was standing over Eldin.

"I think they ought to teach manners to ladies," Draccart said, panting. His hood had fallen over his face and he jerked it aside, leering down at her. Will saw a dark string of blood rising at the corner of Draccart's mouth. Eldin, on the ground, was clutching her arm and gasping.

"Touch her and I'll murder you!" Will snarled. He made to swing from Admere's back only to find a blade pressed against his chest from one of the riders. He didn't bother turning to see who. All he could do was focus his eyes on Draccart. He hated him far more than he hated The Cutthroat Prince in that moment. For the first time in his life, he wanted a sword in order to kill.

"Go ahead and teach them both a lesson." Will turned his head to see The Cutthroat Prince standing behind him, holding the reins of his horse. T laughter in The Cutthroat Prince's voice only fueled his fury.

"Let her go," Will ordered.

"Calm down there, heir," Draccart chuckled darkly.

Will's attention was jerked back to Eldin and her captor. Draccart was standing over her, his fingers caressing the sword at his side as he watched the girl on the forest floor, cradling her arm and gasping for breath. Will saw the color draining from Eldin's face. She'd broken it, he was certain.

"Let her go," Will snarled again, this time directing his words at Draccart.

Around him, he heard the faint laughter of riders, the whisper of a blade being drawn by one of them. He didn't care. Suddenly it seemed worth a knife in his flesh to attack Draccart.

"Settle down there," Draccart shook his head.

"I swear, if you hurt her," Will said, fighting to keep his voice even. "If you kill her-"

"I'm not going to kill your girlfriend, just teach her how to respect her betters." He raised a hand to strike, and Will bared his teeth in a snarl, the blade at his chest pressing closer, ready to slice through his heart if he moved.

"I don't recommend that."

Will, Draccart, Eldin, and all the Cutthroats turned in unison. Standing on the ground, a dagger pressed to The Cutthroat Prince's neck, the shadow of a man tilted his head. "Anything you do to Eldin, I promise you, your Prince here will feel tenfold," rasped the Ranger of Kings.

CHAPTER TWENTY-FOUR

No one moved. Every eye was fixed on the Ranger. Will's heart slammed in his chest and relief washed over him. The Ranger had come for them. They were safe. So long as the Ranger was with them, they'd get out of this.

His relief faltered as he noticed the Ranger sway slightly, one knee threatening to buckle. It seemed he was still weak, too weak. Before Will could think of anything to do or say, the Ranger was speaking.

"Firstly." The Ranger turned his head, nodding to the man holding Will at sword point. "Stow that blade. We'll find out if The Cutthroat Prince bleeds red like the rest of the royals if you don't."

The man hesitated but, at a nod from Draccart, obeyed and pulled his reins, backing his horse several paces from Will.

"Well done on your listening skills. Now, let the girl go," the Ranger said calmly. "Will, help Eldin onto Admere if you don't mind. By the looks of that arm, it's broken, so move gently."

Will swung from Admere's saddle, rushing toward Eldin on the ground. He had half a mind to turn on Draccart and attack. Resisting, he glowered at the larger boy until he took a step back, allowing Will to crouch at Eldin's side.

"That was stupid of me," Eldin moaned, still gripping her arm. She squeezed her eyes shut, inhaling through gritted teeth. "I thought I could stay in the saddle, I threw out my arm and it caught the saddle."

"Eldin, focus," Will hissed. He flinched inwardly at his harsh tone. There wasn't another way to go about it though. He needed to get her to Admere, to get her out of here. He couldn't imagine it'd be long until the Cutthroats decided to attack regardless of the Ranger's captive. "Please, come on, Eldin, we have to go."

She grabbed onto his arm with her left hand, her fingers biting into his muscles. A whimper of pain escaped her tightly pressed lips as she pushed herself to her feet. Will could feel eyes flitting from them to the Ranger, Cutthroats unsure of whether to attack or wait.

"Will, get her on your horse. Now," the Ranger said, his voice cool and even. Will nodded, not turning to see the Ranger. He could feel Eldin shaking as she slung her unbroken arm over his shoulder for support. The few yards between them and Admere might have been miles. Will's heart slammed in his chest, expecting someone to rush forward, to try to stop them. But it seemed the Ranger's prisoner was worth more to them than capturing Will and Eldin. They only waited and watched in silence.

At last, Eldin scrambled onto Admere's back, gasping in pain when her arm struck the front of the saddle. Will flinched, remembering his own ride with broken ribs and knowing in a moment things would be worse for Eldin. The movement of the horse would promise that.

Once settled onto Admere's back behind the saddle, Will turned to the Ranger, waiting for instruction.

The Ranger snorted. "Please start riding now, Will. I think it best you squires not stick around at the moment."

"Don't you need-"

"I said ride, Will," the Ranger warned. "Get out of here."

Will hesitated only a moment before nodding. The Ranger would have a plan and he and Eldin would be a bother and in the way now. She couldn't fight and if he tried to use Admere as a weapon and she fell…well this would have all been for nothing.

Turning Admere toward the trees, Will urged the horse into a canter, ducking the low branches, unable to believe their luck. The Ranger had done it! He had saved them all again! The thought of his bitter words toward the Ranger, his anger, pressed on the edges of his mind and a taunting voice seemed to whisper in his ear; *he saved you to save himself. You're his way to a crown, that's the only reason he saved you tonight.*

No. He couldn't think that way. He had to focus on riding, on keeping Eldin upright in the saddle.

"Oi, Will!"

Will started so hard that he jerked Admere in a half turn, almost colliding with the horseman stepping between the trees.

"Rowan! I'm going to murder you!"

"Chill out." Rowan held up his hands. "You two alright? Did they–hold up, what's wrong with Eldin? Where's the Ranger?"

Eldin managed a muffled whimper and Will shook his head. "Her arm's broken and he was behind us. He's holding The Cutthroat Prince and told us to get out of there. But I feel like we need to go back to help the Ranger get-"

Before he could finish his thought, Niet was emerging between the trees, gripping the reins of Eldin's horse, his face contorted. "Eldin's been hurt?"

"Look, much as I love to chitchat, I'm pretty sure the Ranger said our job was to scatter and cause a diversion," Rowan cut across. "We should probably do that before they come after you two."

All of them started as a roar of fury echoed in the forest behind them. "Well, before that, actually," Rowan finished, somewhat lamely.

"Will, pass Eldin here," Niet said hurriedly. "She can ride with me; this horse can handle the weight."

"What about the Ranger?" Will demanded, even as he helped Eldin bridge the distance between the two animals.

"He wanted us to scatter to get them on our tail," Niet barked. "We have to ride."

"You and me, Will! Adventuring! Causing chaos! Being brilliant!" Rowan said eager. He punched the air. "Onwards on our quest! Listen to that sweet call of-"

His rant was brought up short by the arrow that flew past them while Eldin was settling into the saddle of her horse in front of Niet. Niet swore in Kelkorian. "RIDE!"

There wasn't time to debate, to discuss it further. Will dug both heels into Admere's side and jerked the reins, leading him to the left, off the trail, through the thick branches and trunks. Diving forward through the dark, Will wondered if he might not die by decapitation as trees reached downwards. He had to lean against Admere's lashing mane, flattening against the feel of twigs snagging on his tunic, scratching along his boots.

Admere thankfully seemed intent on keeping him in the saddle and avoided knocking his knees on any trees–though how the horse could see in the darkness, Will had no idea. All he could make out was the pain of thorns biting through his clothing, the rush of air, the deafening slam of hooves. He couldn't tell if they were being pursued, if it was only Admere he was hearing or others. And if it was others, knowing if it were the Ranger or one of his friends was equally impossible.

Admere flattened himself out, running with strides of a larger horse, leaping fallen branches and ditches, his breath heaving from his sides. A light caught Will's eye ahead through the trees and his heart leapt. The distant castle was drawing nearer, he could see windows. Another flash of light. He just barely ducked his face in time to avoid a low branch and vowed not to look up again until he was clear of the forest. It couldn't be long now, not long...

A hunting horn bellowed in the night and Admere increased his speed, the animal careening through darkness at breakneck speed. Another blast of the horn. Will didn't understand but couldn't twist round to see without risking his seat on the horse or—more likely—breaking his head on a rock.

They launched into the valley and fresh air and freedom rushed over his body. Will straightened, pulling Admere back into a canter and twisting round to see the forest behind him. The blood froze in his veins a moment, realizing he was alone. Then, through the darkness, another rider appeared some fifty feet to his right. The whoop that cut through the night told him it was Rowan. Laughing, barely believing their luck, Will reined Admere to a trot at the path to Alamore and patted the horse's sweaty neck. "You're not bad, horse, not bad at all."

"That was brilliant!" Rowan laughed, bringing Naja to a prancing gait at Will's side. "Brilliant, I tell you! One of them nearly caught me—Naja, walk you moron, stop prancing—nearly got me though and I turned, and he hit straight into a tree!"

"What was the horn about? Where are the others?" Will demanded.

"They were a bit behind me and then cut further to the south. So, they'll be behind, but Will, best we can do right now is get to the castle and get help and..." Rowan's voice drifted and Will turned his attention from the forest to his friend. In a faint orange glow, he saw the bewildered horror on his friend's face.

"What is it?" Will asked tensing.

"We might have escaped the Cutthroats, mate, but I'm pretty sure we're dead meat now."

Will followed Rowan's gaze and felt his stomach drop. The castle ahead of them was alive with movement on the walls, light flaring. Now that Rowan had fallen silent, he could hear people shouting. A pool of flickering orange and gold shadow poured from the open drawbridge into the valley and in the courtyard, he saw men running around, horses being saddled.

"All this because we're missing?" Will asked slowly. "Seems a bit extreme for a couple of squires."

Rowan snorted. "You mean four squires–two of whom are the last of the Kelkorian squires loyal to protecting Kalia, one of which is the extremely good-looking son of a powerful Lord, and the last twerp is the heir of our enemy Kingdom, and Kelkor, and somehow of Alamore too."

Will forced a hollow laugh. They were near enough now that the light was reflecting on Admere's sweat-darkened neck, glowing red over the horse's hair. A shout rose up from someone on the walls and were echoed through the courtyard.

"Riders! Riders approaching!"

"No crap we're approaching. What, you think they thought we'd camp out here?" Rowan demanded indignantly.

Will frowned, an uneasy feeling pressing on his shoulders. "I'm not sure they're expecting it to be *us*."

"What's that supposed to mean?"

Will didn't answer. They were close enough now to make out the three people standing on the drawbridge, peering at them through the darkness. In the glow of torches, the thatch of red hair was too recognizable. Haru gave a shout and sprinted toward them, ignoring Rockwood's yell.

"Will!"

Will reined in Admere to keep the horse from stepping on his knight at the foot of the bridge as Haru reached him. Before Will could open his mouth to form a question, Haru had grabbed him around the middle and was pulling him off of the horse and into a tight embrace.

"Walls of Thornten! You're alive, you're alive!"

"Course he's alive you daft rat," Rowan said somewhere above. "But you keep crushing him like that and he's not going to be alive much longer."

Haru released Will from his hug, grabbing him by the shoulders and looking him up and down. "Are you hurt? Did they hurt you?"

"What?" Will blinked, bewildered. How had Haru already received news of their attack? There was no way that Eldin and Niet had returned first. Rowan said they'd cut south to avoid the Cutthroats.

Haru ignored his question, shaking his head and dropping his hands back to his sides. "Thank Alamore, I didn't think that we'd see you back here...we were getting horses ready...and..."

Will stared at his knight. Haru seemed frantic. He'd expected a tongue lashing for being an idiot but Haru was shaking, running a hand over his face.

"For future reference, Haru." Rockwood had jogged to their side, panting slightly. "Don't run toward unannounced riders. It's a damn fine way to get murdered."

Haru gave a halfhearted laugh which Rockwood ignored, already grabbing the reins to Rowan's horse and peering up at his squire. "Alright, how the blazes were you drug into all of this? Where are the others?"

"All of them are right behind us. And all of what?" Rowan demanded. "What are you on about?"

"The Cutthroat Prince's attack," Rockwood said flatly. When Will and Rowan only stared at him, openmouthed, Rockwood groaned. "Don't tell me you left the castle of your own free will. Seriously?"

"What happened?" Will repeated, turning to Haru. "What-"

"Get your reunion off the drawbridge and into the walls!" Laster's voice called down from the gatehouse above. "If you haven't yet understood the concept of a drawbridge, it's made to be shut to keep people safe *inside* and unless you care to tumble in, get off of it."

"Mangy git," Rowan huffed but didn't protest to Rockwood pulling Naja forward into a trot.

Will and Haru walked together the remaining distance into the courtyard, leading a sweat-soaked Admere behind them. Serena still stood on the bridge, eyes blazing.

"Where are my charges, Haru?" she demanded. "Where are Eldin and Niet?"

"They're coming," Will assured her. "They weren't far behind us and-"

"And you left them?" she snarled. "You left them behind?"

"Niet's practically a knight, have some faith in the lad," Rockwood retorted. "Will and Rowan are thirteen. They can't do much to help him anyhow."

"We all got away anyways," Rowan told Serena, swinging off of his horse in the courtyard. "They were right behind me. Then we heard a horn blow and the rider chasing me turned back, so I am guessing the one chasing them did the same."

Serena seemed on the verge of retorting when two more people approached them. one of them broke into a run, colliding with Will and Rowan in a streak of golden hair and a cry of relief.

"You're alive!"

"Blazes, Colin!" Rowan staggered, trying to free himself of their friend's grip. "If the Cutthroats don't kill us, you seem about to!"

Will struggled to break out of Colin's embrace as well, taking in their surroundings. The courtyard was crawling with activity, guards rushing up the stairwell to the top of the battlements while scrambling to pull on leather jerkins or fasten sword belts.

"Well," Serena said, stepping back slightly and glancing back toward the drawbridge. "We need to go find them."

"I quite agree." Rockwood nodded. "And that's something we can actually go do. Colin–see to it your two friends here don't go getting themselves killed or anything for twenty minutes while Haru and I saddle horses."

"Wait," Haru hesitated. "Should we-"

"Come on, Haru," Rockwood cut across him. "I imagine Ross is already about done saddling his horse and we need to get out there and help Serena."

The knights strode away, Haru throwing an anxious glance back at the three squires.

Will shook his head, stepping away from Rowan and Colin to pat Admere's neck and take in their surroundings. The change to the courtyard since they left could not have been more drastic.

"What happened here? How did you all know we were gone?" Rowan demanded of Colin.

Colin took a shaky breath, shaking his head. "I'm not sure how the knights really found out. All I know is that one minute I was asleep, the next Laster was shaking me awake demanding to know where you– Will–were."

"He didn't ask about me?" Rowan asked, offended. They crossed the courtyard toward one of the hitching rails. Will slung Admere's reins over the top of the rail, the horse nearly knocking him aside as he itched his sweaty face on Will's back.

"We noticed you were gone soon as I was up," Colin continued, reaching to help Will with unsaddling Admere. "That's when the panic really set it. I tried to get Laster to let me help look for you, but he made me go wake the knights and he came out here to the gatehouse since the guards..." Colin paused, and Will saw his face twist in a pained look. "Well..."

"What guards?" Will asked, frowning. "We didn't see any."

"They were behind the barracks," Colin explained. Now he looked ready to be sick.

"Behind the barracks? What? Like having a drink fest or some stupid dance that they didn't invite me to?" Rowan asked, addressing them with his head under Naja's stomach as he uncinched the horse's girth. "Why weren't they at their post?"

"They're dead," Colin said, and Will suddenly understood his friend's green tinge. He himself felt ready to be ill.

"What?" Rowan gawked up at Colin. "Dead? How?"

"Someone knew which guards would be on night watch it seemed." Colin ran a hand through his hair, closing his eyes a moment as if trying to forget something terrible. "Someone slit their throats... but after Laster came out here, I went to wake the knights. They roused the other guards and that's when Serena woke up and found that Eldin and Niet were gone." Colin shook his head. "And that didn't make sense to me. I get that The Cutthroat Prince and his followers somehow got into Alamore and caught you all."

"That's not what happened," Will cut across Colin. "The Cutthroat Prince wasn't in the castle, he was in the woods and it was-" Before he could finish recounting the true version of events, however, a shout rose up from the wall.

"Rider coming in and looks like someone is injured," Laster called down.

Will spun round, heart slamming in his chest, and started at the open mouth of the drawbridge. Eldin had been hurt, he knew that, but what if it was something else. What if Niet or the Ranger...the Ranger. A sick weight dropped in his stomach. How had he forgotten the Ranger?

The Ranger had just saved them and Will had been so caught up in the escape, in what had happened in the walls, that he hadn't spared a thought of the Ranger of Kings. The clatter of hooves rose before the single horse appeared. Will saw Eldin slumped forward, Niet's hair sticking to his forehead with sweat, struggling to keep her on the grey horse with one hand, controlling the animal with the other. A shout from the barn announced Serena's reappearance. She ran toward her squire and Eldin, reaching up to help Niet lower Eldin out of the saddle.

"What's happened?" Serena was asked, her voice shaking. "What happened to her?"

"She fainted," Niet panted. "Her arm is broken–careful of it please. She fainted as we fled and..."

"Will, where you going?" Rowan called.

Will didn't bother responding, darting the distance between the hitching rail and Niet, reaching up to grab the reins of the grey horse. "Did you see the Ranger?" Will demanded. "Did you-"

His question was strangled in his throat by Niet's head shake. "All we saw was Rowan for a while, then we turned. They were after us," he hurried on, and Will could hear the pleading in his voice. "They were on our tail. I thought they had us, then the horn blew and we were riding for our lives."

"I get it." Will nodded. And he did. They had been fleeing for their lives.

"The Ranger?" Serena asked sharply. "What about the Ranger? Did he have something to do with this?"

"He saved us." Niet shot her accusation down with a sharp look. "He saved us. *Again.*"

Serena snorted, her lip curling, and whirled round. Carrying Eldin like a child, the woman stalked back across the courtyard and through the double doors into the castle.

"The Ranger is out there?"

Will hadn't heard or seen Ross leave the barn, leading his black and white stallion, a stony expression on his face. Will nodded, still struggling to speak through the knot in his throat.

With a growl, Ross turned, swinging himself easily onto the warhorse. Tilting his head upwards, he waved to Laster on the wall. "Keep the bridge down, I'm going to find the Ranger."

"Ranger?" Laster shouted back. "Why is the Ranger out there? Isn't he supposed to be in the healing chamber, being dramatic about a bit of poisoning?"

Ross didn't craft a response, digging his heels into his horse's sides and charging into the darkness. Will watched him go, dread seeping through his veins. A moment later, Rockwood and Haru were leading their horses from the barn as well, grim expressions on their faces.

Haru's face lightened at the sight of Niet and Eldin. "You're safe!"

"Ross went after the Ranger," Will said, unable to keep his silence. "He's still out there."

Rockwood swore, spinning round and vaulting onto his chestnut horse. "Haru, come on. It'd be just like Ross to try to murder the lot of Cutthroats."

Haru didn't hesitate, pulling himself onto his roan and the two knights thundered after Ross into the darkness.

"He says murder the lot of them like it's a bad thing," Rowan commented casually. Will hadn't noticed his friend come to stand behind him. "But if they were all dead, I honestly wouldn't give two farts."

"Your way with words is astonishing." Niet shook his head, sliding down from his palomino. Exhaustion was drawing on his features, making him look older.

Will turned away from his friends, glancing back over the bridge. His skin was crawling, his mind still reeling from the night's events. Surely the Ranger had a plan to escape. He had just assumed the Ranger would get away like they had but if so, why wasn't he here? What had the horn been about? His stomach churned sickeningly. Had it been a signal that the hunt was over? They had their caught quarry?

"Healer, all of you."

Will started, turning to see Laster striding down the steps, his amber eyes narrowed at the group of squires. "The younger squires can tend your horses, but you need to get inside and taken care of. I have no doubt you'll need to be in a council before dawn."

"A council?" Will asked. "What for?"

Laster raised his eyebrows, pausing on the bottom step. "Use your head, Will. Soldiers are dead, our defenses breached, and the King will probably want to know where his Ranger ran off too since we all thought he was intelligent enough to give himself time to heal. Colin, see to it that Kelkor and the two troublemakers get to the healer, won't you?"

"Yes, Sir." Colin dropped the brush he'd been using to untangle Admere's mane and gave Rowan and Will a firm look. Will hesitated, torn between the comforting warmth of a bed and the desire to wait, the need to see the Ranger return. He'd been terrible to the Ranger, and again the man had come through and saved his life. He had to be sure the Ranger was okay.

"I'll make sure Ross comes up when they return," Laster said, and for the first time his words were edged in a softer tone, more comforting than Will had ever heard them. He seemed to catch the tone himself because his sneer curled his lip a moment later. "And I can only hope the Ranger returns with him, so I have the chance to throttle him myself."

Will nodded. There wasn't anything else for them to do. Even if he had wanted to help find the Ranger, he knew the knights would never let him and what good would it do anyhow? He'd put them in more danger. All because of his stupid blood.

He waited as Gabe appeared–blurry eyed and tousled hair–to take Niet's horse. Then the four of them, Colin in the lead, started across the courtyard. They had just reached the double doors when a guard shouted something from the top of the wall. All of them turned, Will's heart swelling in his throat. The dark forms of two horses were returning. Instantly, he recognized the roan as Haru's horse. His heart leapt and he pulled away from the others, moving toward the bridge again.

"Will, wait!" Colin grabbed Will by the back of his collar and Will turned, confused. His friends were staring ahead, their faces unusually grave. Even Rowan was wide-eyed in horror, his mouth falling open, all traces of his smile gone.

Turning back to the bridge, Will's heart froze. Haru was leading the second horse. He recognized the slight built black mare, her head high in panic, twisting to look behind them with each step. Her eyes were ringed in white and her coat glistened in the torch light. It wasn't until they had stopped in the center of a now silent courtyard that comprehension crashed into Will's chest. Someone grabbed him as his knees buckled a step. He stared in disbelief at the Ranger's mare, at the blood that had been spilt over her shoulder and neck and, worst of all, at the hauntingly empty saddle.

CHAPTER TWENTY-FIVE

"I need to get back out there, I can help, I can-" Will was babbling and he knew it, but he still struggled to get free of Rowan and Colin, dragging him backwards through the doors and into the entry hall.

"Like the blazes you will," Rowan snarled. "Let the knights find him! Niet, mate, either give a hand or get out of the way won't you?"

Niet was standing in the corridor, his face twisted in a mixture of anger and shock. He shook himself and nodded, stepping aside. "They'll find him, Will."

"But I need to help, it's my fault," Will pressed on.

Colin grunted as Will pulled to break free, his elbow catching his friend in the stomach. "Don't be a fool, Will! That's what The Cutthroat Prince will want. He'll want you to get back out there."

"Elbow Colin again and I'll knock your block off," Rowan grunted, heaving Will toward the stairs of the healing chamber. "We're trying to help you!"

Niet grabbed Will around the middle, hoisting him out of Rowan and Colin's grip. "Come on, we're getting upstairs and checking on Eldin. You need doctored anyway."

"I'm fine! I need to help find the Ranger! We need to go! We need to help!" Will struggled but Niet didn't budge, gripping Will tight enough to press the air from his lungs. He carried Will up the stairs like a protesting toddler, growling a few choice words in Kelkorian until they were pushing through the door to the healing chamber. It wasn't until Rowan had slammed and barred the door that Niet unceremoniously dropped Will onto the floor.

His knee collided with the ground painfully, but he barely noticed, scrambling upright and spinning to face Rowan and Colin. He stared between them, desperate. "Come on, please."

"You'll cause more problems than you'll solve being out there right now," Colin said flatly. "If you want to help the knights find the Ranger, then the best thing you can do is stay here."

Will looked at Rowan, pleading in silence. With a pained look, Rowan shook his head. "Col's right, Will. We can't help, we screwed up and bad this time."

Will opened his mouth, ready to argue but someone cleared their throat behind him and he turned. Serena was standing beside one of the beds, watching them with a dangerous gleam in her eyes. "What's going on out there?"

Will turned from his friends to Niet to Serena and, when it became clear that none of them were going to answer, he straightened, matching her glower. "The Ranger's horse returned without him."

The orange light of the torches in the room cast a shadow across her face as she turned away, snorting. "So, it seems he's pulling a trick again."

Anger crawled up Will's back but Niet spoke before he could retort. "The horse is blood covered."

Serena turned back to them, eyes flashing. "What?"

"Haru just brought her back," Will explained, now desperate. "And we need to help. I can help, I'm not hurt, I just-"

Serena cut across him with a hollow laugh. "Help? Help? Do you see what you've done tonight?" She waved a hand behind her at Eldin's feebly stirring form, her face still dirt streaked and unconscious. Serena took a step nearer to them, anger twisting her features. "Your help could have got my squire and Eldin both killed. The Cutthroat Prince was in these walls. It could have just as easily been Kalia who he captured."

"The Cutthroat Prince wasn't in these walls," Will retorted, ignoring Rowan's hushing movement. Colin groaned behind him. It didn't matter. He was terrified for the Ranger, frustrated with the knights, and livid with the whole castle for keeping him locked away like a child right now when he should be helping right what was wrong. What he'd done by being stupid enough to get Niet that information about Marl in the first place. "We left the walls, we-"

"Then it was your fault the bridge was wide open?" Serena snarled. "Your fault that my squires were out? You realize what you risked? Because you can't control your own stupidity–just like the Ranger. You think that a bit of Royal Thornten blood makes you better, makes you above the rest of us, and thought it'd be fun to ride after The Cutthroat Prince? Is that it?"

"No, I-"

"And what about the guards then, eh? Was it that you didn't notice they were dying and dead or that you didn't care? Maybe you knew and-"

"Serena!" Niet reached out a hand to stop her as she approached Will, a murderous glower in her green eyes, teeth bared. "It wasn't him."

But Serena either didn't hear him or didn't care. She was raising her voice, straining against Niet to take another step toward Will. He took a half step back, between Rowan and Colin, his own instinct to fight hesitating. Serena was a knight, a furious knight, armed with a sword. Hadn't she already proven she'd throw a knife at him when they broke into her chambers? Whether she was the spy or not, she might try to kill him or, worse, Rowan and Colin.

"Maybe you thought you'd earn some further favor being an idiot, or you just like to flaunt your stupid blood rights. Or maybe you decided to go back to your father, back to being an heir, but I don't care. I don't trust you. You're just like the Ranger. He's probably out there now, reporting to his brother, causing this panic as a diversion." She pulled her arm free of Niet, her hand leaping to her sword. Will reached out an arm to block Rowan behind him, his other hand diving for his dagger, heart slamming in his throat.

"Serena!" Niet's voice boomed through the room. He stepped between the three squires and his knight, sword in hand, barring her way.

"Out of my way, squire," Serena snarled. "Get out of my way!"

"It wasn't his fault!" Niet bellowed. "It was mine! I led them out, it's my fault Eldin's arm is broken. And the Ranger didn't just ride off. He saved our lives. He saved Eldin and all of us. I'm the one who took us outside the wall."

Serena took a step back, confusion breaking the mask of anger. "What?"

"Yeah, it was me." Niet lowered his voice but still stook braced between Serena and the Alamore squires, blade at the ready to fight. "I climbed the walls. Eldin realized I was gone and Will and Rowan helped her come after me."

"What about the guards then?" Serena demanded. "What about..." She shook her head. "What?"

"The spy," Colin said firmly. "It must have been the spy who killed the guards. They were trying to make it easy for the Cutthroats to either get in or for them to get out."

Serena looked past Niet, at Will, then back at her squire and took a hesitant step backwards. "And what of the Ranger then?" she asked, some of the anger leaching from her voice.

"He must have heard us leave or something before the knights did," Niet continued in a tone of forced calm. "He came after us. The Cutthroat Prince and his riders separated our group. They took Eldin as bait to make Will ride with them. The Ranger found Rowan and I riding back and ordered us to come with him, to cause a diversion while he got them out. Rowan threw some rocks and then Will showed up with Eldin a short while later. We scattered. I don't know where he went but Haru's just returned with his horse. Rockwood and Ross are out looking for him still."

Serena snorted, releasing the hilt of her sword and moving to step past Niet. He sidestepped, blocking her way and she gave him a cool look, brows raised. "Out of my way, squire."

"You're not touching Will," Niet growled. "It's not his fault what he was born to be."

The shadow of a smirk flitted over the knight's lips then faded to a grim thin pressed line. "I don't intend to harm him. If you all would move." Her eyes drifted back to Will's and she gave the smallest of nods. "I intend to help find the Ranger." When all four squires fixed her with distrusting glowers, she sighed. "I don't intend to be in any debt to that man for saving my squire's life from his own stupidity. Now step aside. They'll need more help to search the forest."

"Come on," Colin muttered, pulling on Will's sleeve.

Will paused, watching Niet step away, not sure he trusted Serena to be anywhere near the Ranger. She seemed to hate him enough she might just murder him to simplify her life. He stood steadfast in front of the door as she approached. It was she who had planted his doubt of the Ranger, she who had known his truth and plans. She had never lied but she'd been the reason for so much mistrust between him and the Ranger now. They glowered at one another a long moment before she rolled her eyes to the ceiling.

"Storms of the sea, I swear I won't kill him, boy."

"I don't trust you."

She fixed him with a green glower and shook her head. "I never said you had to."

"Why do you hate him?" Will demanded. "What did he do to you?"

It was Serena's turn to falter. She looked away from Will, toward the dancing flames of the hearth, then back at the squire and shrugged. "This isn't the time for old stories. If the knights are to find the Ranger, they'll need my help. Please move."

Will finally stepped aside, his chest tight, and watched the knight pull open the healing chamber door. She almost collided with the round-nosed healer who was on the verge of pushing through the door on the other side, his arms full of bandaging and clean sticks. He yelped in surprise, leaping aside and Serena pushed past wordlessly, stalking down the steps.

The healer turned to the four squires, scowling as though it was their fault for his surprise. "Well, if you're hurt, pick a bed and let me look you over. If you're not, get out of my way or assist."

"I can help." Colin stepped forward, ducking his head politely and relieving the man of his armful of bandages.

None of them spoke after that. Will walked to one of the beds, his mind humming with empty panic and exhaustion. He didn't protest or fight against the healer when he was forced to drink a bitter tea that was supposed to help him sleep. He didn't even notice the stinging pain when the healer applied salve to the slices over his face and arms. When the medicine in the tea took hold and started to pull him into sleep, he still felt that strange numbness. The last thought to cross his mind was the sight of the Ranger swaying as he held the knife to The Cutthroat Prince's neck and the realization of how weak he had still been. The Ranger had been too weak to run…and he'd known that even before he arrived to save them.

246

CHAPTER TWENTY-SIX

Will first thought it was the faint grey light in the eastern window that woke him until the hand lifted from his shoulder. Turning and blinking against the heavy exhaustion that clouded his vision, he saw the broad shouldered and towering form of Ross lowering himself into the chair beside his bed. Standing behind Ross was Colin, bouncing nervously on the balls of his feet. The knight looked haggard and exhausted. His blue eyes were bloodshot with lack of sleep, dark shadows resting beneath them, and the lines in his brow were deepened by its furrow as he frowned at Will.

"How are you feeling?" Ross growled.

Will blinked again, trying to make sense of his surroundings. He wasn't in the squire chamber. Why wasn't he? Why did Ross look so grim? Was this the healer chamber and, if so, was the Ranger...the Ranger...

Will sat up with a yelp, causing Colin to take a step back and, in one of the other beds, he heard Rowan's small shriek of surprise and a string of swearing. "Did you find him?"

Ross held up a silencing hand, his stony features impossible to read. "Steady, Will."

"Did you find the Ranger?" Will pressed. He didn't need to be treated like a patient. He was fine. He'd had a few scrapes from trees but that was it. "Is he back?"

"No," Ross said bluntly, and Will stared, mouth falling open in silent horror. "We found the scene of the fight not long after the mare found us in the forest. But they were gone, all of them. There was some blood but not enough to track by."

"So maybe he was hiding?" Will offered wildly. "Or..."

Ross shook his head and Will's voice died in his throat. "He wasn't. We've searched nearly all night–Serena, Haru, Rockwood, me and Laster. Not a sign of him anywhere with the exception of that horse."

"Did you try to track the riders to see if maybe-"

"As far as Thornten's line," Ross said, interrupting his questions. "But that's it. We can't risk riding to Thornten right now. It would have left the castle under defended."

Will remembered the guards and his stomach churned sickeningly. He turned away from Ross, feeling ill, and took in his surroundings. Three of the other beds were occupied. Rowan, Eldin, and Niet were all sitting upright and listening. Their faces echoed the horror he felt.

"We're still searching though," Ross added hastily. "We've employed the help of a few people from the town as well, anyone who can ride and track halfway well. We're not giving up looking for him."

Will nodded mutely, unable to speak through the knot in his throat.

Ross pushed himself to his feet, sighing. "But for now, if you are all up for it, the council would like you to join us. We need to sort out what's happened. Colin tried to fill me in, but the King wants you to speak for yourselves."

Without a moment's hesitation, Will scrambled from the bed, grabbing up his torn cloak from the foot of his bed and throwing it over the pale sleeping tunic. From the other beds, Rowan and Niet were already springing to their feet, grabbing up their tunics and weapons. Ross watched in silence until Eldin reached her unbandaged arm to grab her dagger from the side table.

"Not you, Eldin."

"What?" Eldin stared at him, openmouthed. "I was out last night; I should be there."

"Your arm is broken. If it heals wrong, your days of a knight will never begin," Ross growled dangerously. "You're staying here. That's not a discussion."

With a snort of disgust, Eldin dropped back against her pillows and scowled at the knight but held her tongue.

"I'll be back as soon as we're out," Niet promised. "And I'll bring Kalia so you can tell her your story."

Eldin didn't answer and Will hurried to look away. She seemed on the verge of frustrated tears.

"Right then," Ross said, striding toward the door. "They're waiting." He held it open, his blue eyes unreadable, jaw set. Without a word, Will led the way through, Rowan and Colin at his back and Niet stepping out with Ross. None of them spoke in the journey down the steps. The castle was eerie and still, though outside the walls Will could hear the clamor of voices, the sounds of guards going through training. It had to be early morning still, he was certain. *So not too long. The Ranger still might be out there...*

"Did we miss breakfast?" Rowan asked, pausing in the dinner hall. He looked between them, clearly crestfallen.

Ross snorted, not bothering to slow his stride. "No, it's delayed. The cooks have been feeding the soldiers on the walls. You'll go out to the courtyard for breakfast *after* the council."

"Yeah, that's fine," Rowan grumbled, breaking into a trot to catch up with Will and Colin. "Just let this poor squire wither and die, that's fine."

Ross ignored him, pushing through the door to the squire chamber. Will was surprised to find that all their fellow squires were gone, their beds already made. He couldn't form a question of where they had gone but it seemed unnecessary as Ross grunted, jerking his head toward the bed he was passing.

"Squires are on wall guard for the morning, learning under some of the soldiers."

At the door to the council, Ross hesitated for the first time, glancing back at the four squires. His brow furrowed, dark eyes hardening. "All you need to do is tell what happened. Don't elaborate and, for the love of Alamore." His eyes shifted to Niet, "Don't bring anger and emotion into it. We just need to know what's happened. We aren't hunting Marl. This isn't the time for revenge or hatred. We're trying to understand how you were out and what happened to the soldiers. You're not in trouble," he added when Rowan opened his mouth. "You're being questioned. That's all."

Turning away, he opened the door and waved them through. Feeling as though the weight of the world pressed on his shoulders, Will stepped into the council chamber followed by his friends.

All of the knights sat in silence, with expressions of weariness similar to Ross's own. Kalia sat to the right of King Revlan, her face pale and drawn, her eyes haunted. Catching Will's eye, she shot him the ghost of a smile which he attempted to return though it felt more like a spasm over his lips.

Catching sight of Haru, Will hurried to the empty chair at his knight's right. His knight gave him an exhausted half smile that did not quite reach his grey-green eyes.

"How are you?" Haru muttered, his eyes following Ross across the room to the seat beside the King.

Will grimaced. "Not bad," he lied.

Haru's grim smile was enough for Will to know the knight hadn't been fooled but there wasn't a chance to speak further as the King rose to his feet.

"Council, we are gathered to discuss the events of last night." The power that always surrounded the King was present, though Will could feel the cold fury crackling around him like storm clouds. "Last night the castle was attacked from within our walls. We lost twelve soldiers–the entirety of the night guard–and never knew we were under attack."

"Which means the guards didn't see it coming either," Bane said flatly.

The King inclined his head in agreement. "Indeed. Which leads me to believe it was our spy that killed the guards."

"A spy who is, more than likely, in this very room." Laster sneered. His amber eyes narrowed, flitting from face to face. "Anyone care to admit it now?"

"They might be in this room or they have already left the castle," Serena added coolly. All eyes shifted to the Kelkor knight, seated on Kalia's other side, her arms folded over her chest. She met the gazes with a proud look of defiance, brows raised. "Don't pretend it hasn't occurred to any of you."

"That what hasn't occurred to us?" Ross asked. Will pressed slightly back in his seat. Ross's voice warned of danger.

Serena snorted. "The Ranger." When no one spoke she continued, arms still clamped tightly over her chest. "He's known about every plan; he knew the route he would be taking with Kalia and the others. He's the only one not in the castle today and-"

"And he's the reason we're here," Niet cut across his knight, giving her a scathing glower. "He saved us last night, I've already told you. He's how we escaped."

"And the best actors make the best spies," Serena pressed, lip curling in disgust.

"Enough," the King barked, cutting across Niet who'd opened his mouth to retort. Turning to the squires in the room, the King sighed, seeming older than ever. "I think it best we know exactly what happened last night from those who might have seen anything. Would you mind explaining, if you weren't captured from within Alamore's walls, what you were doing out? And how did you leave the castle?"

Will shifted uncomfortably, shooting Niet a sideways look. Anything he said would sound like an accusation. Even if they had been after Niet, it wasn't his fault they hadn't gone for help. That'd been their stupidity.

To his relief, Niet rose, clearing his throat and gripping his hands behind his back. "It was my fault, King. I'm the reason the others left the castle, they came looking for me."

The King's expression remained calm and unchanged as he asked. "And why, Niet, would you leave Alamore?"

"I wanted to find Marl, King." Niet hung his head. Will saw Kalia's eyes brighten and her fingers curl into tight fists in her lap. "I wanted to kill him for killing King Azric."

"Don't we all," Laster said quietly.

The King nodded. "Understandably. But Niet, why would you leave last night? What made you pick them to go?"

Niet straightened, raising himself to his full height and Will felt a stab of admiration for the squire's bravery as he met the King's eye with a defiant glower. "Because I had Will find out where Marl would be. I helped him get to the healing chamber to speak to the Ranger yesterday."

Next to Will, Haru swore under his breath and Will closed his eyes a moment. He could feel all eyes shift to him. When he opened his eyes, Colin was watching him in confusion, Rowan was frowning, and Haru had shifted his gaze forward to Niet again. His grey-green eyes were stone cold.

"You helped him speak with the Ranger?" the King asked, frowning. "How so?"

"One of the guards was saying he was tired of guarding the Ranger, that he couldn't be bothered with it," Niet continued. "I heard him say that. Haru was on patrol, and I offered to train with Will. But I told him that the Ranger was unguarded, and I lied to him, King. I told him I needed to know where Marl was because I was concerned for Kalia's safety. Will went to the Ranger..." Here Niet paused and Will braced himself. All the knights knew who he was now but this was the moment the Ranger's motives could come out.

Niet shook his head and continued slowly. "He told me that Marl would be heading back to Thornten. I figured my best bet was to meet him in the forest. I told Serena I felt unwell with the news she had given us of Kelkor's fall and I went to the Hall of Records. I went through maps all day then left that night. I scaled the wall to leave the castle."

"When was that?" Ross asked in his growling voice. "And did you see anything?"

Niet shook his head, turning to Ross. "Not long after sunset. I'd hoped to go between the change of the guards, so I didn't think much of the silence. Someone was on the wall when I started to go down the rope, but I was worried I'd be stopped. I went faster and didn't see who it was."

Laster swore under his breath and Rockwood groaned, running a hand over his face. "You got lucky there, squire. That person was probably the same one who killed the guards. He would probably have come to kill you," said Rockwood, dropping his hand back to his lap. "Real lucky on that."

Niet nodded. "I realize that now, Sir."

The King's gaze shifted to Will and something in his face softened slightly. "So that's when you went to find Niet?"

"Yes, King." Will nodded. Haru gave him an elbow in the ribs and the slightest jerk of his head, gesturing Will to stand. He did so, his knees feeling unsteady under his weight. Swallowing, Will continued. "Eldin came and woke me. She knew I was training with Niet that morning and said she'd gone to check on him and he was gone. She found the maps and got worried, so we went searching for him. We ran into Rowan in the entry hall-"

"And I volunteered to protect them," Rowan piped in, despite Rockwood stepping very obviously and intentionally on his foot.

Will nodded. "He came with us. We got in the courtyard and realized it was quiet. No one had lit the evening torches. We went to the wall and found the rope that Niet had used to drop down the wall. It was us, King, who opened the drawbridge. I realized what Niet had done, why he had left, and we knew we needed to find him."

"And it didn't occur to you to get a knight?" Laster asked, smirking.

"Well, you see, there's a murderous Cutthroat Prince outside these walls and we thought we should probably find him first," Rowan growled, glowering at Laster. "You know? Like fast? Rather than take time to explain everything happening."

Will ignored Laster and Rowan, who were shooting daggers at one another, and continued. "We rode out and found Niet in the forest. We were getting set to return when we were surrounded by The Cutthroat Prince." Will paused, racking his memory. The night had been a blur, but hadn't The Cutthroat Prince said something about them making it easier for him? *"And here I was, imagining I would have to ride all the way to the walls myself."* "I think," Will said slowly, "I think they'd intended to come to the castle to…to come after me." He choked on the last few words, hating himself for them.

A silence fell across the room. Will noticed Bane's brow furrow, Henry throw a fleeting look to Ross, and Richard's face soften with pity. That was perhaps the worst. Worse even then the sharp look from Serena, the flames in her green eyes.

"If they intended to come to the castle, they knew the guards were dead," Rockwood finally said. Will had the sense the knight was speaking more to break the quiet than anything else. "Which means, honestly, you lot getting out was luck for us. Who knows what damage they might have done if they got in."

"True." The King nodded and gave Will the ghost of a smile. "You can sit, Will. Thank you for your honesty."

Will nodded, sinking back into his seat. Haru patted him on the shoulder and, at last, Will chanced a glance at his knight. Haru raised his brow and gave a heart-hearted grin.

"But this isn't without damages," Richard rasped, turning his gaze away from Will at last and facing the King. "We haven't found anything of the Ranger apart from his horse." Serena snorted and Richard shot her a cool look before continuing. "Which means that either they killed him and brought him along–which seems a waste of energy–or they captured him alive. But, this is the Ranger. He might very well be tracking them afoot."

"Or he's going with them of his own free will," Serena muttered, as though unable to resist.

"Did you not hear that your squire say that the Ranger is the reason they all made it back alive last night?" Laster shot. "Or were you too busy hating him to listen."

Will caught Rowan's indignant look out of the corner of his eye and suppressed a mad urge to laugh. Laster lecturing another knight on hating the Ranger? It seemed too much an irony. He could see even Ross looked taken aback.

"Again, that could be a ploy," Serena snapped. "We have no reason to trust-"

"You have no reason to trust him, perhaps," the King said, cutting across Serena. "But I do. Your suspicions have been heard, Serena, but I have no reason to think the Ranger has been the spy."

"He's the reason I even got to Alamore," Kalia said in a low voice. She straightened in her seat, seeming only now to notice that the attention had shifted to her. Clearing her throat, she continued. "The Ranger was nearly killed getting us here. Actor or not, he wouldn't have done that. That would be too much to risk. Serena, I understand your mistrust of the Ranger, but he did his best to protect me, and I am in his debt for that. We are also in his debt for the safe return of Niet and Eldin."

Serena huffed, shaking her head. "Perhaps but, that brings us to a new worry. If the Ranger isn't the spy, we can't keep risking our lives for the Thornten heirs." Her eyes flitted toward Will, and he tensed, already sure he knew what she was about to say. "You're risking lives, you're spending lives, protecting an heir whose father killed your brother, Revlan."

The King didn't have a chance to speak before Haru had shot to his feet, closely followed by Ross, Rockwood and Niet. All four of them moved to stand between Serena and Will. "And what's that supposed to mean?" Haru snarled. His hands had curled into fists at his sides.

"It means his being here is a danger for us, for the King, and for Princess Kalia. It's my duty to protect the Princess, Haru, and his being here is a threat!" Serena retorted, springing to her own feet. "He doesn't belong here. He's like the Ranger, he's Thornten."

"And you're Kelkor," Ross growled. "You want to get rid of him, you'll have to go through us."

"Yeah." Rockwood nodded. "All of us."

Robin and Miller rose as one, both reaching to grip their sword hilts. Then Richard, Henry, Bane... last to rise was Laster, fixing Serena with a spiteful sneer.

"You're walking thin ice," Ross growled. "I don't know what you do in Kelkor but in Alamore we don't throw a boy to the wolves for what his blood makes him."

"Nor do we in Kelkor," Kalia said sharply, standing as well. Spinning on Serena, Kalia shook her head. "I'm not a Princess anymore. Don't use my prior title as your excuse."

"What?" Serena turned to Kalia, face falling. "My lady..."

"I'm not your anything," Kalia snapped. "I'm not Princess, or Lady. My father *was* the King. He isn't any longer, which means I'm not a Princess."

"We don't know for sure," Serena said, sounding suddenly desperate. "We might-"

"Sit, all of you," the King ordered, running a hand through his hair. "I won't have my council at one another's throats. I don't believe the Ranger is a spy, nor more do I believe that making Will leave would change anything. It would be a sign of weakness, not a parlay and his blood doesn't make him any less worthy to be a knight than any other Alamore squire. I've had enough of this fighting." The King waved a hand. "Sit down. That's an order."

The knights sank into their seats, though Haru's gaze never left Serena, his hands shaking in his lap.

"For now, we must focus on the guard," the King continued. "I don't believe our spy is in this chamber. I do believe, however, that he knows too much. If The Cutthroat Prince had intended the murder of the guards to be his chance to strike, he'll be disappointed and he'll know that we're more attentive inside of Alamore now. I want knights in every guard around the clock. Any soldiers acting out of line are to be reported. Any strange behavior, anything out of the normal, I will hear about. Is that understood?"

Will watched the others nod and waited, heart slamming. This didn't matter to him. There was only one thing that mattered.

"Then, in that case, this council is dismissed." The King clapped his hands.

Will shot to his feet, feeling Haru grab at the back of his tunic. "What about the Ranger? We're still looking for him, aren't we?"

The King's face fell, the lines in the corners of his eyes deepening. For the first time since the council had begun, the anger faded from his black eyes. Shaking his head, he ran a hand through his hair. "We can't exhaust the guard on finding the Ranger, Will. We will keep those willing to search from the town looking but I won't send any more guards or knights. We need every armed man here, protecting Alamore. I'm sorry, it's the best I can offer you."

Will looked from the King to the knights. None of them met his gaze. Even Ross turned his face away, bowing his head as if in defeat. There wasn't anything else to say then. The King had spoken and the knights of Alamore would obey. Will turned to his friends, and saw his same shock etched in their faces.

Then chairs were scraping over the floor, people rising to leave. Rockwood patted Will on the back as he passed, and Laster averted his eyes. Serena swept from the room in silence. Will didn't move, letting people move past him. His feet were stone, planted in the earth. He couldn't move. Moving now would be taking the order of the King as truth. Admitting that they had lost the Ranger.

"Come on, Will, we have to go." Rowan was pulling his sleeve, his face drained of color. Colin stood beside him, still openmouthed, shaking his head, apparently not sure what he could say to help.

"Hold on a minute."

They turned. Haru was standing behind them, running a hand through his hair. "Will, you alright? The healer said you didn't seem hurt, but I know there's a lot going on, a lot happened…"

"I'm fine," Will managed to force the words through his numb lips. "Just some scratches."

"Right." Haru nodded, glancing toward the retreating knights. "Look, I need to get some sleep but then I'm taking you three for training. Ross and Rockwood will be taking one of the patrols after they get rest, so we'll be on the walls. I'd recommend you three get any sleep you can, as we'll be up there all afternoon."

Will nodded, waiting. He could tell Haru wanted to say more but was struggling to find the words. After a pause Will raised his eyebrows in a silent question.

With a sigh, Haru grabbed Will with one arm in a side hug. "You about scared me to death last night. Don't do that again or I'll murder you. Deal?"

"That's my threat," Rowan complained.

Haru raised his eyebrows. "I'll murder you too, twit. Blazes, when Laster said you were gone." Haru shook his head as words failed him again. "Never mind that. Look, you get rest but then it's onto the walls for training and guarding. We'll work on battle tactics for defense as well as some archery from the wall. Just promise me you'll stay out of trouble."

"We will," said Will, nodding and stepping aside as Haru released him.

"One more thing." Haru fixed Will with a stern look. "You're working with Rowan in the kitchens for the rest of this week."

Will nodded and turned, letting Rowan and Colin lead him from the room. He barely noticed the route they took, the twists of corridors, the stairs they climbed. It wasn't until they were stepping into the grey light cast by heavy clouds above that Will blinked in his surroundings. They were on the wall he'd scaled down with Eldin two nights earlier. Two nights...it might have been a lifetime.

Rowan flopped onto the ground running both hands over his face with a groan. "I can't believe it."

"Nor I," Colin said, somewhat shakily. He lowered himself next to Rowan, closing his eyes.

"Might be that this is all a bad dream," Rowan offered, raising his brows. "Maybe we'll wake up and find we've imagined this stupid Cutthroat Prince and that the Ranger is fine and-" He stopped, catching sight of Will, still standing, staring out over the courtyard. "Will, it's not your fault. If anything, it's mine. I was the idiot who said we shouldn't go for knights."

Will shook his head, not turning from the drop. His eyes were being pulled toward the innocent stand of trees that marked the edge of the forest. "I should have known better. I should have realized something was wrong."

"Who the blazes would have thought they were going to kill twelve guards inside the walls?" Rowan demanded. "Will, you heard them. There's a chance that he's still out there. They didn't find a body. Richard's right, it'd be just like the Ranger to try tracking them."

"Yeah, maybe," Will muttered without conviction. He turned from the drop to see both his friends watching him. They looked like the knights—worn from the night's events, exhausted by more than just lack of sleep. It was as though the events of the past few weeks had aged them years. Maybe they had. "Look, I need to tell you two something. When I talked to the Ranger, when I found out about Marl, he told me something else too. He told me…he admitted more like…" How were the words so hard to find, to tangled, when the anger and reality had been so real? Straightening, Will inhaled slowly. "The Ranger wants me to fight Tollien someday. He thinks I should battle him for Right of Blood."

He realized the reason the words had been so difficult the moment he spoke them. It was painful to see the dawning looks on both his friends' faces, Rowan's shock, Colin's terror. "You? Fight Tollien?" Colin asked slowly. "For the crown of Thornten?"

"Yeah." Will nodded, sinking to sit in front of them, his back pressing against the battlements. "He wasn't going to tell me, but Serena made me curious. She kept talking about him always having a reason of his own, a way for personal gain. I guess this time, it was me."

"I don't believe that," Colin said stoutly. "I don't think he brought you to Alamore just for his own gain."

"Then why did he?" Will demanded. He stared at Colin, hoping his friend would have an answer.

Colin shook his head. "I don't know but the Ranger isn't that way. Serena sees him that way because of…well because of something that happened but that doesn't mean…" It was Colin's turn to struggle with words.

"If the Ranger was doing this for his own gain, why wouldn't he just go fight Tollien himself? He's royal blood, right?" Rowan asked, frowning. "Surely he can go murder him, make our lives easier."

"He said it wasn't his right," Will huffed, running his fingers over the stone floor beside him. "He keeps acting like he can't tell me the truth. And I got mad." He squeezed his eyes shut, shame and the empty panic twisting in his throat. "I got mad and stormed off. And now he's missing. He might even be dead because he was trying to save us."

"Wait a minute!" Rowan said excitedly. Will looked up to see Rowan bouncing, rubbing his hands together, a broad grin stretching his face. "Maybe the Ranger decided you're right! Maybe he's gone to challenge Tollien to Right of Blood."

"On foot?" Colin asked skeptically.

"He might have? It'd be harder for The Cutthroat Prince to track him," Rowan pointed out. "He could be even now almost to Thornten on foot and then challenging Tollien at dawn!"

Will glanced between his friends, his spirits lifting despite his mind insisting the thought was absurd. "You know, maybe…"

"He'd have to have a following in Thornten," Colin said flatly, shaking his head. "And I don't think he'd do that without talking to the King."

"You're really being a downer right now," Rowan complained. "Look, let's just say that the Ranger did go there, and challenges Tollien. It's his right and, I mean, Marl got a following pretty fast in Kelkor…"

Will was barely listening. He had leaned his head back against the wall to stare up at the churning grey clouds, heavy with the promise of storms. His friends were putting on a brave face, he knew it. The prospect of being expected to fight Tollien, of taking his crown, was enough to make Will sick.

It was some time later that Colin, finally resigning and agreeing there was a small chance that Rowan had a point but that they needed to get to the lower floors to help out, that they all stood. Rowan gave Will a one-armed hug, grinning.

"Maybe by this time tomorrow, the Ranger will be a King. King Ranger of Thornten," Rowan pronounced it as though introducing a royal to court.

"King Ranger?" Colin snorted. "He's got a name, Rowan."

"Yeah well, I don't know it so he's King Ranger of Kings, which is a long and somewhat confusing name." Rowan rolled his eyes and bounded toward the door.

Will hesitated, hanging back with Colin a moment. "I'm sorry, Colin. Sorry we left. It was just…"

"Don't apologize." Colin waved a hand. "You were doing the right thing. Niet needed to be saved. Sometimes the right decisions don't have easy answers. Come on now, or Rowan will eat all the breakfast and we'll train on empty stomachs."

"You think the Ranger is in Thornten?" Will asked him, following Colin toward the door.

"I think I have no idea where the Ranger is," Colin replied, shrugging. "If he doesn't want to be found, he won't be. But I don't feel that The Cutthroat Prince would keep it a secret either if they'd killed him. Honestly, Will, all we can do is wait."

Will nodded and followed them through the door, onto the twisting stairwell.

CHAPTER TWENTY-SEVEN

Waiting was a form of torture. Will was certain of that by the time night fell. The only good thing was that the waiting had been full of training and, after the training, a night of helping Rowan in the kitchens cleaning dishes. Rowan hadn't made any friends in the kitchen due to his unhelpful habit of randomly quacking like a duck and splashing water over passersby. This meant that by the time they had washed all the dishes on their own, it was late, and Will was drenched from head to toe.

"Don't look so grumpy, you should feel honored," Rowan said, climbing the stairs from the kitchen next to Will.

Will glowered at him, wringing the hem of his tunic. "Honored?"

"Yeah, you got to see a Rowan Duck in the wild. Pretty rare creatures."

Half snarling, half laughing, Will took a swipe at Rowan's head with one hand but Rowan had already bounced up two steps, out of his reach. "You're a prat," Will called up, grinning for what seemed the first time since the Ranger's disappearance.

"I am amazing!" Rowan bounded up the remaining steps, waiting for Will at the landing that would lead into the dinner hall.

"Yeah, well, amazing one–you've got a potato skin in your hair."

"Oh, gross," Rowan groaned, shaking like a dog and spraying the landing with water and the single potato skin. "This is ridiculous. Laster is a real prat for making me do this. All I did was check that he was on his guard. I'm keeping him alive, really."

Once they'd changed into dry clothing and climbed into their beds, Will was glad for the exhaustion. His eyelids grew heavy and pulled him deep into sleep before the nightmares had a chance to plague at his mind.

When nightmares did arrive, Marl leered above the Ranger's crumpled form. The Cutthroat Prince's laughter rang through his head and the forest, dark and empty, spun around him. He couldn't stand to fight Marl, to help the Ranger. Marl was lifting his sword and...

Will woke with a start to the sound of a horn being blown. Rowan in the next bed swore and fell to the floor in surprise while Colin was sitting upright, reaching for his boots.

"The blazes is that?" Will demanded groggily, reaching for the dagger on his side table.

"Royal messenger," Colin snapped. "Seriously, do you two study anything ever?"

"Why bother? Studying hasn't yet made me happy as food does," Rowan grumbled, pulling himself back onto his bed.

But Will was awake and scrambling into his boots, grabbing up his cloak, a sick knot in his stomach. The Ranger. Colin seemed to be having the same thought and was hurriedly buckling his dagger belt over his sleeping tunic. "Come on, Rowan."

"You can't be serious right now?" Rowan demanded. When neither Will or Colin answered, only continued to dress while other squires blinked in bewilderment, Rowan pulled himself out of bed with a groan and grabbed up his own boots.

The three ran across the castle, through the corridors, and into the courtyard. A party of riders was standing on the bridge, a white banner of parlay fluttering feebly beneath another banner–the sea green fabric with a bronze kelpie. In front of the riders, blocking their way forward, were four Alamore knights. They stood to either side of the King, their hands resting on their weapons, faces set– Laster, Ross, Haru, and Rockwood.

Will slid to a halt, staggering a step forward as Rowan collided with his back. Colin came to a halt at his side and the color fled from his face.

"Blazes, why'd you two stop?" Rowan demanded.

But Will wasn't listening. He couldn't break his gaze from the rider in the center, astride a fine black horse. His chest plate gleamed silver even in the feeble light breaking through the clouds above, his black eyes dancing in triumph above his black beard. He was speaking to the King of Alamore, a humorless smile showing white teeth. On his black hair, a thin bronze crown glinted with green and blue stones, giving the sense that the crown was alive with the water of an ocean. The man paused, seeming to sense squires' gazes on him, and his eyes shifted past the King, resting on Will.

"Well, if it isn't my own *heir,*" hissed King Marl of Kelkor.

"Oh, damn." Rowan grabbed the back of Will's tunic as though expecting him to rush forward but there was no need. Will's legs had turned to lead, and he couldn't move a muscle. His mind was screaming for him to turn away and run from this man, the monster, while the part of him that had driven to hunt The Cutthroat Prince, was the same part of him that wanted to dive forward for an attack. But Marl seemed prepared for a fight, his hand gripping the hilt of his sword, the riders on his either side alert and armed.

"He's not your heir," Ross growled, stepping sideways to stand between Will and Marl.

Marl laughed coldly, raising his brows. "And you intend to stop me from reclaiming him?"

Ross nodded and Haru moved as well to Ross's side. "You'd have to go through me as well."

"Boy, don't think spilling your blood would, for a heartbeat, bother me," Marl sneered. "I've no problem killing an infant knight."

"Yeah, well you've got to get by me and Laster as well, and I doubt you'd manage it, but I welcome you to get off that horse and give it a go. Believe me, we'd love the chance to tear you apart," Rockwood snarled.

"This is enough," the King snapped. "Marl, I decline your offer of an alliance negotiation. Alamore will not side with the man who murdered my brother."

The dark eyes shifted from Will to the King. "No? You would rather war between us than see sense? Lives will be lost, Revlan, if you don't step down from pride and see reason instead."

One of the riders behind Marl gave a snort of derisive laughter. Colin gasped and Will felt his elbow dig into his ribs.

"What?" Will hissed, glancing toward his friend.

Colin wasn't looking at him but rather the rider to Marl's right, his face taut. "Look at that rider."

Will didn't get the chance as something large and solid barreled past him, nearly knocking him to the ground. A moment later he realized that it was Niet, bounding toward Marl.

"No!" Will's cry made Haru spin. The young knight grabbed Niet before he could reach Marl, struggling to hold him back as he snarled and kicked, eyes fixed on the man that had murdered his King.

Marl let out a bark of humorless mirth. "One of my own subjects seems too eager to greet me!"

"Niet, knock it off! Quit!" Haru was struggling, red faced, and straining to keep Niet from springing at Marl. "Will, Rowan, Colin, help me!"

Will broke the ice that had frozen him to the spot, sprinting to Haru's side and grabbing one of Niet's writhing arms. He was nearly lifted from the ground with the force of Niet's struggle. A moment later, Rowan was clinging to the arm on his other side. Then Colin's hands were grappling to help Haru.

The riders were laughing at the struggle and the grief stricken Kelkor squire battling the four of them to get to Marl. Will felt himself dragged forward several inches and planted his heels in the ground, pulling back with all of his strength. "Niet, he'll kill you!"

"I don't care, let me go, I want to kill him. He killed Azric, Paranella, Paxrin..." Niet was grunting between breaths, white faced with fury.

"That's enough, lad," Ross growled. He pushed past Will and Rowan, grabbing Niet's shoulders in a pincer grip.

"Marl, get your circus out of here." Laster sneered, amber eyes flashing. "If you think you can intimidate us into an alliance, then you clearly are more of a moron than you look."

Marl's face contorted with hatred and for a wild moment Will felt certain Marl would strike down to kill Laster where he stood. But, after a long pause, he gave a forced and horrible smile. "How no one has killed you is a miracle, Laster. That is one thing I will consider to be a benefit if Revlan decides against alliance with Kelkor's new rule."

"I have decided against it," the King said coolly.

"You would rather risk this country falling in war than form an alliance with the new King of Kelkor?" Marl laughed coldly. "You value the life of that boy." He waved a hand toward Will. "And the death of your brother more than the lives of your people? Perhaps you are more like your brother than I believed… only difference is that you have a pulse, for now."

"They are among my people," King Revlan growled. "And I value honor and trust, two things I could never believe you have. An alliance with you is postponing an inevitable betrayal."

Marl's face darkened. "I wouldn't be so hasty in making your decision. Not until, of course, you know what's at risk."

"And what would that be? The chance to see you make a fool of yourself firsthand?" Laster asked, smirking.

Marl spun toward him, dark eyes flashing, and reached to draw his sword. Laster was faster, his blade drawn and pointed toward the earth. Marl didn't move, sword half drawn, torn between attack and composure.

"Draw the sword, Marl. Draw it and you break the parlay," Laster snarled. "Then we can see which of us is the better swordsman once and for all."

"That won't be necessary," Marl hissed, shoving the sword back into its scabbard. He turned to the King and the malice in his smile made Will want to recoil. It was a look that promised suffering. "I will have you know that your failure to be more progressive, your failure to see that perhaps an alliance would suit you, will cost lives. The first of which will dead in five days with the execution of your precious Ranger of Kings."

"What?" Will didn't realize he had spoken until Marl's black eyes flitted to him instead and the leering smile stretched broader over his face. Rowan grabbed Will's arm with a death grip.

"Don't do anything stupid, Will," Rowan hissed.

"Yes, boy. The Ranger of Kings will die at the celebration that King Tollien is hosting for my coronation. Perhaps if you would see sense, take your duty as my heir, swear your loyalties where they are due, then he might live. But you seem as daft as the King you follow. Perhaps one day you'll be a proper heir, like my brother's son. If you're not, you'll meet the same fate as my other brother, won't you?" He waved a hand to the rider on his right and Will noticed the young guard that Colin had been trying to point out to him before. Beady eyes were gleaming with cold humor, his round freckled face red with excitement. The young rider was sixteen or so, but Will recognized the sandy hair and that leer.

He didn't need to glance to the saddle to see the jagged edged sword. He knew this rider. The blood in Will's veins turned to ice.

"Have you met my brother's new squire?" Marl asked, dark eyes dancing with suppressed mirth. "He seems a bit more loyal than the last, doesn't he? He was one of those who helped capture the Ranger after all."

"And what proof do you have of that?" demanded Ross.

Marl nodded to the boy at his side. "Show them, Draccart."

The Cutthroat didn't respond, only reached into his saddle bag and withdrew a length of black fabric. Will's heart stopped in his chest as he watched the Ranger's cloak slip from Draccart's hand and flutter to the ground.

"If you want your Ranger of Kings back alive, then I think it only fitting we trade him for another royal," chuckled Draccart, his mouth twisting into an evil smile.

Will moved to grab the dagger at his side and Rowan's fingers bit harder into his shoulder. Draccart spat on the ground, his horse shying slightly sideways.

"Seems fair enough, doesn't it?" Marl offered, his black eyes boring into Will's even as he addressed the King.

"Leave," King Revlan said, his voice low and dangerous. "Get out of here."

Marl snorted, wheeling his horse in a tight circle. "The offer stands, Revlan, for four days. You have five days to change your mind or it's the Ranger's blood on your hands."

And with that he dug his heels into the sides of his dark horse, the other riders spinning to follow. In a thunder of hooves over the drawbridge and a deafening silence that followed, no one moved. They could only watch as the King of Kelkor and Draccart vanished from sight.

CHAPTER TWENTY-EIGHT

For the second time in as many days, Will found himself sitting in the council chamber, shifting uneasily. This time, however, it was Rowan on his left side instead of Haru, while Colin sat stiffly to his right. Niet, his expression still murderous, sat hunched in a seat beside Serena.

The door snapped open again and Will looked up, his heart leaping as, for one wild moment, he was sure it would be the Ranger sweeping through it, sneering at the gullible nature of knights. For the first time, he didn't notice the power that emanated from the King as he strode into the chamber, slamming the door behind him and glowering around the room.

"How did this happen?" he asked and, though his voice was low, Will could hear the note of raw fury shaking beneath. "How have we been played for fools to this extent by Tollien? His own squire and the rest of these so-called Cutthroats have been running amok in Alamore and done this much damage. How can this have happened? And to the Ranger?"

For a long moment, no one moved, everyone staring at the King with mixtures of apprehension and foreboding. Finally, Laster stood, crossing his arms over his chest.

"I think we all would like to know that, though we shouldn't be too surprised." His amber eyes flashing in Serena's direction and his lip curled into his custom sneer, "there are those who are so determined to be blinded by their own theories that they will go to any extent not to see the truth or help others see it."

"If you are saying this is my fault," Serena started, half rising.

"In part, yes," Laster snapped. "You have been pushing from the start that it is that boy there." He pointed toward Will. "That is our biggest threat. You have been so determined that you get revenge from the

Ranger that you are blind and keep pushing discord and issues that have nothing to do with you because you're blaming Kelkor on the Ranger rather than Marl. It wouldn't surprise me in the least if you are the spy, the reason he was caught."

"How dare you!" Serena sprang to her feet, teeth bared in a snarl, her hand reaching for the curved sword on her hip. "You think I had anything to do with this? It's bold of you to assume I'm the one holding these petty grudges when we all know about your history. Or did you think that story never traveled to Kelkor? About Marl killing Sir Dasroch because of-"

Laster launched himself to his feet and reached for his sword. Before he could draw the blade, however, Ross and Kalia had sprang to their feet as well, stepping between Laster and Serena. "Sit down, Laster!" Ross barked.

"Serena, take your seat," Kalia commanded.

"Laster, that does nothing for us," the King snapped, striding across the room and lowering himself into his seat. "So, what is it we know then?"

"That the Ranger will be dead in five days," said Laster and Will could tell he was struggling not to roll his eyes as he lowered himself into his seat.

"I mean," the King said, his tone betraying a snarl, "what do we know that might help."

"I know my way around Thornten," Robin offered, raising his eyebrows. "I mean, I lived there until last year. I could sneak in, try to rescue him."

"That would be a death sentence," Ross snapped. "Laster and I know our way around that castle as well. Even if the three of us go in, there's not much chance of getting him out alive. We would have to somehow sneak in with the crowd on execution day. They'll make it a spectacle for certain—how often do you get to kill a traitor Prince?"

"You know they'll be expecting that," Sir Don said, shaking his head. "They'll be guarded with an army and that path from the city to the castle is empty of trees. There wouldn't be any sneaking toward them, just a mad charge in which time he'd slit his throat."

"We could attempt to ambush one of the royals in the city, trade hostages," Ross retorted.

"That's impossible as well," Sir Henry said doubtfully.

"No, it's not." Sir Miller shook his head. "We did it last year, don't you remember? Laster, the Ranger, Rockwood, Ross, and I. We got into that city and saved those three!" He waved a hand dismissively at Will, Rowan, and Colin. "We could do it again! Those royals are bound to ride out between now and then and we'd just have to ambush them."

"Just have to ambush them? Do you hear yourselves? And of course, you could make it then, you said it yourself," Sir Henry said evenly. "You had the Ranger. We don't stand much chance there without the Ranger. He has more influence in that city than any of us can ever truly explain."

"We don't need influence, we need swords!" Haru snapped. "And I'd go too. He got captured saving our squires, I want to help."

"I don't doubt you would all love to volunteer," Laster said, sinking back into his seat and eyeing Serena, still glowering at him, "but that leaves a little matter of an undefended castle. In case you've forgotten, I'll remind you that is exactly how they struck over the winter. If we all gallivant to save the Ranger, we are setting ourselves up to die here. We've lost twelve soldiers in a single night. If we all leave, the castle will be left wide open for attack."

"So, you're saying you won't save him?" fired Haru, eyes flashing.

"Did I say that?" This time Laster didn't resist rolling his eyes, a contemptuous look on his face. "I believe I said we can't *all* go parading off to save the Ranger. If there is to be any party going to save him, I will be with it, if only for the joy of holding it over his head for the rest of his life. Not to mention, as Ross already stated, I've been in that castle. I know my way around well enough."

Haru said nothing in response but Will saw his knuckles whiten as he gripped his knees.

"You aren't serious right now!" Serena demanded, turning to look from the knights to the King, every eye on her. "You can't be considering throwing away more lives in an *attempt* to save the Ranger! We are talking knights swarming in and attacking when outnumbered? Listen to reason!"

"Listen to reason?" Haru stood, standing eye to eye with the Kelkorian woman, his face set and eyes narrowed. "Reason? You think not trying to save a man who's sacrificed himself for my squire, who nearly died bringing the last Kelkorian royal here alive, is *reason*? Are

269

you so childish as to let some feud between the two of you sign his death warrant?"

She stepped nearer to Haru, her hand gripping the sword at her side. "Child, am I? Coming from the boy who hasn't had his sword long enough to know how to sharpen it? If I were you, I'd keep my mouth shut on things that didn't concern me. Ignorance is unbecoming of a knight, *boy.*"

Will's hand shifted to his dagger automatically, not sure what to do but, to his relief, Richard clapped his hands, breaking the tension. "If you'd both resume your seats, I think we'd all appreciate it. Serena, your lecture on keeping lives would make more sense if you aren't threatening to kill people who just disagree. Haru; you're a knight of Alamore. Act it."

Both threw themselves into their seats with sidelong looks of purest loathing at one another.

"We can't let him just be killed."

Will started. He had almost forgotten that Niet was in the room at all, seated quietly in the shadows, watching with his arms folded.

"Don't speak of things above your status, squire," Serena snapped.

"Haru's right," Niet said, his voice still quiet, smooth and even, the musical accent slipping between the words. "You're so ready to throw his life to Thornten because of the past."

"Some men don't deserve saving," Serena snapped. "And even if he did, even if he wasn't the filth and traitor that he is, it would still be stupid."

"But you would try if it was someone else! If it had been me or Kalia or Eldin, you would have tried!" Niet's voice was raising, color flushing his cheeks.

The room fell silent, eyes flitting from Serena to Niet, waiting.

"Leave this chamber," Serena snarled at last. "This isn't a place for any squire, so you should all leave."

"I'd thank you to keep your orders to your own squire," Rockwood broke his silence. "Rowan, stay in your seat. This concerns you as much as the knights."

"Same with you, Colin," Ross growled, glowering at Serena.

"And the Ranger is your uncle," Haru muttered to Will, the words so quiet that even he barely caught them. "So, if you would like to stay, I ask that you do."

Will nodded, not sure he could trust himself to speak.

Serena looked to the King who raised his eyebrows then she snorted in disgust and turned to Niet again. "You're still my squire. Get out."

He stood, face twisted with fury, and stalked from the room. He slammed the door hard enough that the frame trembled, the iron ring handle crashing against the wood again.

"Then we should make our plan of who will ride," Ross said, as though nothing had happened. "Laster has already volunteered, as have Robin and Haru. I will go as well. Rockwood and Miller, I would be happy to have you along as well if you choose."

"Of course," Rockwood said, and Miller nodded firmly.

Serena scoffed, shaking her head. "On your own heads be it then, fools."

"Bold of you to call us fools when it was your squire who caused us to be here in the first place, darling," Laster purred.

Serena gripped her sword, half rising, and Laster opened his arms–halfway between a challenge and some mocking embrace. Will tensed, sure that someone was going to get killed before the meeting was out, before they could save the Ranger.

The King stood first, however, his dark eyes warning both knights to resume their seats. Something in the way he stood before them was ominous and an icy tension ran up Will's spine. He wasn't the only one who felt it, he was sure, as Rowan, on his other side, gave a slight shiver.

"We can't risk it," the King's voice shattered the still that had fallen over the roof. Will's mouth fell slightly open, a buzzing filling his head, as he stared at the King and saw the grief in the dark eyes.

"The Ranger knew the risks, he knew what it might mean to turn spy for us, to be my Ranger. To send knights to save him means risking more lives than just one, and I would never dream of sending Will, even as bait. The Ranger would not want it either. No. I'm afraid..." He swallowed hard, closing his eyes, and years lined his face in the time it took to inhale an uneven breath. "we must leave things as they lie."

"But King," Ross started, standing and stepping toward him, brows furrowing.

The King opened his eyes, staring at Ross sternly. "Do you have a suggestion that doesn't risk the lives of others? Because if you do, I beg for you to speak it. But I can't let you and the other knights tear into Thornten by force and try to release him. If you have an idea though…"

Ross closed his mouth, his face closing again, and the King nodded solemnly. The room had gone still. Even Sir Laster seemed speechless at the King's decision, his lips pressed thin, posture rigid. Only Lady Serena nodded her agreement, her eyes blazing. Will's loathing of her twisted: a knife slicing through his chest, white hot and poisoned.

"Very well." The King ran his hand through his dark hair, looking haggard and tired. "This council is adjourned."

Will didn't move, frozen to his seat as knights stood to file from the room. His ears were ringing, horror rising inside him. This couldn't be real. This was a bad dream. They were not just leaving the Ranger of Kings to be killed in Thornten. Where was the rescue he was so used to, a knight, any knight, to stand for the Ranger?

"Will?" a great distance away, he could hear Rowan's voice, feel his hand shaking his shoulder. "Will, we have to leave. Come on."

Will broke his eyes from the wall he hadn't realized he was staring at and blinked up at Rowan's face. Breathing felt strange, rattling air through his lungs, through his body. Next to Rowan, Colin looked how he felt; pale and dazed. "We aren't going to save him?" Will heard the question but wasn't aware of asking it.

Rowan swallowed hard and nodded, pulling his arm. "We can't."

In a dreamlike state, Will stood and followed Rowan and Colin back across the squires' chamber where curious faces turned up to them, not knowing that their King had condemned the Ranger to die, ignorant of what had been decided. He didn't know where Rowan was taking him and didn't know that it mattered. If anything mattered.

"I can't believe it," Colin said at last, breaking their silence when Rowan pushed open the doors of the castle, leading them into the courtyard. The sun was sinking, painting the sky with the blood of the dying day. "I can't believe this happened."

Will shook his head, fighting the buzzing in his mind. "It can't be happening."

"It is though," Rowan muttered. "I mean, you heard the King. If we go charging to his rescue, we're risking too many people."

"But look how many times the Ranger risked his life for us," Will snapped, turning on Rowan, anger fighting to break the fog in his mind. "And we're just going to let him die? Just like that? We're not even going to try to save him?"

"How are we supposed to take on an army of men expecting us?" Rowan retorted. "Do you honestly think you're the only one who doesn't want the Ranger killed? Don't be such a selfish prat!"

Will's hands balled into fist and a mad urge to punch Rowan right in the face rose inside him. It would release some of the tension in him, the grief, the fury.

"Stop it, both of you!" Colin stepped between them, eyes flashing. "This isn't helping anything."

"That's the point! I can't help anything! I can't help the Ranger!" Will threw his hands in the air. "I can't help him and it's my fault they took him! My fault that he had to come for us, that the soldiers are dead! It's my fault he's going to die!" His voice broke on the last words.

Rowan and Colin stared at him and he hated the pity in their faces. At last, Rowan shook his head, rolling his eyes. "Don't be thick, you moron," he said, his voice gentle. "I mean, you honestly think they weren't wanting the Ranger nearly as much as you? He's been a right pain in Tollien's left buttock for about all our lives. Plus, I was there too, and Eldin, and Niet for that matter. It's all our faults."

"But they would have released him if I'd just given myself up." Will strode to one of the water tanks at the edge of the courtyard, sinking onto the edge in sudden exhaustion.

"I doubt that's what they wanted at all," Colin said, shaking his head and joining Will on the edge of the tank. "I think this is what they wanted–to play some mind game to make you think you were the reason for this when it's them. It's always been them."

"The Ranger wouldn't want you to beat yourself up anyway," Rowan said, shrugging. "He'd want you to train so you could beat them up instead. Come to think of it, I want that too at this point. Wish I could punch that Prince right now."

Will snorted an unbidden laugh and, to his horror, felt a knot constrict his throat. Quickly, he looked down at his hands on his lap, blinking back the burning feeling of tears in his eyes.

"I hate to admit it, but Rowan's got a point." Colin patted Will on the back. "We'll just keep training harder, figure out a way to get our revenge."

"Yeah, we'll get our revenge on the whole lot of those prats," said Rowan, laughing darkly.

Will nodded, not trusting his voice. After a long moment, Colin broke the still with a hollow laugh. Will and Rowan turned to him, bewildered.

"Alright, Will." Colin ran a hand through his hair with a resigned grin. "You might as well tell us your stupid idea this time."

"What stupid idea?" Will asked, somewhat defensively.

"To save the Ranger," Colin said.

Will stared between them. "What? I hadn't come up with anything! The knights will suspect I'm up to something, honestly, and look what happened last time. Plus you heard the King–there's going to be knights guarding the wall. We'd never get out of here."

"And has that ever stopped us before?" Rowan said, winking. "This time, I'm going to make sure this goes off without a hitch."

"Alamore, I hope you're not thinking you're in charge," Colin snapped. "We'd be better off without a plan."

"Which we are at now." Will shook his head. "Look what happened when I tried to help! The Ranger is going to die because of me. What if this ends up with one of you captured or dead? What if it's Ross, or Haru, or Rockwood, or Laster…"

"Well, that last one wouldn't be much of a loss," Rowan interjected. When Will didn't laugh, he rolled his eyes. "Lighten up. We'll think of something."

"You're not seeing how serious this is," Will pressed on. "And the only thing I've come up with is turning myself over and you two are right, that won't work. They'd never keep their word. Plus, I don't see how the blazes we are going to get out of Alamore. Haru's going to be watching me like a hawk."

"Right," Colin said, his jaw set in a determined way. "Then that's where we need to start, finding our way out of Alamore."

CHAPTER TWENTY-NINE

No ideas came to them even after hours of plotting. Rowan threw out several schemes, each crazier than the last, and Colin insisted on reading through a stack of old volumes that might assist them in planning an escape, but they found nothing. Will's head was throbbing and each time he rested his forehead in his palms he had a terrible vision–the Ranger lying on the ground in a pool of growing blood.

"This is stupid," Rowan announced as the sunlight faded to red, snapping the book he had been reading shut.

Will lifted his head to blink blurred eyes at his two friends and take in their surroundings. They had taken shelter at the very back of the Hall of Records, as far from the doors and prying eyes as they could get. Not that anyone was searching for them. The castle was eerily silent, and Will felt sure it was the news of what had happened, of the Ranger's capture, Kelkor's collapse, that brought the deadly still.

"There has to be something in here," Colin said, setting aside his own book and glowering at the shelves. "People have escaped before!"

"I mean, Will and Niet showed it can be done, but I don't think the answer is in a book," Rowan complained. "It would take more than that to get us out and, Will's right. Haru is going to be watching him."

"He's right," Colin moaned, running his hands through his hair. "I don't see us getting over that wall or through the gates."

Will smacked himself in the forehead, causing his two friends to jump in surprise.

"What the blazes did you do that for?" Rowan demanded.

"I've been an idiot!" Will hissed. He glanced over his shoulder before leaning across the table, eyes gleaming with mischief. "We can't get through the gates or over the walls, I agree with that."

"Yeah, Colin just said that," Rowan complained. Will and Colin both made hushing motions at their friend. Will's heart was picking up speed, excitement running through his veins.

"So, what are you saying?" Colin asked, furrowing his brow.

"What about under the walls?" Will watched the comprehension wash over Colin's face, a grin starting to turn the corners of his mouth. "What if we got out of the castle that way?"

"You know," Colin said, nodding, his grin broadening, "that could work. We could get you out from the tunnels and meet you with the horses on the other side. We already know that the tunnels lead out of the castle.

"Hold up a minute!" Rowan held up his hands, looking between them with an indignant expression. "Don't tell me I'm about to have to be the voice of reason? Because that means we've crossed the line of insanity."

"It's the only thing that makes sense!" Will pressed.

"Only thing that makes sense? It doesn't make any damn sense at all!" Rowan snarled. "Those tunnels were locked for a reason, Will! They're dangerous! Up until this winter, there were murderous traitors living in them and, for all we know, there might be still! We almost died the last time we went in that tunnel, or have you forgotten?"

"Of course I haven't," Will snapped. "If I remember right, that last time was your idea and all because you were bored. This is different, we're not doing this because we're bored, we're doing it to save the Ranger."

"Oh yes." Rowan rolled his eyes. "The tunnel people would totally be on board with that. It's all about the honor of the quest, naturally. If they know you're going to go save your uncle, of course they won't want to kill you."

"The tunnel people are probably well away in Thornten now," Will argued. "The tunnels are just sitting there, empty. If we can get through the gate in the tunnel that's in the King's Crypt…"

"Which we can't," Rowan insisted.

"We can." Will grinned wolfishly. "The blacksmith who built the gates? He's the same one who made Airagon's sword."

"So, what? Because Airagon got a sword we're all suddenly going to be best friends?" Rowan rolled his eyes.

"No." Will felt his smile stretch across his face, the rush of hope and excitement making his hands shake as he rested them on the table. "But his apprentice and I are friends from when I was in the city."

Colin clapped his hands together with a laugh, the sound so strange and loud in the silence of the castle that it made even him start with surprise. Red faced and sheepish, he grimaced apologetically. "Sorry, but that's just too good. You reckon we can get a key for the gate from him then? Or a copy?"

"I think we could." Will nodded.

"No," Rowan said flatly. "You can't. You can't even get out of the damn castle, that's why we are considering this madness in the first place."

"You're right." Will's heart sank, and he leaned his elbows on the table again, the excitement ebbing as quickly as it had come. "Alright...I'll try to think of something else."

Silence settled over them again, somehow stranger and heavier than it had been before. After a long and excoriating moment Rowan sighed dramatically, pushing himself to his feet. "Fine, since you two are all set on this madness, I might as well get on board. Let's get into the tunnels."

"We can't get to the city," Will said, raising his brows. "You just pointed that out."

"We can't," Rowan agreed. "But when the blazes has any soldier told a Princess no before?"

***

Will scrawled the note before they left the Hall of Records. It was Rowan who led the way, a jaunty spring in his step, humming and swinging his arms, all the way through the castle and the twisting maze of corridors. The halls of the castle seemed to be holding their breath and their footfalls echoed strangely as they twisted through a network of corridors that Rowan claimed were a shortcut. Whether or not they were, Will wasn't sure. Time was acting most strangely–somewhere between frozen in a moment and flying through the seconds.

Eventually they were stepping into the guest wing and Rowan was leading them toward the banners that marked the Kelkorian visitors.

Will's eyes flitted to Serena's door and he tensed. What if she came out? Or what if she was in Kalia's room? Which even was Kalia's room?

They weren't left wondering long as one of the doors was pushed open and Niet stepped out, red faced and still looking murderous. He paused, taking in their appearances. "What are you doing here?"

"Looking for Kalia," Rowan said, somewhat boldly.

"Well, she's not here." Niet pulled his door shut behind him. "She's in the healing chamber, visiting with Eldin. I was going there myself." He forced a stiff smile. "I just needed a chance to calm down first."

Will nodded, not sure what to say. The four of them stood in an awkward silence until Niet cleared his throat, raising his eyebrows. "Want to come with?"

"Depends," Rowan said slowly. "Is Serena going to be there?"

"No, she's on patrol." Niet's face darkened.

"Then, yeah." Rowan beamed, striding to lead the way back down the hall. "Let's go together!"

"I'm sorry," Will muttered, falling into step next to Niet as they proceeded down the hall.

Niet shrugged, snorting. "Don't be. Serena has a hard time being pleasant of late. She wasn't like this in Kelkor–but there's a lot happening and…" He shook his head. "She's changed since coming here. She doesn't seem to know how to trust Alamore now. Especially with the Ranger."

"Do you know what that's all about?" Will asked, frowning.

Niet paused then nodded. "Yeah, I do." But he didn't continue and Will, feeling uncomfortably aware of anger still in Niet's face, didn't push the matter.

Before long they were mounting the steps to the healing chamber and Rowan was pulling the door open, announcing. "You've got company, fair maiden!"

Kalia and Eldin both turned toward them. Kalia shook her head, a sad smile playing at her lips, and leaned back in her chair. "No welcome for me then, Rowan?"

"Eh, hi," Rowan offered lamely.

Kalia laughed. "I feel honored." Her smile faltered at the sight of Niet stepping into the room behind them. "How are you doing?"

"Fine," Niet said coolly. "I'm fine."

"Niet, I should have told Serena off and," Kalia hurried to add but he held up a hand.

"It's not your fault, Kalia." His eyes softened as he took in Eldin, sitting upright and wearing a bemused expression as she turned between her Princess and the squire she admired. "How's the arm?"

"Believe it or not, still broken, despite having an entire two days to heal," Eldin offered dryly, wincing as she tried to lift it and show off her bandaging.

"Don't move it," Niet ordered. He strode to Eldin's bed, sinking onto the foot of it and turning to the Alamore squires. "You three wanted to talk to Kalia?"

"Yeah," Rowan muttered, now seeming hesitant.

"We've got an idea," Will said, stepping forward. He glanced at Rowan and Colin then continued. "We want to save the Ranger."

Niet's brows raised, vanishing in his fringe of black hair. "And do you have a plan?"

"Save the Ranger?" Eldin looked from Kalia, who was gnawing on her lip, to Niet. "What's going on? Why are you two hiding things?"

"We weren't hiding them," Kalia protested. "I just hadn't told you yet."

"The Ranger was captured and Marl himself came to tell us that they're going to execute him if we don't hand Will over," Niet interjected. Turning back to Will, he narrowed his eyes. "That better not be part of the plan."

"It's not," Will assured him. He didn't admit that he hadn't even considered that far into his plan. They'd only been planning how to get out of the walls. "But we need to be outside of Alamore to do anything."

"And that's not going to happen." Kalia shook her head. "Haru won't let it."

Niet smirked, glancing at Kalia who had reddened. "Maybe they intend to have you ask him for them?" he asked, sweetly.

"Eldin, can I borrow your pillow?" Kalia asked, in the perfect picture of a composed Princess. Taking the pillow, she leaned forward, belting Niet in the face with it. "You're a rat."

Eldin giggled, reaching her good arm forward to grab the pillow back. "Knock it off, I'm sure Will's got a plan."

They turned to Will again and he shifted uncomfortably. "We do… but it means, Kalia, we would need your help. See, there's tunnels under the castle…"

"I've heard," Kalia assured him. Her brow furrowed. "I've heard they're locked."

"They are," Will agreed quickly. "But the locks were made by a local blacksmith and his apprentice is a friend of mine. I was thinking, if I could get a message to him, he might bring me the key, or a copy of the key…" His spirits started to sink. She was looking at him quizzically, her eyes unreadable.

After a moment, she gave a small nod. "And you'd get out of the castle and walk to Thornten?"

"Blazes," Rowan groaned. "Hadn't considered that part."

"No," Colin muttered. "We hadn't."

"If I ride with Kalia, we could bring horses to the blacksmith and say they need reshod?" Niet offered, grinning. "We could even pull the shoes off some of your horses then leave them in the city. The soldiers at the gate won't notice."

"But our knights would," Colin pointed out. "They know which horses are ours."

"Your knights are on the same guard as Haru tonight," Kalia said and reddened as they all turned to her again. "He told me he was guarding. That's it. Niet, if you keep smirking I'll murder you."

"So, then you'd have to leave sooner rather than later," Colin said, forcing the matter on track again. "Probably before Serena comes back. I think she'd recognize our horses as well."

"Do you think they'd let me leave?" Kalia asked, shaking her head. "I mean, there's danger of Cutthroats."

"I don't think they'd stop you, you're a Princess," Will pressed. "You just have to have a good reason. Would there be a reason for you to go to the blacksmith?"

Kalia paused a moment, her eyes hardening. "One. I have my crown." She looked up at them and the grief and pain in her eyes shone in unshed tears. "My crown as Princess. I want it turned into a dagger handle. If I can't rule Kelkor, then it should be mine to defend those I have left, I think."

Niet reached over, his smirk dropping, and gripped her shoulder. "Kalia, that's your crown. When we win it back…"

"I don't want the throne." Kalia shook her head. "Look what it cost us to try to keep Kelkor. My parents, your brother... I don't want to be the heir of anywhere ever again." A tear tracked down her face and she wiped it with the back of her hand in frustration. "I'll do it. You just tell me where I can find him, and I'll go."

"I'm coming with you," Niet said, rising to his feet.

Will looked between them, torn between a need to comfort Kalia and the urgency of saving the Ranger. Urgency won out and he uncurled his fist which he hadn't realized he'd clenched. The parchment was wrinkled but the words were still legible as he held it out to Kalia. "Glimmern's shop. Any guard or person can point you there once you're in the town. You're looking for his apprentice, Zudin."

Kalia took the note, rising to her feet. "Very well." She seemed older, more powerful, and Will appreciated for the first time that she was Revlan's niece. "Come on, Niet. We'd best leave before Serena comes back." Turning to the Kelkor squires, she gave another shadowed smile. "I think it best we keep the horses in the city with us. I'll come up with some excuse for staying there. Haru mentioned there's a safe tavern, we'll just stay there until dark and Niet can bring you the horses or something."

"The Dancing Stag." Will nodded then hesitated again. Was he putting another person in danger for his foolishness?

"We'll be fine," Niet assured Will, gripping his shoulder and striding toward the door. "We have the help. The Ranger saved us, it's the least we can do."

"You better come back and say bye," Eldin said, looking sulky. "Since I'm guessing I can't come along."

Niet turned, beaming. "I'll come say bye and then it's your job to act ignorant. Have we a deal?"

She smiled, her eyes dancing with mischief. "Ignorant of what?" she asked, innocently.

***

They watched Niet and Kalia ride through the gates, Niet leading Admere and Strider, Kalia riding Naja, from one of the high windows. Will was surprised when none of the guards questioned their departure and relieved to see that Henry–the knight on duty with the guards–was too preoccupied trying to get up the stairs with his cast foot.

"You reckon Niet can get back here on foot with that key?" Rowan asked, glancing toward Will and Colin.

"He's got to," Colin said, somewhat nervous.

"He will," Will said firmly.

The three of them did their best to stay busy and out from underfoot. Unfortunately for them, this strategy didn't work well and Richard was soon taking charge of their lessons for the day. He handed each of them a thick and very boring book, ordering them to read the first chapter of each book and summarize the battle strategies discussed. Then he'd strode away to take over the guard duty from Henry. Within the first hour, Will was certain he never wanted to see the inside of the Hall of Records again.

Overhead, the gathering clouds of the past two days finally shattered, bringing with them a crash of thunder and forked lightning that split the sky. Curtains of rain pounded down over the castle, making the comfort of the Hall of Records more bearable even as Will's nerves frayed. Would Niet even get back to the castle in this? What if he and Kalia couldn't find Glimmern? What if Zudin ignored his plea for help?

"Will, you've got a guest."

Will looked up from the page he'd been studying for the past quarter hour to see Miller, dripping with rainwater, stepping from between two rows of shelves. He jerked his head behind him, and Will sprang to his feet as Zudin appeared, gazing around in awe, water pooling at his feet.

"Zudin!" Will beamed, his relief making his reaction of surprise seem genuine.

"Your friend here let us know that Kalia and Niet will be staying with Glimmern till this rain passes," Miller said, looking annoyed. "I guess some of the guards didn't think that they should, perhaps, clear it with the King before letting a Princess leave…morons…"

"She'll be fine with Glimmern," Zudin assured, bowing his head to Miller nervously. "He used to be a soldier here and all."

"Well, nevertheless, thanks for getting here with that news. I'll tell Serena," Miller said, raising his eyes to the ceiling. "Alamore help me, she might try to murder me for this. It'd be just like her to kill the messenger."

With a glum wave, Miller turned away and strode from the Hall of Records, leaving nothing but a patch of wet footfalls in his wake.

"This place is huge," Zudin said, turning and whistling. "Mean books everywhere, ain't there?"

"Yeah, and most of them are boring," Rowan grumbled, pushing himself to his feet. He held out his hand, grinning. "I'm Rowan, that there bookworm finishing his page is Colin."

Colin looked over the top of his book, scowling. "If I don't finish the page I'll waste time rereading it." But he still set aside the tome and stood, shaking Zudin's hand after Rowan.

"Nice to meet you." Zudin ducked his head again and turned to Will, raising his bushy brows. "Blimey, you asked a lot in that letter there, Will."

Will reddened. "I'm sorry, Zudin. I just was hoping,"

Zudin held up a hand and grinned, stopping him. "Don't 'pologize. That squire, Niet, said it's 'cause you're gonna save the Ranger. That true?"

"Yes." Will nodded. "It is."

Zudin whistled again, running a hand over his drenched hair and making it stand on end. "Wish I could do somethin' like that. Glimmern'd kill me though, if I was out or anything. But here." He reached into his pocket and withdrew something small, wrapped in a brown rag that seemed as sopping wet as he was. "Least I could do an' all."

Will took it, surprised to find his own hand shaking and pulled away the cloth. The key was small and made of simple black iron, already shot through with red rust from its short journey. He looked up at Zudin, grinning. "I seriously can't thank you enough, Zu. If I can repay it in any way, let me know."

"Just don't get killed," Zudin offered. "And," he added, almost as an afterthought, "destroy that when yer done. It's a copy I made today but still, only Glimmern and the King are supposed to have keys like that now. It's pretty important to keep that gate to the tunnel locked. Throw it in the moat when you get back, that way Glimmern don't throttle me."

"Got it." Will slid the key into his pocket. "Thank you again. Want to see the castle? We can show you round?"

Zudin shook his head, already pulling his hood up again. "I got to get back to the shop. My horse is down there getting soaked through in this rain and doubt he takes well to it neither. Good luck, you three."

Once Zudin had left, Will turned to his friends, grinning. "We've got our key."

Rowan whooped but Colin only managed a small smile. He looked ready to be sick. "Just what I've always dreamed of," he said, running a hand over his face. "We're going back into the tunnels."

CHAPTER THIRTY

For the second night Will found himself climbing the stairs with Rowan after washing dishes. Only this time, they climbed them in silence. He could almost hear Rowan's heart slamming like his own as they mounted each step. Outside, thunder growled and the storm continued in all its fury.

"Think Niet's going to be able to find us in those woods?" Rowan asked, breaking the silence.

Will shrugged, closing the door to the kitchens at their back. "Hope so. I mean, I'm not sure where the tunnel even comes out. It's just a rough estimate."

"And we won't have torches in this." Rowan jerked a thumb toward the window as more lightning illuminated the dinner hall in ghostly white light, leaving them temporarily blinded.

"Yeah, I don't imagine we will," Will agreed in a whisper. They waited until another flash of lightning before stealing across the dinner hall and sneaking into the squire chamber. Will had to stop himself from yelping as he almost collided with Colin.

"Blazes, Col," Will gasped, stepping back. "You nearly scared me to death."

"Sorry," Colin whispered. "I was coming to look for you two. You ready?"

"To get soaked? Not hardly," Rowan moaned. "It's pouring out there."

"You literally said you were a duck last night," Will pointed out, backing through the door again into the dinner hall.

"But that was on my terms, I like it better when it's on my terms," Rowan explained. In the dinner hall, Will held out a hand as Colin passed

285

around the three saddle bags he'd slung over his shoulder. Will was taken aback by the weight.

"What's in here?" he asked, opening the flap. It was too dark to make out much, but his chest tightened as, on the top, Will saw the diving dagger falcon he'd taken from The Cutthroat Prince. He'd nearly forgotten it was in the chest by his bed.

"Everything I thought was useful of your stuff, plus anything else I could find," Colin hissed. "But come on. We've got to get moving before a knight comes poking round."

"The quest begins then!" Rowan said boldly, throwing his bag over his shoulders. "You packed dry clothing, right? Because we'll need it."

"Yeah, and a hot meal," Colin said dryly. "Rowan, everything's going to get soaked. We just have to accept that."

"Well bugger all," Rowan grumbled.

"Let's stop wasting time," Will whispered. "Come on." He strode forward, skin crawling, and led them toward one of the doors leading off the dinner hall. Not the double doors to the entry hall but the side door that he'd avoided for months. He hadn't been through here since the battle of the crypt when he had fought Marl to save Haru's life.

Haru. A stab in his stomach made him hesitate and Colin passed him, gingerly pushing through the door. What would happen if Haru decided he didn't want to be Will's knight after this? He was hiding secrets again from Haru. He doubted the knight would forgive him again so easily.

"Will!"

He started. Rowan and Colin were peering at him through the door. Rowan had grabbed a torch from the wall, its orange glow pouring over him.

"Coming." He pushed down the regrets, the worries, and hurried to join them. He would have time for regrets later. There were things more important than that now. Even if he was thrown from the castle, if he was excused from his training to be a knight, this was more important than that.

They didn't speak but Will could feel the uneasiness of his two friends when he led them through the door that branched to the right of the corridor. This chamber seemed to swallow the light of Rowan's torch when they entered; black drapes like endless shadows hanging from the walls, lines of dark benches facing forward, toward a dais and beyond the dais, the door. The door that would take them into the cemetery.

"You know," Rowan grumbled, throwing a dark look about the room, "if I die, go ahead and skip this whole part. I just want to have a bright sunshine and daylight place, not this creepy room. No wonder people come here to be sad, it's dead depressing."

"Let's not plan to bury anyone," Colin growled.

"We aren't getting killed," Will assured him.

"No, course not," Rowan agreed, grinning. "I'm just saying, when that does happen, in about a hundred years, once I've become master of the entire world, I want you to make my death like a party. Cake for everyone and a box of kittens to be set loose during the speeches that talk about how fantastic I was."

"Shut up," Will said, half laughing–from nerves more than from humor.

He pushed through the door at the end of the chamber at the same moment another fork of lightning illuminated the sky, bringing with it a deafening boom of thunder. The three of them jumped, taking a step back from the courtyard before them where gravestones stood–long dead sentries–guarding the resting places of those who had already gone before them.

"Bloody Thornten," Rowan hissed. "Forgot how damn creepy this place is."

"Lucky you," Will grumbled. He watched the sheets of icy rain throw themselves at the earth, spraying mud into the air, and shattering over the gravestones. Shivering, he pulled his hood lower and squeezed his eyes shut a moment. "Right." He opened his eyes and took the first steps into the storm. "Let's go."

Rain soaked through his cloak even before he was halfway across the graveyard, moving slow to avoid tripping over any of the stone markers. Judging by the string of oaths behind him, Rowan hadn't been as careful. Ahead, he could see the crypt–a large stone plinth which he knew would open to a crypt beneath the earth where all the Kings before had been laid to rest.

Will was the first to reach it, already crouched and running his hands over the stone before Rowan and Colin arrived, Rowan holding aloft the spluttering torch. Eyes straining to make out anything in the dark, Will's heart leapt as his fingers brushed over an indentation in the stone. It took him and Colin both to heave the heavy stone upwards, revealing the top few stairs in the dying torchlight and the darkness that gaped ahead.

"I better go first," Will said, raising his voice to be heard over the howling of the wind. "Rowan, give me the torch."

"No argument here," Rowan huffed, offering his hand forward.

Will took the torch and, swallowing the misgivings that tangled in his throat, lowered himself onto the first step. The blackness rose around him and the light, the rain overhead thudding on the stone ceiling as he descended into the gloom. Behind him, Rowan and Colin were nothing more than half silent footfalls on solid stone.

Raising the torch higher the better to see their surroundings, Will turned his head to take in the chamber they were entering. The crypt was massive. The steps were straight and narrow, no handrails blocking them from the plummet to either side. He could hear water dripping continue beneath the earth and, stillseveral feet below them, he could just make out the torch reflecting off of puddles gathering on the crypt floor. He shivered, remembering the attack over the winter, the knights who had fought on these steps. It was a miracle none of them had been slaughtered.

At the bottom of the stairs, his feet hit solid dirt floor, damp earth muffling his steps. Will turned on the spot, taking in the narrow corridor they had entered, lined with large stones, each about the length of a human, that each had a name etched into it.

"These must be the Kings before," Colin whispered interestedly, approaching one of the stones. "I wonder…"

"We don't have the time to explore right now," Will cut across him. "We've got to get to the end of the tunnel and get out to meet Niet."

"Right," Colin mumbled sheepishly.

The three moved closely together, Will's knuckles white on the torch handle as they moved down the corridor, twisting along the narrow tunnel. Etchings in the stones cast darker shadows, reminding Will forcefully of claw marks gouged in rock. Their own shadows moving ahead made the hair rise on the back of his neck, tricking him into feeling that they weren't alone beneath the earth.

More than once, Will thought he heard something and froze, heart slamming in his throat, only to see water trickling down the walls into a puddle or a mouse scurrying over the floor and away from the invading light. To his relief, neither Rowan nor Colin seemed to notice. They were both as jumpy as he was, Rowan grabbing his arm once and yelping as a rock Will's boot had kicked rolled ahead of them.

"You know," Rowan said, in an obvious attempt to seem casual, releasing his death grip from Will's arm. "It's honestly quite spacious down here. I was expecting more dead people to be taking up the room."

"They're behind the stones," Colin said flatly. "That's why there's carvings in the rocks, it's the name and date of the Kings, Queens, and heirs who've died in Alamore."

"Well, now this is creepy," Rowan grumbled. "Thanks, thanks a lot. I was really considering moving down here, starting a family, but now that I know the walls are filled with dead people, I don't think I'll be doing that."

"We shouldn't be down here anyway," Colin snapped. "It's only royals and their trusted few who are supposed to enter."

Will grimaced. "We don't have a lot of choices."

"Anyway," Rowan pointed out. "Will's royal and we're his trusted few so we're fine. Stop being such a stickler for rules, won't you?"

"Where's this tunnel entrance?" Will hissed, breaking the argument he knew was about to start behind him.

"Can't be much further, can it?" Colin muttered. "I'd expect we'll be there in a moment."

Sure enough, when they turned around the next twist in the corridor, they were met with an iron gate that spanned the height and width of the tunnel. The black metal bars twisted, each the thickness of Will's arm. Set at the center of the gate, reflecting silver in the dark, was a small keyhole. Will reached into his pocket with his torch free hand, his fingers shaking as they rested on the replica key that Zudin had given him. Silently begging that it would work, he pulled it from his pocket and slipped it into the lock, twisting it.

A faint click echoed through the tunnel behind them and Will stepped back as the gate swung wide on groaning hinges, opening into more darkness. None of them moved, each rigid while the echoing sound of the gate opening faded into distant echoes. Will swallowed, finding it difficult through his dry mouth, and turned, brows raised.

"Reckon we should leave it open for coming back?

"No," Colin said firmly. "We can't risk the castle for this. I say we lock it and slide the key underneath so no one can take it from us. If we're caught, it'll at least be on the right side of the gate then."

"In terms of the castle security, that seems the best decision," Rowan agreed nervously. "Though, I don't much care for the idea of being trapped in this damned tunnel."

"We aren't coming back this way anyway," Will said firmly. He stepped through and, once the others had entered, pushed the gate closed. The hinges moaned again, causing a shiver to run down his spine. "We'll be riding back through the gates."

"Before breakfast, I hope," Rowan said, his stomach growling loudly in agreement.

Will did what Colin had suggested, locking the gate and sliding the key as far and hard underneath it as he could before straightening and turning to the chamber they had entered. Beside him, Colin gave a low whistle and Rowan swore. The chamber was a vast cave, the walls fading from sight on either side in darkness and the ceiling a distant shadow that flickered in the torch's light.

"How big is this place?" Will asked, turning to stare at the shadows that flitted along the edges of the room.

"Has to be massive, especially as it leads into the tunnels," Colin pointed out.

"It gives me the creeps," Rowan announced, drawing his dagger. "But, seeing as it does meet the tunnels, don't you reckon we should keep moving? Not sure about you two, but I'm not really looking forward to a reunion with the tunnel people if any are still in here."

"Right." Will shivered at the very prospect of meeting tunnel people in the near darkness. Feeling both of his friends waiting on him to lead, he straightened and strode forward with as much confidence as he could muster, silently hoping they were moving in the right direction. "Keep your eyes open for any hatches that lead back up to the surface–offshoots of the tunnel, stairs, ladders, anything."

Being on this side of the gate made Will's skin crawl. They were soon ducking into another branch of tunnels, lower than the first, and narrower, but with obvious boot prints. Colin thought the tracks seemed several months old and Will hoped he was right. If so, this had to be the branch that led to Thornten.

None of them spoke, moving in silence, all too aware of the flickering light shining as a beacon in the dark, telling the world they were beneath it. Will imagined several times he could hear distant voices or the scuff of boots, making him spin round, raising the torch. Rowan and Colin were on edge as well and, at one point, a distant sound made all three of them jump, raising their daggers and the torch.

When the silence returned, stretching for several minutes, Rowan laughed nervously. "I'm guessing that was a rat."

"Rats don't sound like that," Will hissed. He waited, listening, but the sound had been brief and some distance behind them.

"Maybe an animal fell down into the crypt," Colin muttered. "We left it open. I don't hear anything now, do you?"

Will had to agree he didn't, and they continued, though Colin and Rowan still clutched their daggers and Will silently cursed himself for not thinking to grab better weapons. How stupid had he been to forget that? He'd thought of an escape from the castle but what were they supposed to do against Thornten with knives? He should have at least tried to barter for some from Zudin but, knowing Glimmern, they wouldn't have been able to afford them anyhow.

"What's that up there?"

Will was yanked from his thoughts by Rowan's voice hissing to his left. Raising the torch higher to spread its shadow further, Will's heart sank. Ahead was what seemed to be a solid wall, no passage leading beyond it, slanting at an angle upwards. A dead-end. He had led them down the wrong branch of the tunnel.

"We could double back," Colin offered.

Will stepped closer to the wall, reaching out his fingers to brush the surface, his eyes still fixed on the floor. The tracks of soldiers from the winter ended here. It didn't make any sense. Pressing his hand against the wall, he pushed. Nothing happened. He pushed harder, shoving his shoulder against the wall. There had to be a way out, they couldn't just be trapped underground. He thought of the key on the far side of the gate, out of their reach, and pushed harder, panic rising in his throat.

"Hold up, look," Colin whispered.

Will turned to his friend, fighting to hide his fear and saw Colin was pointing to the low ceiling above them. Twisting his head upward, Will saw it as well. Almost hidden in the ceiling was a square patch that did not match the rest of the tunnel.

"Will, Row, give me a foot up," Colin ordered, stowing his dagger back in his belt.

Will propped the torch carefully against the dirt wall and moved to help Rowan. Together, they lifted Colin toward the ceiling. Swearing under his breath, Colin pushed against the center of the off-colored ceiling with all his strength. A breath of fresh air broke through the stale tunnel along with a shower of water sprayed down on them.

Rowan let out a whoop, almost dropping Colin in his attempt to punch the air. "It's a door! Yes! Brilliant!"

"Focus, Rowan, or you'll break someone's neck," Will grunted, staggering under Colin's weight to keep him from falling.

"Sorry." Rowan reddened, reaching to support Colin better.

"If you two can push me a bit higher, I can get through," Colin said, apparently not noticing Rowan's lapse in support.

Straining, Will and Rowan pushed Colin as high as they could. There was a resounding thud of a hatch being open and rain began to pour through the hole in the tunnel ceiling. A moment later, the weight lifted from Will's shoulder and Colin was pulling himself out. "Alright, I'll throw down a rope," Colin's voice called down to them. "I just have to find it in my bag."

"You next," Will ordered Rowan, stepping back to grab up the torch again.

"You sure?" Rowan frowned. "I mean, I don't mind being last up."

"This is my plan." Will shook his head. "I'll go last. It's fine."

A moment later a rope was falling to the floor at their feet. With a salute, Rowan turned from Will and grabbed onto the line. Will watched Rowan struggle his way up the rope until he could grab the edge of the hatch. With a kick and grunt, Rowan's feet were pulled from sight.

"Right, Will, we just heard Niet hollering nearby so looks like we're set. Colin's going to get him. It's you now," Rowan called down.

Will nodded, glancing at the torch in his hand, then at the rope. If they were going to keep the torch he'd have to be pulled up with the rope. Otherwise, he'd have to keep the torch here. The prospect of continuing without light wasn't one he cared for, so he tilted his head up to the hatch. He had just opened his mouth to call up to his friends when an icy chill ran down his spine. Even before he turned, he knew the cold had nothing to do with the rain trickling down his collar and everything to do with the fingers that were biting into his shoulder.

"Drop the torch, boy," hissed a voice behind him. "I'm afraid your little adventure is over."

CHAPTER THIRTY-ONE

Jerking round, Will swung the torch up with all his strength and the hand released him with a string of oaths. The man staggered backwards, stumbling out of his reach. The man threw one hand out to catch his fall, bracing himself against the tunnel wall and looking up at Will with bloodshot blue eyes.

"Will! Will! What's going on?" Rowan was shouting above him.

"Stay up there," Will ordered, backing a step away from the man, who was straightening now, one hand reaching to grab the sword from his side. The last thing he needed was to have Rowan here. Gripping the torch in both hands, Will tried to place the man before him; the pale, gaunt face surrounded with stringy white-blond hair, the eyes that burned too bright above dark shadows. He was certain he'd seen this man before, but the features were different, nightmarish now.

"I can't let you go, not that way." The man swayed, a smile curling the edges of thin, pale, lips. He looked like a man driven to the brink of madness. "If you get away, if you escape, they'll kill me."

The man took a step nearer and Will stared at him, his mind racing to place where he had seen the face before. "Who are you?" Will demanded, raising his voice. He needed Rowan to know someone was down here so he wouldn't do anything stupid.

"Oberoan," the man answered, running his sword-free hand over his stubble-lined jaw.

"Who's down there? Will! Will!" Rowan was bellowing above the sound of the storm. "Colin! Niet! Help! We need help!"

A string of memories flashed before Will's eyes: the man standing by the cart the day he'd first met The Cutthroat Prince, the one guarding the Ranger, the one hurrying to report to Ross in the dinner hall.

"You're a soldier," Will said, stepping back and raising the torch. And understanding washed over Will. "You're the spy."

"Yes." The soldier's eyelid twitched and something between a smile and grimace spasmed over his lips. "I didn't want to be, you got to understand that I'm not doing this to be a traitor. They'd kill me. They *will* kill me if I don't do this…"

Will took another step back. Above him, he heard Rowan swearing between shouts for help. Will guessed he was trying to figure a way back into the tunnel without falling. He silently hoped he wouldn't find one. This wasn't their fight; they didn't need to be in here. But what if Oberoan heard them? Would he hunt them next?

"You are a traitor of Alamore," Will said, raising his voice. He had to drown out the noises above, keep this soldier distracted. He edged backwards. If he could figure a way to grab the rope without being noticed, perhaps Rowan and Colin could pull him out of this tunnel, if Colin was back yet.

"No, I didn't want to have to do this." The man shook his head, as though bothered by a fly. "But that Cutthroat Prince, he's got more control than anyone can say. He'd have killed me for entertainment, as a message to the others…"

"Others? Like other spies? Like whom?" Will stopped, quite forgetting about the rope behind him for a moment. "Who are his other spies?"

"He never lets me know," the man whimpered. His tongue flitted over his teeth and his smile spasmed again. What sanity he held seemed to be slipping away. "He's always waiting for me. He's been angry with me a few times for not knowing more… When you and your friends got away the first time, I thought he might kill me. Then the knight attacked him… he was furious. When I didn't manage to catch you in the castle, that's when he came closest to killing me. If I hadn't had the maps of the Princess's journey, he would have. I'd have been dead."

Will stared at Oberoan, trying to make sense of what he was saying. "You stole maps? You're the one who got the Ranger ambushed? How…" He stopped and wished he could kick himself. The hooded figure who had been coming into Serena's chamber the night he and Colin had. It had been their distraction that gave him time to get there. And this was the cloaked figure. He hadn't been there to hunt them. He'd been after those maps, those lines that trailed from Kelkor to Alamore.

That's how he'd known. "So, Serena hasn't had anything to do with this?"

"Nothing." The man twitched his head to the side, panting, and took a step nearer. "She hasn't trusted me. She doesn't trust anyone. I was worried her squire would be the same when I told him I didn't want to watch the Ranger, thought he even saw me on the walls the other night."

"And you killed all the soldiers!" Will snarled. He didn't move as Oberoan took another step in his direction. Anger was coursing up his back, making his hands shake. "You killed guards and they trusted you."

Something like pain flickered in the eyes then Oberoan shook his head. "It was my life or theirs. I've been a soldier here for years. It was simple enough to walk past them. I wasn't in the night guard, I was never suspected…though I think the Ranger saw me too. He was leaving through and when he didn't come back, I knew he wouldn't come back. You see, if I keep myself a secret, I get to live. That's the deal The Cutthroat Prince has. He wants information, he wants power. And that's why he wants you, because he could gain power.

"All of it's been easy. When you would leave the castle, it was me who would signal toward the forest by dropping a banner from the side of the castle. The night you left, I was terrified. I thought I would lose my life, cause you weren't supposed to leave. You were supposed to be there. But when they caught the Ranger, I knew I had this one more chance.

So tonight, I saw you and your friends coming here and I followed. I had intended to take you from Alamore myself tonight, under the cover of the storm. I waited, I watched. I've heard that you were working in the kitchens. Then you didn't go to the squire chamber to sleep. Instead, you all came down here and when you stepped through the gate I was terrified, certain that was the end of my life." The man was rambling, the skin under his eye twitching. "Then I heard that key, heard you slide it under the door. And this is it. This is my chance. I'll bring you to Thornten, to The Cutthroat Prince, and he will reward me. I'll be a knight under his rule, I won't have to live in fear of being discovered by Revlan or of disappointing him. I will be free of this and you will get to be a Prince. It's best for us both."

"Right, I'm not certain that I want that, but I appreciate the offer," Will snapped. He took another uneasy step and rain splashed over his back. The torch in his hands hissed angrily, sputtering in the water and Oberoan straightened. His eyes shifted for the first time from Will to the rope, his face contorting in a snarl of understanding.

"No!"

Will pulled on the rope but it was too late. Oberoan was lunging forward. Rowan gave a cry of pain as the rope burned through his hands. Oberoan's shoulder had collided with Will, both of them sprawling onto the earth. The torch flew in a brilliant arch from Will's hand, falling into the stream of water that still poured from the tunnel opening.

Scrambling to his feet, Will saw it flicker then the light died, plunging him into darkness. Overhead, Rowan was yelling something, a distant voice that he could barely make out responding back.

Shaking himself, Will strained to see anything through the black that pressed against his eyes. He couldn't see or hear Oberoan, but the man had to be around here somewhere. Slowly, Will reached his hand for the dagger at his side, fighting to keep his racing heart calm. When his fingers brushed nothing, he bit back the urge to swear. The dagger must have flown from his sheath when he'd hit the ground.

"Come out, come out, wherever you are. Come out, boy, or I'll climb the rope, let your little friend pay for you not listening. Come out, there's no point in hiding, boy."

The sing-song voice sent a chill through Will's blood and he gritted his teeth against the sickening terror. A hiss of cloak over the tunnel floor. The man was several paces away and moving toward him but if Will moved at all, he'd give away his position.

"If you go with me, if you go alive, think of the power you stand to gain. You can become a Prince of Kelkor, and I can join The Cutthroat Prince. There is nothing to lose, boy, nothing. Your destiny, your blood, you were born to be a King."

Another step. This one dragging and followed by a sharp hiss of pain. So, the fall had hurt Oberoan. Good. At least if he was going to get caught he'd made this traitor miserable.

The clash of steel against stone several feet to Will's left made him jump, sparks flaring from where the blade of Oberoan's sword struck against the walls. The momentary light burned into Will's vision and he had to blink several times to clear his eyes.

"If I can't bring you to him alive, I can't leave you here to be a threat either. You'd tell Revlan about me, you'd ruin everything."

Another strike of steel on stone and Will crouched down, heart slamming. *Alright, so I guess he's decided killing me is easier,* Will thought grimly. Above, there was a commotion, Rowan shouting, the sound of someone yelling back further away. What was going on? Will ran a hand over the floor. He needed his dagger, or the torch, or anything to use as a weapon.

"Give up, boy," Oberoan rasped. "I'm tired of these games. I'm tired of being a spy. Give up." The voice was drawing nearer, low and soothing. "Give up and take your blood right, let me earn my place at the Cutthroat's side."

Will turned his face slowly. Oberoan had to be there, only feet away. If he ran, he'd give away his position and risk being killed, but if he stood, Oberoan's next furious strike stood a good chance of plunging into his chest. Mind reeling, Will froze. The bag still tied over his shoulder. Moving carefully as not to make a noise, Will twisted, reaching one hand into the bag.

"Hiding? Like a child? Come now, boy." Oberoan's voice was shaking. "Don't hide. Don't be a coward."

Will's fingers brushed over the hilt and a new shiver ran through him at the feel of intricate steel in the shape of a diving falcon.

"Come out, boy. Think of the power we'll have. If you come with me, you survive and become King, but you know I can't let you live if you don't come. Come out, come out... I hear you breathing..."

Will moved at the same time that the soldier in the dark lunged again. Will felt something sharp slice through the air where he had been a heartbeat before, catching on his cloak, tearing fabric in place of skin. With every ounce of strength and memory from training, Will let the dagger fly from his hand, the falcon blade diving through the darkness toward the shape of a man.

There was a terrible gurgling cry, a thud and Will staggered, panting, and wheeled round, fists raised, ready to fight. Nothing moved. The only sound apart from the rain above and Rowan's yells coming nearer was something guttural, gasping through the dark.

Heart slamming in his ribs, Will took a tentative step forward and felt his foot land on something solid and shaking. He sprang back with a cry of panic and waited, half expecting the man to rise again, to strike. There was nothing, only another shaking breath.

Will took another step back, away from the form on the floor and felt the rain running down his back. Looking up, he winced as water ran over his face and into his eyes.

"Rowan!" His voice cracked, hoarse even to his own ears. "Rowan!"

"Colin! He needs help! Hurry up!" Rowan bellowed. Will could have laughed with relief as a face appeared, hanging upside down from the tunnel hatch. "Will! Where are you? Will!"

"Quit shouting, I'm right here." Will ran a hand over his forehead, eyes still straining in the direction of the uneven breaths at his feet. "Where's Colin?"

"Getting Niet. I don't have another rope. I didn't mean to let go, I swear. I just couldn't keep hold of it. Who's down there, what's-"

"I'll explain when you get me out of here," Will snapped. The smell of blood was mixing with the stale air of the tunnel, rising around him in suffocating waves.

"Right." Rowan's head disappeared. "Colin! Hurry up! I need rope!" Rowan's voice was hoarse from screaming. "Will, you scared me half to death. Colin wasn't here, and then I heard you fighting someone and didn't know how to help!"

"It's fine." Will shook his head, knowing Rowan couldn't see his face and hoping his voice hid the lie. "I'm okay."

"What's going on?" Colin had returned, standing above Rowan.

"Someone was down there with Will and-" Rowan started.

"What?" Colin demanded.

"Look, someone throw me a rope," Will barked. "I want out of here."

He barely sprang aside in time as the rope fell from above, one end landing neatly on the other rope. Without a moment's hesitation, Will grabbed onto the rope and felt it tighten. They were pulling him up. At the edge of the tunnel door, Will grabbed onto the wonderfully solid feel of wet grass and hoisted himself out. He sprawled on the ground on his back, the rain washing over. Closing his eyes, he inhaled the fresh smell of forest, of rain.

"Will, who was down there? Was it tunnel people?" Colin asked. "If it was, we need to go warn the castle."

Will shook his head, wiping sweat and rain from his forehead and sitting upright. "It was the spy."

"What? Seriously?" Rowan gawked at Will, astonished. "Who was it?"

"A soldier, Oberoan," Will said and scooted away from the black hole in the earth where the tunnel had let out. He could feel his body beginning to shake with a mixture of fear, cold, and adrenaline. "He's that soldier who let me go see the Ranger, the one who's been hanging round and…" He stopped, shaking his head. "I don't think he's alive."

"Blazes, we're lucky you are," Rowan said, laughing nervously and pounding Will on the back. "You might have been Will soup down there in the mud."

Someone moved in the shadow of a tree and Will half rose, reaching again for his empty dagger sheath. He recognized the tall teenager, even with his black hair plastered to his forehead, and relaxed.

"You got the horses here, then?"

"Yeah, I did," Niet said, coming to stand beside Will at the edge of the tunnel hatch. "I tried to get here sooner but Serena ended up in town."

Will winced. "I'm betting that didn't go over well."

Niet shook his head. "Not bad, actually. She and I needed a chance to talk and she's finally starting to see sense, I think. It's been a lot for her to come here and realize that she left and Kelkor fell without her there." A muscle tightened in his jaw. "It's been hard on us all."

Will hesitated, not sure what to say, but Niet was shrugging already. "That doesn't matter right now though. You said the spy is down there. Will, was he armed?"

Will nodded. "Yeah, he's got a sword…and I dropped my dagger down there."

"By the sounds of it you dropped your dagger in his neck," Rowan said, cracking a grin. When none of the others laughed, he rolled his eyes. "One day you'll appreciate my humor."

"We should get his weapons. All we have right now are my sword and bow, and Rowan and Colin's daggers," Niet said, sinking onto the ground and swinging his legs over the hole in the ground. "Colin, on my saddle is a lantern. Can you light it and bring it here?"

Will eyed the hole in the ground suspiciously as light flared from several paces away, brilliant gold cutting through the darkness. Crossing toward them, Colin wordlessly handed the lantern to Niet. "Want one of us to go with you?" Colin asked, concerned.

Niet grinned. "I think I can handle a corpse on my own but thank you."

Will shivered, pulling himself further from the tunnel entrance as Niet, the lantern gripped in one hand, inhaled deeply and jumped down, the light vanishing with him. The three squires waited in tense silence.

After an eternity, the light bobbed back beneath the tunnel mouth and Will, Rowan, and Colin braced on the end of the rope as Niet appeared, the handle of the lantern clutched in his teeth, a second sword slung over his back. Dropping back onto the earth, he grabbed the lantern from his mouth and spat, his face disgusted.

"That tastes revolting," he grumbled. Rising, he reached into his belt and drew two daggers, holding them out to Will, brows raised. "These yours, I take it?"

Will took them both, half tempted to chuck the falcon dagger back into the hole that Rowan and Colin were sealing once more with a moss-covered hatch.

"Nice throw, by the way. It was in his throat," Niet said, looking impressed.

Will turned away, busying himself with making sure that both daggers were tucked safely on his side. The thought of the dead man made him feel sick. He'd murdered soldiers. Traitor or not, he hadn't meant to murder Oberoan, just to get away without being killed himself.

"Right then," Colin said, turning and raising his voice as thunder growled in the distance. "We should get as far as we can in this. When the knights find out we're gone, they might send someone looking."

"Or just send an assassin and have done with it," Rowan added, grinning and pulling his hood over his head. "Niet, you look stupid with two swords. Hand one to Colin, he's better than Will and I are because he's a prat."

"I think you mean because I practice," Colin said coolly, accepting the traitor's sword from Niet with a look of mild disgust. "Not sure I want this sword anyway."

"We can't be picky about blades." Niet shook his head. "Come on you three. We've got ground to cover. The horses are just in the thicker trees there, they aren't really appreciating the rain so far."

"Me neither," Will said, straightening and following Niet back through the trees. He grinned at the sight of the familiar red horse who blinked at him through a rain sodden forelock. Will gave Admere a pat on the neck before swinging into his wet saddle and gathering his reins. Overhead, the sky flashed with brilliant white lightning before plunging them back into darkness.

"And now we go save the Ranger!" Rowan announced grandly, punching the air. His words were almost drowned in another growl of thunder.

CHAPTER THIRTY-TWO

By the time that the four of them decided to dismount, the rain had lightened to a drizzle and the sky visible through the trees was turning from black to a murky grey. It seemed Niet had come more prepared than any of them had and was quick to set up two make-shift tents, though Will wasn't sure there was much point. They were all already drenched, and the ground squelched under their feet. Still, Will helped him set them up and when Niet offered to take the first shift of guard duty, Will was quick to volunteer to help.

It was a mark of Rowan and Colin's exhaustion that they didn't argue. They ducked from sight into the tents while Niet tended to his horse and Will sank onto the driest patch of earth he could find. He stared at the forest around them, dark and cold, trying to clear his frantic mind. He kept seeing Oberoan's haunted face, imagining him stepping between trees toward him, a blade in hand.

The man had been driven to the brink of madness in his own attempt to save his skin. He'd been terrified and Will felt a stab of pity. The feeling fleeted almost at once as he thought of the twelve soldiers. Soldiers who Oberoan had served alongside, all dead because they'd trusted him. Anger twisted with disgust and Will's hand balled into fists on the ground beside him. The Cutthroat Prince had chosen his spy well. Someone who would risk anything to save himself.

And yet had he deserved to die? Will understood the fear, but the betrayal? If he had been in Oberoan's place, would he have betrayed Alamore? *No*, he thought firmly. *I'd die before I'd betray Alamore, I'd never kill any of the squires to save myself.*

But maybe, said another voice in his mind, *maybe it's different when you truly must face death. Maybe you wouldn't be as brave if you'd seen whatever Oberoan had. Afterall, The Cutthroat Prince had to have convinced him somehow. He was terrified of The Cutthroat Prince.*

"A puddle for your thoughts?"

Will started as Niet flopped onto the ground beside him. He hadn't even heard the older squire approach, and he was supposed to be the guard. Reddening, Will shrugged, trying to seem unsurprised. "Oh, nothing of much interest."

Niet fixed Will with a dark eyed frown. "I'm not an idiot, Will. It's the soldier. You're thinking about the spy aren't you?"

Will nodded, turning his gaze back toward the forest. "Yeah, a bit I guess."

Niet sighed, tilting his head back. "You did what you had to do, Will. He'd have killed you." Niet spluttered and straightened, wiping the rain from his face. "Storms of the sea, I hope this weather lets up."

"I know he would have," Will muttered. He ran a hand over the ground beside him, finding a small stick and turning it in his finger. "But I don't know… I didn't mean to kill him."

"You meant to survive," Niet said firmly. "He was a murderer already. If it had been Rowan or Colin who were last from that tunnel, he'd have killed them."

Will shivered. He'd thought about that. He'd again risked their lives. Turning to Niet, he shook his head. "Why are you going with us? Aren't you worried about what Serena will do, or…what could happen to us all?" He had teetered on the verge of saying dying but, somehow, it didn't seem the right thing to say with the dangers ahead.

Niet snorted and Will was surprised to see a grin curl the edge of his lips. "Storms of the sea, no. I'm not worried. Serena will be livid, but she's not that bad, really."

When Will's only response was a baffled look of disbelief, Niet groaned, stretching his legs forward and shook his head. "You've only seen her at her worst, and honestly, I don't like her much when she's like that. No one does. She can be stubborn and unreasonable but she's one of the best knights Kelkor has ever had. She'd die for the crown, she'd die for those she loves and is loyal to."

Not sure what to say, Will only gave a slight hum of acknowledgement and turned the stick in his hands again.

Niet chuckled. "You get it worse than most of the others in Alamore because of your blood."

"Because I'm related to Marl," Will growled, scowling at the stick.

"No, it's because you're related to the Ranger," Niet said, still half laughing.

Will turned to Niet, raising his eyebrows. "The Ranger? She hates the Ranger more than Marl?"

"It's a different kind of hate," Niet clarified. "She hates Marl, she wants to kill him and get revenge–we all do. But she has hated Marl since she met him, years before all this. She hates the Ranger for…eh." He paused and Will saw a red hue creep up his neck. "Other reasons."

"Well, not sure what *other reasons* are but I'm getting really tired of her hating me for it," Will grumbled. "And how can you stick up for her? After how she treated you in the council?"

Running a hand over the back of his neck, Niet let out a long breath. "Because I know that's not how she is. She and I actually got to talk about training in Alamore, about everything that's happened. When she came into the city, I thought she was there to murder me for leaving with Kalia. Instead, she and I just talked. It's why I was late–I ended up sneaking out of a window because she and Kalia were in the tavern downstairs later. She's going to be livid that I left, but I think, deep down, she understands. She just can't forgive the Ranger for what he did."

"Which was what?" Will demanded. "What could he have done that was that bad?"

"He broke her trust," Niet said, grimacing. When Will only watched him, Niet continued, shaking his head. "She doesn't like to talk about it, she doesn't even know I know. She always told me that the Ranger of Kings was never to be trusted, that he's proven that time and time again. When we were leaving Kelkor, I tried to convince Paxrin not to take the route we were on because I thought we'd run into the Ranger and he ended up telling me the truth.

"Years ago, before the Ranger was, well, the Ranger, he came up to Kelkor with Marl. He was there to try to convince Paranella to marry him because of the alliance. Serena was still a squire and ended up hanging around the Ranger most of the time they were there. I guess they were really good friends and then, when it came time for Paranella to decide who she would marry, Marl came forward with more support from the country. Serena had told the Ranger stuff she shouldn't have, things about the unrest to the east due to Shadow Dale and Marl had spent all of

305

his time in Kelkor causing trouble there, getting the Lords, Counts, Dukes, and Earls of the eastern lands on his side.

"Paranella was livid. She told Marl never to return to Kelkor again because he'd torn the country with that information, had promised bloodshed and war against Shadow Dale, which was exactly what she wanted to avoid. Then she went after the council in Kelkor to find out how Marl had learned that, and it came down on Serena. She was accused of being a Thornten spy for telling the Ranger all of that. But she had really believed that she could trust the Ranger, I honestly think she loved him. It had turned out that Marl had set him to learn what he could, and, after that, Serena and he had a fight. Like drawn blades and everything, she tried to kill him. Which didn't go over well with King Temrod of Thornten, the Ranger's father. He threatened to support Shadow Dale in attacking if Serena wasn't condemned. I'm not sure how, though, but eventually he dropped that threat."

Niet grimaced. "And because of that, she nearly didn't get to become a knight. She spent two years on probation, she had to live and fight in the Eastern Lands for that time, to defend the border against Shadow Dale. Only after she'd proven herself did Paranella let her come back. And by then, she was one of the best knights. She's never let anyone doubt her loyalties since then. She's hated the Ranger ever since and now, with Kelkor falling because of the uprisings, I think she thinks it's still her fault."

"Thornten," Will whispered. He leaned back against the tree behind him, staring at the lightening forest, and felt confusion, pain, betrayal, all twist inside his chest. He'd known that the Ranger had served other Kings, that he had been a Prince of Thornten, but somehow he had never imagined him doing something this terrible. He thought of Serena's fury, of her hatred, and of all that the Ranger had done and felt a stab of pity. "I can't blame her for hating him."

"Nor can I," Niet agreed somberly. "But I wish, sometimes, she could just let the past be in the past. He's proven he'd do anything to make it right. He nearly died getting Kalia to safety, and now he's been captured because of us."

Will nodded, thinking of his discussion with Serena, of her insisting the Ranger would use him for personal gain. This was why then. Because she felt that she'd been used in that way.

"You'd better get some sleep, Will, you look awful," Niet said.

Will snorted, grinning in spite of himself. "Thanks for the compliment."

"You're welcome." Niet pushed himself to his feet, stretching. "Come on, go get some rest. You'll need it. We have more distance to cover after this and I'm not tired yet."

Will nodded and climbed to his own feet, his body aching. Even though his mind was teeming with this new information, with the events of the night, he had to admit that Niet was right. He needed rest. They would be reaching the edge of the forest by that night and he'd need to be prepared. They'd have to come up with plans, with ways to rescue the Ranger.

Again, the image of Serena's anger flashed before Will's eyes and his stomach clenched painfully. There were those, like Serena, who wouldn't think the Ranger deserved this rescue, deserved a second chance.

***

He woke to the faint smell of smoke and, opening his eyes, sat up to see that the other three were clustered around a fire, talking in low voices. Glancing upwards, Will was surprised to find that the sun had shifted to the west, its light reflecting on the pools of water that surrounded their makeshift camp.

"We were starting to wonder when you'd wake up," Rowan called, grinning, as Will joined them at the fire's edge. He pushed a bag toward Will, brows raised. "Want some breakfast...maybe it's dinner...oh bloody blazes of Thornten's walls–want some food? It's dried beef I nicked from the kitchen when we were working."

"Smart move, Rowan. Thanks," Will said, pulling out a handful of dried beef. His stomach growled at the tangy smell. "You all should have woke me, you must be exhausted," he said, turning to Niet.

Niet shook his head, smirking. "I've already slept. Rowan and Colin watched a while. We decided you needed sleep, though, after the last few days."

Feeling somewhat sheepish, Will nodded, chewing the dried beef and taking in their surroundings again. The forest here was thick, the trees close together, heavy with spring foliage. Somewhere in the undergrowth, he could hear the whisper of running water, a small creek, perhaps the result of the deluge the night before.

"We need to get closer to Thornten," Will said at last, turning to the others. "We need to be prepared."

"What we need is a plan," Colin countered. "We can move closer when it's dark again, it'll be safer that way. My concern is that we've spent so much time trying to get out of Alamore that we didn't even bargain on what would happen when we got here."

"I thought the plan was just to walk in, pick up the Ranger, find a nice place for a cup of tea, and get back before dinner," Rowan said, grinning. He had to duck as Colin picked up a handful of muddy earth and chucked it at him.

"So, the execution, it's to take place in the castle then?" Niet asked, turning to Will.

"It's not going to take place," Colin growled, and Will felt a mad urge to laugh at the squire's sudden resemblance to Ross.

"The courtyard, at least that's what Robin figured, and he used to be Tollien's squire." Will ran a hand through his hair. "But I've never been in the castle. We've only been as far as Thorwal and…well…" His voice drifted as the painful memory of that day rushed back.

"This won't be like that," Rowan assured him, still wiping mud from his shoulder. "We know Marl's a prat now, so that's a big difference."

"Our best bet is to either come in with the crowds who enter to celebrate or with the help that arrives beforehand," Niet said flatly. "Either way, Will, they will be looking for you."

"Yeah, so what?" Will demanded, annoyed. "I'm not staying behind if that's what you're suggesting."

"It'd be safer if…" Colin started but catching Will's eye he stopped.

"For the very least, when we ride in to check what's going on, I don't think you should be there," Niet insisted, leveling Will with a steely glower. "You'll be a liability while we are trying to understand the layout of the castle. They know what you look like-"

"They know what Rowan and Colin look like!"

"*And,*" continued Niet, raising his voice over Will's protest. "They are looking for you in particular."

Will crossed his arms over his chest, biting back the urge to sneer. "Right, let's just think of some plans, shall we? Perhaps we should see what all supplies we have in case that helps us think of anything?"

They did so, emptying their bags onto Colin's damp cloak. Will was grudgingly impressed with the supplies that Niet had brought. He'd brought the same essentials as they had as well as a rope that was at least four times longer than the one that he'd stashed in his bag, a bow, two replacement strings, two dozen arrows, several cloaks of varying colors, several different flasks and bottles, of what Will had no idea, more dried foods, several strips of bandage, and an assortment of odds and ends including needles and thread.

"Overachiever," Rowan huffed when they had sorted through it.

"What are these?" Colin asked curiously, picking up one of the small vials and holding it to the sun.

"Careful with those," Niet warned, holding out his hand for one of the bottles. "It's not a pleasant thing to get on your skin. The dark bottles there are Sadalius–it's used in Kelkor for pain and to ward off infection, but it will sting your skin. The green bottles are Meldona, a draft for sea sickness and upset stomachs."

"And that one?" Colin asked, placing the last pale bottle into Niet's palm.

A wicked smile curled the older squire's lips. "Inanimus. It's used to help those dying fall asleep, to rest easily, or used on the living to calm them."

Will found himself gazing at the small bottle, a sick feeling in his chest at the thought of Visra and the Ranger. "We know that one."

Niet's jaw tightened. "I know you do." Picking up the bottle, Niet dropped it into Will's hand. "That's enough for us to coat our blades. Unless we deal a killing strike, I don't think it'll be fatal. It'll just give us an upper hand."

Will turned the bottle in his hand, resisting the instinct screaming in his ears, begging him to throw it as far as he could. After a moment he reached over, handing it back to Niet. "I don't want to use it."

All three of the others turned to Will: Niet seemed annoyed, Rowan's mouth hung open in shock, and Colin frowned, his green eyes unreadable.

"What?" Rowan demanded. "Will, you saw how much power it has! The Ranger and Visra both, plus it knocked us out from inhaling it last year!"

"Yeah, and it feels like we're sinking to their level," Will said firmly. "I don't want to do that."

"I don't like it either, Will, but the truth of the matter is that we are outnumbered," Niet growled, shaking his head and scowling. "And, if we can get close enough to kill Marl, one strike with this and he'd be down. Think about it–we could use it to help us."

Will shook his head again. "You go ahead and use it, but I don't want anything to do with it."

"Me either," Colin said, turning his gaze from Will and nodding decisively. "He's right. It is sinking to their level."

Niet snorted, stowing the bottle back in his bag. "How about you two decide after we see how many guards are there? That'll change your mind on wanting an upper hand. Anyway–Marl would deserve a death by Inanimus."

"It kills?" Rowan asked, frowning. "Hang on, I thought it just makes people fall off into a really bad lala land of sleep."

"If you use enough it slows the heart rate, causes hallucinations, and death," Niet explained, rocking back to sit on his heels. He gave a wolfish grin. "If Marl got enough of it in his blood, he'd die. Even if the blow from a sword didn't kill the snake–a large dose of Inanimus would. It takes longer, much longer, days even–and I've heard it's supposed to be terrible." The grin slipped, and pain flitted through his dark gaze. "But he'd deserve just that."

An awkward silence fell, and Will found himself glowering at the bag. Now he really wished he had smashed that vial.

"It'll be handy for us if we need captives to get out," Colin said at last, breaking through Will's thoughts and turning his attention to his friend. Colin was glowering at Niet, as if daring him to argue. "I'm not dosing a blade in it, but Marl used a rag with that stuff last year to catch us. If we carry rags, we can knock people out."

"Fair enough." Niet nodded. "We'll do that."

"I like that better anyway," Rowan agreed, relaxing. "I mean, it'd be more entertaining to take down a kingdom with a washrag than a poisoned blade. Makes for a better story."

"Just don't go licking the washrag," Niet said, and Will was relieved to see the broad grin that he threw toward Rowan lacked the iciness of moments before. "Otherwise, we'll be carrying your moronic arse out of the castle."

Rowan waved a dismissive hand. "Tempting as that stuff sounds to eat, I already have plans for my rag. Over Tollien's mouth it goes, then we can carry him out and be safe and sound to get to Alamore. He'd be a human shield!"

"You really think that we are going to somehow not only get the Ranger but get the King of Thornten out of there?" Will asked, snorting derisively.

Rowan raised his brows. "Don't go crushing my dreams just because you woke up grumpy from your nap."

"Knock it off, the both of you," Colin interjected. "We still need a plan and we're losing light fast. I don't think we have far yet to go until we're in sight of the castle. It's a straight shot east and should have been a single day of riding but we walked a fair chunk of it last night in the tunnels."

They all agreed and, after clearing all signs of their camp, were back in their saddles again. Will wondered if he would ever feel entirely dry ever again as they moved through darkening woods. It wasn't until they caught the first glimpses of distant lights flickering through the thinning trees that they decided to halt for the night and he and Rowan opted to take the first shift of watching.

All through the night he perched on a fallen tree, staring down the hillside at the distant shadowed form of the city and, rising above it, a shadow that blotted the stars, the towers and turrets of a castle. Thornten.

The place that he was so tied to by blood. Seeing it now, for the first time, Will felt a strange twisting in his chest. He had known for almost a year now that he was a royal but knowing and actually seeing the walls that his family controlled were two different matters.

The castle was as large as Alamore, though with more towers, sharper angles of walls jutting into the sky. But the walls seemed colder, and Will wondered if it was the design of the castle or the truth that he knew. Even though it was where his blood tied him, all he felt was a cold hatred. It lacked the warmth of Alamore, the feeling of home.

He sat in silence pondering long after the breathing of his companions drifted into gentle snores, even Rowan's head bobbing to rest on his chest.

Only when the first golden rays of the sun started to rise did he rouse Colin and Niet to take their shift, curling on his cloak and falling asleep.

CHAPTER THIRTY-THREE

Midmorning sun found the four squires staring from the forest edge down toward the city. Will couldn't keep his eyes from drifting past Thorwal, resting again on the looming castle beyond it. In the light of day it was somehow even more intimidating, the shadow of the castle falling over the majority of the winding streets.

"Right," Niet said at last, breaking the glum silence and turning to the others. "Our best chance is to gather as much information as we can about this castle and this city before we are in there trying to get the Ranger out."

"Agreed." Will nodded. "We could go in groups of two so we can see more but be keeping an eye on..." His voice drifted as he noticed his friends exchange tense looks. "What?"

"Will," Colin said, running a hand over the back of his neck and grimacing. "I don't think you should go, not on this one."

"What?" Will stared between them, fighting the annoyance building in his chest. He'd hoped they'd forgotten their concerns of the night before, that they'd come to see sense, but instead Rowan and Colin were exchanging tense looks. Will gritted his teeth, understanding. They had discussed this, all three of them, probably yesterday when he slept and again today as he gathered wood to dry out for their fire.

"I'm here, aren't I?" Will demanded. "I should be there!"

"I mean, you should be there when we are rescuing, but for now, for scouting," Rowan hurried to say, speaking faster as Will's face became stony. "You should stay here because they'll be looking for you more than any of us. You can start coming up with plans and such."

"Plans? We don't even know what the Thornten we are facing over there!" Will snarled, stabbing a finger in the direction of the distant castle. "How am I supposed to do anything helpful by being stuck here?"

"You're being helpful by not getting us noticed," Niet cut across him before either of his friends could, fixing Will with the steely gaze he normally reserved for Eldin when she argued. "If you are seen with us, we're more likely to get killed or caught. If we go without you, then we can see more of what's happening without having to watch you."

Will looked desperately between them, heart sinking as Rowan refused to meet his eyes. Finally, he threw his hands in the air with an annoyed snarl. "Fine! I'll stay here while you get information but, I swear to Alamore, first sign of anything going wrong and I'm coming, you got that?"

"Agreed," Colin said, grinning. "If we aren't back by sunset you can come looking but only so long as you're wearing your hood. I wouldn't put it past Marl to have every soldier in the city searching for you."

Will turned away, disgusted with all of them, and stalked to Admere's side. He pretended to be focused on untangling the horse's mane as he listened to his friends prepare to walk the distance to the city, changing into different outfits without the Alamore crest.

"We'll leave the soldier's swords and such here," Niet called, making Will turn away from Admere at last. "It'll attract too much attention if we're all obviously armed. Plus, if something happens here, you'll be armed."

"Fine," Will said coolly. A savage part of him was glad to see that Colin and Rowan were both refusing to meet his gaze, staring guiltily at their boots instead.

"And," Niet continued, alone ignoring Will's attitude. "We'll leave our horses as well. We won't blend in on war animals."

"Great." Will forced a smile. "I'll take care of them till you're all back then, shall I?"

"Oh, get over yourself," Rowan said at last, rolling his eyes. "Look, none of us want your father to be a murdering git but he is and that's that. You can't keep copping a bad attitude with us for keeping you alive. Makes you seem a real prat when you do that. We're out here risking our lives too, you know. So don't be such an ungrateful carrot of a human."

Will looked away, hot shame rushing over his face. "I'm sorry."

"We get you're mad," Colin said in a soothing voice. "I would be too if it were me but we're trying to help Will. We really are."

Not sure of what to say, Will only nodded and watched from the edge of the trees as the three others left, striding down the hill and toward the city with hoods drawn and in silence. The guilt writhed still worse in his chest as they at last vanished over a ridge. How childish was he to hold this against him? They were here, weren't they? They were risking everything just as much as he was to save the Ranger.

The shame continued to eat at him for the hours that drug on, each slower than the last, while he cleaned up the camp, drew dirt diagrams and tried, and failed, to come up with plans as to how they might save the Ranger. It was hard to formulate ideas when unsure if the Ranger was to be held in a tower or in a dungeon, in the castle or perhaps hidden somewhere in a barrack or even in the city.

Several times, Will thought he heard the distant rumble of voices and bolted toward Admere, snatching up the sword, only to hold his breath and wait for the silence to stretch once more. By afternoon, his nerves were on edge and he had paced a thin track in the soft earth from the camp to the forest edge, searching the roads below for the return of his three friends. Where were they? Surely he should see them coming back by now?

Frustrated, he spun round and caught sight of the bag Niet had brought with assorted tunics and cloaks. He only hesitated a moment before changing into one and grabbing from the depths of his own bag his grey cloak. Throwing it over his shoulders he half ran from the camp, through the last trees, and into the open light of the valley that stood between him and Thorwal.

He would meet them outside of town because they had to be on their way back by now, surely. It couldn't be taking them that much time. He would only make it halfway, perhaps, and Rowan would come bounding toward him or Colin would roll his eyes and demand to know why Will had to be so thick as to come out here.

When each step didn't bring them into sight, he had to swallow a new mounting fear that they had all been captured too. That he would have to turn himself in not just for the Ranger, but for all his friends.

He was almost to the city's edge, the sound reaching his ears, when he noticed something on one of the trees that bordered the path. Slowing, he stared at the parchment and anger flared in his chest. Drawn over the parchment was a poor illustration of a boy with dark hair and pale eyes.

Wanted Alive–Runaway Prince. Son of Marl, King of Kelkor

Reward for his safe return. May be armed and dangerous if provoked. If sighted, please alert Thornten or Kelkorian guards.

Signed, King Marl of Kelkor.

Will's hand had reached for the poster, prepared to rip it to shreds, before good sense returned, and he let his fingers drop back to his sides.

To destroy it would be a giveaway that someone was in the area that knew him, that perhaps he was there. Very well. If Marl was going to hunt him like this, using the full power of the city, he would have to take after the Ranger. He would have to become invisible. Pulling his hood lower, he ducked his head and continued toward the city, hoping against hope that no one would notice him.

Luck was on his side. No one even seemed to see him through the bustle of life, the rumbling of carts over uneven footing, the hollers of vendors selling the last of their stores. Judging by the multiple different color banners Will saw on saddle blankets, it seemed guests were rolling in from other courts for the celebration of Marl's crowning and the death of the Ranger.

The moment he entered the outskirts of the city, he could feel the excitement buzzing around him. Wherever he walked, he caught snatches of conversation, people eager for the execution of the Traitor Prince. Anger made Will grit his teeth and he had to hide his hands in his pockets to conceal that they were balled into fists and shaking. What he wouldn't do to punch even just one of the teenagers laughing on the side street, pulling grotesque faces as if they were being executed.

But that would have to be for another adventure. Right now, he had to keep people from noticing him and he had to find the others. Once he found them, they could sit down and plan how they were going to save the Ranger. That would wipe the smirks off every face, even if he couldn't punch anyone.

Not sure of where to go, Will followed the streams of people that still flocked forward, toward the distant towers of the castle that hovered above the city. He had to keep himself from gawking up at the cold walls, a sick feeling in his chest. That was where they were keeping the Ranger and that was where Marl hid...

"Out of the way, business of the crown!"

Will jerked round and automatically his hand dove into the folds of his cloak, to the hilt of his dagger. Three horsemen were riding through the throng of people, toward Thornten. Young riders, their hoods barely concealing their faces, their grey cloaks fluttering over their dark horses. Cutthroats. The Cutthroats were here, in Thornten.

Moving as quickly as he could without attracting attention, Will ducked his head and hurried toward a vendor at the side of the street, pretending to be interested in the assortment of vegetables for sale. Instinct was screaming at him to run, flee back toward the forest, as the riders neared then passed. Only when they were out of sight did he wave away the vendor's insistence that he needed the bundle of carrots he'd been looking over and start moving again. Now he was more alert. The Cutthroats were out here. Were they looking for him then? Would they be patrolling the forest?

He was so caught up in his own thoughts that he barely noticed the people around him. It wasn't until an arm fell over his shoulders that he was yanked back to reality, leaping into the air and biting back a scream.

"Why the long face, eh?"

"Rowan!" Will hissed, glowering from under his cloak at the grinning face next to him. "You trying to kill me?"

"I thought that bossy one and bossy two told you not to be here?" Rowan said, winking and taking a large bite out of the apple he was holding.

"You all said you'd be back by afternoon," Will pointed out, stepping sideways. He blinked, taking in Rowan's appearance fully. "What the blazes have you got on your face?"

"What? This?" Rowan ran a hand over his jaw, which was stained a dark brown color, cocking one eyebrow. "It's a disguise."

Unable to help himself, Will snorted with a stifled laugh. "You look like an idiot."

"Yeah, well look who snuck up on who? I'm practically a master spy now, thank you very much," Rowan snapped, rolling his eyes. "Now I'm not sharing my apple."

"Doesn't faze me," Will shrugged, turning on the spot. "Where are the others?"

"Dunno," Rowan said through his mouthful. "Wannared off tis mor and haffin seen em."

Will stared at Rowan, torn between amusement, disgust, and frustration. "You all split up this morning?"

"Oh, don't be a spoil sport, they're round here somewhere. We'd know by now if they were caught," Rowan said, rolling his eyes again and shoving the half-eaten apple in his pocket. "Come on, if we don't get back before them they'll panic."

Will threw a glance back toward the darkening towers of the castle then nodded grudgingly and fell into step beside Rowan, retracing the route he'd only just taken. "You see the Cutthroats are here?"

Rowan's lip curled in a sneer. "They've been crawling around all day, the sleazy little prats."

Will let out a hollow laugh. "Probably looking to see if I'm going to do exactly what I'm doing."

"What? Coming into a city plastered with posters of your face and a fat reward? Probably." Rowan smirked, bumping Will with his shoulder. "You look simply dashing in those portraits with that hooked nose and thin face they're giving you."

"Shut up."

"I even took one, thought we could hang it on the wall in Alamore as a way to remember that time we vacationed in Thornten."

"Did you find out anything useful?" Will asked, deciding it was best to change the subject.

"Of course I did," Rowan huffed, looking mildly offended. "I just told you, haven't I, that I'm a master of spying now? Kelkor guards are helping man the castle with Thornten ones, as the gates were open all morning. They closed them just as the sun started to sink. But they've been letting people in and out of there, they have stalls along the edges of the courtyard–which is really quite a pretentious size, honestly, makes me think they're trying to prove a point–and they've set up a stage. I didn't see your darling concerned father, your sweet uncle, or that hooded bloke we're trying to save. But I did see our Cutthroat friends. Even heard our darling Cutthroat Prince screaming orders at people…prat."

Will nodded, jaw clenching. "The stage, that's where they plan to execute him then?"

"Or hold a breathtaking performance of a soppy love play, one of the two. Considering the talk round town though, yeah, probably the murdery one."

"Did you hear where they are keeping him or anything?" Will pressed. They were on the edge of town now, at the base of the hill, and the last brilliant of the light of the sun was just visible above the dark treetops.

"No luck there." Rowan shook his head. "I was mostly helping out some old chap selling food in the courtyard, it seemed a good place to stand round and listen and I got to eat. Colin and Niet were trying to get a more in-depth idea as to where…"

Rowan's voice drifted and it was a moment before Will realized he had stopped. Turning to him, frowning, Will was surprised to see Rowan's face reddening with guilt. "You alright?"

"Eh not good…we're in trouble now," Rowan whispered, eyes fixed ahead.

Will turned and felt his stomach swoop. Striding toward them, one hand resting on the blue stone of the sword at his side, the man paused on the dirt track and gave a cold and dangerous growl of laughter. "If I wasn't here to keep people from getting killed," Ross growled, blue eyes flashing, "I might very well murder you myself."

CHAPTER THIRTY-FOUR

They didn't speak the rest of their walk back up the path. Ross's fingers digging into Will's shoulder felt like an iron manacle. On Ross's other side, Rowan was still swearing under his breath.

Once in the forest, without any word from them, Ross pushed them forward through the thickets to their small camp. Will felt another jolt of unpleasant surprise as they entered the camp to see Colin and Niet seated beside a fire, both with glum expressions, while above them stood Sir Laster, his arms crossed over his chest, amber eyes narrowed.

"Oh blazes, couldn't you have at least just brought Rockwood?" Rowan demanded, breaking his silence at last.

Ross didn't answer, pushing them forward toward Niet and Colin with a grunt. Staggering a step, Will caught himself and moved to sit on Colin's other side. Colin shot him a scathing look. "What happened to staying here?"

"You lot were late," Will hissed. "And I don't think that's the issue right now."

"You should probably realize that none of you are good at staying where you ought to." Laster sneered. "That he left shouldn't be a surprise given that all of you should have stayed in the castle, where you belong."

"How did you find us?" Niet demanded, scowling at Ross.

"We've been tracking you since last night," Ross growled.

"Since before you left, really," Laster added, moving to stand beside Ross.

"What? That makes no sense," Rowan interjected, shaking his head. "How can that be the case?"

"Because," Ross growled, eyes flashing. "When we were leaving, I noticed which horses weren't in the barn. The soldier told me that Kalia and her squire friend had brought them to town to be reshod." His eyes flitted to Niet. "That'd be you then, wouldn't it." It wasn't a question, but Ross waited and when Niet didn't answer, the knight nodded. "In future, perhaps it's best you take a few extra horses to make it less suspicious or, better yet, not help these three out of the castle."

"Why were you two leaving?" Will demanded. "Your patrol was in the morning, wasn't it?"

"You did pay attention a bit then, didn't you?" Laster asked, lip curling. "We weren't going on patrol."

"Then why-" Will started.

Laster cut across him, sneering. "Didn't you listen at all in the council the other day? Ross and I know our way around Thornten, the castle and the lands."

Will stared at them. "I thought the King said no one was to go for the Ranger."

Ross gave a hollow laugh. "The King didn't know we were leaving."

"So," Rowan said, a sly grin curling his mouth. "You two are learning from us, eh? Decided to get out, stretch your legs, try your hand at escaping? I could teach you a thing or two about being a spy too, if you'd like. I'm somewhat of a master."

Laster shot Rowan a scathing look. "Whatever you've painted your face with looks ridiculous, Lonric. Anyway, that the King didn't know we were leaving isn't any of your concern. We are *knights*. We don't need permission to leave. We came armed with more than daggers."

"We have two swords and a bow," Rowan protested.

"So, if you weren't tracking us, you came for the same reason we did," Will said, hurrying to break through the argument he knew Rowan was about to start.

Ross nodded, running a hand through his brown hair and closing his eyes a moment. "Yes. That was the plan."

"What do you mean *was*?" Will asked sharply. "It's still the plan. We've got time, we can save him."

"*We* aren't doing a damn thing. This rescue of the Ranger just became the rescue of four squires," Laster snapped.

"What?" Will stared between them in disbelief. "Because we're here you're just going to give up and escort us back?"

"Will, they are after you." Ross's eyes opened, reflecting the flames of the small fire. "They are after you, they want you if anything more than they want the Ranger and we are not risking that happening."

"They won't catch me!" Will insisted, rising to his feet. "We can help save the Ranger."

"You think you could do anything but get in the way?" Laster asked, smirking. "That is a childish thought indeed."

"We made it this far, haven't we?" Will pressed. "We got here didn't we?"

"And you're lucky you're not already dead," Ross growled.

Niet rose to his feet, shaking his head. "We're not leaving. We're going to get the Ranger out of here."

Laster raised his eyebrows. "I'm sure your knight would appreciate that sentiment, considering her love for the Ranger."

Niet's face darkened. "Last I heard, Laster, she doesn't think you're too fond of the Ranger either. I bet you loved finding us here, it's a good excuse to turn tail and leave him to die. From what she's said, you've always been spiteful, been jealous, hated the Ranger for being in Alamore as much or more than she has."

Silence fell over the small group. Will started between Laster and Niet, suddenly wishing he had one of the swords so he could stand between them. The look that Laster was giving Niet was terrifying; a cold, calculating, smile. It held more danger than any sneer or snarl Will had ever seen.

"Jealous, am I?" His voice was as cool as his smile, even, and low. "You think it's jealousy that makes me hate the Ranger? Think it's envy that makes me despise him? Tell me, boy, do you think your knight tells you everything? Do you think your little act of saving the Ranger fools any of us? You're after revenge against Marl, and this happens to be an excuse in your own mind. It makes you feel like you're doing something for the better, doesn't it? Do you think you're the only one that Marl has ever tormented? Your brother, Paxrin, was killed by a Kelkor rebel, wasn't he? Yes. And you're going to kill Marl for causing that traitor? I imagine that will bring you some relief in your mind.

"But you see, the difference is that when I lost someone to Marl, I saw Marl murder them. When it came down to steel on steel, I watched my knight fall, unarmed, with a sword through his chest, while I was held back from taking his place."

Laster took a step nearer, amber eyes blazing and Niet took a step back, the anger melting to horror in his face.

"You lost your brother, and I might as well have lost my father. He was the one who cared if I lived or died. Imagine watching Serena die, begging attackers to let her squire go. Or if it had been Paxrin, begging on his knees for your safety? Do you know what it's like to be captured and taken into Thornten? Because, boy, you won't enjoy it if it's you. You'd learn to hate the Ranger too if he'd been the one holding you back. You'd hate him for being the reason you couldn't sacrifice yourself to save your knight. Even if he's how you got out of Thornten, even if he turned his back on his family to help you escape, it'd be too late. You'd hate him for being on Marl's side as he killed a pleading man."

None of them spoke. Will stared at Laster, ice in his veins freezing him to the ground. The amber eyes had shifted to his blue ones, and they blazed with the same fury that filled Serena's own.

Will imagined for a moment a young version of Laster struggling to break free of the Ranger, to save his knight from Marl. And a small piece of Laster's hatred, his cool mannerism and sarcasm, seemed to break away before him as Will imagined Haru being killed. He would hate the Ranger if it were him. He'd want to kill the Ranger, Marl, all of them. He'd want them all to feel some semblance of his agony.

"Why are you here then?" The question came from Will unbidden, a low whisper.

Laster's face contorted into its sneer again and he took a step back, straightening. "Because there's nothing worse than owing your life to someone you hate. The Ranger saved me from Thornten." He snorted, lip curling back into its usual sneer. "Marl captured me to ransom me to *my father*." He spat the word as though it were poison. "I'm the fourth son of a powerful Duke in the mountains that border Alamore and Shadow Dale. They thought they could turn him spy against the old King, against Paradon. Their father must have loved them more than mine loved me to think that would work. My father's response took two weeks longer than expected and was only four words. *"I'll mourn my son."*"

"No," Colin whispered, looking horror struck.

"Yes." Laster laughed, taking a step back from them and turning. "I told you that my knight may as well have been my father. I was a fourth son, a back-up heir if my brothers had all somehow died. My life meant nothing.

Thornten's King at the time, Temrod, decided to execute me after that." He stopped, turning his head upward to stare at the few stars starting to appear through the tangle of branches and Will nodded, understanding.

"The Ranger...he let you go."

"That was the day the youngest Prince of Thornten turned traitor to his bloodlines and joined Alamore," Ross growled. "He helped Laster escape."

"Surely the knights of Alamore tried to save him," Rowan interjected. "Like you two are here now."

Laster raised his brows, turning to them again. "Knights don't defy the King often. Revlan's father, King Paradon, was a fair King but also knew that his brother, the King of Thornten, would take any excuse to wage a war against Alamore.

He told his knights not to attempt a rescue of one squire. When the Ranger and I reached the woods, however, we found three people hadn't obeyed Paradon. They captured the Ranger and helped us get to Alamore." He lifted a hand, ticking names off on his fingers. "Ross, Richard, and your father." His eyes fixed on Colin. "Cavian Greyhead, Count of Lonnac."

"My father?" Colin said, mouth falling slightly open. "He..." he looked between Ross and Laster, both of whom nodded.

"Seems only fitting, then, that Colin and us help out this time, too, doesn't it?" Rowan said, pushing himself upright and glowering at the two knights.

"What?" Ross growled, eyes flashing.

"We're saving the Ranger," Niet said firmly, meeting Ross's eyes with a defiant glower. "None of us came all this way to turn around."

"Laster and I initially came this way thinking all we had to worry about was ourselves," Ross snarled. "Not a bunch of runaway squires."

"But we can help," Will insisted, stepping forward to stand at Niet's side. "We've already gone to the city and started getting information. If we're already here we should be helping."

"And when you were browsing the vendor stalls on the high street, did you see your face plastered to the sides of buildings? Did you see the money offered for your head?" Ross demanded, wheeling on Will.

Will braced himself, fighting the urge to step back, away from the intimidating knight. "Yeah, but I'm not living my life in the walls of Alamore, and Marl isn't going away, so I better learn to get around him, shouldn't I?"

Laster let out a derisive snort, but Will refused to turn from Ross, glowering into the dark blue eyes. After a moment, it was the knight who stepped back, face darkening. He turned from Will and stalked to the tree trunk where only Colin sat now, lowering himself to his squire's side.

"Right then," he growled, scowling into the flames. "Did you find anything useful to our rescuing the Ranger on your little day trip, boys?"

CHAPTER THIRTY-FIVE

Will couldn't help but feel jealous of how much his friends had done in the day that he was stuck at camp. Niet had managed to convince the soldiers on the wall that he was a Kelkorian guard sent to relieve one of them and patrolled along the outer walls of the castle all morning, learning the schedules and ins and outs of where people were positioned. Rowan, even for just being with the food vendor all day, still had an idea of when they would be bringing the Ranger to the stage to kill, the events beforehand, as well as also having several more apples shoved in various pockets.

"Alright, Colin," Ross said, turning to his squire and waving away Rowan's proffered apple. "What did you find?"

"They're not keeping the Ranger in the dungeons," Colin muttered, staring transfixed into the fire.

"What?" Will stared at him. "How do you know that?"

"Because," said Colin, straightening and shaking his head. "I heard Marl say it."

All five of them gawked at Colin whose face turned beetroot red. "What?" he asked, somewhat defensively.

"How the bloody Thornten did you get up close and personal with Marl without getting recognized?" Rowan demanded, crossing his arms. "You didn't even have a fabulous beard!"

Colin grinned sheepishly, nodding to Ross. "I kept my head down and the attention off myself, like when you're telling me not to show off with swords. Just keep my head down and keep focused. I decided the best way to get in was to act like I belonged in there, so I managed to get into the kitchens and help serve the afternoon meal to the Thornten council."

Will noticed Laster look grudgingly impressed, running a hand over the stubble on his jaw. "And none of them recognized you?"

"They wouldn't." It was Ross who answered in his low growl, leaning back and chuckling darkly. "The kitchen help would be beneath their notice. But, if it was a full council planning the execution day, I'm sure there were interesting tidbits to hear."

"There were," Colin nodded, now addressing Ross. "They're keeping him in whatever wing of the castle he used to live in as a Prince."

"Sixth floor, southeast wing," Ross said automatically. Will stared at him, taken aback. How did Ross know his way about the castle that well?

There wasn't a chance to ask as Colin continued. "They seem to think it an entertaining irony that he gets to be what he refused to be–a Prince–until his execution, as well as thinking it'll wrong foot a rescue."

"Which means they're expecting a rescue," Niet said, face falling.

"Of course they are," Laster snapped. "Have you met the knights of Alamore? It would be stupid to assume any didn't decide to come out and give this rescue an attempt. Greyhead, continue."

"They're planning an armed escort of fifteen guards to bring him down to the courtyard and Tollien plans to kill him himself."

"Tollien?" Will asked, bewildered. "Not Marl?"

"No." Ross chuckled again. "No, Tollien will want to have that power as he is the King of Thornten, and the Ranger is a threat to his throne more than Marl's. The country knows that. He's a traitor to Thornten and his death should belong to their King. Anyway, Marl is a pawn to Tollien's power. His seat on Kelkor's throne was won with Tollien's men. It was to build an alliance without having to stretch his powers thin. He knows Marl will make sure that throne stays loyal now to Thornten, so long as he's in it."

Will shivered at the words. He had never considered Tollien's hand playing above Marl, ordering him about, even if he had known Marl was his spy before. Somehow that made Tollien much more threatening.

"It doesn't sound like we have much chance of saving him from fifteen guards," Laster said, sneering. "Did they mention if there are guards outside his chambers?"

"Four," Niet answered this time. "The guards I was on the wall with were discussing that they found it comical that an unarmed man, weak with poison, needed four guards. They seemed to think it a waste."

"Because they don't know the Ranger," Ross growled. He pushed his hands through his hair, sighing. "Very well, we have to get him before the guards get there then, but I'm not sure how to get us in the castle, let alone to that wing. It's far from any of the doors."

"What about windows?" Niet offered.

The knights stared at him a moment, Laster's expression contemptuous, Ross's dark. "I'm not letting you through any window into that castle without my supervision. You've already snuck off once to kill Marl, and given the chance, my guess is you'd do it again. Anyway, it's six stories up, we can't climb that high."

"What about being lowered down?" Will asked. He could feel the old excitement stirring again. "What if we lowered someone down with a way to cut the Ranger free. Then other people could pull him upwards if he's too weak to climb. Two people could lift the Ranger." He noticed Niet's half smile and knew the older squire had understood his thinking.

"Which comes back to the fact we still won't let Niet enter that castle without Ross or myself," Laster scoffed. "And you'd need to know what you were doing to get in and out down a rope."

"If you won't trust me, I understand. But that doesn't mean we can't do it. Will could get through that window," said Niet.

"No." Ross shook his head. "We aren't putting him in harm's way about this. The Ranger won't thank us."

"Well, Ranger won't thank anyone if he's dead either," Rowan pointed out with a half grin. "Plus, I agree, Will's already scaled down some walls, what's another?"

Ross glowered at Rowan a long moment until Laster sighed and stood, rolling his amber eyes. "I've had enough of this. How about we get turned in for the night? We still have time. Tomorrow we will patrol for another way in and, if by tomorrow morning we don't have a different solution, we'll see if Niet's mad scheme is our only option."

"I can take the first shift of watch," Ross growled, turning away from the squires and pushing himself upright. "You all get some rest. You'll need it."

CHAPTER THIRTY-SIX

Laster's story haunted Will's dreams that night. In nightmares he watched, helpless to escape the Ranger's grip, as Marl struck at Haru with Ross's blue hilted sword. His screams were mute even to his sleeping ears and, when he finally woke, he could taste blood in his mouth from biting the inside of his cheek.

"You alright?"

Will blinked, peering upwards through the gloom of the half-light before dawn. Niet stood over him, brow furrowed in concern.

"Fine," Will mumbled, sitting upright and wincing. His muscles ached from being taut most the night. "What time is it? Did I miss my watch?"

"No." Niet shook his head, sinking to sit next to Will. "We opted not to give you one."

"What? But you need sleep and-"

Niet held up a hand, cutting him off. "Laster and Ross took the first two shifts. They wanted you three rested up. Ross is worried and I think it makes him feel better to know you're rested."

"Are you about to suggest I stay here?" Will asked, gritting his teeth.

Niet snorted. "Not hardly. Who was it who suggested you scale the wall in the first place?"

"Right." Will grinned sheepishly. "But you also thought I should stay here before."

"That was because we didn't know what to expect," Niet pointed out. A shadow crossed his face and he grimaced. "Now we know we need you out there too."

Will nodded and glanced around at their silent companions. He saw Colin had curled into a tight ball, wrapped in not only his cloak but another. One glance toward Ross, lying on his back, eyes closed, one hand gripping the hilt of his sword, told him who had covered Colin.

"I keep thinking about Laster." The words slipped from Will unbidden. Turning to Niet he saw the older squire was nodding, a grim look in his dark eyes.

"Same here," Niet admitted.

"Like, I never knew that about him." Will ran a hand through his hair. Now that he was speaking it seemed impossible to stop. "I always figured that his hatred of the Ranger was about something stupid, like jealousy, like you said, or something but…" His throat tightened. It was hard to admit that he had never cared to think about what the Ranger had done before joining Alamore.

"He probably saved Laster's life holding him back," Niet said, though his tone was still dark. "But, no, I shouldn't have pushed him. I should have realized he'd have a better reason to hate the Ranger than that… just like Serena…"

"Yeah." Will nodded. "Just like Serena."

They slipped into silence, both lost in their own thoughts. After a moment, Niet exhaled, shaking his head. "It makes me wish more than ever that I could kill Marl."

"Yeah, but he'll be too well protected now. He's a King, after all," Will muttered.

Niet shrugged. "So was Azric."

"He died in one-on-one combat," Will argued. He didn't like the shadow that was crossing Niet's face. "You heard the knights, Niet. They won't let you out of their sight in there. We have to stay focused. Marl would kill us in a heartbeat without any regret. Save vengeance for another day, we need to get the Ranger." When Niet didn't answer, Will narrowed his eyes. "Niet."

"Fine," Niet huffed, lip curling. "I won't go looking for him, but if he turns up, if he's in our way, I'm going to take the chance I get to kill him."

"Yeah, well," Will grumbled, readjusting himself on the uneven ground. "Just don't go looking for him."

***

Preparing to enter the castle and celebrations felt strange. Will wasn't sure if it was the appearance of the knights, the days in the unfamiliar forest camp, the nightmares that played through his mind, or the failure to find a new plan.

It was evident that Ross was taking this last truth harder than the rest of them. For the past day, he had barely spoken, leaving every so often in a cloak to prowl through the city streets, seeking new information or ideas.

On the morning of the execution, he sat apart from them, where the trees thinned, and the distant castle could be seen. It was strange to see him brooding and when Will brought his breakfast, his only response was a low growled thanks.

"Your knight is the grouchiest creature I have ever met," Rowan told Colin as Will returned to their small group, several paces out of ear shot of the knights.

Colin grimaced, running his bread-free hand through his golden hair. "He's worried."

"We all are, but you don't see me quietly sulking in a corner, do you?" Rowan demanded, then frowned, turning to Will. "Do forests have corners? I guess it'd be edge, wouldn't it?"

Will stifled a snort of laughter in his elbow, shaking his head. "You're an idiot."

"Alright, Will, for that sass, I propose you go sit on the Grump Stump with Ross there!" Rowan said dramatically, pointing toward Ross's hunched figure.

Will playfully punched Rowan in the arm, rolling his eyes. "Only after you, because I believe in ladies first, Rowan."

The others laughed and some of the tension seemed to ease from the knot suffocating him. This was how it was supposed to be. They had a plan to rescue the Ranger and there was nothing else they truly needed now. Worrying wouldn't get him anywhere.

"I never knew any of that stuff about Laster, did you?" Colin asked, turning the bread in his hands.

"No," Will and Rowan both answered, Rowan's grin slipping several notches.

"Your father never mentioned it or anything?" Rowan asked, raising an eyebrow.

Colin shook his head. "He died when I was still young, so he might have thought it too much for me at that time."

The sound of the knights approaching ended any further conversation. Ross's face was resigned, Laster's sneer set, as they stopped above the squires.

"We've come to a decision," Ross growled.

Though Will suspected what they had decided by Ross's expression he asked anyway. "And what's the plan then?"

"We'll proceed with Niet's idea," Laster responded coolly. "As Ross and I know our ways about but are more likely to be recognized than most of you…" His eyes hesitated a moment longer on Will, his lip curling still further. "That means he and I should stand guard where we are less noticeable. The crowds, that is. Which means Niet should resume his act of yesterday, pretending to be a guard. Ross will take you and Niet both through the castle in the less traveled routes inside, while I put up with Rowan and Colin." His expression changed to one of pained annoyance.

"Right." Will stood, no longer interested in the remaining piece of bread and shoving it into his pocket. "Then we should head off."

"Not so fast." Ross's hand clamped down on Will's shoulder, jerking him to a halt. "Laster and I won't just be here to watch. We want our exit to be as assured as possible in the event you or Niet are caught in the castle." His dark eyes stared into Will's, chips of sapphire ice in stony features. "We have to be able to get out safely which will be what Laster and I will try to ensure."

"How can you do that?" Colin asked, bewildered.

"With Tollien's heir," Laster answered again. "Ross and I will make it our tactic to capture and escape with him."

Will stared at the two knights in utter disbelief. "Tollien's heir?"

"Yes." Ross nodded. "From the rumors we've caught, it seems Tollien's son has returned to Thornten. The celebration would be the time that Tollien introduces him to court as his heir."

"You're going to kidnap a Prince?" Will demanded, turning from Laster to Ross. "No one ever said anything about kidnapping. We can't do that."

"And why not?" Laster raised an eyebrow, sneering.

"It's wrong," Will said flatly.

"Did they not just kidnap a Prince themselves?" Laster fired back. "Now that's the plan, like it or not. If we manage to take him with us, it will ensure you all get out alive. Unless, of course, you prefer the alternative of being captured, tortured, and turned into Tollien's puppet for the throne of Kelkor?"

"Laster," Ross growled. Turning to Will again he nodded. "If we can capture and remove the Prince with us, that will keep eyes away from you and give us a strong negotiation in the event you're caught."

"But you two have to be mental to do that," Rowan said, throwing his hands in the air. "That Prince will be guarded! And using him as a diversion will get someone killed!"

"We clearly have something wrong with us as we are allowing four squires, not knights, to attempt this," Laster replied scathingly. "I will be the one attempting the capture, while Ross sees to it that Will can get the Ranger out of his chambers. Niet, don't leave Ross's side. If the Ranger is weak, he'll need your assistance in getting away.

Once we are in the courtyard, Ross or I will take the Prince on our horses and scatter in the other direction out of the gate. When we make to escape, we will take our horses from the castle and cut south and west, back toward Alamore. When you break, go north and west with the Ranger. They'll have to divide, and they won't be expecting that necessity."

Will bit down on the inside of his cheek, frowning at the forest floor, brow furrowed. It felt wrong, as though they were sinking to Thornten's levels, to attempt the capture of a Prince. What did he have to do with any of this? He was new to Thornten's castles, sent away as a child. He couldn't be much older than Will himself and they were going to drag him from the castle with a knife at his throat.

A hand settled on his shoulder and Will lifted his gaze to find that Ross was looking down at him, the ice melting from his eyes. "We won't allow anything to happen to him, Will. It's to escape."

"It feels dishonest somehow," Colin said, voicing Will's feelings.

"Dishonest?" Rowan gawked at him. "How the blazes is that dishonest? It's Marl and Tollien who landed us in this mess, them and their little Cutthroats. I think it's brilliant. I get not liking the Inanimus, but taking the Prince?"

"Yeah, but the Prince, doesn't have anything to do with this. It's not his fault that all of this is happening, so why should he be drug into it?" Will insisted.

He let the words hang a moment, noticing Ross's brow furrow and broke his gaze quickly from the knight. He had voiced his feelings, not just about the Prince of Thornten, but himself. It felt as if they were throwing this unknown Prince into the same position he was in; they were using him, after him, only because of his blood.

"It's either we do this to escape, or we let them kill the Ranger." Laster sneered. "You get to pick which evil seems the worse of the two, boy."

Will nodded. They were right. Leaving the Ranger wasn't an option. "Fine."

"Very well." Ross sighed, running a hand over his jaw. "We will get dressed to ride out then. Again, to avoid the attention, we'll break into groups. Will, Niet, you mentioned you have Inanimus? See to it that Laster has some of that before we split ways. When you, Will, and me go in, we'll be wearing Kelkor colors to keep attention off of us. Laster, you're in charge of-"

"I know," Laster snapped, scowling. "I'm in charge of your squire and the brat."

"You let anything happen to either of them and Rockwood and I will see to it you suffer," Ross warned.

"Would I let something happen to them?" Laster demanded. "Their biggest worry is that I might do something to them myself."

They packed their camp in silence, the excitement and worry churning in each of them as they scattered the burned wood in the mud, kicked branches over the flat earth where they had slept. In the east, the sun's light was rising behind the castle, throwing a dark shadow across the city and the hillside. Will couldn't help but feel that shadow was Marl standing over them, ready to strike, to kill.

***

"Stick close," Ross snapped as again, Will had to steer Admere sideways to avoid the rattling wheel of a cart. The red horse reached his nose out with interest to sniff the man seated in the cart and Will tightened his reins.

"He's curious," Will said, half apologetically.

"He's a young horse," Ross growled. "They are either curious or terrified, and I prefer the ones intelligent enough to be inquisitive."

Will couldn't argue with that as Niet was having a harder time with his palomino. The horse was prancing, arching his neck, as though the excitement and chatter around them were contagious.

Not that Niet seemed to notice. Will had seen him reach to his side several times to rest his fingers over the bundle of cloaks that Will knew concealed his bow and arrow. Ross's black and white paint moved through the crowd with his ears pinned, baring his teeth at the few foolish vendors who had tried to slow their party. If the horse wasn't enough to make the salesmen slink back, Ross's face, shrouded by the shadow of his cowl, certainly was.

Will turned his eyes upwards, craning his head to see the castle towers rising above them with each stride. This was the nearest he had ever been to Thornten's wall and the fortress, built of solid dark stones. It was stranger and more threatening than before. Ahead, the crowds were pressing tight to squeeze over the bridge that spanned between the city edge and the castle wall.

"Try to not ride too near the edge," Ross recommended.

"How come?" Will asked, craning to see the edges of the bridge.

Ross chuckled darkly. "A fall from there will break your bones, if that is, you're lucky. It's a thirty-foot ditch with stone at the bottom, not a moat."

On that note, Will stopped trying to see over the sides of the bridge, steering Admere to press nearer to Ross's large horse and keeping his eyes fixed straight ahead. This was seeming more impossible by the moment.

The stones of the bridge clicked under the horses' shoes, and Will had to focus all of his energy not to try to peer over the low walls of the bridge, to the drop below. Instead, he tried to see the gates ahead. Immediately he wished he'd chosen to stare at the drop instead. Standing on either side of the gates, grey hoods drawn, were more Cutthroats.

Next to him, Niet swore under his breath. Ross on the other hand merely glowered forward, an almost defiant tilt to his lifted chin. "Don't look at them long and they won't notice you. Will, keep your head low. Niet, wash your mouth out."

Will ducked his face, as much to hide his silent laughter at the affronted expression Niet wore, as to conceal his features. To his relief, the two Cutthroats standing at the gates seemed unfamiliar. Neither had the beady eyes of Draccart nor the haughty mannerisms of The Cutthroat Prince himself.

As they approached the gates, Niet held up a hand, muttering something in Kelkorian and the two Cutthroats nodded. Out of the corner of his eye, Will noticed one of them sneer and spit on the ground in front of Niet's horse. Niet's jaw tightened but Will was glad to see he didn't reach for his sword.

In the courtyard, Will couldn't help but gape at his surroundings. Where Alamore's front courtyard was reserved namely for the barn, soldier barracks, and gatehouse, this courtyard was massive. Ahead he could see what was clearly the jousting arena to one side, flanked by two smaller barns and, to the other, a fountain where water poured from the beak of a diving falcon. The gurgle of the water was drown though by the people. So many people. Will twisted in his saddle, seeing if he could glimpse Rowan, Colin, and Laster. It was impossible. Horses of all colors were clustered at hitching rails, ridden by soldiers and Cutthroats.

"Sickening," Ross huffed.

Will didn't understand at first but, turning his attention from the fountain, he saw it. There, at the back end of the jousting arena, hidden from his view at first by the nearer of the two barns, was the stage. Three throne-like chairs had been set upon it while to the front, centered for all to see, was a solid dark block of highly polished wood, decorated with ornate gold engravings. Will didn't understand at first, then comprehension made him want to be sick. That was where they would kill the Ranger, where anyone could see it.

"People really gather to see this?" Will asked, turning to take in the crowds.

"Yes," Ross growled. "They will have traveled for days when they heard the news that the traitor Prince is to die here. It's not every day you see a man kill his own brother, let alone a King kill his brother the Prince."

"What did the Ranger do here to make so many people hate him?" Niet asked, raising his brows.

336

"They don't hate him," Ross said, laughing hoarsely. "They love a scene. There are many who aren't here because they think it wrong to kill the youngest son of the late King. There are those who even sympathize for the Ranger."

"So, others might help?" Will asked hopefully.

"No." Ross shook his head, face darkening. "They won't help. They might not agree with the death of the Ranger but that doesn't mean that they value his life more than their own."

"We should get to the castle," Niet hissed, pulling their attention from the grisly sight. "We can't risk going too late or we'll have the extra guards to contend with."

"Right." Ross nodded, swinging from his horse, and reaching into the bundle of cloaks. Will couldn't help but be impressed with how the knight moved the sword from its hiding place on the horse into the fold of his cloak in a fluid motion that seemed as natural as breathing. It was more of a struggle for Will when he dismounted to extricate the traitor soldier's blade from his saddle and even more problematic to hide it in his cloak.

Once he finally had managed it, he straightened to find the other two were waiting on him. Niet was barely suppressing a wolfish smirk, which Will tried to ignore.

"We'll tie our horses here," Ross growled, jerking his head toward the nearest rail. "Laster will move my horse when we're out of sight to where he needs to be, Rowan and Colin will collect your two. For speed, make sure that you get on Niet's horse with him, Will. The Ranger can get Admere out of here, that horse will look after him. Then, Will, you're getting on a horse with Rowan as he's the smallest and Naja's big enough to handle you both at speed."

"I know," Will mumbled. How many times had they gone over the plan and Ross still felt it necessary to tell them again? Still, it was better than the brooding attitude the knight had had that morning.

No soldiers tried to stop them, not bothering to notice them more than to throw sneers at the three people in Kelkor cloaks of sea green. Twice more guards spat in their direction and Will couldn't help wondering how the Kelkor soldiers that were truly there with Marl hadn't snapped and started fighting. If they were anything like short tempered Serena, that was a miracle. Each time someone sidestepped and whispered about them to a companion, Will could see Niet's fingers tighten over the handle of the bow he carried now at his side.

It was too simple, Will knew. Too simple that they were able to stride between guards that flanked tall double doors, carved with a bronze falcon on each, and stride into the open air of a grand entry hall. Will tried to not let his attention wander, half jogging to keep up with Ross and Niet. Niet seemed just as in awe as he did but Ross, his face set and eyes blazing, didn't even pause to take in their surroundings. Instead, he led them to the stairs that rose to the left of the hall, taking them two at a time, Will and Niet scrambling to keep up.

At the top, Ross led them through the second door on the landing, into a narrow passage. They passed through door after door, twisting and turning through corridors in a spiderweb that Will quickly lost track of. Left, left, right, another left, up a flight of steps here, pause to glance around them there, down passage after passage until they were pushing through another door, one that looked ancient, forgotten in its frame, the hinges groaning when Ross shoved his shoulder into it.

Cool air rushed over their faces and Will gulped in the freeing relief of escaping the castle as they stepped onto what seemed to be a narrow balcony, with two other doors leading off of it.

"This is above his chamber," Ross said, turning to Will and Niet and pulling his hood from his face. "Now, how do we do this?"

"Hold up, I'll get us set on the rope. You help Will make sure he's ready," said Niet, dropping the bag from his shoulder and kneeling on the ground as he began to rummage through. Will glanced toward the edge of the balcony and his stomach churned.

"You going to be okay doing this?"

Will turned to see Ross was watching him with a worried look in his dark eyes, brow furrowed. He nodded, trying to make himself seem more assured than he was. "As Niet said, I've already done it before in a way. This won't be bad."

Ross grunted, clearly unconvinced, but seemed to decide it worthless to press the point. "Sword attached right?"

"I think so," Will said, checking the buckle on the sheath again.

"Do you have the lockpicks?"

Will pressed a hand to his chest, where he could feel the small leather pouch of tools pressing into his skin. "Got it."

"Right then, just take it slow with those. It'll be a simple enough lock on manacles. If we're lucky, he's just tied up. You get in there and make sure you and the Ranger can get out fast, is that understood? Soon as you are in, Niet and I will start counting. If you're longer than ten minutes, we're coming to find you."

"I know."

"Good. Niet, how's the rope coming along?"

"I've got it ready now," Niet said, testing the knots again as he stood, surveying his handy work. "We just need to lower him and soon as you tug on that rope, we'll start pulling up the Ranger then you."

"Great," Will said and winced at the squeak in his voice. The prospect of lowering down the side of an enemy castle floors above stone cobbles, in broad daylight, made him regret the meager breakfast he'd eaten. It might very well fall on a passerby.

"Let's get a move on," Ross ordered, clapping his hands together. "We haven't all day."

They did so, Will sliding into the rope harness and standing stalk still as Niet adjusted ropes and triple checked his knots. His nod of approval felt more of a death sentence, but Will turned away, hoping Ross wouldn't see his face and order a stop to their plan.

Moving to the wall, the air rushed from his lungs. Dizzying distance fell beneath him, empty space that swallowed his heart. The climb to the sickroom felt like child's play compared to this drop.

Niet's hand gripped his shoulder in a bracing way, the wind whipping around them. "Should be a memorable event, eh?"

"Yeah, you could call it that," Will said, laughing hoarsely. "Memorable, deadly, what's the difference?"

Feeling Ross's uncertainty was the drive he needed to place both hands on the wall and lift himself, so his legs dangled over the drop. The rope around him tightened, Niet and Ross stepping into position, ready to lower him the four floors to the Ranger's window.

Taking another deep breath, Will closed his eyes and turned, pushing himself backwards down the wall. He didn't open his eyes again until he could feel the rope clinging behind his legs and against his back, a presence that told him he wasn't falling to crash onto the cobbles. At least, not yet.

He stared at the dark stone in front of him, reminding himself not to look down and kicked off the stone again. The rope lowered several feet. Again, and again, he kicked off the wall, forcing himself to stare straight ahead, both hands gripping the rope in front of him, until he was passing a set of windows, then another, then a third set.

The next one. He would need to be going through the next one. He reached out his fingers soon as he saw the window rushing up to greet him and grabbed the sill. The rope jerked, stopping suddenly and twisting, turning him so that for a moment he faced the open drop. He swallowed his scream and waited for his weight to turn back to the narrow window, peering inside.

He was looking into what seemed to be a grand bed chamber. From what he could see from his vantage, the room was empty, no fire burning in the hearth, the foot of an untouched bed, dust collecting across an ornate rug.

Grabbing the windowsill more firmly this time, he pulled himself through, swearing under his breath as he struggled to get the sword hilt through the opening, before lowering himself to the floor as silently as he could. Holding his breath, he moved to slip the rope from his body and, relieved for the solid floor under his boots. As soon as he'd stepped from the rope, he let it drop to the rug with a dull thud and turned, taking in his surroundings.

As it had seemed on the outside, he was in a bedroom though now that he stood in it, he wasn't sure grand was the right word. It seemed forgotten. The grey bedding with gold threads was faded, a layer of dust resting over the pillows and floors. Across from the bed, the wardrobe was wide open, the rail inside of it torn at an angle, clothing heaped on the floor around it as though someone had cleared it as best, they could in a hurry. Grime clung to a mirror on one wall, making Will's reflection seem more ghost than human.

Two doors led from the room. The one to his left was ajar, revealing a once fine bathing chamber with stone floors and a copper wash basin while the other door, in the wall in front of him, was closed.

He crossed the room and reached for the sealed door, heart rattling in his mouth. As his fingers closed on it, ready to rip it open, a voice seemed to whisper in his own head. *"Don't be an idiot, boy."* What would the Ranger say if he ever found out that Will had been so careless as to barge into an unknown room in Thornten? For all he knew, Marl might be in there. He stopped, leaning forward, his ears straining to hear.

At first, he could hear nothing but, pressing his ear tighter to the door, he froze. There. The rasp of breath. Someone in pain. That might be the Ranger. He gripped the door handle tighter. If they had hurt the Ranger, if they had done something terrible to him…what if he couldn't stand or was delirious and didn't recognize Will? Why hadn't he thought of these things before agreeing this was a good idea? Stupid!

The click boots over wood floor made Will stiffen. Someone was walking across the room beyond. The footfalls stopped and there was a thud followed by a grunt of pain.

"Sorry to rouse you."

Will froze, recognizing the sneering voice and felt anger flare to mingle with the panic.

"I wanted to see if you've changed your mind about being useful. You haven't long to decide to save your own life," said The Cutthroat Prince.

A raspy laugh followed the words. "As tempting as it would be to become a traitor to those things I've sworn my life to in exchange to become your lapdog, I think I'd sooner be dead. You'll have to make do with your current dog." The Ranger's voice was weak, dry, but Will recognized the cool tone.

Another thud and a sharp intake of breath. Will knew someone had struck the Ranger.

"I'd watch my mouth, traitor scum," Draccart snarled.

"Leave it, Draccart," The Cutthroat Prince snapped. "He'll be paying for his tongue soon enough. Well then, *Prince Esrin,* you best be prepared to die for your foolishness because your darling King has refused our demands as well as failed to send help. It seems he takes the safety of a child more seriously than the safety of his right hand."

"There are things worse than dying," the Ranger said dryly. "You would do well to remember that, as it's something too many of your kind take for granted. Perhaps you should look at me and remember that even *Princes* are left for dead at times."

Another thud. "Do not speak to me as an equal, traitor," hissed The Cutthroat Prince. Then in a louder voice, as though trying to compose himself. "There will be no more chances. By sundown tonight, you will be dead and for nothing. We will still take him as an heir for Kelkor, we will still ensure that the crown is passed to an ally in the future. All you've done is throw away your life like a fool."

Will listened as the footfalls crossed the room again and then a sharp crack echoed, the sound of a door being snapped shut. He waited, wondering if Draccart had perhaps stayed in the room as a guard. Or other guards who had stayed silent. After a few moments of silence, he braced himself, drawing the sword at his side. Waiting would get him nowhere. It was best to save the Ranger now, before someone arrived to escort him to his own execution.

Pushing the door open softly, Will took in the next room. This chamber was twice the size of the bedroom he stood in, with tapestries hanging from the wall, shelves flanking either side of a fireplace. A few chairs were pushed out of the way against the walls and a single door led from this room. And there, leaning against the wall between two of the chairs, head bowed against his chest, arms behind his back and clothing matted with dried blood, was a man.

Will took a tentative step into the room, eyes fixed on the unmoving figure, half afraid that the man was unconscious or already dead. The man's head jerked up, eyes flashing, and Will froze, staring. He had never seen the Ranger's face and yet he recognized the high cheek boned features, the cool dark eyes, the dark hair, though it fell in tangles around his regal features. Even with the bruising along his stubbled jaw and his unkempt appearance, there was no denying the similarities of this man and King Tollien of Thornten.

The man's mouth fell open as he stared at Will, what little color was in his face washing away. Closing his mouth, he squeezed his eyes shut and Will took another step forward, wondering if the Ranger was about to pass out.

"When I have opened my eyes, I am very much hoping you won't be here because I'm hoping you're not stupid enough to have broken into Thornten."

The eyes opened and Will noticed their depths were dark blue, not black like Tollien. Even the hair was lighter, a deep brown rather than midnight darkness. The Ranger's face shadowed. "What are you doing here?"

"Saving you," Will snapped, striding the distance between them. He crouched beside the Ranger, setting the sword on the floor, and reaching for the dagger at his side. Luck was on their side. He could see the binding biting into the Ranger's hands was the same style of rope that The Cutthroat Prince had used on him.

"Considering you came from the bedchamber, I take it you came through the window," the Ranger said, eyes narrowed. "Which means your Kelkor friend is helping you get into trouble again."

"Yeah, well, so are Rowan and Colin. Ross and Laster aren't doing much to stop us either."

"Remind me, if I get out of here, to kill you myself just to simplify matters."

"Great, will do. Now, do you mind leaning forward? I can cut your hands free."

He couldn't watch the Ranger's face as the man leaned forward but still he saw the body flinch in pain. They had clearly beaten him. Trying to keep his hands from shaking, Will sliced through the rope in a matter of never-ending seconds.

The Ranger brought his hands forward and rubbed the raw burns on his wrists. "I must say, I didn't expect that Ross and Laster would have brought you of all people."

Will grinned guiltily. "They didn't. We all just sort of showed up at the same place."

The Ranger rolled his eyes to the ceiling, inhaling deeply. "There are days I don't know why I bother trying to keep alive those so intent on getting themselves killed."

"Well, dwell on that later. We have to go. Can you stand?"

"Of course, I can stand," the Ranger growled. He pushed away Will's offered hand and, teeth bared, climbed to his feet. Will waited, holding his breath, as the Ranger swayed a moment. If he fell, all Thornten might rush through that door. Inhaling deeply, the Ranger straightened, face tightening with pain. "What is the plan from here then?"

"Ross will pull us back up, him and Niet."

"They can't lift us at the same time," the Ranger said, frowning. "Where is Laster? He should be up there."

"Planning our get away," Will said, shaking his head. "We haven't got time, we got to go now. When they come back for you, they are bringing fifteen guards."

He scrambled to his own feet, grabbing the sword, and forcing it into the Ranger's hands. "Let's get out of here."

"Right." The Ranger nodded, grabbing the sword in trembling fingers. Pain spasmed over his face but he didn't allow it to slow him, leading Will back across the room on cat silent feet. In the bedchamber, Will was glad to see the rope still trailing from the window, waiting for them with its looped harness. "You first, Will."

Will shook his head. "No."

The Ranger's eyes flashed dangerously. "You have to get out of here."

"I will but you have to go first," Will snapped. "They're expecting you first and you're not strong enough to tie yourself in right. We can't have them getting worn out lifting me first either. You weigh more. It'd be a really worthless rescue if you dropped off a rope and died halfway through."

The Ranger looked at Will with a strange frown, then shook his head, turning his face away but not before Will had caught a glimpse of his smirk. "You're getting rather bossy. I never thought I would miss the days when you were scared to be in my presence."

"Yeah, well those days are over." Will laughed ruefully and glanced back to the empty room they had just left. "We need to hurry up though, or Ross is going to charge down here himself to see what's going on."

"Nearly worth my life to see that," the Ranger said coolly but grabbed the rope all the same. Will helped adjust the knots, checking the harness was secured correctly before watching the Ranger lift himself through the window. A moment later, the rope moved, pulling the Ranger upwards, one hand clutching the rope, the other the sword. Another pull and he was almost out of sight of the window.

Will's chest swelled with pride, with success. This was it. They were saving the Ranger.

A crash behind him made Will whip round. Draccart was standing in the doorway of the other room. For a moment they stared at one another, shock and realization dawning on Draccart's pale features. Out the window, Will heard the Ranger yelling something, his voice weak, hoarse, too quiet for Niet and Ross to hear above the roar of the wind, the distance of four floors.

Draccart's shock broke and an evil leer pulled his mouth. He moved to step forward, reaching for the jagged edged sword on his side. Will's hand dove for his own blade and dread washed over him. The sword was in the Ranger's hand and his dagger was on the floor where he'd cut the Ranger free. He'd been so intent on getting away he hadn't thought to grab it. Plunging a hand into his pocket, Will drew the falcon blade, gripping it in a shaking hand.

"We've got him!" Draccart yelled, his voice shattering the silence of the room. "We've got the heir we wanted!"

CHAPTER THIRTY-SEVEN

Will dove away from the window, vaulting and rolling across the bed before crashing to the floor next to the wardrobe. He could hear Draccart running flat-footedly toward the room and scrambled to his feet, grabbing the clothing rod from the closet and gripping it in his dagger-free hand like a staff. The few garments that remained slid to the floor at his feet as Draccart appeared, swinging the sword lazily in one hand.

Catching sight of Will's makeshift weapon, he let out a bark of laughter. "Sticks against swords? They keep saying you're a threat but now I'm doubting that."

Without answering, Will threw the falcon dagger as he had in the tunnels. His stomach clenched as Draccart batted it away with a swat of his own weapon, barking in laughter.

Will glanced to his side, desperate for anything else to use as a weapon and grabbed up a pillow from the bed, still clutching the make-shift staff in his other hand, thinking desperately of Rowan and their pillow fights.

Draccart's laughter redoubled, and he shook his head, glancing the way he had come. "If they didn't want you alive so bad, I'd do it myself. Kill you here, like I did that horse."

"You didn't manage that too well," Will snapped. He glanced toward the window, hoping to see the rope drop back into sight. If he could grab it and jump, maybe he could hold on. Out of the corner of his eye he saw Draccart take a step forward and, without thinking, he wheeled round and threw the pillow at Draccart's face with all the force he had.

Draccart swung his sword up to stop the pillow and white feathers burst into the air like snow, scattering around the Cutthroat and blinding his vision. Will didn't hesitate but leapt up, onto the bed again, and dove forward, bringing the rod in his hands crashing down on Draccart's flaying arm. There was a howl of pain and before Draccart could strike, Will was on the floor again, bounding past him, out the door.

There were no guards coming. Maybe Draccart had been the guard! He might still stand a chance! He was across the room now at a sprint, rushing toward the door that would lead him out into the castle. He was crossing the threshold, stunned with his own thinking and luck.

His foot caught on something solid and unmoving, and the ground rushed to catch him as he crashed onto his chest, the closet rod flying from his hands and rattling over the floor ahead. Pain split up one leg, over the hand he had thrown out to break his fall, but he didn't care. There was time for pain when an angry teenager with a sword wasn't chasing him. He made to scramble upright, and a foot collided with his back, dropping him forward again.

"Come now, did you really think you could get away that easily?" laughed a snide voice above him. Will rolled onto his back, spitting blood from his split lip, and glowered in the dark eyes of The Cutthroat Prince above him.

Only The Cutthroat Prince wasn't wearing his grey hood and dark clothing. In fact, he wasn't hiding his face at all. He stood over Will with a gloating smile on his handsome face, black hair falling over his black eyes, somewhat disheveled from his springing forward to trip Will. His dark grey and gold tunic were perfectly tailored, his black boots polished to a high sheen, and one hand rested on the ornate handle of an expensive sword. Will stared up at the boy above him with a mixture of horror and comprehension freezing him in place.

"I must say," purred the boy, tilting his head to one side, "this is a pleasant surprise."

Will scrambled back as Draccart pounded through the door, panting, and came to an abrupt halt, murder dancing in his small eyes. The boy beside him held out an arm to stop him, smirking.

"Don't kill our guest quite yet."

"He let the Ranger get away," Draccart panted, turning from Will to the boy next to him.

The boy raised his dark eyebrows, seeming grudgingly impressed. "That is unexpected. No matter, go alert the guards. They'll find him and whoever else helped him to get away. Then bring my father and Marl here. They will want to see what we've managed to catch."

"What about him?" Draccart asked, jerking his head toward where Will still lay.

"I can handle him," snapped The Cutthroat Prince. "I want some time alone with my dear *cousin*."

"You're the Prince of Thornten then," Will snarled, trying to push himself into a seated position as Draccart strode past, down the corridor.

The boy gave a mocking bow, eyes never leaving Will's own. "With distinction. Allow me to formally introduce myself. I am Prince Tabius of Thornten, heir to the throne of my father, Tollien." He straightened dark eyes dancing, daring Will to rise to the bait.

"I'd bow but I'm afraid I don't actually care," Will growled.

He glanced behind him, toward the out of reach closet rod. He had a mad urge to lunge for it, just to knock this Prince around the ears. And to think he had felt bad that Ross and Laster intended to kidnap him when, all along, he had been the Ranger's captor. That feeling was gone. Now he wanted to see Laster burst through a door and tackle this fiend. But that was unlikely, and the closet rod was so close…

"If you move for it, I can promise you'll regret it."

Will turned his eyes back to the Prince to see the hungry black gaze was fixed on him. Tabius gave a humorless smile, raising his brows.

"Go for it, if you're feeling brave, I won't kill you. But what I can promise is that you will regret it. You see," he said, drawing his sword, his voice casual, more like he was discussing the weather than Will's fate. "This blade is from my uncle, a gift that he got in *Kelkor* when I first arrived at the castle this spring. It's imbued with Inanimus. Do you know what that is?"

When Will refused to answer, Tabius continued, turning the sword in his gloved hands and smirking. "You should know what it is. My father says that it was used on you last year, when they caught you before. It's what we used on the Ranger to slow him down when we were trying to capture him before on his way back from Kelkor. Only then we almost killed him. He wasn't meant to get struck with two blades, but he took the arrow meant for the Kelkor squire as well as the one meant for himself.

You see, this Inanimus is a poison. If inhaled, it can render a person unconscious in time and, if in the bloodstream, it can cause the victim paralysis." His smile grew more delighted, his dark eyes fixed on Will's blue ones. "Sometimes temporary but, in high doses, perhaps permanent. It will shut down the body slowly until the person dies in the most agonizing way. Their body will fail on them, their own body will attack and kill them."

"You nearly killed the Ranger," Will snarled, furious. "You almost killed him with that stuff."

"As I said." The Prince shrugged, lowering the sword point to rest on the floor. "That wasn't my intention. We wanted to use him as bait before, when we realized attacking you wasn't getting us where we needed to be. I wanted to capture your knight too but, I guess he and I will have to catch up another way. I haven't forgotten that he humiliated me."

"He should have killed you," Will spat. He wanted to kick out, to strike, even if it meant getting struck with this blade. It would be worth it just to kick him right in the shins and see him hop around like a moron.

"Lucky for Alamore that he didn't," Tabius chuckled, shaking his head. "You see, there would have been war. My father wouldn't have stood for it, nor would our allies in Phersal, Bronswick, and now Kelkor. But your King already knew that. He knew that The Cutthroat Prince couldn't be killed so easily. He gave the orders that your knights not try to kill me but rather capture me and, by never showing my face, it protected all of my Cutthroats as well."

"How did he know that?" Will demanded.

"Why from your Ranger, of course," Tabius said, raising his brows.

"The Ranger?" Will frowned, furrowing his brow. "He wasn't even around."

"Oh, he was for our earliest attacks. You see, you weren't my first target. Before I went for you, I needed to see to it that the Ranger was out of the way, that I had a clear shot at you because he's kept you protected more than you ever would know. What I needed was the ability to track your movements, give me insight into everything in Alamore."

Will snorted, rage making him bold. "Right, about that. That bloke, Oberoan? Your spy? He's dead."

"Oberoan? He's dead?" Tabius frowned then nodded thoughtfully. "I'm honestly surprised he lived as long as he did. He's been torn between betraying me and joining me for months now. But no matter. I planned for a few casualties. He's not my only set of ears in that castle."

The sound of approaching feet cut off any response from Will and he sat up, forgetting about the sword in Tabius's hand, and twisted round. Immediately he wished he hadn't as his mouth went dry, and hands curled into fists on the floor.

Draccart was half running toward them, his face alight with excitement while behind him strode two men. The taller of the men shared Tabius's features, which might have been handsome had they not be so cold, his black eyes more like bottomless pits. Tollien's brow furrowed as they approached, his lips pulling into a frown at the sight of Will on the ground. Beside him, his beard groomed and looking strange in a rich green tunic and bronze cloak, Marl's face was transported with delight.

"We've got a new guest, father," Tabius called. Will grunted as Tabius shoved a boot into his chest, knocking him almost to the ground again.

"Well done, Tabius." Marl leered down at Will, his chest rising and falling excitedly. "And here I was heartbroken that I would have to celebrate becoming King without my heir at my side. I'm glad to see you've come to your senses and decided to bring your loyalties where you truly belong, *son*."

Will scrambled away, his hands slipping over the floor, not daring to take his eyes off Marl. "I'd sooner die than swear loyalty to you."

"That could be arranged," Tollien said smoothly, coming to stand next to Marl. His dark eyes roved over Will's face, his eyes, and the frown deepened. He turned to his son, raising one brow. "Am I to understand that you lost the Ranger?"

"What does it matter?" Marl snapped before Tabius could answer, his eyes still narrowed at Will. "We've got the boy, haven't we?"

Tollien's lip curled in a snarl. "You might be a King, brother, but this is my Kingdom, and you will not question my concerns or leadership. If he's here and managed to help the Ranger escape into the castle it means others are here too."

That broke Marl's attention from Will and he turned to Tollien, the smile turning into a twisted expression. "Then send guards to find them. Kill them. I don't care."

"Most of my guards are in the courtyard," Tollien snarled. His eyes shifted to Will and the frown lessened. "I don't see them leaving the boy here. But, to be sure, perhaps he can give us names. So, boy, who all came with you? How many of your *King's* knights are in my castle?"

Will shrugged. "Anywhere between none and a thousand, I'd say."

He didn't get to enjoy Tollien's reaction as Marl struck. The back of his hand collided with the side of Will's face, knocking him nearly flat to the floor again. Catching himself on one elbow, Will spat a pink string of bloody saliva, his face and lip throbbing and something hot and sticky running down his chin. Beside him, he sensed rather than saw Marl stoop, crouching at his side. Lifting his gaze, Will looked up into the smirking face, the bottomless cruel eyes, and hatred and rage flooded through his bones. He wanted to strike back, to fight, even if it meant getting killed.

"You'll learn quickly that I won't stand for your impertinence, William. If you're to live long, if you're to be my successor, you'll have to start listening to me. Is that understood?"

Will said nothing, blinking against the sting in his right eye. He wouldn't show weakness. He refused to.

"If you tell us who is in the castle, Will, it's the first step to earning your freedoms here." Tollien spoke, coming to stand behind Marl, surveying Will with cool curiosity. "You'll stand a better chance of surviving. Work with us, boy, and one day you might be like Tabius here–a Prince."

"I'm not telling you a thing," Will hissed between gritted teeth.

Tollien's face darkened and he gave a curt nod, turning from Will to Draccart. "Find the guards. Search the entire castle and tell them to seal off the gates."

Will's stomach clenched. There was no way the others had gotten away yet and, knowing Ross, he would still be trying to get Will out of here. If Rowan and Colin knew he'd been caught, they'd be trying to help.

"As for the boy." Tollien turned to Marl, raising one eyebrow. "You might want to teach him some manners if he's your last option for an heir of Kelkor."

"Understood," Marl said, dark eyes narrowing to slits. Reaching into his belt, Marl drew a dagger. Will half expected it to be the diving falcon that he'd thrown at Draccart, but this blade was different. The metal shone strangely in the light of the torches, as if wet. Will's muscles tightened, his heart plummeting with understanding.

Marl's teeth shone white in his snarling smile. "Let's see how much better you handle poisons than the Ranger does, shall we?"

Will brought his knees into his chest and struck out, nearly managing to kick Marl. He sprang back with a string of oaths, Tabius and Tollien both taking steps back in surprise. Bracing himself to strike again, Will waited, eyes fixed on Marl's glower. If they thought that he was going to give up that easily, they were wrong. He would go down fighting.

A sound behind Marl made Will start, glancing back and he saw Tollien and Tabius wheel round, the King of Thornten reaching for his sword.

Marl turned his head, his murderous expression twisting into a look of purest loathing at the sight of the man stepping through a door and into the corridor behind them.

Lip curled in his sneer, sword lifted in challenge, Laster snorted derisively. "If you're enjoying being alive and King of Kelkor, then I don't recommend taking another step toward the boy. Otherwise, yours will be the shortest reign any kingdom has ever seen."

CHAPTER THIRTY-EIGHT

Marl tossed his dagger to his left hand, his right reaching for the sword on his side. It was clear in his blazing eyes that he no longer cared about Will. The furious snarl was fixed on Laster and he was stepping forwards, his blade lifted to strike.

Before he could move more than a stride, Tollien stepped forward, blocking his way, and throwing Marl a threatening look. "Your concern is the boy," he snapped, then turned to Laster, raising his voice. "Foolish of you to return here, Laster. You should have realized that escaping from here once was luck and twice impossible."

Marl moved toward Will again, lowering his sword point so it rested at Will's throat. "Any closer and his blood is on your hands, Laster."

"Let him go and I might let you live, how about that instead?" Laster offered disparagingly.

"You might let me live?" asked Marl, laughing. His hand was shaking with fury and Will scooted slightly to the side, eyes trained on the now quivering sword point. If he could reach the closet rod and help Laster, maybe they could get out of this.

"Your guards aren't coming, Tollien." Laster took a half step forward, amber eyes blazing. Will inched to the side, aware that all eyes were on Laster now. "You should train your squires to be a bit more alert of their surroundings or they might run right in front of a door as it's being thrown open." The sneer twitched into the shadow of a smirk. "He'll be fine in a few hours I expect."

"By which time you'll be a corpse," snarled Marl.

"How about you quit talking and show if you're even a decent swordsman anymore instead?" Laster asked. "I imagine that crown you stole made you worse, if that was possible."

Will rolled as Marl's sword jerked, feeling the edge of the blade just catch his shoulder. Marl was rising to his full height, seeming to have forgotten about Will, stalking toward Laster.

"Marl, the boy!" Tollien's shout was drown in the clash of steel on steel as Laster brought his sword up with deft speed to parry Marl's strike.

But Tabius had heard his father. Will saw him whip round and swore, scrambling to his feet and diving for the wooden rod. Tabius was bounding toward him, sword raised. Will's fingers closed on the wooden rod. He spun, bringing it up at the same moment that Tabius struck. Wood shattered in Will's hand, showering him with splintered fragments.

But the blow had been knocked aside, giving Will a moment to step back, still clutching the short remainder of his makeshift staff. Another rapid clash of blades made Will glance toward Laster. Tollien had joined the fight. His heart slammed in his ears. Laster couldn't hold them both off, not for long.

The momentary distraction was all that Tabius had needed. Out of the corner of his eye, Will saw the Prince move and spun round, bringing the rod upwards to block but he was too slow. The edge of Tabius's sword sliced along his shoulder, tearing through tunic and flesh. Will felt hot blood running down his arm, dripping over his fingers, but didn't dare to take his eyes of Tabius again. He took a step back. The Prince followed, hungry eyes gleaming.

"You have the chance at everything, Will. You have the chance to be what you should have been, a Prince," Tabius rasped. "You can be like me; you can have power and-"

"I don't want any of that," Will snapped. "I don't want your throne or your power."

He could feel a dull ache creeping into his arm and blinked hard against it. He had to focus. The cut wasn't that deep, not enough to kill him. If this was his body reacting to the pain, he had to ignore it, to focus. He took another step backwards, his toes sliding on the floor. His body was starting to weigh too much.

"How can you not want this power? You should want all of this; you should always have wanted to be what I am!" Tabius's words were distant, echoing in his ears and around his skull but not stringing together enough to make sense.

Will made to strike but something strange was happening. His body was moving slowly, too slowly. The attack seemed pathetic, the staff descending toward Tabius as if through water. With a bark of laughter, Tabius batted the staff away as easily as if it were a fly. "Father hasn't cared as much as Marl. He sees you as what you are–a threat to my crown. And now that I know what you are like, what you are, I think he's right."

Will's body wasn't listening. The sword was lunging forward, and he could only stare stupidly at the blade lunging toward his chest.

"ALAMORE!"

Something barreled into Tabius, knocking him nearly to the ground. In a flash of golden hair, a second figure joined the first and Tabius crashed to the floor, sword slithering over the ground.

Will blinked, shadows filling the edges of his visions, and tried to make sense of what had happened. He shook his head, trying to clear it and saw the two people fighting Tabius.

Rowan was straightening, grabbing up the sword and stepping out of Tabius's reach while Tabius himself wrestled to free himself from Colin, who had pinned one arm up and behind his back. Then Colin twisted and Will saw the flicker of silver and tried to shout a warning, but it was Colin's dagger. Colin pressed the blade to Tabius's neck.

"HEY! BONEHEAD! We've got your Prince!" Rowan shouted, his voice loud enough to break over the scream of swords and the spinning in Will's own head. Laster and Marl took no notice, but Will saw Tollien spin.

At the sight of Tabius, half kneeling on the floor, Colin's dagger at his neck, Tollien's face became a mask of fury. He made to move forward, and Colin shook his head, pressing the dagger tighter.

"Call off Marl," Colin ordered. "And stay back, or you'll be having to hunt down an heir for yourself as well."

"MARL!" Tollien shouted, blazing eyes never leaving Colin's face. Marl faltered, turning, and Will saw Laster take a step back. Will frowned, bewildered. Why hadn't he struck? Marl's back was turned. He could have struck and killed Marl. Marl's eyes flitted from Colin to Tollien to Tabius.

"Drop the sword, Marl," Tollien snarled.

"But Tollien," Marl protested.

"I said drop your weapon!" Tollien's voice boomed through the corridor, commanding and crackling with rage.

Marl's sword fell from his fingers, ringing off the floor as his dark eyes rested on where Will stood, swaying. "This isn't the end."

"For now it is," Laster snapped, sheathing his sword. "Arms behind you, now."

Will stepped sideways, leaning against the stone wall for support and watched as Laster forced Marl's arms behind his back and tied them with a length of rope. Next he did the same with Tollien. "Rowan, gather their swords," Laster ordered. "Throw that one you're holding out the window."

"Why?" Rowan demanded obstinately. "I like this one."

"Look at Will. It's covered in that Kelkorian poison," Laster snapped, jerking his head toward Will. "I've seen you in practice. You'll end up poisoning yourself and being useless to me and I need you and Colin to help with Will."

"Git," Rowan grumbled but did as he was told, scooping up Marl's and Tollien's swords as the Alamore knight pushed the two Kings to the ground against one wall. Will watched through his fading eyes as Rowan darted into the other room, returning in moments without the poisoned blade.

"Let go of my son," Tollien hissed, eyes still fixated on Colin.

"You'll get him back when we're safely at Alamore." Laster sneered. "I don't trust you half as far as I could throw you. Here, Colin, let me deal with that one. You and Rowan get Will upright. We don't have long until guards get here."

"But I thought you knocked that squire out," Rowan said, looking annoyed.

Laster rolled his eyes to the ceiling. "Did you not hear the swords echoing or are you truly as stupid as you look? Someone will have heard it and have the brain to piece together what's happening. We have to catch up with the others. Come on."

Will squeezed his eyes shut, trying to stop the spinning in his head. He wanted to be sick. A moment later he felt a hand gently grab his arm and lift it over solid shoulders. "Lean on me, Will. I've got you." Colin's voice was low, soothing.

Opening his eyes, Will saw that now Laster had bound and gagged the Prince of Thornten and was lifting him over one shoulder.

Rowan moved to Will's other side, still gripping one sword. Colin held the other.

"Scream for help before we're out of sight and I'll kill the Prince just to spite you," Laster commented to Tollien, smirking. "But go ahead and plea for your soldiers to find him when I'm gone. I only wish I could see it."

"You'll die for this, knight," hissed Tollien.

Laster rolled his eyes again. "You haven't managed to kill me yet, so your threats are starting to lose their bite. You three, let's get out of here."

Will leaned against Colin and Rowan, staggering down the corridor. Like his way up the tower with Ross, it was impossible to keep track of their route. His feet dragged down steep steps, his head spun, and it took all of his strength not to get sick on his friends. Each window they passed brought with it a relief of fresh air to his choking throat but the darkness between them grew blacker. Once in a while he felt Rowan or Colin elbow him gently, trying to get him to stay awake.

"Bit further, just a bit."

Somewhere in the castle, Will heard the shouts of voices, the din of feet running. Laster swore under his breath. "Either they have found our darling Kings, or they met Ross."

"I don't think Ross was in a mood to keep them alive," Colin commented wryly. "So, I'm guessing the former."

"Probably." Laster smirked.

"How did you know where I was?" Will asked, trying to keep his mind from the tantalizing dark that welcomed it.

"Ross," Rowan answered simply. He looked unusually grim. "When they got the Ranger, he must have realized something was wrong. He started a fire on the tower and Laster drug us this way."

"It was our signal for something went wrong," Laster said coolly, leading through yet another door.

"Why didn't you tell us the signal?" Rowan asked, affronted.

"Because telling you all that we expected something to fail wasn't really helping the confidence level of the group," Laster snapped. "Now shut up and pick up the pace."

Will could tell his weight was leaning more on his two friends and he tried to place his feet under himself, lift his weight. They were on another narrow set of stairs, steps that seemed long forgotten. Thick dust clung to the banister and floated in the slanting shafts of light that streamed through windows. They had nearly reached the bottom step when the door below was yanked open and blinding sunlight streamed through it. Will tensed, expecting the cry of soldiers or Marl's furious howl.

"Storms of the sea, I thought you all would be dead by now."

"Nice to see you too, Niet," Rowan grumbled.

Niet stepped into the tower, reaching hand forward to grab Will as they reached the bottom step. "Will? You alright?"

"Does he look alright?" Rowan demanded.

Niet ignored Rowan, turning to Laster. "Ross and the Ranger are out but we have to hurry. They're trying to clear the gateways and get them closed. Only thing that's stopping them a group of civilians and I'm not sure why."

"Supporters of Alamore and the Ranger," Laster said stiffly. "They will pay for what they're doing, and they can't hold long. Niet, take Will. You two, get on the horses and go. We'll follow. Once in the city, scatter. They will be hunting me and the Prince, I'll try to keep them off of your trail as long as I can."

"We want to go with Will!" Colin said, pulling closer to Will's side.

"Either you scatter and separate from him or die next to him, your choice, but I'm not bringing flowers to your grave if you die for being a moron," Laster barked. "I said go!"

Niet grabbed Will and stepped aside, allowing for Rowan and Colin to barrel past, out the door and into the courtyard. Will could hear it now. The hubbub of voices, screaming, hooves and the chaos.

"What happened to him, Laster?"

"Inamimus. This darling Princeling got him with a blade coated in it."

Niet swore and Will felt himself lifted up. Embarrassed and annoyed by his own weakness, he tried to pull himself upright, to move, but Niet didn't seem to notice.

Something was draped over him, covering his sight and Will squeezed his eyes shut, feeling the older squire break into a run. He wanted to vomit. The noise of people grew louder, echoing around him. Someone screamed, Laster yelled a string of orders that he couldn't make out, hands lifting him upwards. Then the jerk of movement, familiar movement. He was in the saddle, or rather thrown over the front like a ragdoll.

"Hold on, Will," Niet yelled then another twisting and they were launching forward. Will grappled to grab onto the saddle as the cloak covering him flapped away in the wind. Beneath them, the golden horse surged forward, scattering people who got in their way.

He saw a man in rich robes scream and leap into a horse tank to avoid being run over, a guard bellowed something and tried to grab at them but recoiled as an arrow struck his arm. Will turned his head, fighting to keep conscious, and saw Laster's horse surging next to him, the Prince of Thornten slung like he was.

They broke through the gates, onto the stone bridge, the horses never hesitating a moment. Will was glad he couldn't see the drop. He didn't want to imagine it right now. All he wanted was for the throbbing starting in his arm to lessen, the spinning to stop. Niet was holding him in the saddle with one arm, and they were turning into the city. They scattered chickens and children as they burst into a side street. Behind them, some ways off, Will could hear more horses. The chase had started.

"Hold on, Will, hold on, we're nearly to the forest." Niet was saying. Will had a feeling the squire was talking to himself more than Will. "They're chasing Laster, not us."

Will tried to nod, only managing to knock his already spinning head on the saddle. It must have been hard as the world blinked out into nothing.

CHAPTER THIRTY-NINE

It was the still that roused him. Will opened his eyes, blinking at the red sky that peaked through high tree boughs. His mouth was dry and, judging by the taste of his own tongue, he hadn't managed to keep himself from vomiting. Rolling onto his stomach, he pushed himself up on shaking arms and spat onto the forest floor. Forest. They shouldn't be on the forest floor, should they?

He turned, trying to see his surroundings but the light was piercing his eyes, the still of the woods deafening. They were in the heart of the forest and the soft earth was ladened in dead leaves.

"Don't move much or you'll get the poison going through your body again."

Will started, dropping onto one elbow, and craned his neck to blink upwards. Niet was standing over him, dark hair a mess, his face exhausted but elated.

"Where are we?"

Niet shrugged. "Somewhere in the forest. I thought it best you get your arm treated before we carried on."

"But we were being chased," Will mumbled. He ran his tongue over the roof of his mouth. Alamore. Had he been chewing on the rotting leaves?

"Here." Niet crouched, holding a water skin out to Will. "Drink. You drink, it'll help your body recover from the toxin. Laster was right, the knights all were on his tail. I can only hope that either he dropped the Prince, or his horse is strong enough to lose them."

Will guzzled the water. He wasn't sure he had ever had anything that tasted as good. After a moment he pulled it from his mouth, processing Niet's words. "But Rowan and Colin?"

"They got out ahead of us," Niet said, grinning. "They actually caused the chaos that gave us a way out. Rowan ended up lighting that stage on fire on his way out. I guess it's his version of a grand exit, eh?"

Will managed a weak laugh. "Sounds like Rowan."

"But we did it." Niet beamed down at Will. "We saved the Ranger. We actually did it."

The Ranger. Will sat up, immediately wishing he hadn't as his head spun again. He turned, ready to be sick, then relaxed as the churning in his stomach settled. "The Ranger and Ross?"

"They were the first out. We made Ross get the Ranger out on Admere. That's why I was in the courtyard still instead of with Laster and the others, I was waiting on them. Ross showed up and was going to charge right back in, but I told him to get the Ranger out and start the chase, so we'd stand a better chance."

"We did it," repeated Will softly. For the first time in days, Will allowed himself to relax, leaning his head back on his sore neck to stare at the sunset stained sky overhead. They had done it. It was all over now. A distant sound snapped him back to reality and he glanced around them. "We shouldn't be here. We should still be riding."

"You needed treatment," Niet said, pushing himself to his feet.

Will touched the thick bandaging on his arm. "Thanks."

"You're welcome." Niet straightened, brushing leaves from his tunic. "The only thing that would have made this escape better was the chance for me to come face to face with Marl. I could have had the chance to kill him then."

"You don't want to cross Marl," Will said, shaking his head. "He's…he's evil."

Niet snorted, his nose wrinkling in disgust. "And evil shouldn't survive, let alone rule Kelkor. It would be worth my life to end his."

Will shivered at his words. "Yeah, well, you're alive still so I think that's good enough. Maybe when we're knights you can go kill him and we'll host a party or something. Right now, though, I want to move."

He pushed himself up, trying to stand. His legs were still weak, too weak to hold his weight, and they buckled. The forest floor sent a throb of pain through his bruised body as he crashed to his knees.

"Easy, Will. That poison can cause serious issues. I'll get Cerlan saddled, and we'll be out of here, but you just sit." Niet pushed down firmly on Will's uninjured shoulder. "I said sit. And I will come back here and deal with you in a moment, alright?"

Will grudgingly stopped his attempts to rise, contenting himself with another pull from the waterskin as Niet stomped across the clearing to where the palomino horse stood, his coat matted in dried sweat, his blanket and saddle hanging from a nearby tree. Will frowned, staring at the horse. They had to have been here a while if the sweat had dried. It made him uneasy. Even with the knights after Laster, someone might have followed them. He could still remember the last time he'd been to Thornten and rested. Had it not been for the arrival of Ross, Laster, Miller, and Rockwood, he would have been captured again by Robin on that adventure.

Another sound in the woods, this time nearer, made him stiffen. He noticed Niet do the same, turning toward the wall of trees and reaching for his sword. There was a low sound carrying toward them now, growing closer. Will tried again to push himself upright, panic rising. He knew that sound. The gentle jingle of tack, the soft thud of horses hooves.

Niet seemed to recognize it at the same moment. He grabbed the horse, pulling it over toward Will without the saddle. "We got to go."

Will could hear some of his panic now echoed in the older squire's voice. Niet grabbed him by the arm, half lifting him, and pushed him onto the horse's bareback. A moment later, he swung up behind Will and dug his heels into the golden horse's side. The palomino surged forward, and Will ducked his head, grabbing handfuls of the white mane. They were plunging into the forest and, over the crack of breaking thicket. The rumble of hooves, Will heard the second horse. It too seemed to be gaining speed.

"Come on, Cerlan," Niet hissed to his horse. The horse stretched out, covering the ground in great bounds. Will squeezed his legs tight around the animal's sides, half certain he'd fall each time the horse leapt a felled tree or small twisting offshoot of creek. "Come on!"

Ahead the trees were thickening. Will flattened himself forward, trying to keep out of Niet's way. They could lose their pursuer in the forest, through these trees. If they could just hide where the foliage was the thickest...

The horse stumbled and Niet's arm tightened around Will's chest. All peace was broken. Invisible in the tangle of trees, the horse was plunging off the edge of the earth itself. The ravine was sharp, breaking into the clearing beneath. Will tried to pull himself straight, bracing himself backwards against the animal's withers but the horse fell onto his front leg, stumbled up, then fell again. A loud burst of swearing and he felt Niet's arm break free.

He'd hit one of the low hanging branches of a tree. Will tried to twist, to see where he had landed, and the horse staggered again.

In a blur of color, sound, the smell of dirt, everything rushed toward Will. He fell for either seconds or an eternity, he couldn't be sure. His plunge ended as hard earth crushed the air from his ribcage, ripped the skin from his palms. He rolled down the steep incline, struggling to stop himself. Hard earth battered his body, thickets tearing his skin and clothing, in an endless fall that seemed never to end. It was a tree that stopped him, colliding with his bandaged shoulder and the pain and darkness swallowed his surroundings.

CHAPTER FORTY

The world was spinning, hot blood slid down the side of Will's face when he tried to open his eyes. The Inanimus was coursing through his aching shoulder and his head throbbed with pain. What little recovery he had made when they stopped was gone, the feeling of being sick churning in his stomach again as if the poison had taken hold again when he and Niet had fallen.

Niet!

He tried to move, to sit up, to see anything but the spinning forest floor. His body seemed to be broken, limbs twitching and convulsing each time he tried to move. He lay back on the ground, breathing hard. Niet would find him. Perhaps he was catching the horse. He would find him, and they would get back to Alamore before the rider could catch them. Now that he was this weak, Niet wouldn't argue or pause. They would ride without stopping.

The clash of steel on steel made Will try to rise. His body failed and he crashed back to the earth, the skin breaking across his palms. He heard a familiar bark of cold laughter and tried to rise again, this time to his hands and knees, his body shaking. This time he knew the shaking wasn't all because of the poison as terror clawed through his throat, tightened on his lungs.

"Is that the best you've got, boy?"

Marl. Marl's voice. Marl's laughing, hateful, voice. He had found them. He had found Niet.

Niet!

He tried to crawl forward, but his limbs weren't working, they shook under his weight. Another deafening sound of blades colliding split through Will's head as if it had been struck. He lifted his face, swaying, and blinked the blurriness from his eyes. Niet was standing several paces away, his sword gripped in both hands, panting, watching Marl.

Marl looked unphased, as though this were nothing more than simple training. His black eyes were empty of emotion and he wore a smile that showed his teeth like a snarl.

"You've got to learn to fight better than this, boy," Marl hissed. "You won't live long, just like your King. Go back to Alamore, why don't you? Let them teach you to fight and then, maybe, I'll let you crawl back to Kelkor, let you join my armies."

He turned his back on Niet and Will's arms buckled, half in exhaustion, half in disbelief and relief. Marl was truly striding away, moving to sheath his sword and reaching for the reins of his black horse that stood, sweaty and waiting. Hidden in the undergrowth, Will held his breath. Maybe Marl thought Niet was riding alone, that he wasn't worth his time.

Glancing toward Niet, Will's muscles went rigid. A shadow had crossed the older squire's face, twisting the features in furious hatred that rose in storm clouds behind dark eyes. Marl had just reached to mount his horse, his back turned to them, when Niet lunged forward. Marl seemed to sense the attack and spun so the blade meant for his heart only sliced into upper arm, biting deep into the outside of his left shoulder.

With an animalistic roar of fury, Marl unsheathed his sword again with his good arm and swung. Niet was forced to block blow after heavy blow that made his arms visibly shake. Will could do nothing but watch, transfixed with horror.

Niet took a step back, then another, then another. He was being backed against the thicker vines that lined the clearing. His foot caught one and he threw his blade forward wildly to block Marl's strike. Steel screamed, snapped under Marl's own sword, and the shards of Niet's blade fell into the dirt, useless. Marl struck without hesitation and scarlet blood rose to the gash across Niet's shoulder.

"No! Leave him alone!" Will didn't recognize his own voice, hoarse, cracking.

But Marl stopped. He wheeled round, eyes landing on Will. His lips twisted into a smile and he stepped toward him, leaving Niet gasping on the forest floor. Will braced himself, staring at the blood-stained steel of the blade. Instead of striking, Marl crouched, bringing his face low so he could look into Will's face. Will refused to look away and fought the urge to blink. He had never hated anyone as much as he hated this man standing before him. With the burning in Marl's eyes, he knew his father felt the same spite.

"You cause death, boy," Marl hissed. "You bring about death better than any sword I've ever held. Are you saying I should kill you in his place? Offering your life up for his?"

Will struggled to keep his voice from shaking. The poison in his blood was making everything hazy again, the edges of his vision darkening.

"Leave him alone," Will repeated, his voice low now. "I don't care if you kill me but leave him alone."

Something in the dark eyes flickered and Marl hesitated. Will longed for the broken portion of Niet's sword or even his dagger, lost somewhere in Thornten castle. He could strike now, kill Marl. It would be worth his life.

"No." Marl straightened, shaking his head. "You can't decide who lives and dies, boy. This squire, this *boy*." He was striding toward Niet, lifting his sword. "He chose to defend you. I would never disrespect his dying wish by letting him see you killed."

And the sword plunged down. Will's scream never left his throat, it couldn't, but he felt it tear through his body. He tried to stand and crumpled. Again, and again, he fought to reach Niet, the poison and the blow to his head dragging at him, attempting to pull him under its darkness.

By the time he had reached Niet's side, Marl had vanished, his horse's hooves a distant echo that resounded in Will's ringing ears. He stared down at Niet's blood, staining the front of his sea green tunic, the corner of his mouth, and thought of Sir Dannix's mutilated body.

"Niet," Will whispered, pleading, trying to make his hands stop the blood. "Niet!"

"Will." Niet's voice was gravelly, too soft, too tired, too strained with pain.

"Don't talk, we got to get you to the castle, to the Ranger, a healer, someone," Will whispered. "We have to-"

"Will," Niet insisted, interrupting. His voice was growing weaker, and Will leaned in, desperate to catch the words, fighting the burning in his eyes and throat. "Will, take care of Eldin, won't you? Her...and Kalia..."

"You're going to be okay; you'll be fine, you're going to get back to the castle." Will knew the words were a lie, but he tried his hardest not to see the blood running down Niet's chest, his face, into his dark eyes.

Niet laughed, the sound weak, choked. "Don't gamble, ever. You're not a good liar." His fingers reached up to grab Will's arm, clenching around them. He could feel them shaking, weak and in shock. Niet's dark eyes flitted between Will's and he swallowed hard, color leaching from his face. "Don't tell Serena…I acted a coward…struck at a man's back…"

"Marl isn't a man, he's a snake." Will shook his head. "We won't tell her, you're going to be okay, we're going to get back to Alamore, it's going to be okay."

Niet gave a shadow of his wolfish smile and let his hand fall to his side, his eyes shifting to the sky. "I miss the ocean."

"We'll go to the ocean. Maybe you, me, Rowan, Colin, Eldin, Kalia, we can all go Please," Will whispered. Niet's face was pale, his lips tinged with blue. His eyelids flickered, sails in a heavy wind, then closed. His chest stopped rising, the silence that had been filled moments ago with the sound of his breath was deafening.

He was dead.

Will stared at him, not sure what to do, a ringing filling his ears. Around him the forest was still, even the wind held its breath.

"No," he whispered, grabbing Niet's shoulders. He wanted to shake him, to make him wake up. Something told him he couldn't, though. He couldn't shake him hard enough to wake him. Those eyes wouldn't open again.

"No!" His voice broke and he released Niet's tunic, his hands shaking too badly to hold on any longer.

Everything was wrong. This was wrong. It was a nightmare, a terrible nightmare. He would wake up in the squires' chamber, it would be dawn again and this whole nightmare wouldn't happen. It wouldn't happen because it wasn't real.

Something hot and wet was dripping down the side of his face. He saw his blood fall onto Niet's chest, mixing with the scarlet that stained his hands. Niet's blood. It was real. It wasn't a nightmare. This was death and he, Will, had brought it about. He had been helpless to save Niet's life.

Grief tore at his chest, ripping deep claws through his heart, up his throat, until he thought he might scream with the suffocating pain of it all. His breathing was coming in ragged gasps and, somewhere, an animal's cry to the night seemed to echo the agony inside of him.

It was only as he bit down, hard, on his own sleeve and the keening stopped that he realized there was no animal. Nothing in the world moved. His cries had stopped, now trapped behind his teeth, desperate to escape once more.

He lay like that in the dark of the forest, night wrapping cold and dark around him, his body shaking with sobs that seemed unwilling to escape. It was as though the pain bit deeper than tears could understand. Nothing mattered. The world was gone. He wanted to be anywhere else but here, be anyone else. Because it wasn't anyone else who had caused this. It was his fault. Marl had killed Niet to spite him, only to waste a life from pure hatred. Somehow he felt certain that steel could not bite as deep into his body as the emptiness that consumed him and the poison that gripped tight over his mind and forced him back into unconsciousness once again.

CHAPTER FORTY-ONE

"Ross, he's here! He's over here!"

Hands grabbed at Will's uninjured shoulder, but he tried to push them away and squeezed his eyes tighter. If he didn't open them, this would be a nightmare. He had hoped that reality would pause a moment, not flood back over him, but give him even a lung full of air as reprieve. It hadn't. Under his hands, he could feel the stiffness of drying blood on the front of the tunic.

"Will." The voice had become softer. He wasn't sure he had ever heard it so gentle. "Will, you need to let go of him."

At last, he opened his eyes and met the blue eyes of the Ranger, his face drawn and pale, the hood of the cloak he wore pulled away. Bruising still marred his face, fresh blood beading over his broken lip, but somehow he looked stronger than he had the day before in the Thornten. The day before. Had it only been the day before?

Will blinked again at the face swimming in front of him. There was a sadness in the eyes that made his resemblance to Tollien lessen and their reality crushed down on Will without turning to see the body he was sprawled over.

"It's my fault," Will rasped. "My fault."

"It's not your fault." The Ranger sighed and grabbed Will tighter, pulling him away from Niet. He grunted with pain, lifting Will onto his feet but his knees buckled, and the Ranger grunted, catching his weight. "Try to stand, Will, you have to try to walk."

Will nodded and tried to force his legs beneath him, trying to stand. He swayed, his muscles giving way again. His bones had turned to stone. Between the emotions rising again in his chest and the poison, he could feel his muscles spasming, twitching and weak.

Someone crashed through the undergrowth near them, and Will heard Ross's voice break. "Is he...?"

"He's alive. Ross, we have to get Will out of here. I can't carry him...my leg." The Ranger's arms were shaking, and the world was starting to tilt.

Arms embraced Will and he felt himself lifted more securely. He barely noticed the light filtering between tree branches as Ross carried him out of the clearing, toward the path.

"Are you hurt, Will?" Ross asked, his growl soft. Will wondered if the man might cry then wondered if it mattered. His own eyes seemed heavy, his face swollen with the tears he had sobbed, and nothing had happened. They hadn't brought Niet back. Nothing could bring back the dead. "Will?"

"No," his voice rasped again, still unfamiliar, a stranger speaking through his mouth.

"Ross! Ross!" Haru's voice, panicked, desperate, rushing toward them.

"He's alive," Ross growled. "Haru, get the horses. You'll have to bring Will back to the castle. The Ranger and I...we will get Niet."

"Where is he?"

"He's in the clearing, down the ravine behind us. The horse must have fallen, and someone caught them." Ross's voice tightened.

Haru didn't ask and Will wondered if he already knew. Did news of death travel in silence? In the look on Ross's face above him? In the blood that stained his tunic?

"Will, can you stand?" Ross asked huskily.

He nodded, pain rushing to his head with the small movement. "I can try," he whispered.

Ross lowered him, seeming reluctant, but Will's knees still weren't working right. They shook, his body threatening to rush to the ground. Hands grabbed him by the unscathed shoulder, and he lifted his face to see Haru's face, bloodless and tired, his red hair falling over his grey-green eyes. Ross, next to him, looked no better with dark shadows of exhaustion, several days of beard darkening his jaw.

"Get him to Alamore, he needs a healer," Ross growled then spun away, stomping back down the edge of the ravine, to the clearing below.

"Come on, Will, lean on me," Haru whispered, pulling Will's arm over his broad shoulders. Trying to walk felt as unfamiliar as his own voice had sounded. This wasn't his body. Everything was so wrong with it that it couldn't be his body.

"The horses are just up there," Haru encouraged, and Will lifted his heavy head, staring up the path.

A cluster of horses was tied along the path: Laster's grey, Rockwood's lanky chestnut, the Ranger's slight black mare, and Haru's broad roan, and a small red horse with a thick neck. Admere's ears pricked forward, his eyes fastened on Will. The sight of the animal brought the grief rushing to his throat.

When they had neared him, Will pulled away from Haru and wrapped his arms around the horse's thick neck. He fought to swallow the knot that choked the air from his lungs, the tears but, try as he might, he couldn't control the shaking. Admere stood, steadfast, his neck curved around Will. His hot breath warmed Will's back and he managed a choked laugh.

"It's good to see you, old boy," Will muttered, lifting his face. The brown eyes blinked back at him, and he thought he could see worry in their dark depths.

"Can you ride?" Haru asked softly.

Will nodded, not trusting his voice to speak again. He didn't protest when Haru held the stirrup steady and braced a hand on Will's back to help him into the saddle. Admere stood unnaturally still with none of his normal fidgeting. Will gathered the reins and saw the dark stains over his pale fingers. He tried not to think of whose blood it might be. His. The Ranger's. Niet's.

"I'll lead Admere, you just stay on," ordered Haru. It sounded to Will like Haru expected him to argue but he didn't. He was too tired to argue. Instead, he gripped the front of the saddle and stared firmly at the red ears of the small horse. He wouldn't look down at his hands. He wouldn't see the blood again.

The ride didn't take long enough. Will wanted to ride forever, through forest in silence. Haru's only words were to his horse and there was a peace in not speaking. Too soon Alamore's walls were visible, lit in the early hours of sunrise. His home, full of the people he loved and who cared about him. Rowan and Colin would be there demanding answers, wanting to find him.

And those who loved Niet would be waiting for answers as well. Serena, Eldin, Kalia. They would be waiting too. Had Niet's horse made it back to the castle when they'd fallen? Had they seen the blood and assumed? The idea of telling them that Niet was dead made him want Admere's reins back so he could turn around and ride far away.

"I'll talk to people first," Haru said, answering Will's unasked fears.

"Thank you," Will whispered.

"Will, what you did, you and the others, saving the Ranger..." Haru was struggling for words and Will noticed his eyes shone unnaturally bright. "I thought all of you were dead. When I found you were gone...but the King wouldn't let me leave, wouldn't let any of us leave...then when the others got back last night..." His voice broke and Will watched a tear roll down Haru's cheek.

"Haru, I'm fine," Will choked on the lie. He knew he wasn't convincing his knight.

In the courtyard, Haru's face kept the soldiers and stable hands at bay. None of them dared to look at Will under his knight's protective glower. It was only when Will had patted Admere's neck again in thanks that one of the braver stable hands collected enough courage to rush forward. He grabbed the reins to Admere and Haru's roan and Will watched the red horse led away, head low, tail rippling with each step.

"Healing chambers, now," Haru grunted, grabbing Will's arm again as he swayed.

"Haru!"

Haru swore under his breath and Will squeezed his eyes shut. Serena's voice, demanding, full of broken emotion; anger, desperation.

"Where is he, Haru?" Will opened his eyes again and looked up. She was stalking toward them from the black doors, her hair falling from its braid, framing her snarling face.

Haru opened his mouth to answer, then closed it, struggling for any sound, any words. Her green eyes moved to Will's and Will felt his throat close again. His face must have been answer enough because she staggered several steps back, shaking her head. "No."

"Ross," Haru managed.

She wheeled away, shaking her head. "Someone bring me a horse, now!"

"Serena, they're bringing him here," Haru called after her. But it was useless. She was already storming into the barn.

Will ducked his head quickly to wipe his tears on the sleeve of his tunic without Haru noticing. His knight let out a shaky breath and pulled gently for Will to follow. People cleared as they strode into the entry hall, past familiar doors, to the familiar stairs. Haru half carried him up the steps and into the healing chamber. As soon as they had entered, he drew the bolt across it and turned to the startled healer who was making one of the nearby beds. The bed Eldin had been in. Pain tightened over Will's chest. Where were she and Kalia? When would they know the truth?

"No one is to enter this chamber, got it?" Haru growled threateningly at the healer.

The healer raised his eyebrows but didn't protest, only waving to the bed he had just made. "Just cleaned this so might as well get him in this one. But only after he changes. Come along, squire. A clean tunic then bed, what do you say?" His voice was firm yet caring.

Will saw the hesitation in Haru's face when the healer pried the knight's fingers from his sleeve. "If you want to see to it that no one enters, then stand guard outside. Standing guard inside doesn't do us much good. People will pound upon that door, I know this boy's friends, I've dealt with them. They'll climb through windows to get in here if we aren't diligent."

"Right. I guess they'd have help from some of our Kelkor residents on that too if there isn't someone to stop them." Haru smiled, the gesture not quite reaching his eyes.

Will watched him leave then allowed the healer to herd him behind curtains where he changed into one of the sleeping tunics, discarding his stained clothing in a pile. He wished he could burn them, but the hearth was unlit, no torches nearby offered their flames. He had to content himself with washing his bloody hands in a basin of warm water and wiping his face with a cloth brought to him by a quiet woman with almond eyes and premature silver in her auburn hair.

When he was clean enough that the healer allowed him into the bed, the round nosed man stood over him, hands on his hips, to ensure that Will drank the tea he was given—bitter herbs stinging his nose and throat even through the honey that someone had generously added. After he placed aside the cup, the healer busied himself cleaning the cut on Will's shoulder and pressing a compress on one of the scratches across his forehead. He couldn't remember the skin tearing. Had it been in the fall? Did it even matter? The pain of his wounds was somehow disconnected from his body, as if it were a memory.

He drank more of the bitter herbs, listened to the sounds in the courtyard of returning horsemen. Everything was hazy and, eventually, unconsciousness caught up with him once again. This time it was not dark and hungry, however. This time, when he closed his eyes, it was warm, caring, and felt like sleep.

CHAPTER FORTY-TWO

Rowan and Colin made exactly twenty-four attempts to sneak, slip, trick, and push, their way past Haru before the knight finally allowed them to enter. It was mid-afternoon of the same day and Will was propped on his pillows, wishing he could run his hand over his stitched forehead and shoulder. The healer had already yelled at him for it once then rambled on darkly about infection for a quarter of an hour while he reapplied a stinging salve to the injuries. He threw his hands in the air and cursed under his breath when Haru opened the door, letting Rowan and Colin in and entering himself.

"I thought you said the boy needed peace!"

"You tell that to them," Haru snapped. "I'm too tired to keep fighting them."

"I thought you were supposed to be a knight! Fighting is your duty!" the healer retorted and rolled his eyes, stalking through the curtain at the back of the room and grumbling about squires.

Will grinned at his two friends, glad to see both looked uninjured, apart from a few superficial scratches. He imagined they must have been from the twigs trying to grab at them while riding the day before.

"You two making Haru crazy, then?"

Haru growled behind them, flopping fully clothing onto the bed across the room.

"Naturally," Colin said, grinning and lowering himself into the chair beside Will's bed. Rowan grabbed the chair from the bed next to Haru's and carried it over, flopping onto it backwards and crossing his arms across the backrest.

"What happened to you two when we got out?" Will asked. He was determined to keep the subject away from Niet and himself.

"Well, Naja bolted, wasn't going to slow down for anything when that stage just happened to catch fire. It turns out my horse is absolutely terrified of fire. Not that I mind, as we ended up running over one of the Cutthroats. He got up, so I guess we didn't hurt him too bad, unfortunately.

But we got loose of the courtyard and came back along the same trail as we did last year, I think, but hard to tell because the trees all look the same. I rode about an hour and a half then my path found Colin's. We were the second group back, Ross and the Ranger had already got here and rounded up Rockwood and Haru to come back out on the search for the rest of us." He hesitated, his eyes glinting with mischief. "Then Laster showed up with our guest."

"Guest?" Will asked, looking between them.

"Oh, come on, you didn't think we were going to give back our new darling friend did you?" Rowan asked, grinning. "Laster showed up, right? And he literally dropped him on the ground in the courtyard! Made my day! I think I like Laster now, because he had the nerve to *drop* a Prince like a sack of potatoes."

"He brought him all the way back here?" Will asked, astonished. "Seriously?"

"That wasn't part of your stupid plan all along?" Haru asked, sitting up in his bed across the room.

"Shove off, we're story telling over here," Rowan snapped.

Haru made a rude hand gesture and lowered himself back to the bed with a groan.

"So," Will said slowly, his brain sluggish and tired, "the Prince…he's here?"

"He's in the finest dungeon that villainy can buy," Rowan said proudly. "All thanks to Laster and Greyhead. Seriously, I don't think I ever have been more impressed than with how you threatened the King of Thornten!" He gave Colin a playful punch in the arm. "You backtalked a King! You deserve a crown, you deserve a castle, you deserve-"

"We get it!" Colin shoved Rowan, nearly toppling him from the chair. "All that matters is that it got us out of there!"

"It did, and it was impressive at that!" Rowan agreed. "And don't try to be modest, it makes you seem more pigheaded than you already are, you prat."

Will laughed, shaking his head. "And here I thought you'd be the first telling us not to do anything rash and that Laster would have advised against anything as moronic as kidnapping a Prince."

"The plan was to rescue the Ranger. We merely reevaluated the probability of that and revised the plan accordingly," said Colin, smirking. Behind him, Rowan rolled his eyes and pretended to cuff him in the back of the head.

"We got back here about midnight and the castle was all awake, since Ross and the Ranger were back and someone's knight was in an uproar trying to leave," Rowan continued, raising his eyebrows at Will. Across the room, Haru's arm lifted, making the same gesture, this time at Will.

Will's face reddened. "We had to save the Ranger," he muttered, somewhat apologetic.

"Yeah, by doing something stupid," Haru grumbled.

"Well, it was good we did because it worked, didn't it?" Rowan snapped. Turning back to Will, he continued. "Once Laster got back and we realized something was wrong, Haru and Ross took off without waiting on the others. Poor Laster had to switch horses and actually took off bareback to catch up. If you ever want to hear that man swear, hear him get on a horse bareback and fall off the other side. Any other time, I'd have made fun of the bugger. But then the Ranger was already getting his horse and taking off again. That wasn't so funny."

"None of it was funny," said Colin quietly. Will noticed he was staring at his hands again, face drawn, and Will knew he was thinking of how close they had all come to dying. They had all been so close to death...

Niet's face flashed before Will's eyes and he had to bite back the urge to yell out in pain and grief. His teeth dug into the inside of his cheek and the coppery taste of blood filled his mouth.

"But we got the Ranger! And we got the Prince," said Rowan in a forced cheerful voice. "We got him, and, with that, we can negotiate. They can take back their Cutthroat Prince, the heir to being a complete and utter prat."

"What are we going to negotiate for with the heir to Thornten?" Will asked, glad for the change in subject. He would think of Niet again, he knew, but he wasn't ready for it yet. Not right now.

"Maybe a year's supply of fine wine and steaks?" said Rowan, eyes wistful.

"Maybe a brain for that one," Haru chimed in. from across the room.

"This is squire time, go somewhere else to be dislikeable and judgmental, won't you?" snapped Rowan.

"I asked the King that when Sir Miller and I brought the Prince to the dungeon and Revlan met us there," Colin muttered. He looked up, his face tired. "Revlan is going to tell them two years of peace–no Cutthroats, no raids, not even patrols within a mile of the border."

The idea of peace for two years after so much fighting made Will stare at the ceiling, sinking deeper into his pillows. "That sounds amazing."

"Tollien will never go for that, not that long, he'd break his word and attack," said Rowan spitefully.

"I doubt it," said Colin seriously. "A treaty like that means he would have to tell each of the castles that follows him that there will be peace for two years and if he broke that, their alliances would be forfeit. They'd be free to refuse to send him horses, men, and food for an army. It's how the laws and traditions of powers that support him work."

"You read too much, it's making you pompous and smart and I don't rightly like it," Rowan grumbled.

They talked a while longer and Will was relieved when neither asked how he was, what had happened. They didn't mention the new King of Kelkor, that Will was next in line for the throne of a country he had never seen. They didn't even discuss Thornten at all, instead recounting stupid tricks Rowan had played, what pranks he would teach Gabe and Jerram, and how much the two newest squires hated the ponies.

When the healer returned it was to light the torches and heard Rowan and Colin away. He snapped at Haru for defiling the clean healing bed but Haru ignored him and refused to leave. Will was glad when the healer gave up and left. He didn't think he could handle lying awake in the darkness alone again. The sound of Haru's breathing, deepening to sleep, was a comfort. A reminder that someone else was alive in the world. Someone else who would stand guard over him no matter what his life twisted by his lineage would bring forward next.

***

A weight pressing on the foot of his bed made Will wake, blinking against the darkness that surrounded him. It took a moment for his eyes to adjust and make out the form of a man seated at the edge of his bed. Scrambling upright, Will reached automatically for the empty dagger sheath that rested on his side table before the figure let out a low laugh and he relaxed. He sat up straighter, gazing at the familiar figure in his black cloak, the hood drawn low to hide his face.

"The blacksmith is going to hate you for going through daggers as fast as you have this year," the Ranger said coolly, shaking his head. "It must be a record."

"Shouldn't you be in a healing bed too?" Will asked, frowning and glancing around the room. Across the room, Haru was snoring gently in a pool of silver light that filtered through the windows above. The hearth had turned to glowing embers, the torches almost entirely dead. "What time is it?"

"Late." The Ranger shrugged. "And as for staying in here, I'm rather like you. I don't care to listen to rules."

Though it was impossible to see the Ranger's face, Will imagined the shadow of a smirk flit over the man's mouth. He grinned sheepishly. "Well, you didn't expect I'd just leave you there, did you?"

"I rather hoped you would," the Ranger grumbled. "Seeing you in that castle made me wonder why I haven't throttled you before now." He sighed. "But you did very well, Will. You did more yesterday than most knights manage in a lifetime. And you got away with it. You survived."

Will closed his eyes, thankful for the night as pain gripped his heart. *He* had survived. But Niet was dead. Marl had killed Niet with Will right there. He'd left Will...

His eyes shot open, and he frowned, confused. "Ranger?"

"Yes?"

"Marl...Marl killed Niet."

There was a long pause then the figure in the darkness nodded. "I gathered as much."

"How?" Will asked, bewildered.

379

"When I saw the tracks by Niet's body. It seemed the attacker moved away, went to leave, and Niet struck. I can't think of anyone else that boy would have tried to stab in the back."

Will's jaw tightened and he thought of Niet, pleading with him to never tell Serena. "Marl would have deserved it. But please, please don't tell Serena or any or…"

The Ranger held up a silencing hand. "Niet was courageous. He acted out of fury and as far as I am concerned, you and I will go to our graves with the secret of what happened."

"He wasn't going to kill Niet." Will's throat tightened, and he swallowed the lump that had started to rise. "He struck Niet down, but it wasn't a killing blow. I thought he would, and I yelled…and…and…" he remembered Marl stepping toward him, the hatred that contorted his face.

The Ranger waited in silence, rigid as a statue.

Composing himself, Will forced the words out. "He killed Niet only when he knew I was there. He killed him and he left. He left me. But I don't get it. Why? Why wouldn't he kill me instead?"

With a low exhale, the Ranger ran a hand over his jaw, seeming to weigh Will's words. After a long moment he spoke, his voice low, cold. "He did it to torture you."

"What?" Will asked, feeling if anything more lost.

"He's done it to people before. If he knows you care about someone–a friend, a brother, a sister, a wife, an infant–if he knows that someone wants to save another person, he kills them. He lets them see it because that pain will haunt you far longer than any wound."

"But they wanted me dead," Will whispered. "They tried to kill me."

"He wants you as his heir," the Ranger growled. "He wants you as a puppet for Tollien when he either stands down as King of Kelkor or is killed. If you were dead, Tollien would have to task him with finding another heir."

"Another heir?" Will stiffened. Surely there weren't more, more people would think his being an heir was something to be jealous of.

The Ranger chuckled. "They were considering me."

"You?" Will asked, frowning. He thought of the fury he'd felt toward the Ranger and a shiver ran down his spine. "Would you become his heir?"

"Not if my life depended on it," the Ranger snapped. He shifted, seeming uncomfortable then added, his voice lower. "They knew that. They knew someone else's life would have to depend on it. It's part of why I've avoided people since coming here. I know how they work, what they would do to those I loved or cared about. Unless they could capture you, they couldn't control me."

"Me?" Will asked.

Across the room, Haru huffed and rolled over, making them both fall silent. The Ranger turned back to Will. "Yes. If they had you, I would die to protect you and they know that. And before you ask, no, it's not because of your blood. It's because you're the only person they know I care about seeing survive–whether you're royal or not."

"You said you wanted me to challenge Tollien for the throne," Will mumbled, turning his face away from the Ranger.

"What I said was it was your right," the Ranger retorted. "Whether you pursue that right or not, that is your decision. Will, if you want to be a knight of Alamore, then I will keep you alive to be a knight of Alamore."

Will nodded, feeling the knot tighten in his chest again. Only this time it seemed different. It wasn't grief for what was lost but for what had been found. Finally trusting his voice, Will cleared his throat and grinned ruefully at the Ranger. "I'll be a knight and I'll help you go after the throne. It's as much your right as mine."

The Ranger laughed hollowly again. "Not exactly but, that's not the point. That is a discussion for another day, when you're rested and not on the verge of death with your bulldog of a knight keeping guard."

Will glanced toward Haru, still sound asleep. "Yeah, he hasn't let me out of his sight yet."

"I can't blame him," the Ranger huffed. "He took his eye off you thinking the walls would keep you in and you still got out. From what Miller told me, when Haru found out you were gone, he tried to disobey orders and find you. He and Rockwood both have been kept under lock and key since you left. The King couldn't afford more knights leaving, not after Ross and Laster."

Will nodded, the thought of Laster stirring more thoughts. "Laster…" he started but stopped, not sure what to say.

"Laster has his reasons for hating me and I can't say I don't deserve them," the Ranger said flatly. "He's never forgiven me for stopping him from leaping between his knight and Marl. He most likely never will forgive me for it. But I knew my brother by then. Had Laster tried to stop Marl, they both would have died. His knight would have suffered the pain you feel now–Marl would have killed Laster first just to cause his knight agony."

"But Marl wanted to ransom Laster," Will pressed. "He wouldn't have killed him."

The Ranger snorted. "Marl wanted to kill knights for entertainment. He wanted to prove the Alamore knights weren't immortal. It was I who said we should ransom Laster when Marl killed his knight. It was my idea to keep him alive."

"Why?" demanded Will. "You were Thornten then? Weren't you?"

"I was but my allegiance had started to shake. I'd seen what Tollien was capable of doing, what measures he'd take for power, and I didn't like it. It made me uneasy. Marl has always followed his orders well, always let Tollien be in charge.

What I did bought me time to decide between staying in Thornten and betraying everything I knew to come to Alamore. I couldn't decide, it tortured me, until Laster's father responded. Then I heard my father's plan to make his execution a lesson, and I made my decision. I snuck Laster from the dungeon that night on my horse, while I pretended to be Tollien. We rode from the gates without question. No one stops a Prince or Princess, as I know you've learned."

"You've never told Laster that?" Will shook his head. "Why?"

"What difference would it make?" the Ranger asked coolly. "He wanted to die for his knight. He wanted to keep alive the only person he cared about in the entire world. I stopped him from doing so. It's not something he will easily forgive. I've told you before, Will. I used to serve other Kings. I am not proud of all I've done."

"And Serena?"

The Ranger chuckled though there was no humor in the laugh. "Serena had the misfortune of meeting me three years before that–when I was young and arrogant, I thought I was above the world because I was a Prince. That was back when I didn't care because I supported Tollien, I thought he would be the rightful heir for Thornten and all I wanted to do was please him. Marl didn't care about Kelkor, but it had been an idea between Tollien and my father. I went to see how I could help. Even then,

I was the one who could slip through halls unseen. I was the Prince who might as well have been a shadow.

"Serena trusted me. I got her to open up, to tell me far more than she should have. She was the star of all the squires, the only one trusted with duties of a knight, but she was young, she was naive. We both were.

"She told me that the east had unrest and Marl left Kelvane to ride east, to gain the support of rebels. He was good at that, as he promised war. Men who feel they are being trod upon love the idea of killing their enemies, even if that solves nothing. They will get a new oppressor, a new iron hand.

"When it came time for Paranella to pick a husband, she announced she was in love with Azric. That was when Marl returned to court, with Kelkor Lords, Dukes, and Earls at his back giving him support. They announced they wanted him as King. It nearly brought the country to war that much sooner to see how many of their nobles betrayed the crown. But it was settled, and Marl and I fled back to Thornten, we laughed about it and thought it was fun."

The Ranger sounded disgusted with his younger self and Will imagined the sneer curling his lip. "I didn't care that I'd left a squire to take the fall. She'd trusted me as her best friend, and she'd wanted me to stay in Kelkor. I left her to go through her trial where she was accused of betraying the crown. It was probably Azric's merciful nature that had her go east to settle the feuds rather than be marched to a gallows.

There are things I did for Tollien, for my father, I will never forgive myself for. But to remember them and live in the past will do me little good."

Haru grunted and turned again, and the Ranger stood, his cloak falling like shadow around him. "I better let you sleep, Will, or your knight will be baying for my blood like a hound."

Will shook his head. "I want more answers."

"And I've told you," the Ranger murmured, his voice low but gentle. "Some answers are not mine to give you. You will get them, Will, when the time is right. I promise you; I'll make sure of that. For now, however, sleep. There are long days ahead of you, I am sure."

Before Will could protest, the Ranger was striding across the room and slipping from the chamber. There was a faint click of the door closing at his back and Will was left again in the darkness.

CHAPTER FORTY-THREE

The following morning Will had no choice but to face the reality of Niet's death when a soft knock on the door was followed by the appearance of Lady Serena, Eldin, and Kalia. All of them had bloodshot eyes and Kalia's cheeks glistened with tears. Serena's tears seemed to have morphed into an anger, deep in her green eyes, that burned like flames. Haru sprang from his bed, still wearing his filthy clothing from the night before, and moved to stand between Will and Serena, one hand resting on his sword, eyes narrowed.

"Serena," Haru said warily.

"Haru, don't worry." She gave a small smile and the flames in her eyes quieted some. "I'm not here to attack Will."

She turned back to Will, the smile sliding from her lips. She didn't have to say anything else; he already knew. She wanted the truth. She had come to find who had killed her squire, one of the few people who had escaped Kelkor's uprisings and fall.

"It was Marl." Again, his voice was different, like someone else spoke through his lips.

She moved past Haru in silence and sank onto the foot of his bed. Her shoulders sagged, the light in her eyes fading. Somehow she seemed much worse, much more intimidating. Blank, cold.

"First Azric, then Paxrin, now Niet," she whispered.

"He was trying to save me, and then." Will shook his head, fighting to keep his composure, "Marl caught up with us, but was going to let him go. He was going to let Niet go, he didn't know I was there and..." Will's voice failed. He remembered the fury in Niet's face, so similar to the anger in Serena's when discussing Marl before. "He tried to kill Marl...he tried to kill him because of Kelkor. For Kelkor. He struck at Marl, but it only injured him, he didn't manage to kill him or stop him striking back and then Marl broke his sword…"

Behind Serena, Kalia was pulling Eldin into a hug while Eldin tried to keep her bandaged arm from being crushed between them. The older girl was crying in silence, tears racing down her cheeks but Eldin was listening, her expression hollow. Will had the sense that her grief was deeper than tears and that she, like Niet's knight, needed to hear what had happened.

Will glanced beyond them to where Haru sat, face taut. He shook his head, just barely, but Will understood. He was telling him to stop. He didn't have to continue. And it was a relief. He didn't want to tell Serena that Marl had struck again to kill Niet when discovering Will in the undergrowth, too weak to stand.

He would never mar Niet's memory by describing how, as Marl had turned away from him, he'd tried to drive his sword into Marl's back. The Ranger was right. That secret would go to the grave with them both. The pain in the faces of Niet's friends, of Serena, Kalia, Eldin, and Haru, was too much. They would never need to know how he had died.

There wasn't anything to be earned telling Serena that Niet might have been alive, would have been alive, if not for his temper. If he had just let Marl walk away, back to his horse…

"He died a hero, a knight by his blood if not by his King's sword," said Serena, her voice shaking.

Will nodded and glanced back toward Eldin. The stony features were fracturing, her lips beginning to tremble and Will wished he could slip from his bed and wrap his arms around Eldin. It was hardest to see her–Niet's small shadow–breaking.

But he could see her trying so hard to hold onto the moment, to not completely fall apart, trying to be brave for Kalia. Kalia…she was sobbing at last, her heart shattered again; first she had lost her family, her parents, the King and the Queen, and now she had lost her best friend, the boy who might as well have been her brother. There were no words to ease their pain, so he offered none.

Serena rose suddenly, eyes filling with tears, and spun away. She was shaking with rage and grief, the muscles in her face jumping, her hands balled into fists. "I will kill him for this, I will kill Marl for this!" she stormed from the room slamming the door with enough force that the cup of water on Will's side table rattled.

Her rage had broken apart Kalia and Eldin. Eldin looked at Will and tried to smile, hugging her broken arm against her chest. "You stayed with him...you stayed with him when he...?"

He nodded and watched the tears start to roll down her cheeks. "I didn't leave his side till they found us," Will promised.

She nodded. Kalia wasn't listening, staring blankly at the open window in the respite before another wave of grief. Will understood the expression. He had been ladened with it through the night.

Haru stood stiffly, a man older than nineteen, and crossed toward them. He ran a hand through his hair, clearly struggling for the words. "Kalia, Niet was of your court and saved my squire's life, saved the Ranger's life." He hesitated, opening his mouth to try again but Kalia shook her head. "I won't let anything happen to you or Eldin. I promise, whatever you two need." His voice choked, and Will looked away, at his own hands. He knew Haru wouldn't want him to see him cry.

When he chanced a glance again, Kalia had thrown her arms around the knight and Haru was staring steadfastly ahead, his eyes overly bright, but strong as steel while Kalia shook with renewed sobs.

"Your Ranger, he saved us–me, Kalia, Niet–he got us to Alamore, he nearly died doing it," Eldin whispered. "I know Niet wanted to save him, and he died knowing...knowing he'd saved the Ranger."

Will nodded and Eldin leaned in, giving him a half hug before turning and slipping her arm around Kalia's waist. Will had to admire the small girl's grit. She didn't waver, taking the Princess slowly from Haru and leading her away. It was as though she were suddenly the older one tending the child.

"She's going to be a bloody good knight," Haru said, his voice constricted.

Will gave a raspy laugh. "She will be." He tilted his head back, fighting to keep his own grief inside.

"You will be too, Will."

Will stared at the ceiling, feeling the tears slip from the corner of his eyes, down his cheeks. "I hope so, Haru."

Haru chuckled and Will glanced at him, taken aback. The knight was sinking back onto the bed he had claimed, giving Will a wry smile. "You will be, providing I don't murder you before then, that is."

The last person to visit Will that day arrived in the evening, when the grey light was fading to darkness, stars blinking to life beyond the healing chamber windows. Haru had left to wash up, mostly due to the healer kicking him out. Will was waiting for his return, staring out the window and trying to keep his own mind from the haunting nightmares that lurked at its edges when he heard the door opening.

Sitting upright he turned, expecting to see his knight, but his grin faltered. The King closed the door and straightened, a small smile pulling the edges of his lips as his eyes settled on Will. "There's no need to look so unsettled, William."

"I," Will stopped, trying to think of what he should say. *Sorry? I could say sorry? Yeah, sorry for ignoring and disregarding your royal orders...* that seemed a bit lame.

The King held up a hand, shaking his head. "I don't need to hear apologies. You're not the first, nor will you be the last, to ignore a King's order to do what you think is right. It's not easy to obey orders when they are doomed either way."

"I couldn't leave the Ranger to die like that, King," Will said, the words coming from him in a flood. "I couldn't. I know that I've caused a lot of issues, but even if I can't train here anymore, I couldn't leave him to-"

"Will," the King had to raise his voice to stop him. "I am not here to condemn you. I'm here to thank you."

"Oh," Will mumbled, looking down at his hands on the bed, a red heat creeping into his face. Then he frowned, confused and glanced back at the King. "I disobeyed though."

"You did." The King nodded. "And I would rather you never do so again. Deciding to disregard orders too many times sows doubt into a commander's mind. But your two friends, and Ross and Laster told me what happened, they told me about the spy, and about saving the Ranger." The King's eyes darkened, and the muscles clenched in his jaw. "That decision to not save the Ranger was one of the hardest I've made as King of Alamore. It's impossible at times to do what is right for the majority when it means the death of another, especially when that other is a friend. There is nothing worse than to be helpless in such a situation."

Will's throat tightened and he blinked hard. Niet. Even without saying it the King was reminding him that they still had lost a life. "We nearly got away, King."

"I've heard. Where Marl found you was Alamore land even."

Will nodded, not trusting his voice. *We were on Alamore land...we were almost back.* If Niet hadn't stopped, or if the horse hadn't fallen or if even one thing had been different than perhaps Niet would have lived.

"I have spoken with the knights of the council regarding the fate of you, Rowan, and Colin for disobeying orders."

Will looked up again, his heart sinking. It was impossible to read anything in the dark eyes now, a frown creasing the brows. After a moment Will cleared his throat. "C-could I train as a soldier then? Or maybe even in the barns, I can help out there."

"There won't be a need for that," the King chuckled, his composure softening. "It was a unanimous decision that you and your friends continue to train as squires. The newest knight of Alamore was perhaps the most avid in that defense. Instead, what we agreed was that the kitchen can't handle any more torment from Rowan, and you three will spend an hour a day over the next two weeks assisting in morning wall watch while we bring more soldiers to Alamore."

Will nodded. "That seems fair." Then the rest of the King's words sank in and he furrowed his brow. "The newest knight?"

"Serena." The King smiled slightly at Will's look of disbelief. "She swore fealty to my crown. Now that my brother is gone, she can never return to Kelkor–her, Kalia, Eldin. They will continue to train, serve, and stay in Alamore. Kalia requested this morning to be made a squire but I think that decision came from a place of loss rather than actual interest and I don't see my brother resting in his grave under the knowledge his daughter became a knight. For now, I've convinced her that she should perhaps go to Finnwick and train under Earl Kenta in strategy and the rule of a small castle. As for Eldin, she will be Serena's squire now."

Will relaxed against his pillows. "Thank you, King."

The King reached forward, squeezing Will's shoulder a moment. "You've done more than I could ever imagine of a squire your age. Now." He straightened, his voice booming as he smiled down at Will. "Get to healing so you might catch up on training. I've got a hostage to negotiate with Tollien and you've got things to learn." He turned, his cloak billowing out behind him.

He was almost at the door when Will thought of something. "King."

The King paused, one hand resting on the door hand, and turned to Will. "Yes?"

"Niet." Will swallowed the knot that rose in his throat, forcing himself to talk on. "Niet...he said he missed the ocean, and I was wondering if perhaps someone could...if they might bring him there. You know, to rest." His voice broke and he felt his eyes sting.

The King's face softened, and he nodded. "I will tell Serena and see what we might arrange."

Will nodded and looked away. He heard the door click shut and closed his eyes. When Haru returned he was feigning sleep as to hide his burning eyes.

CHAPTER FORTY-FOUR

The healer seemed less concerned with the physical injury than Will's mental state when he allowed him to leave the healing chamber that afternoon. Will heard him tell Haru not to let people question Will, to give him his time and space to heal on his own. It was a job that Haru took seriously, growling at everyone who approached Will when they descended the stairs into the entry hall a few minutes later. Will laughed, shaking his head.

"You're acting like a dog, Haru. I'll be okay."

"I don't want people to push you. I don't want anyone to talk to you about any of it," Haru growled.

"Does that include me?" purred a cool voice. They turned. Leaning against the wall at the bottom step, arms crossed, the Ranger was watching them from the shadow of his hood. Will could see the faint smirk twitch over his mouth. "I would have come to visit you this morning, but I didn't want to risk the Lady Serena and I being in close proximity. I didn't think it would do either of our health well."

Before logic could protest and disregarding the ache and bandages on his shoulder, Will stepped off the final stair and grabbed the Ranger in an embrace. The man grunted in surprise but, after a moment, folded his arms around Will tightly. "You might be daft enough to be a knight, but at least you've inherited some of your uncle's good sense."

"Don't go telling him crazy things, Ranger," said Haru, grinning. "I can't believe I'm saying this, but I'm glad to have you back again."

"You know, when you say it, it doesn't concern me nearly as much as when Laster says it," the Ranger said coolly. "Finding out that he was one of the people who was in Thornten has me torn between concern for his sanity and annoyance. I can't continue to just blindly loathe him. The most worrisome part is that he actually seems to have missed me."

Will laughed in spite of himself, breaking away from the Ranger. "Laster? Miss you?"

"We are both in the same amount of disbelief, I see."

"Might be the first sign that the world is ending," Haru chuckled. "Did he say that verbatim?"

"Not verbatim, but he implied it." The Ranger's eyes glinted in the shadow of his hood, the smirk broadening to a grin.

Will couldn't keep the grin from his own face. "Oh yeah? What, exactly, did he say?"

"He said that at least he gets the chance to kill me himself someday, since Tollien couldn't manage it himself."

Haru let out a bark of laughter and pulled the Ranger into a hug as well, which the hooded man tried to extricate himself from. "Get off of me, child knight."

"I've missed your snide and sarcastic ways, Ranger," Haru said, letting the man stagger back.

"Touch me again and I'll slit your throat in your sleep," the Ranger snapped.

"What exactly did you want to talk to me about?" Will asked, watching the Ranger. He knew the Ranger too well. He hadn't come to say hello. He had already done that the night before. This was something else.

The smile under the hood slipped away and the Ranger sighed heavily. "If your guard dog will allow it, I want you to come with me to see the Prince."

Cold gripped the back of Will's neck.

"Ranger, he's not supposed to talk about what happened or do much today," Haru growled. "It can wait."

"I wish it could, but Tollien and Revlan have already started hostage negotiations and I think it best that Will knows what he's facing for the future now rather than when he's safe in his father's armies again."

"Ranger, I don't think-"

"I'll go," said Will, cutting off Haru's protest.

"You don't have to, Will," Haru said. All traces of his grin were gone, replaced with a heavy glower at the Ranger.

"I know that," said Will. He glanced between the two men. "Haru, I'll be fine. I'll be in the dinner hall in the next hour and, if I'm not, I'll let you carry me back to the healing chamber and I'll stay there for a week without arguing."

"Seems like a good deal if you ask me," the Ranger said sarcastically.

"No one asked you, Ranger," Haru snapped. He looked down at Will and Will could see the misgivings behind his gaze. Finally, Haru straightened, glowering at the Ranger again. "One hour or I find you and Will both, and I will put you both in the healing chamber for a week."

"The dog certainly can bark," the Ranger muttered, but only loud enough that Will caught the words. He rested a hand on Will's shoulder, half guiding, half leaning on him. Will could hear the uneven step of the Ranger's limp, his leg dragging slightly on every step. They paused at one of the doors Will hadn't ever passed through. He already could imagine what it was before the Ranger pulled it wide, cool air rushing up the dark stairwell and engulfing them. This was the dungeons then. Will chanced a glance over his shoulder to see that Haru was still watching them, his face grim.

"At least he worries about you. It actually makes me glad he's your knight. He might be naive and a fool," the Ranger said, pulling open the door and waving Will toward the stairwell. "But he's a fool who would die to keep you safe, as proven by his childish comment. Injured or not, he should know by now I would beat him."

"Yeah, but then you'd have to take on Ross and I'm not sure that'd be a good fight when injured," Will said, grinning slightly.

The Ranger chuckled. "Perhaps not."

The stairwell beyond the door was narrow, lit with flickering torches that sputtered in the drafty air. Neither of them spoke, the silence deepening with each stride as the cold of the dungeons closed in around him. Will glanced back a few times, torn if he was making the right decision. He didn't want anything to do with this Prince, with Thornten. He didn't want to be an heir.

At the bottom of the steps, they were met by Sir Richard and one of the soldiers, both standing sentry at a heavy door. Richard gave Will the ghost of a sad smile and a nod as he gestured Will and the Ranger through the door and into a narrow corridor. A sudden thought made Will start, turning to the Ranger.

"Didn't the tunnels reach the dungeons last year? Didn't Vonnic help them do that?"

"Yes," the Ranger growled. "But we learn from our mistakes. Your friend the blacksmith also helped us redesign the dungeons." When Will continued to look perplexed, the Ranger continued. "Iron bars on all walls, the floor, and the ceiling. It would take more than digging to escape the cells anymore. Now, this is our stop."

They had reach another set of guards; two soldiers Will didn't recognize. After his experience with Oberoan he shifted, uncomfortable. Hadn't Tabius said he had more spies in the castle? What if one of these was a spy?

But they didn't move to attack. Instead, they shot nervous looks at the Ranger and stepped aside, revealing another door that the Ranger opened for Will. He stepped in first, followed by the Ranger.

The room was small, dark, lit with four torches, one on each wall. Someone had thrown an old rug over the floor but even through it Will could make out the thick bars that the Ranger had mentioned.

"So, looks like you survived just fine, doesn't it?"

Will started, spinning on his heel. He hadn't noticed Tabius, but the Prince was striding toward them, a manacle around one ankle and a heavy chain dragging on the floor. He smirked at Will's surprise. "And here I was worried you'd been murdered."

"Thanks for the concern," Will said dryly.

"But I heard someone died." Tabius ran a hand over his jaw. "One of the squires. Was it your two friends? The annoying ones? Maybe the smart mouth?"

Will's chest constricted but the Ranger spoke in a dangerous growl. "Prince or not, I can promise I'll silence you."

Tabius snorted with laughter. "You seem to have more of a backbone when you get to hide away under your hood and pretend not to be what you are."

"On the contrary I wear the hood because I'll never forget what I am," the Ranger replied coldly. "Will, I'll stay with you if you-"

"I'm fine," Will cut across the Ranger. "I want to talk to him."

The Ranger nodded, stepping back through the door. Neither Will nor Tabius moved as it clicked shut behind Will. They eyed one another warily.

"So," Tabius said at last, smirking. "Are you going to hide your face to forget what you are, too, then?"

"I don't need to because I'm just a squire," Will said flatly. "And that's all I want to be."

"Shame," Tabius said, sounding almost bored. He crossed his arms, leaning against the nearest wall and taking Will in. After a moment, he looked away, shaking his head. "I know it was the Kelkor squire who died. But what I don't get is why he was even there with you, why he didn't dump you from the horse."

"Because he was my friend," Will said flatly.

Tabius shot Will a sharp look then shook his head. "You weren't friends. He was Kelkorian, he should hate you and the Ranger for what you are."

"I'm a squire," Will repeated, annoyed. "Nothing more, nothing less."

Tabius's lip curled in a sneer that reminded Will forcibly of Tollien. "Come now, don't play games. He knew that Marl wanted to name you heir of Kelkor, he knew that Marl killed Azric. He should have been delighted at the chance to see you or the Ranger dead."

"Yeah, well, the thing with people is not all of them see you as just the blood in your veins," Will snapped. His mind flashed to Serena's hate, to Eldin's distrust as they climbed the tower wall again, Marl's attempts to kill him, Tabius's own attempts to use him. "You see me as what my blood is because that's all you've been seen as–a Prince, not a person."

"You sound like a moron," the Prince purred, breaking his eyes from Will to examine his own fingers. "Talking of princes and people when you refuse to acknowledge what you are yourself."

"I told you, I'm a squire! I'm a squire and I'm going to be a knight of Alamore!" Will snarled, taking a step toward the Prince. At his sides, his hands had balled into fists. He had an urge to vent some of his feelings by punching this Prince square in the face for all that he had caused, for trying to kill the Ranger, him, for being the reason that he and Niet had gone to save the Ranger in the first place. If they hadn't needed to go there then Niet wouldn't have…wouldn't have…

"Don't play a fool," Tabius's scoffing tone broke Will's thoughts from Niet. His eyes were hungry as they had been back in the castle. "You have the chance at power. You and I can work together, you can rule Kelkor someday, and I'll rule Thornten. We'd be unstoppable. What better position would you be in to help Alamore than as a King? And if I helped you onto that throne…you could take up some of that mantle that you should have. If you settle for Kelkor, I can help you become a King. If you and I work together we could be unstoppable."

"I don't want to work with you," Will said, his voice flat, uncaring. "I don't want anything to do with the crown or…" He stopped, realizing what Tabius had said. "What do you mean settle?"

It was Tabius's turn to look confused. "Haven't you realized?"

"Realized what?" Will asked, stepping closer.

The Prince of Thornten let out a bark of laughter. "You don't know? You haven't realized? Or is it that no one has thought you're ready for that little secret yet?"

Icy cold shot through Will and he waited, holding his breath. "What secret?"

"I think that this little chat is over."

Will started. He hadn't heard the Ranger return. Judging by how Tabius sprang into the air, color draining from his face, he hadn't either. The Ranger leaned against the open door, one hand resting on his sword, the other running along the jaw hidden in shadows under his hood.

Tabius recovered his composure quickly, shooting the Ranger a venomous look. "Are you afraid what will happen when the truth comes out? Is that why you're hiding it from him?"

The Ranger huffed, straightening. "Like your father, you live to cause chaos and strife. I'm sure your people will love having that in a King again. Will, come on, before I have to prove to Haru that even injured I can defeat him."

Will nodded, turning away from the Prince and following the Ranger back out of the cell and into the corridor beyond. The Ranger rested a hand on Will's shoulder, guiding him back through the twisting maze, back past Richard, and up the steps. They were nearly at the top of the stairs when Will pulled free, turning to the Ranger.

"What was he talking about?"

"Nothing that concerns you."

Annoyed, Will braced himself on the step, crossing his arms. "You can't keep lying to me, Ranger. What was he on about?"

The Ranger sighed heavily, stopping one stair above Will. "He, like Tollien, is trying to use the secrets of others to cause mayhem. What he was saying is something that's not my place to tell you."

"Then who can tell me?" Will demanded, frustrated.

"All you need to know is that he will tell you, Will. He will tell you when the time is right. I can't imagine it will be much longer but, for now." The Ranger turned away, striding up another step. "I'm not spilling the secrets of others."

CHAPTER FORTY- FIVE

"I could eat a cow."

"You literally just ate two apples. Holding off till lunch isn't about to kill you."

"Yeah, but like I could eat more. I'm not saying I'm hungry, but, if there was a cow and someone offered me a bit of money, I could probably eat the whole thing," Rowan said, as though this were perfectly logical.

Colin rolled his eyes to the ceiling. "You are ridiculous."

Will hid his smile by ducking his head, rummaging through the chest at the foot of his bed. After a moment, he withdrew his black cloak and pulled it over his dark tunic, his fingers fumbling with the fastenings.

"You okay, Will?" Colin asked, concerned.

Will nodded, straightening and facing his friends. "I'll be fine."

"Course he will, he's got us." Rowan clapped Will on the back.

They were in the empty squire chamber, the last to leave. Outside, the rays of the morning sun cast brilliant shadows. Will could hear voices in the dinner hall beyond and half wished he could stay inside the squire chamber.

But Rowan was already striding toward the door and Colin was waiting, jaw set. So, Will walked with them out into the dinner hall and toward the squire table. It was the most silent it had ever been. No one was joking around or telling stories about training. Instead, the squires were grim faced, all shrouded in dark clothing.

Will immediately spotted Eldin, seated steadfastly in Niet's chair. Will lowered himself into the empty seat beside her. She gave him the shadow of a grin, which he returned before focusing his attention on the knights table. Serena had pushed herself to her feet, green eyes shadowed and exhausted.

"Today, we say our farewell to one of the bravest squires Kelkor, or Alamore, has ever known. Niet trained under me for five years in Kelkor, earning his sword, his shield, and his spurs. Had Kelkor not fallen, he would have been a knight by now." Her voice quavered. Inhaling she continued in a stronger tone, eyes flashing. "Niet was killed by the man who now claims he's King of Kelkor, by the same man that killed my King. His memory will burn on in our hearts and drive us to never forget what has been taken from us, to never rest until we have settled the scores.

Now, I ask you to raise your glass in honor of a squire who died with all the honor and bravery of a knight." Serena lifted her own goblet and each person followed suit. "Niet the Brave."

"Niet the Brave."

The words resounded around the hall and the memory of Niet's death flashed before Will's eyes again, of him lunging for Marl's back, of Marl killing him to spite Will. His fingers tightened on his goblet as he lowered it to his mouth then set it on the table, staring unseeingly at the knights table.

"If you would all rise," King Revlan said, standing and waving an arm toward the door that led off the chamber.

They did so, chairs scraping over stone in a deafening scream. Next to him, Rowan recoiled, clamping his hands over his ears a moment and grumbling a string of Kelkorian words no doubt taught to him by Niet. Colin grabbed Rowan's arm and shot him a disapproving look, but Will had to bite down on his smile. It would have made Niet laugh, he was sure. A small snort of laughter made him glance at Eldin again. She was burying her own giggles in her elbow. For the first time in days there was the fire of mischief in her eyes.

The squires fell into step behind the knights through the door that led off the dinner hall. No one said where they were going but Will already knew–through the Final Farewell and into the graveyard.

There they would have their chance at saying their goodbyes before the funeral pyre was lit and later Serena, Kalia, and Eldin would ride to the west, to the ocean, and scatter his ashes. Haru had explained it all the night before, taking Will aside so he would be prepared for what was to come.

"If you don't want to come, Will, it'll be alright," Haru had said, face drawn with concern.

"I'm coming." Will hadn't hesitated. "I want to say my goodbyes. He saved my life, Haru. He's the reason we were able to get the Ranger out alive too. I...I owe it to him to be there."

But now, stepping through the doors and striding down the hallway of the Final Farewell, doubt niggled at the edges of his mind. What would it be like to see Niet one more time? He had an image of death in his mind now, Niet's cold body, his blood. He wasn't certain he could do this.

Next to him, Colin gripped his shoulder in a bracing way and Will saw that the green eyes were overly bright, though his friend's face was set. He didn't say anything but gave Will the slightest of nods.

Then they were stepping through the doors at the end of the Final Farewell, into the brilliant light of the sun. Warmth spread over Will like comfort and, craning to see ahead, his eyes rested on the center of the graveyard.

A plinth had been erected there, covered in thatch and timbers, with buckets of water surrounding it. Will could see the body lying on the pyre, but it wasn't the same corpse that had been left in the forest.

Someone had cleaned the blood from his features, changed him into Kelkor green, and placed the shattered fragments of his sword over his chest. The eyes were closed, the face unmoving, too still to be thought of as sleeping.

Ahead, Kalia was lightly crying while Haru wrapped one arm awkwardly over her shoulders. Ross's face was stone though grief flickered in the blue eyes. Laster's sneer was gone, replaced with an unusual expression of sadness. Serena's anguish had morphed to that cold fury again, her anger and pain twisting her lips, making her eyes bright even as they became chips of frozen green ice. Will blinked, frowning. The Ranger. Where was the Ranger? *He should be here. Niet was saving him, he went there to help save him. At the very least he should be here.*

There. Will saw a shadow at the edge of the graveyard shift, the flutter of a dark cloak. The Ranger was standing away from them, face concealed under his hood, one hand resting on his sword. Like a statue guarding over the grieving group, he didn't move.

Will turned away, aware suddenly that the King was speaking, his soothing voice booming around the group.

"Let us never forget that Niet died to defend others, to save others, and to keep Alamore safe. He embodied all that a Kelkorian knight should ever strive to be. We will mourn his loss, our loss, and celebrate his memory in the time of peace that he helped us to attain. Thornten has agreed to lay aside the blade for a year and a half and, in this time, we shall rebuild, we shall all strive to be stronger, better, more prepared for what the future may bring."

Serena stepped toward the pyre, a torch wavering in one shaking hand, and touched the flames to the wood that surrounded Niet's body. Fire flared to life, igniting the dried timbers, devouring the Kelkor banner and, swallowing Niet from sight. Will heard someone let out a dry sob and had to force himself to stand where he was and not push toward the three Kelkorians. Pain stabbed through his chest and he stared ahead, knowing that Eldin had finally broken.

***

The Kelkor riders left before the Thornten riders appeared. Will was in the barns, grooming down Visra who had finally been cleared for light exercise. He saw the banners of the bronze falcon on the grey backdrop and reached instinctively for his dagger.

"There's nothing to worry about, Will."

He started, turning. Ross was stepping from the feed room, his own eyes trained on the double doors as well. After a moment he turned to Will. "They've come to get the Prince."

"Well, they're welcome to him," Will grumbled, turning back to Visra. He hadn't forgotten what the Prince had said but, in light of Niet, of everything else, it seemed unimportant. The Ranger wasn't going to give him answers either way.

"It'll be good for us to have the time to rebuild," Ross growled. "We've been at war or in fighting too long. A year and a half of peace will do well to rebuild."

"Year and a half?" Will asked, frowning. "Rowan said the King was asking for two years."

Ross laughed coldly. "Tollien isn't so easily won over in negotiation. However, even this time will be welcome. The fighting has exhausted us. It's taken its toll on everyone. Even that horse there."

Will nodded and patted Visra's neck. The bay pinned his ears and reached to nip at Will, which he avoided with long practiced ease, grinning. "Yeah, well, it didn't change him much."

"But it's changed others," Ross said calmly.

His eyes bored into Will, but he refused to meet them, pretending to be more intent on gently cleaning the raw and hairless scar where Visra's stitches had been. After a moment, Will straightened and met Ross's stony blue eyes. "We'll be stronger for it."

"Perhaps," Ross agreed. He hesitated, a frown creasing his forehead. "I hear that horse is about sound to start working again."

"Yeah." Will forced a smile. "So you will be able to take your horse back." His eyes flitted to Admere's stall, where the red horse watched them curiously and his chest tightened.

Ross hummed, coming forward to pat Visra's shoulder. "I'm not certain now is the time for me to work with another hunt horse. I might do better to get a second warhorse, something a bit bigger, to face whatever Thornten throws at us next."

"So, you'll get rid of Admere?" Will's heart plummeted. At least if Admere were with Ross he'd get to see him but now...

"I think that'd be best. At the very least, finding someone who can work him until I've got the time for such leisure as hunting." Ross nodded firmly. He raised his eyebrows at Will, a shadowed smile flitting over his mouth. "That is, of course, if you're up for handling two animals at once.

Will gawked at the knight, unable to believe what he was hearing. "M-me, Sir?"

"I don't believe I was talking to Visra," Ross growled but his eyes were bright with a grin.

"I don't have money."

"I didn't ask if you did." Ross shook his head. "I asked if you'd take care of two horses. At least, for the time being."

"I, well, yeah, yeah I could do that." Will grinned.

"Good." Ross clapped him on the shoulder, glancing toward the door. "If I'm not mistaken, trouble itself and my squire are heading our way and I've just got off a night patrol. I'd rather not deal with them."

He was gone before Will had time to thank him, striding out of sight through the doors.

A moment later Rowan and Colin appeared, breathless from running, Colin's face bright red while Rowan was howling with laughter.

"What?" Will asked, laughing too.

"Colin!" Rowan doubled over, breaking into more laughter.

"It wasn't my idea!" Colin said, face reddening still more. "You're the one who dared me."

"But you did it!" Rowan was wheezing. He reached to grab Visra for support but recoiled as the bay took a nip at him. "Thornten, I forgot you're a dragon." He straightened, eyes watering from laughter and inhaled deeply. "Colin just tripped the Prince of Thornten, and he fell flat on his face in the courtyard. It was brilliant."

Will snorted. "You did?"

Colin grinned sheepishly, running a hand over the back of his neck. "I didn't really think about it. Just stuck out a foot and..." He clapped his hands, miming someone falling.

Will broke into laughter, shaking his head. "Alamore, Colin! Rowan's rubbed off on you!"

"It's for the best that I rub off on you two, you both need it. Otherwise you'd walk around thinking you're better than the world because you don't break rules or have any fun," Rowan said decisively.

"So then," Will said when he finally stopped laughing. "He's gone?"

"Yup." Rowan nodded. "Him, his father, and his little Cutthroats band are up and out of Alamore and we've got a signed peace arrangement where forfeiting the arrangement means they forfeit all alliances. It's going to be a bit weird though."

"How so?"

"Well, we've had fighting and all, it's always been watching our back and now." Rowan shrugged. "There's a respite."

"We need it," Colin said firmly.

"That we do," Rowan agreed. "But it's still weird."

"It won't last." Will shook his head. "They'll be back–Tollien, Tabius, Marl. They'll be back and we'll all be plunged right back into it all."

"Only this time we're going to be older and cooler and stuff," Rowan said, smirking. "Like knights or like assassins or like-"

"Idiots?" Colin supplied innocently.

Rowan suggested Colin kiss Visra somewhere not only inappropriate but dangerous and they all broke into laughter again. Will leaned against the familiar bay horse, sighing. "Well, we're going to just have to train as hard as we can for now then, so we're ready."

"Ready to fight Thornten," Colin agreed.

"Ready to be awesome," Rowan corrected.

Will nodded. In his mind however, he was picturing himself battling Marl. He would have to be ready to fight Marl, Tabius, and Tollien. He'd be ready to fight the war that his bloodlines made him part of, whether he wanted a throne or not.

"But in the meantime." Rowan slapped him on the back, grinning. "Who's down to see Will get thrown off this dragon, eh? I am. I have missed the show."

And, laughing and shaking his head, Will turned away, toward the tack room. "Fine, I'll get him saddled," he called over his shoulder. The idea of fighting Visra made him feel lighthearted. There were, after all, worse battles than that of a boy and his horse.

Dear Reader,

I truly hope you enjoyed The Cutthroat Prince, book two in the William of Alamore series. This adventure has been a long time in the making.

If you enjoyed this book, I would ask that you please leave it a review on Amazon and Goodreads so that others can also discover this series.

Additionally, be sure to subscribe so you never miss a beat at www.cjrisely.com. There you will find book updates, character art, and additional information about characters. By subscribing, you will get sneak peeks at future stories and extra chapters, plus a free e-book of The Falcon and The Stag: A Tale of Alamore.

Thank you once again,

C. J. R. Isely

NEXT IN THE WILLIAM OF ALAMORE SERIES

BOOK THREE:

THE FALLEN HEIR